To Barbara,
I hope you love Lander
and return to visit many
times

CHRISTOPHER

THE LANDER SERIES

A NOVEL BY

CARRIE CHESNEY

Carrie Chesney

CHRISTOPHER

THE LANDER SERIES

A NOVEL BY

CARRIE CHESNEY

Copyright 2005 by Carrie Chesney

ISBN: 1-59507-073-7

ArcheBooks Publishing Incorporated

www.archebooks.com

9101 W. Sahara Ave.

Suite 105-112

Las Vegas, NV 89117

Hardcover First Edition: 2005

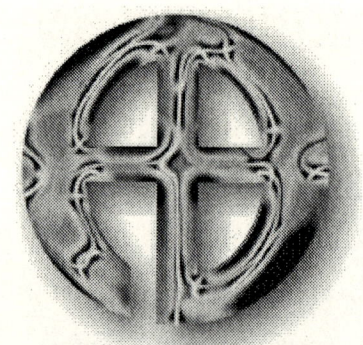

ArcheBooks Publishing

DEDICATION

For all the love, encouragement, support and advice you've given through this whole ordeal, this book could never belong to anyone but you, Bill. You put up with the headaches, the tirades, and the tears, and never once, not even for a moment, did you ever stop believing in me. You have lifted me and shown me horizons I never dreamed existed.

Yours from Chapter One. All ways, always.

ACKNOWLEDGEMENTS

My undying gratitude goes to my two very dear friends who worked un-ceasingly to help me prepare this work for publication, Tom Lynn and Bill Avery.

Tom is my writing partner on other projects, but he supported me every step of the way on this novel—always ready to help edit, sustaining whatever decisions I made, making me laugh each and every day without fail, and for-ever telling me I'm the best little writer on the planet. Remember when - ily.

Bill built me the most fabulous website there is and works to keep it ever-changing, ever-growing, and always a reflection of me. He was the first writer to ever lay eyes on the CHRISTOPHER manuscript and tell me I had talent. That was huge for me and has carried me through. Thank you, Bill, for loving my story and seeing the potential in it. Thank you for sitting through so many readings of it, for making suggestions to improve it, for the laughter and the tears, and most of all, for loving the Abby girl.

My thanks to my daughter, Charlotte, who loves to help name characters and who listens, then bursts out with her own predictions of what's going to happen. Sometimes her ideas were better than mine, so they got worked in and changed the direction of the story. She's also become a terrific proof-reader, and I rely on her. Thanks for always standing by me in everything, Char.

To my family, who out of the blue was deluged with country music 24/7. For the most part they were pretty gracious, and on those lines I have to thank my sons, Taylor and Colin, who both provided me with numerous sets of headphones.

To my daughter, Charity, who gets $50 for leaving me alone to write.

To the Lander Chamber of Commerce and the people of Lander, Wyoming, for all the assistance they gave in helping me to write their hometown. I fell in love with it.

To Canadian country music star, Jason McCoy, for graciously giving me his time and knowledge of the business. It was greatly appreciated.

Thanks to Ed Allen, my authority on all things Wyoming, who never let on how annoying it was to have me calling at all hours of the day and night with bizarre questions.

To Sheila Shackleton who revelled in Maisie's demise, and to Cindy St. Jean who didn't want the story to end and is trying to talk me into a sequel.

To Shara Desrosiers, who patiently did not one, but three photo shoots to get my picture for the book cover. You were amazing, and I'm so grateful. We prayed for a miracle that last day, and we got one. You actually made me look good.

To Clare Douglas for doing the artwork on the front cover. You listened to what I wanted and kept at it until we got Chris and Abby's island. Thank you. I enjoyed the journey and hope to travel it again with you.

Thanks to Dr. Jennifer Caspers of Guelph, and Dr. Doug Austgarden of Hamilton for medical advice. Jennifer also provided a great deal of encouragement as I've struggled on this endeavour. I'm sure she has no idea how much it has meant to me.

To Jennifer Stewart, Sarah Allen, Lesley Sprickerhoff, Lori Joy, Susan Hemmi, Edith Peters, and Carla Cardinell. Your help and encouragement was above and beyond.

For all of my friends at WB who have offered support and laughter and just plain been there for me, no matter what I was going through. Thanks, gang. You're the best.

To Bob Farley, and all my friends at the AB Network. Thanks for the ongoing support and ideas. It's grand to have a group you can rant to, and they know precisely what you mean.

To the members of the Kenny Chesney Forum for teaching me about the world of a dedicated country fan and Fan Fair. Let me say that none of them served as role models for Maisie and Daisy.

To Kenny Chesney and Toby Keith, whose music filled my headphones throughout the writing of this book. They supplied the mood and kept me in the country world.

To my publisher, Bob Gelinas, for wanting the series in the first place, and for allowing me to write outside the box and not making me try to fit into a mold I didn't want to be in. To my editor, Vickie Dubois for her suggestions and advice.

And Denis, who has always been willing to walk a step behind in my shadow so I shine and takes pride in all my accomplishments that have put me in the spotlight over the years.

CHAPTER 1

April 2003

Bright lights flashed in his eyes, blinding him to anything farther than ten feet in front of him. The volume of screaming from the darkness beyond pressured his eardrums to the point of bursting. Sweat dripped from his hair, rolling down his face, chest, and back. Energy vibrated tangibly in the air.

A voice carried through his earpiece above the din, "Good one, Kip!"

He smiled and pulled the monitor from his ear, waving to the thirty thousand fans congregated together. The rush pumping through his veins consumed him. Being onstage was the only thing that did feel good anymore, and he immersed himself in it, wanting to milk the moment for every ounce of joy he could suck from it.

Heading off stage, he pointed a finger of acknowledgement to the two women he spotted in the front row at every single performance on the tour. At the bottom of the steps Julie handed him an iced bottle of water as he passed by on his way to the dressing room.

Security opened the door for him. He had only a few moments to himself before the rest of the band came streaming in. Taking a deep breath, he let his shoulders sag as the adrenalin drained out of him.

He clicked the lock on the bathroom door and started the shower as he heard the others arrive. He knew they were ready for food and beer, but he needed a few minutes to wind down on his own before joining them. It was a good show. He knew it, and the tension eased as the water spilled over his

1

body, cooling him off and rejuvenating his spirits. After toweling dry, he left behind his snug jeans and sweat-dampened Foreigner tee-shirt, donning fresh khakis and a blue shirt.

The band never failed to pour their hearts into their work, so hunger after a show was a given. Hooting and laughter filled the room as beer bottles opened, and food was devoured. The tour was at an end, and the main topic of conversation was the upcoming two-month break. Some planned to use the time to get away while others chose to make some extra money working as studio musicians.

Wandering through the crowd, Kip made his way to his manager's side. "Tug, did you manage to find me anythin'? You know I can't go back to Nashville. Not yet."

Tug Crilley had promised to find him an isolated getaway spot. "I've got a call in, buddy. Should have an answer by tomorrow. Don't worry. Something will be in place by the time the tour is over."

Kip knew it irritated Tug to be asked every day, but he needed to stay clear of Nashville or anywhere else people would think to look for him. Having just come through a nasty divorce, he wasn't ready to go back to a world where his ex still made her presence felt in a big way.

"You keep tellin' me that, but we only have Cincinnati and Toronto left. Time is runnin' out." Kip hung his head in dismay. "I'm gonna go back to the bus. Talk to ya later." Passing the catered table spread with a wide array of foods, he opted for the simplicity of a banana to take with him.

Seeing the defeated slump of Kip's retreating shoulders, Tug shook his head in sympathy. The entire tour had been tough, but he believed it was the only thing holding the kid together. Tansey had taken him for a sizable settlement, in the neighborhood of seventeen million plus the house, but it wasn't the money that hurt. He took a lot of garbage from her for a long time. Tug was glad when Kip finally had enough and divorced her. She spent most of the fortune he made and slept with anyone who could help her climb in society. At least the guys in the band saw her for what she was and steered clear. Tug felt certain if Kip found one of them sleeping with her, the betrayal would be unforgivable.

Relieved to be alone in his traveling home-away-from-home, Kip settled back on the couch and closed his eyes. The CD player provided relaxing piano music, and he swigged at a bottle of juice while letting the melodies of Jim Brickman flow through him. He hated for sleep to come, because he knew Tansey would be there, waiting to torment him. When would she leave his thoughts, his dreams, and his life? She was everywhere. He just wanted his life back—a life without her.

Thinking of the crowd tonight—women grabbing at his legs and screaming his name, posters held up offering him everything—he knew he only had to say the word, and there would be a line-up of women waiting to jump into his bed. Like those two following him the entire tour. It was obvious what they wanted, always wearing low-cut tops that left nothing to the imagination when he looked down from the stage. He wasn't interested in a string of lusty one-nighters. Never had been. He wanted a partner who shared more than just his bed.

His best friend, Jeff Clayton, shared his bus and his values. Growing up on neighboring ranches, the boys had been inseparable since childhood with Jeff's younger sister, Julie, always tagging along. They'd bought their first guitars together, Kip getting a lead and Jeff a bass so they could accompany one another. A developed internal sense of each other's timing kept them always in sync.

In high school they started a band and played at the local nightclub, even though they were under age. One evening a well-known band traveling through town stopped in for a few drinks and heard them play. Impressed with Kip's voice and style, they offered to make some connections to give him a boost. With the bright lights of Nashville beckoning, he made the journey with Jeff and Julie at his side. As Kip's career flourished he needed an assistant, and Julie was the obvious choice.

"Kip? Are you okay?"

His eyes popped open. "Oh, Julie, hey. I didn't hear ya come on. Sneakin' up on me there, huh?"

She stared down at him and thought how bad he looked. Even with the dimmed lights erasing a lot of the weariness and worry lines from his face, he still appeared exhausted.

"Sorry. I just wanted to see how you're doin'. I noticed you didn't stick around backstage again tonight."

"Sit down, and for heaven's sake, get that look off your face. I can't stand the pity. I want you to tell me I'll get over this, that my life ain't over. Buck me up, girl. Where's that cheerleader spirit?"

Sitting beside him on the black leather sofa, one of two that ran along the sides of the front living area, she let her hand rest on his thigh. "Well, now that you bring it up, you will get over it. And in my opinion, your life is just gettin' started. I know you don't want to hear it, but she isn't the one for you. Never was. She's a phony." She watched him turn his head away, and tucking a finger under his chin, turned it back to face her. "Look at the up side of it. You'll have control over the money you work your butt off for, and you won't need a house with four walk-in closets. Best of all, you won't have to wonder whose bed she's crawlin' into every time you turn your back."

He felt the heat rise in his face. "That's enough. You're crossin' the line."

She lay her head on his shoulder and said calmly, "Christopher Adams, I have known you since I was born, long before you became the infamous Kip

Adams. I love you as much as I do Jeff. Get that angry look off your face, cause you know it's what we all think. You can get mad at me for carin', but you can't deny what I'm sayin' is true. Maybe when you start seein' her for who she is instead of who you wanted her to be, you'll be able to put her behind you. I hate watchin' you suffer like this. I know you don't want to hear it, but if not from Jeff or me, then who?"

"I know you think you're helpin', and I love you for it. I'm just not ready yet." He lay his hand on top of hers and squeezed it.

"Honey, if somebody doesn't say somethin', you never will be. Everybody has been walkin' on eggshells around you this entire tour. It hasn't been fun for anyone. I hope this break is gonna help ya heal, because carin' and sympathizin' with ya can only go on for so long." She stood and headed to the front of the bus. Stopping at the steps, she turned back. "Those guys have all gone to the ropes for you, but everyone has a limit to what they can take. I don't want you to lose your band too. Then you will be empty. Even Blake and the boys in Emerson are wishin' they hadn't signed on to tour with you. There's only one solution. Do what all country songwriters do. Write a hit, and get over it."

"Get off my bus, brat."

"Sis-Boom-Bah!" She gave him a coy smile and left.

Kip leaned back, closing his eyes again. He could always count on Julie for honesty. Her words played over in his mind. Had he really been that bad? Every night he sat here on the bus alone instead of partying with the rest of the guys. He didn't share in the games and fun anymore, having become so withdrawn he didn't even see what was going on around him. Darn that Julie. He hated it when she was right. And she was always right.

"That girl needs her backside paddled. She's gettin' too much of a sassmouth. Think I'll leave her home next time. Huh," he muttered, "think I'll get me a new personal assistant."

Paying heed to Julie's words over the next few days, he pretended to be happier whenever he was with the band and saved his moping for private moments.

A few days later as the bus left Cincinnati behind, Tug and Kip wielded their video game controllers like weapons. With the score neck and neck, Tug's cell phone started to sing in his pocket, putting an end to the match. He spoke for a few minutes and smiled as he turned it off. "Kip, my friend, I have got news."

"I take it from that stupid grin you think you've really pulled somethin' off." He turned off the game system and tossed the controller aside.

"Indeed I have. That was my friend, Jim Masterson, who lives up near Toronto. He just happens to own an island in the Kawartha region in Ontario. It's got a great cottage, but he and his wife are going to Australia this summer instead. If you want it longer than the two months I've arranged, it's your option. You can't get any more private than being stranded on your own island."

Kip sat forward, enthused by the turn of events. "I totally love it. Thanks. It's exactly what I was hopin' for."

"Yeah, well I just hope it does you some good. I'm worried about you, Kipper, and I don't mind sayin' so." He pulled on the corners of his mustache as he studied his friend. "We've been together a long time. You sure bein' alone that long is the best thing? I don't want you to get depressed and do something stupid. You're not Elvis, ya know. Kip Adams is an all-star name, but I can't guarantee women'll still be crying over ya in thirty years."

Kip's gaze slipped sideways, giving his manager a hurt look. "I can't believe you said that. I'm countin' on the tears lastin' at least sixty."

Tug burst out laughing, and it felt good. It was the first attempt at humor he'd heard from his young star in months. Damn that Tansey for having ripped him apart. Kip was a great, down-to-earth guy, never letting the fame go to his head. Still the same kid who rustled up cattle back on his daddy's ranch in Wyoming. It was one of the things that made him so popular with the fans. He wrote songs they related to. He sure as heck didn't deserve the crap she threw at him. Tug wanted the kid to heal, and it wouldn't hurt if a few good songs came out of the experience. Seeing Kip reach for his guitar and settle back into the cushions made him smile. Maybe there was hope after all.

Toronto provided one of the largest crowds Kip ever played to at a single event, with sixty one thousand fans packed into the Skydome. He stepped out onto the stage with his guitar. Lights flashed as he picked the first few notes, and the fans went wild. Their frenzy was contagious, and he knew the band would have a great night.

It didn't take long to spot the infamous groupies at the edge of the stage. The band jokingly referred to them as Maisie and Daisy. A few of the boys enjoyed their favors on a regular basis. They were the kind of girls the fellows referred to as HAMSTERS, with changing occupations to suit whoever needed to be impressed at the time. "What do you do, darlin'?" "I'm a Hooker, Actress, Model, Stripper, Trainer, Entertainer, Runway…" Yeah right. Kip knew they were holding out to lasso him, and he wasn't interested. He'd had quite enough of sharing a woman with every other man walking.

Music filled the night air as the crowd danced and sang along. This was the kind of moment he lived for. The music flowed through him, filling him. He was the music. The huge Jumbotron screen over the stage made everyone feel they had a front row seat. Jeff got a lot of screen time, too, as his blond good looks made a sharp contrast to Kip's and earned him a following of his own.

The two friends horsed around during the upbeat songs, laughing throughout the concert, and the fans fed on it. His spirits lifted knowing this was the last night on the tour.

As he crooned the words of a love song, a lull came over the crowd. Men put their arms around their ladies, swaying together. Kip dreamed about moments like this for his own life. He wanted to put his arms around someone and just feel that sense of belonging, of complete contentment. Tansey never gave him that. He realized just how much he missed out on.

Women near the front of the stage reached out to him and called things like "I love you, Kip. I wanna make love to you." Some of the women actually cried when he sang, as though the words were personal between them. He smiled and moved down the stage. Singing about heartbreak had been easy on this tour. Those were the moments he sang the songs of his own heart.

At the end of the last song they left the stage, but instead of heading straight for the dressing rooms as usual, Kip decided to go back on for one more encore. For the first time on the tour, he used his mike to tell the techies not to shut the system down. The band returned to play three more songs and left the audience ecstatic.

While standing in the shower after, he remembered the things Julie said. He would stay and put on a good time for the fellows tonight. Tomorrow they would be heading back to Nashville, and he would be on his own.

Pulling on a pair of comfortable stone-washed jeans and a clean, navy tee shirt, he noticed how loose they seemed. He'd dropped twelve pounds over the past few months, and his frame showed it. Even his snuggest concert jeans no longer required peeling to get them off.

He joined the band and techies as they indulged in the buffet and helped himself to cheesecake. Appreciating all they'd been through on the tour, putting up with his tension and foul moods, he had arranged with his financial manager, Cree McRae, for a sizable bonus for each band member to be waiting in Toronto.

"Can I have everyone's attention?"

A flying Cheesie hit him in the head. He knew without looking who his attacker was. Creeping up behind his friend, he dumped an icy bottle of water over his head. A wet Jeff grabbed him in a headlock, and they wrestled. Julie smiled as she watched, happy to see them acting like the boys she grew up with.

It picked up the mood of the band as they started seeing traces of the old Kip returning. At least it made the past week bearable. He even gotten off the bus and played basketball with them. Many considered the portable nets they took on tour the most important equipment they carried. They were always the last things loaded on the truck and the first thing taken off.

As Kip tussled with his friend, he forgot all about handing out the bonuses, and Tug ended up distributing them. Kip got into the spirit of the party, joking and laughing until his sides hurt. He made a point of sticking to juice and bottled water so he wouldn't wake the next morning with a hangover. Tomorrow he was heading off to paradise.

•

In the parking lot, Maisie and Daisy peeked around the back corner of the stadium to see the limo waiting for Kip. His drummer, Danny, let it slip during after-sex pillow talk with Maisie that Kip would be vacationing in Ontario for the summer—information the two fans considered golden.

While following the band as it zigzagged across the states, the girls discovered a store specializing in surveillance equipment and made a few purchases certain to help them stay near their idol.

Maisie reviewed the plan one more time. "So I go out there first and play up to that chauffeur. When I have his attention, you sneak over and plant the homing device in Kip's things. I saw the roadie leave them by the trunk."

"Right, and I'll get the car so we're ready to follow him. I don't need to wish you luck. You certainly know how to handle men. Now undo those top two buttons, and get your cute little hiney swaying."

Maisie bent over and flipped her hair a few times so it looked full and fluffy as she made her approach. With confidence in hand, she sauntered across the parking lot like a runway model.

Daisy wore all black so she would blend in with the shadows. She noticed Maisie disappearing around the corner with the driver and shook her head in amusement as she slipped the device inside the keyboard case. Maisie would give it up to any guy at the drop of a hat, or a zipper as the case may be. Daisy tended to be more selective, and never lost sight of the goal—to have Kip Adams all to herself on a permanent basis.

Light spilled into the parking lot as the stadium door suddenly opened. She scampered into the shadows for cover.

Julie remained at the door, and Kip turned to say goodbye. "Thanks, Julie."

She hugged him tightly. "If you need anythin', well I know you've got my number. You use it often enough. If you don't check in with me regularly, I'm gonna send Jeff up there after ya."

He gave her a quick kiss on the cheek and turned to find Tug waiting to walk him to the limo.

"Have a good trip, Kip. Call if you need anything. Don't forget about Fan Fair in June. I know you're not ready to deal with Nashville yet, but Donna booked you last summer before you ever talked about divorce. If you're not gonna make it, let her know as soon as you can."

He dropped into the back seat and breathed a huge sigh. Finally. It took a lot of energy to put on a front for the rest of the group the past week. Some moments were genuine fun, like onstage with Jeff tonight, but for the most part it had all been an act. Now, he could be as depressed and withdrawn as he wanted without worrying about offending the sensibilities of others. He glanced at the stereo, but decided that silence after a loud concert had its virtues. He watched the lights of the big city flash by as they left the largest of the skyscrapers behind.

A dark blue Saturn pulled out onto the highway just moments behind the limousine, keeping a close tail.

●

Kip lifted one eyelid to check the clock on the table by the bed. Almost noon. Stretching between the cool clean sheets, he enjoyed a night in a bed not rolling down a highway, and this hotel provided a soft one. He allowed the somnolence to ebb away gradually rather than pushing it off as he usually did. Dreams of begging Tansey to sleep with him only woke him once during the night. A definite improvement.

As rational thought took over, he realized this was his first day of vacation. A smile played at the corners of his mouth as he envisioned it—fishing, swimming in the lake, privacy, and best of all, no women. He hoped this retreat would produce some great music. Emotional highs and lows were the impetus for some of the greatest pieces ever written.

Late April in Ontario could mean cold windy days or sweltering heat. The radio assured him it was a cool morning. After tucking his shirt into jeans, he swigged down some juice and pulled his jacket on. Tucking the car keys into his pocket, he picked up his overnight bag and headed to the elevator. The doors opened in front of him, and there stood Maisie and Daisy. Covering his surprise, he smiled and stepped in.

"Howdy, ladies. Enjoy the tour?"

Daisy moved closer, letting her breast brush against his arm and looked up at him with her large brown eyes, the name of his most recent album blazoned across the front of her white tank top.

"It was fabulous. *You* were fabulous. When do you think you'll tour again?"

"I don't know. There's a lot of work to do before we go out again. Best I can say is keep an eye on the website. It'll be posted there as soon as dates are arranged." The doors opened, and he stepped out. "Have a safe drive home, girls." With a smile and a half-hearted wave, he headed off to find the rental car.

The drive proved pleasant, with the trees in blossom and new green leaves making their debut. Wildlife abounded in Ontario once you left the heavily populated areas, and he took it all in, comparing the differences with his home in Wyoming.

Leaving the main highway at the Peterborough exit, he followed the instructions through a number of small towns until he arrived at the marina.

He parked in front of the office, and extracted his tall body from behind the wheel. Leaping up the three steps in a single bound, he opened the door of the old wooden building. A piece of peeling paint dropped off the door at his foot.

Kip glanced around the small variety store which supplied boaters with last minute necessities. An older gentleman with a two-day beard and graying hair stood behind the counter chewing on a toothpick.

"What can I do for you, young fella?"

"Howdy, I'm Chris Adams. I believe Jim Masterson called about me. I'm rentin' his place for the summer."

"He surely did. Talked to him the other day."

The old man bent and took an envelope and a brochure from under the counter. "Here's a map of the area. This here is the island you're heading off to." He jabbed a finger at the map. "They've got a big two-story redwood with a floor-to-roof window on the west side. Gilda has lots of flowering bushes out front, so you should recognize the place." He pulled a pen from his pocket and marked the spot. "I'll write down our phone number here in case you need anything. You just give a call, eh?"

"Thanks very much. I'm sorry. I didn't catch your name."

"It's Glen. Glen Miner. If I'm not around, my wife Marge will be."

"Thanks a lot." He reached up to tip a hat he wasn't wearing. "Oh, one more thing. Which boat is the Masterson's?"

"They got two of them out there, eh? There's a smaller motorboat they use for skiing, and there's the cabin cruiser. Called *Jim's Toy*. Both are at slip seventeen, right on down the left side of the building. You can leave your car in the parking lot by the docks. Just lock it up, eh? It'll be safe."

"Terrific. Well, have a good day, Glen."

"Right-o, Chris. Glad to meet you."

Using the map Glen supplied, he found the island easily. He docked the boat and followed the flower-decked walkway to the house, unlocked it, and went inside to look around. It wasn't the little summer cottage decorated in third generation Salvation Army decor he expected.

After moving his things inside and unpacking the groceries, he realized the warmth of the afternoon sun. Hat in hand, he headed to the back yard, stretched out on the hammock, and dropped his hat over his face.

Paradise.

•

CHRISTOPHER

The rented canoe skimmed along the lake, the occupants looking both left and right. Up ahead a small empty dock jutted out from the western tip of an island. Paddling along the south shore, they spotted a larger dock with a cabin cruiser, *Jim's Toy*, tied up.

"There it is."

Excitement burgeoned as they drifted in, tying their boat to a tree near the water's edge along the island's bank. Maisie stepped out and held the bow while Daisy climbed out of the precarious vessel.

"He's close by. I can feel it. It won't be long. And after spending some quality time alone with me, he'll realize he loves me. I know he will."

"Of course he will," agreed Daisy. She fully intended to grab Kip's affections for herself, but she let Maisie believe her only purpose was to help with Maisie's fantasy. She felt certain she was the one he really gazed at when singing those love songs. She only went along with Maisie because of her friend's violent temper. When Kip acknowledged his love for her, they would figure out how to dump Maisie together.

The women doused themselves with insect repellant, and Maisie hooked her small but powerful binoculars around her neck, following Daisy who had the thermos. They picked their way through the woods in the direction of the large cottage. Daisy spotted the familiar black cowboy hat in the hammock. They crept a bit closer to determine he was under it. Once certain, Maisie settled in with the thermos and binoculars, ready to spy as long as necessary to see her great love actually move.

"You go into the house, and get back the surveillance thingy before he finds it."

When Daisy failed to move straight away, Maisie raised a stern eyebrow and pointed to the house. Daisy circled around to the front, and finding the door unlocked, let herself in. Wandering through the rooms on the main floor, she set the floor plan in her mind. Off of the living room were three doors and a staircase. The first room opened into an office where she found Kip's instruments stashed. Seeing the keyboard alongside his guitar, she removed the device planted there. Moving through to the open kitchen in the back corner of the living room area, she looked out the window to be certain he was still entombed in the hammock. His lack of mobility gave her the confidence she needed.

Scurrying on tiptoe, she headed to the switchback staircase to peek upstairs. Two large bedrooms, opening onto a balcony running the full length of the house, overlooked the living room and kitchen. She found his luggage in the room at the front end of the house. Twirling around, she gloried in the thrill of being in Kip Adams' bedroom. Her hand ran lovingly over the navy blue spread on the bed, letting it linger at his pillow. She remembered the feeling of his arm brushing against her breast that morning.

"I wonder what you dream of at night? How I'd love to lie beside you and watch you sleep. Oh, Kip, I love you so much." Tears glistened in her eyes as she pondered how very deeply in love she was. Maisie would be full of questions, but she had every intention of keeping this moment a secret. It was too sacred to share.

CHAPTER 2

October 2002

She leaned over the grave and placed her white rose on the casket, aware of everyone watching her as they waited for some show of emotion. They would be disappointed. At the moment she only felt numb, as though this wasn't really happening to her. Like being cast as an extra in a movie, she witnessed the happenings around her but felt nothing. Abigail Lockner was twenty-five years old. Far too young to be burying her husband. After all, he promised her a lifetime of love and companionship.

The minister said some words, but she didn't comprehend them. Those who came to pay Drew their last respects headed to their vehicles, leaving only her sister and herself.

Claire put her arm around Abby, trying to draw her to the car, but she pulled away and stumbled back to the graveside.

"I can't go. Drew might need me. I can't just leave him here all alone." Realization that this was the end of something important finally penetrated her soul.

Reaching out and pulling her back, Claire tried to look her sister in the eye. "Abby, honey, Drew's gone. You can't do anything for him now. It's time we go home."

She jerked away, her breathing becoming deeper and irregular. She wasn't ready for this, and she needed to delay it as long as she could. "No, I can't go. I can't leave him here. Don't you see? If I go now, I'll never have him again. I can't let him go. I can't. He's my husband. I need to be with him."

Standing beside the casket, she stared down at it. "This isn't funny any more. I know you love playing jokes on me, but you're carrying this too far. I'm not going to put up with this. I refuse to be without you. You promised me." Her voice broke. "You promised! Don't you dare leave me. Not now! I won't let you go. Do you hear me? I mean it, Drew. Come back right now. Don't leave me. Please, don't leave me. Please, don't leave me." She collapsed at the side of the casket and buried her head in her arms, sobbing her heart out. "You didn't even say goodbye. Damn you, I don't know how to be without you!"

Claire tried to be strong for her sister, and it was the hardest thing she'd ever done. Now, seeing the agony her sister suffered so blatantly displayed, her own heart broke. Tears spilled down her cheeks, and she lifted Abby back into the shelter of her arm, pulling her to the car. Abby stumbled along in a daze, waiting to wake up from the nightmare.

"It'll take time, honey, but we're here for you. We'll help you through this. Things will be all right in time. You'll see."

Abby stared straight ahead, tears coursing down her cheeks. "You're wrong, Claire. Things will never be all right again. Not ever."

The Lincoln Town Car wound slowly through the hills of the Picton cemetery and exited the front gate, leaving behind all of Abigail Lockner's dreams, and hopes, and laughter to be buried along with her young husband.

•

April 2003

Gilda Masterson gazed out her front window at the pretty, pastel-colored tulips and hyacinths blooming in her front garden. She spoke into her cordless phone with concern. "How is she, Claire? A few times I've called her to go out and do something, but she always makes excuses."

Claire brushed her auburn curls behind her ear. "She's not doing very well. She's really sick with the pregnancy, morning, noon, and night. She still can't believe he's gone. It's been six months, and I would have thought by now she'd at least be trying to live again. I don't mean carrying on as though things are fine, I mean just functioning through the day, doing things that need doing, like on autopilot. Even that would be an improvement. Instead she sits in a far-off daze most of the time."

"I suppose everyone has to mourn at their own rate. Who's to say what goes on in the heart of another person and when it's time to rejoin the human race." Gilda sat on her flowered sofa with a frown creasing her forehead.

"Quite frankly, I don't want to leave on my trip Down Under without helping in some way."

Gilda's French poodle jumped into her lap, and she patted its ribboned hair. "I have an idea. Maybe I can do something for her after all. I'll talk to you later, dear."

With her plan quickly formulated, she placed the call, offering the young widow the use of her summer cottage.

Reluctant to accept at first, Abby finally yielded to Gilda's insistence. Maybe she could deal with things and put her life back together there. Privacy to help her face her new life was a prescription she was willing to take, and she was grateful for the offer.

It was the last week of April when Abby arrived at the marina. The owners, Glen and Marge, were pleased to see her again. Noticing her condition, Glen helped her carry her things to the speedboat, appropriately named the *Miz Gilda*.

The Masterson's island came into view, and she steered the boat to the small dock at the west end. Having visited many times in years past with her parents, she always preferred the rustic guest cabin tucked out of sight from the main house. A steep staircase led to a pathway that meandered through the woods to the small cottage. The trees provided perfect camouflage.

The big house offered little privacy, with a glass wall on the west side. It was a fabulous piece of architecture, but not something she would be terribly comfortable staying in alone.

In her sixth month of pregnancy, she found it more difficult to carry heavy items. A lot of things were becoming harder now. Her feet swelled if she stood too long. Getting up from a chair or bed was awkward. Unable to easily reach the sink to wash the dishes, she needed to stand sideways. If she was this big now, she didn't want to envision the daunting proportions her small frame would reach at nine months.

Setting the last box down on the coffee table, she lowered herself onto the couch to catch her breath. An hour later she opened her eyes, surprised to find she'd fallen asleep.

Deciding to enjoy the fresh, spring afternoon, she picked up her pregnancy diary and her book about fetal development, and went outside. Stretching beneath a large maple in the side yard, she opened the diary and made her entry for the day. Concentrating on her future gave her hope, even though the things to come were inextricably connected with all the things she'd lost. Just the smallest glimmer of hope, but it was there.

As she finished writing, she heard a guitar strumming in the distance. She listened with contentment to the beautiful melody sailing on the breeze until she realized she was supposed to be alone on the island. Setting the diary down, she rolled to her side to get up and went to investigate.

14

Carrie Chesney

As she progressed along the trail, the song grew louder. The music kept starting and stopping, making it difficult to locate the origin. Coming into the clearing, she tilted her head to listen and determined it came from behind the house. She was uncertain which was stronger, her curiosity, or her anger that someone was on the island who had no right to be. Without a moment's thought for her safety, she rounded the corner, ready to confront the interloper.

CHAPTER 3

Chris sat on the deck at the back of the house with his feet propped on the railing and played a few songs from his last CD to get his fingers limbered. A gentle breeze rustled the leaves under the warm sunshine. These last few days of peace had lifted his spirits. His fingers danced over the strings, and he started to play something new, something he'd never heard before. He let the serenity around him guide his fingers across the frets and liked the magic it created. Maybe the writing would come easily after all.

Setting the guitar aside, he dashed into the house and returned with a pad of stave paper and a pencil to get the new piece down. And so with a series of stops and starts, his hands ricocheted back and forth between guitar and paper, sketching out the melody. When he felt he had it just the way it should be, he sat back and played it all the way through again to listen to the flow. It was sweet. It was light. It cried out for uplifting lyrics. It was moments like this every songwriter waited for, when the music revealed itself. He felt awkward taking credit for songs that came this way. It felt more like taking dictation than originating the music himself.

"Excuse me. May I ask who you are and what you're doing here? This island is private property."

Startled by the female voice, he leaped from his chair and faced her. "Hey there, little lady, it's not nice to sneak up on a fella like that. You 'bout gave me a heart attack."

"You haven't answered my questions." She folded her arms under her chest, making her pregnancy obvious.

"No, ma'am, I haven't. But I am aware this is private property, and I'm afraid I'll have to ask you to leave." He stood with his hands on his hips studying the woman. Did she honestly not recognize him, or was it an act to get close to him? He never ceased to be amazed at the things fans would do to get to him. Even with a good security system, he came home on more than one occasion to find naked women in his pool or even his bed. Each one got the same reaction. He picked them up and threw them out. He wouldn't be the least bit surprised to find one of them followed him here. He refused to take any chances, even though her approach was novel, and he gave her a point for creativity.

"Excuse me? I'm sorry to have to tell you this, but you're the one who's going to vamoose." She peered at him, trying to get a good look in case she needed to describe his features to Gilda or the police, but he wore a black cowboy hat shading his face, and she was still distant enough to not see him clearly.

"Vamoose? I haven't heard that one for years. I like it." He shook his head and chuckled. It would make a great song title. He would have to think about it.

"You can laugh all you like, but I'm still asking you to leave." She firmly stood her ground, refusing to let this man push her around. After all, he was the intruder.

"Honey, you can ask all you like, but I paid a lot of money to have this island all to myself, and that's exactly what I expect to get. Privacy."

"Honey? Don't you honey me, mister! Are you trying to patronize me, Mr. ...?" She left her question dangling, hoping to get his name. She advanced a few steps closer trying to get a decent look at his face.

"Don't mean anythin' at all. Where I come from it's natural to call a pretty gal honey. No disrespect intended."

She looked skeptical but decided it would be counterproductive to pursue it. "Well, I'm sorry, but I happen to be a close friend of the owners, and I was assured I would have the island to myself through to the end of the summer."

"Yeah, well, I don't think so. Like I said, I paid a lot of money for this place."

"Well, just who was it you paid?" She felt certain he wouldn't know the owner's name, and then she would have him.

"Jim Masterson. He gave me the keys to the boat and the house. You can check with Glen back at the marina. He'll vouch for me. And by the way, there isn't room for two of us in this house." He quickly dropped his gaze to her belly and back up to her eyes again, "Or three as the case may be."

"You got the keys from Jim?" She looked down where her feet were supposed to be. "I apologize. I really did believe you were trespassing. I tend to get protective of my friends, and unfortunately, this time it caused me to jump to a wrong conclusion."

"That's okay. I considered you a worthy adversary until the 'vamoose' thing." He chuckled.

"Gilda gave me the keys and sent me up here for the season. And by the way, I know it's a two-bedroom house. I've been coming here for years with the Masterson's. But don't worry. I have no plans to stay in the house. I prefer the guest cottage. Jim and Gilda must not have mentioned their plans for the island to one another."

"Well, I'm glad you finally believe me. You're one stubborn lady, but I can appreciate you were defendin' your friends' property. Quite admirable really. The question now is, what are we gonna do about it?" Chris' heart plummeted. He knew this had been too good to be true.

She stared at the ground and kicked at a stone in the grass as she considered her predicament. "Do you mind if we sit down to discuss it?"

"Yeah, sure. Come on up. Can I get you a drink? I've got some cold Fruitopia."

"That sounds wonderful. I seem to be thirsty all the time." She climbed onto the deck and sat on a green Adirondack chair. The good-looking man with dark hair and a western drawl returned with a bottle of juice in each hand. He offered her one and pulled up a chair and sat down. They twisted open their bottles and both took a long drink.

"My name's Abigail Lockner. Abby." She extended her hand to him.

Chris took her delicate hand in his. "Chris Adams."

"You're not from around here, are you? You sound like you're from the American West."

"Why the American West?"

"Because Western Canadians talk the same as we do here. They don't have anything in their enunciation to give them away. Now our Maritimers are a different story. They're very easy to pick out."

"Matter of fact I'm from Wyomin', so that's a point for you."

With introductions out of the way, she got down to business. "What should we do about our problem? It seems we both came here for privacy. I don't think either of us wants to stay locked inside in order to not bother the other one."

He noted the wedding ring on her finger. "Are you alone, or is your husband with you?"

Her eyes fell instantly, and she stared intently at the juice bottle, fighting for control but couldn't keep her eyes from welling with tears. "My husband passed away a few months ago. I'm alone. Just me and the baby."

He couldn't have been more surprised. She was too young to be a widow, and being left to raise a baby on her own was downright sad. Shoot, how could he ask her to leave now? "I'm sorry, Abby. I didn't mean to pry. Are you okay?"

She lifted her brown eyes to meet his blue ones and spoke quietly. "No. I'm not okay. That's actually the reason Gilda, that's Jim's wife, sent me up here. I'm having a hard time dealing with it." She felt the first tear spill over.

"I don't want to be nosy, but can I ask how it happened?"

"He was playing hockey, and when he stepped off the ice, he dropped dead. Just like that. No warning. No pain. He was just…gone. The coroner said Drew had a congenital heart disease. We had no idea he even had it."

"What a shock for you. I think it must be harder when they go so unexpectedly. If there's some kind of sickness, at least you get a sense of gratitude that they're no longer sufferin'. It gets too hard to watch them slippin' away and not be able to help. At least it prepares you for the fact that you're gonna lose 'em."

He watched a tear trail down her cheek and empathized with her. "That's how it was for me when my father went. I still think of him every day and miss him, but I remember that last day, how I just prayed for him to let go." He leaned forward and placed a hand on hers as a gesture of comfort. "It must be even harder for you, bein' pregnant and all. I'm very sorry."

"I didn't even know I was pregnant until after he was gone. It keeps him close to me. I'll have his son or daughter with me." Abby found herself wanting to open up and talk to this man like an old friend. He seemed a sympathetic listener, and he tried to understand how she felt rather than pitying her. She had no use for pity. It was compassion she needed.

"My problem is that I don't know how I'm supposed to go on without him. We were only married two years, but we've been together since I was sixteen. He's always been there at the center of my world. I didn't expect something like this to happen for another sixty years. Now I'm supposed to figure out how to keep on living. It doesn't make sense that the world keeps turning, and life goes on around me."

She reached up and brushed at a tear with her fingertip. "Drew was my first and only love. I can't imagine ever feeling that way again, so I suppose I'll be alone for the rest of my life. I mean, of course I'll have our child, but it's not the same as a partner to grow old with, is it?"

She realized how much she'd been talking, surprised at the flood of words that flowed from her. "I'm sorry. I'm talking too much. I hope I haven't made you uncomfortable by getting so personal. It's strange. I don't usually expose myself like this." She flushed with embarrassment. Maybe it was the philosophy of being easier to talk to a stranger. No, that wasn't it. She was comfortable with him. His eyes reflected a tenderness that made her feel safe.

19

"Hey, don't worry about it. You need to talk about it. I hope I'm a good listener."

"Too good. Thanks. What about you, Chris? What brings you to our little island, and how long are you planning on staying?" Maybe he would only stay a week or two, and they could work out a deal.

"I'm a songwriter, so my time is my own for a while. I planned to spend at least two months here."

"And that's why you're here? To write music? I heard you playing something quite beautiful. I followed it here. Did you write it?"

"Just now. Glad you liked it, but no, it's not the only reason I need solitude." His eyebrows lifted. "Wait a minute, I think I just named the song." He grabbed a pencil and scribbled the word Solitude across the top of the sheet music. She thought it interesting to watch an artist at work.

He dropped the pencil and turned back to face her. She'd opened her heart right there in front of him and trusted him, a stranger, not to harm it. He never knew a woman who allowed herself that vulnerability. If he reciprocated and opened himself to her in return, what would she do? Would she laugh and mock him? He stopped being open a long time ago, knowing it would only bring hurt. Did he dare to chance it now?

Glancing up, he saw her wiping away tears with the back of her hand. He took a deep breath and plunged in. "I'm here because I just went through a nasty, and rather public, divorce. I live in Nashville, and the music world is a rather tight community. Everybody knows everybody, and all the details of your life. It's like livin' in a small town in that respect. I can't stand to be there with her always in my face."

He took a chance and peeked at her. Finding her listening intently, he carried on. "I wasted five years of my life with a woman who was in love with my money and all the things it could buy. She didn't care for me at all right from the beginnin'. It wasn't long after we married that the only thing we shared was my bank account and the house. She gave herself to anyone willin' to help her along on her road of self-importance but not to her own husband. I finally gave up tryin'."

With a sigh he leaned back and took a drink before continuing. "I was alone in the marriage too long. It drained me. I have to do some healin' before I can go back into that world."

She was still listening, her forehead creased with concern. She hadn't strayed off into her own world of thoughts. She mimicked his earlier comfort to her, sitting forward and putting her hand over his, giving it a sympathetic squeeze.

"I'm sorry," she whispered.

It was going to be hard not to like this woman who sat looking at him with kindness.

She summarized their situation. "Looks like we're both here for the same thing. We're each grieving over a marriage that didn't end on our terms. We've both been through a horrific time and need to deal with it before facing the rest of the human race."

He saw the parallels she drew and realized she was right.

"Well, Abby, about who stays and who goes, do you think we could call a truce?" He came to get away from women, and now here he was considering living in seclusion with one. At least in her situation she wouldn't be pursuing him, and it seemed the only solution for him to be able to stay.

"You mean both stay? Learn to get along and share our toys?" Abby started to grin and felt her mood lighten. She couldn't remember the last time anything made her smile.

"I'd like to give it a try. We both need to be here, and we each have our own house for privacy. If we need someone to talk to, well maybe we could be friends?" He smiled in return. For him, being friends with a woman would be a new experience. Well, there was Julie, but she was really a sister. "We can get together for a neighborly visit on occasion, maybe even have dinner together once in awhile. I can't tell you how much better I feel just for havin' talked with you this afternoon. It's like the burden got a bit lighter somehow."

"I know what you mean. I feel the same."

"Hey, you know how to find me, but I don't have a clue where the guest house is." Continuing to lighten the mood, he teased, "You've seen mine, can I see yours?"

She laughed out loud at the double entendre, and he watched her face light up. It was amazing to hear a woman laugh so naturally, without coyness. "Sure, I'll show you the way. But before I go, would you mind playing 'Solitude' for me again? I mean, I understand if you don't like people to hear your work before it gets published or recorded or whatever it is you do with it, but I'd really like to hear it."

He picked up his guitar and took another drink from his juice bottle. "For you, my lady, I will play it."

She lay back on the lounge, and soon her eyes closed as she listened to the changing chords. She let the music run through her, feeling peace inside for the first time in many months. Absolute peace.

After the song finished, he played on, his sweet gentle melodies filling the air. When he observed her relaxed with her eyes closed, he studied her as his fingers so easily found the notes. She was a beautiful woman. Her chestnut brown hair surrounded her face like a halo as it moved slightly, keeping time with the music. It hung down past her shoulders and was layered with a natural bouncy curl. Her long, dark lashes lay like feathers against her cheeks. Her lips weren't overly large, but they were attractive, even as she was biting the bottom one. Her face was free of make up, and he was taken by the natural

21

look. Tansey always applied the entire cosmetic counter from Bloomindales before she let anyone see her.

An hour passed before he placed the instrument on the table. She instantly opened her eyes. "Concert over?"

"For now. I don't want to bore my only audience." Tansey never wanted to sit and listen to him play. It didn't require a credit card.

"No, I'm not bored. I kept my eyes closed hoping you'd forget I was here and keep playing. The music was beautiful. I felt it flowing through me and filling me. I know that sounds dumb. Most people think I'm nuts. I usually listen to music alone, so I can feel it without being teased."

"No, I know what you mean. That's exactly why I write it. I hear it playin' inside of me, just waitin' to get out. Do you listen to country music?" The moment of truth.

"No, actually I don't. I usually just listen to pop. I do prefer the 'classic oldies' to a lot of what's out now. My taste is quite eclectic ranging from Queen to Donny Osmond with a little of the Who and the Beach Boys thrown in. I also know a lot of Broadway music."

"That certainly covers a broad spectrum." He looked at her incredulously.

She laughed. "I've heard some country. Occasionally a song will cross over and hit the pop charts. I like Hope Hilton, but generally there are too many things about it I don't care for."

"Like what?" Accustomed to women throwing themselves at him and praising his work, it startled him to have somebody up front enough to actually deny liking the genre as a whole.

"Well, I don't care for harmonicas, or banjos, or washboards." She paused and thought for a moment. "Or whiskey jugs. And I don't like a lot of twanging and yodeling. And all the lyrics are the same—she stole my truck, my dog, and ran away with my best friend Elmer."

He laughed at her description.

"I hope I haven't offended you. Now, what you were playing was beautiful. It didn't have any of those things. There was nothing hillbilly about it."

Chris knew what she was referring to. "What you don't like is a sub-genre called bluegrass. I don't do bluegrass. Actually, what they refer to as contemporary country often has a more of a rock beat to it, and there are some terrific love songs."

"I like love songs. As much as I love and feel the music, it's the lyrics that win or lose me. The more intimate the lyrics, the better the song. It always amazes me a guy can write such stuff when men are generally so emotionally reserved. It's not often you find a man who actually tells you what he feels. Women are supposed to feel lucky for the crumbs of affection we're thrown. I mean, you can sit and spout off for ten minutes telling him the deepest thoughts of your heart and in return you get something like, 'Yeah, I love you too'. We have to accept that romance is a thing of music and poetry, but it's not reality."

"Your husband wasn't romantic?"

She giggled at the absurdity of the idea. "Not really. He wasn't a man with all the flowery words that women like to hear. Well, some of us women anyway."

Not wanting to overstay her welcome on their first visit together, she started shifting forward in the chair. "I hope you'll play for me again sometime. I don't want to sound like a suck up, but I really thought it was wonderful."

"I'd be happy to. However, you'll have to make me a promise first."

"And what would that be?"

"Honesty."

"Pardon me?"

"When I write new music, I want you to tell me honestly what you think. If you don't like it, say so. Honest criticism. You'd be amazed the junk people applaud because they think it'll make the artist happy. I want an honest critique. I'm a big boy. I can handle it. Agreed?"

"That seems an easy price for the pleasure I get from listening. Of course I'll agree, not that my opinion is worth anything."

Her smile gave him a warm feeling. He began to believe that maybe it was a good thing he would be sharing the island. Here sat someone with no idea of his celebrity status, accepting him for the man inside rather than the persona the tabloids and magazines created. It had been a long time since someone had seen him through those eyes. It would be refreshing. Times like this kept him grounded. He tried to keep in perspective the fact that he was just a rancher's kid who happened to get lucky. A lot of artists began believing the fan hysteria and the praises of the press. He believed once you started to believe the hype, you lost your sense of self.

"Well then, Miz Abby, it would be my pleasure to play for you. Anytime you hear me playin' and wanna mosey on over, you're surely welcome."

"I wouldn't want to bother you if you'd rather be alone."

"Okay, if you come at a time when I need to be by myself, I'll just tell you to vamoose. Honesty. How's that for a deal?"

"Honesty in all things is the only way if we're going to be friends." She reached out a hand, and he helped her to her feet. "I think I'll just vamoose right now before I overstay my welcome."

"All right. Let me put the guitar inside, then I'll walk ya home."

While he took his instrument into the house, Abby stood on the deck and gazed into the woods. Detecting a sudden flash of color, she strained to determine what it was. Seeing nothing out of the ordinary, she decided it must have been a bird. He rejoined her, and they headed to her cottage together.

Reaching around her and over her shoulder, he brushed aside branches that protruded in the pathway. A few twists and turns down the trail brought them to the clearing around the guest cabin. She walked to the maple tree to pick up the books she left there earlier.

He leaped in front of her. "Don't bend over. Let me get that for you."

"Thank you. I'd love to declare independence and capability, but the truth is it's getting harder to bend over. I can't believe how awkward I feel."

"It won't last forever. When's the baby due?

"Middle of July. I'm going to run down to Peterborough to have the baby there, then bring him back here for the rest of the summer. My sister, Claire, will probably come for the last week or so, just to make sure I get to the hospital. She's worried about me being alone when the time comes." She led the way to the verandah and sat on the porch swing.

"Well, Abby, I'm pleased to have made your acquaintance. Give me a call at the house if you need anythin' at all. I'm gonna head on back and work on that song." He stepped off the porch. "Have a good read."

With a wave of his hand, he started down the trail and stuffed his hands into his jeans pockets, muttering, "She stole my truck, my dog, and my best friend, Elmer. Hah, *Elmer*. Where'd she get that one?" He shook his head and laughed all the way back to the big house.

●

Maisie made her way back through the woods to Daisy. "There's another cottage on this stupid island that the broad is staying in. I don't know who she is, but they seem to know each other." She resumed her surveillance position.

"You almost blew our cover. She stood on the deck and stared out here like she was looking for something. I think she spotted you when you left." Daisy was upset by Maisie's carelessness. If their plan was exposed, then all these months were a waste.

"Don't worry about that now. Kip's coming back to the house. Looks like he's laughing about something. Haven't seen that happen before. It's not a good sign. I think we'll have to split up. You go keep watch on her, and I'll stay here and keep an eye on him. We'll get together back at our camp at nine o'clock if nothing's going on."

Irritated, but certainly not surprised at Maisie's division of duties, she replied, "I think it would make more sense for you to watch her since you know where her place is, and I don't."

Maisie took hold of her wrist and squeezed tightly. "I said, you go watch her. Don't argue with me. He's mine. Just walk straight west through the trees, and you'll find her cabin."

"Okay, I'll go." Daisy wrested her wrist out of the tight grasp. If Maisie didn't get hold of that temper she would find herself alone. Daisy refused to put up with her much longer. She took her flask of coffee and headed off toward the cottage where she spent the remainder of the afternoon watching the pregnant woman read a book, then go inside at five o'clock. Darkness crept around the cabin earlier because of the trees acting as barricades against the light of the setting sun.

Peering in the window, she saw the woman sitting on the sofa, her legs curled around her, staring at nothing while listening to a CD repeat over and over. At nine o'clock she rose and turned off the stereo and the lamp before going into the bedroom.

Abby decided a hot shower before bed might help her to sleep better. Carrying her robe and her vanity case into the bathroom, she turned on the faucet. While waiting for the water to heat, she opened the medicine chest to unpack her things.

A single bottle of men's cologne sat on the shelf. Pain tore through her as memories of their last trip together flooded her mind. Drew. He would never share this place with her again. The emptiness consumed her.

Daisy had a hard time changing positions, her muscles cramped from immobility. She stretched and started shaking out her arms and legs in small movements to get her blood circulating again.

The bathroom light went on, and she heard the water from the shower. Nothing worth staying around for. An entire evening wasted that she could have been watching Kip.

As she turned to make her way back to her own campsite she heard a heart stopping wail, clearly the sound of an animal in agony. She debated what to do when the woman returned to the bedroom holding something in her hand, her arms wrapped around herself. She curled up on the bed and sobbed. After ten minutes of watching with concern, Daisy finally determined that while the woman was obviously in great pain, it wasn't physical. She kept crying out the name "Drew," which probably meant the baby was his, not Kip's.

She left the woman to grieve in privacy and made her way to find Maisie.

CHAPTER 4

Nashville sunshine spilled into the bedroom when she pulled the green chintz drapes open. She tucked her pink silk blouse into her black, pleated pants as she crossed the room. Pulling her brush through her long, glossy blonde hair, she studied her face in the mirror. Most of her make-up was still in place. A quick brush of blush and some fresh lipstick would make it perfect again.

"Tansey, I've told you to stay away from the windows. Just because you're divorced now doesn't mean this affair can become public. If anyone, and I mean anyone, finds out we're lovers, the whole game is over. It's the end for both of us. I know you don't want that."

"Of course I don't. It's easier now that I don't have to go home to him. I can actually stay overnight on occasion, but there are still too many people in town who are loyal to him."

"Don't forget I'm s'posed to be one of those people. If Kip ever got wind of this we'd both be dead, and you know it. I do love that body of yours, darlin', but I'd like to keep my own in one piece."

"Don't lecture me, or I'll go share this body with someone else instead."

"You already do. You think I don't know about the others? Go ahead, spread yourself anywhere you please. Just don't go bringin' me any diseases. I don't care who you get it on with, long as you keep your mouth shut about gettin' it here."

"I think I'll go shopping today. I want to redecorate some of the rooms in the mansion. I'm so glad you talked him into letting me have the house. That was right kind of you. It's got the proper address for a woman in my position, and I do love the ballroom for parties." She took one last look in the mirror. She was perfect. As always. "Well, I'm leaving now. Do you have something for me?" She walked to the beside and held her hand out.

"Just a minute, darlin'." He threw the covers off and walked naked across the bedroom to his desk. Opening the top drawer he pulled out a check, already made out and signed, and handed it to her. "You have a good time shoppin'. I'll give you a call in a few days."

Tansey took the check with one hand and reached out her other hand to give him a lingering fondle while counting the number of zeros on the line. It would be enough to keep her busy for a few hours. Folding it neatly in half, she tucked it in her purse as she strolled to the bedroom door, knowing he watched her hips sway in her snugly fitted slacks. At the doorway, she turned and blew him a kiss.

●

Abby grieved more openly for Drew than she had at home; talking to him, screaming, crying, and longing for his arms to comfort her. When tragedy hits, a person turns to their best friend for consolation. The question she still had no answer to was what do you do when it's your best friend who is gone?

She thought of going to Chris but for two days didn't even get dressed, leaving the bed only to be sick. Today she got up and put clothes on. It was only sweats, but she felt as though she was trying. Not having showered since leaving home, she knew she was starting to smell. Her hair hung limp and greasy. All the crying left her with a swollen, red face, a sore throat and a stuffy nose.

Emerging from the house, she sat on the verandah swing with her pregnancy diary in hand, unopened. She knew she was supposed to have joy from this baby, but she thought only of Drew not being there to share it. Having always been so strong, so sure of herself, she now felt she would be forever lost and never find her way to the light.

Chris stayed busy finishing the instrumentation for *Solitude* and started another song, a silly piece called, *I Don't Have a Truck, I Don't Have a Dog, and I've Never Had a Friend Named Elmer*. He hadn't heard a peep from Abby, and after a few days passed he thought he should check on her. After all, she was a nice girl having a rough time.

Coming around the corner of the cabin, he caught sight of her on the swing and was shocked. She looked like she'd been to hell and back. When she lifted her swollen, red eyes he saw there was no sparkle, no life.

He stepped onto the porch and leaned against the post with his hands stuffed in his pockets. "Anythin' I can do for you, Abby?"

"I don't think so."

"Why don't we take a little walk?"

"I don't want to. I don't want to do anything."

He took her book away, set it on the swing beside her, and took both of her hands in his. "I know you don't, but let's go anyway. That baby needs its mama to get some fresh air." He pulled her to her feet and led her down the steps. His instinct wanted to keep hold of her hand or put his arm around her, but he didn't know her well enough to be so forward.

She fell into step alongside him, and they walked the trail to where the *Miz Gilda* sat docked. Beautiful pinks and purples painted across the cloudless sky held their attention. Both lost in their own thoughts, they stood until darkness surrounded them. Realizing the bats had started their nightly swoops to control the bug population, he suggested they head back to her cabin.

"When was the last time you ate?"

"I don't remember," she admitted.

"That's pretty much what I thought. I'm gonna fix dinner for ya tonight."

"No, really, you don't have to do that."

"I know I don't have to. But I would like to spend a bit of time with a friend, so humor me." They climbed the steps, and he opened the front door for her.

"I can fix it. You don't have to," she protested.

"Are you afraid of my cookin'?"

"Should I be?" She didn't notice he went to the bathroom instead of the kitchen, turning on the shower and checking the water temperature. Returning, he took hold of her shoulders and guided her to the bathroom doorway.

"You will feel a million times better after a shower. It always works wonders for me. Just let it wash off the stress and worry. I'll fix dinner while you get cleaned up. Anythin' you need?"

She noticed the towel still sitting on the hamper where she left it three days before. "No, thanks. I have everything I need here."

"All right. I'll leave you to it." He closed the door behind him and headed to the kitchen. Knowing anything heavy wouldn't be welcome in her empty stomach, he steered away from the meat and potatoes route. Welsh Rarebit soon broiled in the oven, and two salads sat on the counter. Grabbing some dishes from the cupboard, he set the table.

He noticed the candlesticks on the fireplace and automatically went for them. Carrying them to the table, he stopped in his tracks and put them back, unlit, on the mantle. Candles implied romance.

He looked through the CD's on the shelf and flipped in a disc of *Elton John's Greatest Hits*. Browsing through the collection, he decided she called it right on. It was so varied it would be difficult to stick her in any particular category. She even had the Mormon Tabernacle Choir.

Interesting woman.

He picked up her book on pregnancy from the coffee table and sat down. Opening it at her bookmark, he found a picture of the fetus at 28 weeks. He became so engrossed he almost didn't notice the water shut off.

Abby used the door connecting the bathroom with the bedroom. What she really wanted was to slip into a fresh nightgown and fall back into bed, but instead put on a blousy smock top and a pair of maternity jeans. She rubbed the excess water out of her hair and brushed it. Feeling considerably fresher, she went to the living room.

He carried the dinner to the table. She sat across from him, looking appreciatively at the food in front of her and began to feel hungry for the first time in days.

"This looks great. Thanks. For everything."

"It's not a problem. Listen, darlin', you should have called me. What happened?"

"The other night, the day we met, I found some of Drew's things, and it took me by surprise. If I'd known those things were there it wouldn't have shaken me so badly. It helped me work a lot out of my system. Stuff I haven't dealt with until now. It's why I came to the island."

He poured them each a glass of milk and took a long drink. "I can understand that. Sometimes you can get through things by yourself that are harder with someone else hangin' around. But, darlin', you gotta remember that little baby there. You can't let it go so long without takin' care of him, ya know. You've got to eat and get some proper sleep. Have you slept at all?"

"Little bits here and there. Nothing solid or replenishing. I'm sure tonight will be better. I think I'm working through this. I can't believe it, but I am."

"At least I have my music. It's therapeutic. Helps me work through things that trouble me."

"You're lucky to have it. I don't have an outlet to pour myself into. Nothing outside of the baby, and that has its connection to Drew. Maybe I need to find an interest to fill my hours. My mother always used to say the best way to get over your problems is to serve someone else who's worse off." She finished her salad and was most of the way through the broiled sandwiches. She still didn't look great, but far better than when he arrived.

"I think when you've worked through the grief, an outside interest will be good. But if you don't work this through first, it'll just build up inside until you eventually fall apart. I think you're doin' it right, Abby. I wish I had the same opportunity. I got the divorce quickly and left right away to go on the road. I've been travelin' four months straight, consumed with the work and not really dealin' with the personal stuff. It made me a pretty miserable person to be with, I can tell ya."

"Why would you have to go on the road? I thought you were a song-writer." She stared at him with a puzzled expression.

He realized he'd put his foot in the puddle now. He wondered how to step out of it gracefully without leaving a muddy trail. "Well, I am a songwriter. I also do some work at the recordin' studio, I produce a band, and I have responsibilities in the CMA." All true. He simply left out the part about being one of the largest names to ever come out of Nashville.

"When do you ever have a minute to yourself? No wonder you needed privacy. Then you turn around and ask why didn't I call you for help? I think you have enough worries without adding me to the list."

"Wrong." He reached across and took her hand. Staring into her eyes he told her, "My friends and family are always a priority over business, and they are never a bother. Never. You're on that list now. You hear me? I don't want you to think twice about callin' if you need me. Especially now. In this world, on this island, there is only us. We've agreed to be there for each other. Don't back out on me now. If you don't call on me when you need to, how can I be comfortable callin' on you? And I promise you, I will."

She saw the look in his eyes. This was important to him. "Okay, I promise the next time I go through something like this, I'll call you. Even if it's just to let you know."

"That's better. My work will never be more important than my friends. It never has been, and I don't plan on changin' my ways now."

"I think that's rather admirable. I don't know many men who let friends and family remain their top priority. I know a lot who live and breathe for their career, though."

He smiled and let go of her hand. Gathering up the dishes, he took them into the kitchen. "I'm lucky to be established enough in my career to have that luxury. I'm just gonna clean up here. Won't take me five minutes. Why don't you go and sit? I'll be right behind you."

He finished in the kitchen and noticed how relaxed she seemed. Her blouse suddenly jumped as he crossed the living room, and his eyes grew large, stunned. "What was that?"

She put her hand on her stomach and smiled. "He's awake. That was just the baby stretching out his legs. Do you want to feel?" She reached for his hand.

He stepped closer and sat beside her. "Can I?" He timidly allowed her to place his hand over her stomach. The baby obliged by rolling over and wiggling right under it. He looked at her with wonder in his eyes. "That's the most incredible thing. I mean, I've been there for foalin' and calfin' an' all, but I've never felt a real baby." The baby moved again, with repetitious thumps as though trying to kick his hand away. She watched his face and giggled.

"I take it you don't have children." She noticed a dark shadow cross his face as he removed his hand.

"No. That was another big disappointment for me. She knew how badly I wanted kids, told me she wanted them too, before we got married that is. Of course afterwards it was a different story. She wouldn't do anythin' that might change her figure. And to get 'fat' as she called it was disgustin'. You're carryin' a child created by your love for one another. What man wouldn't find that a beautiful sight? I sure know what it felt like not to see it. It haunted me for a long time. I suppose in retrospect it's a good thing we never did. Tansey would make a lousy mother."

"Tansey?"

"Yeah, that's her name. Tansey Adams, Nashville's top fundraiser. Not because she's interested in actually helpin' any of the causes. She just sees it as a reason to throw a party with A-list people and get her name in the paper. It makes me sick to watch her in action. Oh, she can schmooze with the best of 'em. Gushin' all over the men to get a sizable check from 'em. With the women she puts on a phony social butterfly act and pretends she's their best friend. When the evenin's over she hasn't got a nice word to say about any of 'em. Her pleasure is in ridiculin' them all. I've learned that she actually despises all other women. It's as though every one out there is competition to her."

"She sounds totally charming. I'm sorry I won't have the opportunity to meet her." Abby realized she didn't know him well enough to display such sarcasm and felt the blush rising in her cheeks. "I'm sorry. I had no right. Obviously you found some redeeming qualities to love her as much as you do."

"No, unfortunately you're right on the mark. I'm just startin' to see that she's not at all the person I thought she was. It took me a long time to recognize the truth. Much too long. And when it all sinks in, I'll be over her."

"Maybe it isn't really her that you're mourning."

"What do you mean?"

"Well, you've been unhappy for such a long time with her, maybe you stopped loving her awhile ago. Maybe the thing that's really hurting is not the loss of Tansey, but the loss of your dreams. The things you hoped she would give you. Love, children, attention, kindness, a companion to share your hopes and dreams, a home where you can go to be safe from the rest of the world. I'm not saying I'm right, I'm only throwing out possibilities, food for thought."

"Abby, that's the smartest thing anyone's said to me in a long time. I'm gonna seriously think about that. What you say makes sense, ya know." He sat back and considered it. "Are you always this insightful?"

"It happens on occasion. I wish I could see my way through my own problems as clearly." She became still and stared down into her hands. "You know, I used to dream of Drew placing his hand on my stomach to feel our baby move, just the way you did. I miss him so much. I still expect him to open the door and come in or be on the other end of the phone if I need to talk to him. Things happen and I automatically think I'll have to remember to tell Drew about that, and then I remember. Sometimes I think this ache will last forever."

He wanted to put his arm around her in comfort. Instead he gave her a moment of silent compassion, then changed her focus to something that made her happier. "You keep referrin' to the baby as *he*. Do you know for certain it's a boy?"

"Actually, I don't. We always talked about a boy first, so I think of it that way. I'd be just as happy with a little girl, though. We wanted four. What about you. How many did you want?"

"Well, I know people are having a lot fewer children these days, but growin' up on the ranch I was real lonely for other kids. My mama had complications after I was born and couldn't have any more. I had friends on the next ranch, but it's not as though we could get together to play every day. Jeff and Julie were eight miles away. I guess I decided then that I wanted a whole passel. I know, that's easy for me to say. I'm not the one who has to go through pregnancy or give birth. But I always planned on doin' my share. You know, bein' there for the long haul, being a real part of their lives."

He stretched his legs out and put his feet on the coffee table before continuing, "I make enough money to easily support a large family. I know a lot of women want a career, and I don't have a problem with that." His brow creased as he thought about it. "I think too many make their job more important than their husband and children. Personally, I always felt the career was just a way to take care of the important things. Not *be* the most important thing."

She thought about his words. Did they sound sexist? Maybe to some women, but not to her. "I always planned to stay home with the children, at least while they were small. As a child, I had a secure feeling that mother would always be there when I got home from school. My father never felt that what she did was less important than his job. He respected that the house didn't clean itself or the dinner get to the table by itself. Now, I'll be a single mother who has to go to work to take care of my child. It's certainly different than the dream."

"What do you do? For a job I mean."

"I graduated from Waterloo as a CPA."

"You're an accountant?"

"Don't sound so surprised. We can't all have creative jobs, Mozart." She saw him grin at her teasing. "Some of us have to tend to the practical side of life."

"No. I think it's fabulous. I admire a woman with a brain."

She gave him a mock frown, and he laughed.

"I've had my accountant for seven years now. He's a good friend, so I'm lucky in that department. But you know, I don't think the books have been audited by an independent agent for a long time, and that's not smart business. Maybe after the baby comes I'll hire you for the job if ya want it. I'll pay ya well with no time limit imposed. That way you can do it as the baby allows ya the time. What do ya think?"

"There are different tax laws between Canada and the States, but I can read up on it if you really want me to. The bookkeeping should be straight-forward. Sure. I'll do it. Give me something to occupy my mind."

"Then it's a deal." He leaned his head back smiling, then realized he couldn't let Abby look at the books until she knew the truth of his identity. Honesty in all things. That is what she said. Already he was lying. He hoped she would forgive him when she found out. If not, he would go home, and she would be here, and they would never see each other again anyway. Would it really matter? Yes, it mattered to his integrity. For some reason he cared what this chestnut-haired, pregnant woman thought of him.

CHAPTER 5

May arrived and with it came rain. Four days in a row thus far. Chris spent the second day of the downpour at Abby's cabin. They played Monopoly, Scrabble, and Risk. She made burgers and fries, and they baked a batch of brownies together. With fun and laughter all day long, the rain fell unnoticed.

Today she would spend the day at the house. She dropped a bunch of CDs into a plastic shopping bag with her slippers, maneuvered into her raincoat, and with both hands picked up the triple layer fudge cake covered with foil.

Chris noticed her scampering across the back yard and opened the door as she came up on the deck. He reached out and confiscated the cake. She stepped inside and hung her coat on a hook in the mudroom.

"You're gonna spoil me, Abs. This looks delicious! Can't remember the last time somebody baked me a cake. You know, this means we'll have to exercise to work it off after we eat it."

"Ha, you work it off. I'll just toss it back up anyway." She took off her shoes at the boot mat and put her slippers on.

"You didn't have to take your shoes off."

"Careful. You're showing your American thinking. This is Canada, eh?" She laughed. "You'd be hard pressed to find one who wears outdoor shoes in the house. Tradition. We always take shoes off when we enter a house."

"You're weird."

"No, we just don't want to get people's carpets and floors dirty. It's a courtesy thing. You know we have a reputation as a courteous nation. Besides, feet are more comfortable without shoes on."

"Yeah, well it wasn't too courteous to try throwin' me off the island that first day, *eh?*"

"Touche'."

He set the cake on the kitchen counter, and they went into the living room. He sat on the sofa, and she put a few CDs into the stereo tray before dropping sideways into an overstuffed chair with one foot tucked beneath her and the other hanging over the arm.

"How you feelin' today? You're lookin' good."

"I'm all right. My little friend is making it uncomfortable to stand for too long. He's been busy this morning. I think he's practicing for track and field. Running, jumping, and hurdles by the feel of it."

"Heck no, he's practicin' for bronc ridin'."

She laughed. "We don't raise too many rodeo cowboys in these parts. I used to think I'd like living on a ranch. What's it really like? There certainly has to be more to it than riding a horse around all day. Tell me about Wyoming."

"It's amazin'ly different from here. First off, there's the vegetation, or lack of it. The space is wide open. Never saw more than a few cottonwood trees Mama planted near the house, except in town. You can see unobstructed for miles. The smell is different, too, because you have a lot of desert and sagebrush. The air is drier. The breeze is hot in the summer, and smells carry a long distance. You don't get to hear leaves rustlin', or the sound of water. Birds are mostly birds of prey, ya know, hawks, eagles, things like that. And colors. Wow, you have so many here in so many different things. Out there the color comes from the soil and rock stratifications. Shades of brown and orange and red. We have mountains to the west of the ranch that make Ontario look pretty flat. Some sections have meadow grassland but it's mostly closer to the Wind River."

She watched the transformation of his features as he talked of home. She could hear his deep affection in the timbre of his voice.

"Now with Daddy gone, it's mine. I go back home when I can to help out with the busy times of year: breedin', birthin', brandin', and castratin'—you know, the fun stuff. Most of the time I have enough men hired on to run it, and Mama's got her eye on things."

"Why do you castrate them?"

"Not good to have too many bulls around, just need enough for reproduction purposes. They get mean and hard to handle, and they don't like bein' around other bulls. So, the rest are castrated. Makes the meat a lot more tender, and that is their purpose. It's a beef ranch."

"Sounds charming. Is it gory?"

"Not at all." He sat forward, his elbows propped on his knees as he warmed to his subject. "We get them in the brandin' stall. While one end is gettin' the ranch brand burned on, the other end gets a little band slipped on. It basically strangulates the blood flow and after a while the testicles just fall off. Then you go collect 'em up and cook 'em. Cowboy delicacy eatin' Rocky Mountain oysters."

Abby covered her mouth and dashed for the bathroom. He followed. His solid stomach didn't get upset by things like this. He'd watched enough friends vomiting like Vesuvius after a night out drinking.

Kneeling on the floor, she hung onto the toilet seat for dear life as her stomach heaved. He ran a face cloth under cold water. Wringing it out, he got down on one knee next to her and laid it across the back of her neck. Cradling the other arm across the front of her shoulders, he supported her while she continued retching. He gently rubbed her back which he knew hurt from the stomach convulsions. When she was through, he pulled her to lean against his chest while he mopped her forehead and wiped her mouth with the cold cloth.

"Thanks," she said gratefully.

"I'm sorry, Abigail. I suspect my big mouth was the cause of that. I should have been more sensitive." Keeping his arm around her, he walked her back to the living room where she lay down on the sofa. He covered her with a mohair throw blanket. Sitting across from her, he hung his head. "I really am sorry."

"Don't worry. I've been doing it for so long now I think I'm actually getting used to it. I'm sorry you had to see me that way."

"Can I get you anythin'?"

"Not right now. I just want to rest my stomach if that's all right."

"Of course. Baby okay?"

She opened her eyes and saw the concern on his face. "Baby's just fine. Doesn't bother him a bit." She closed her eyes again and relaxed. "I'm imagining what Wyoming looks like. The picture in my head is beautiful. Lots of buttes and color patterns in the rock layers. And there must be some waterfalls in those mountains." A smile spread on her lips as she described the images she saw.

"Abs, I was wonderin'," he paused, hardly believing he was considering it, "would you like to come out to Wyomin' sometime and see it? I mean, you could stay at the ranch, not durin' brandin', but maybe durin' birthin' time. I'd like to show you my home. I think you'd love ridin' out on a horse to discover the hidden wonders in the mountains. And the sunsets are absolutely breathtakin'."

"It sounds wonderful! I'd love to go. I've always wanted to travel. But you might decide when your vacation is over that you've had more than enough of me and never want to see me again. I don't want you to feel obliged."

"You're an unusual woman, Abby Lockner."

"Is that a compliment or an insult?"

"You're not like any woman I've ever known. Except maybe my mama."

"Well then, I hope you like your mother."

He laughed. "Yeah, I do."

He couldn't believe he'd invited her into his world. He didn't share Wyoming with anyone. Tansey had only been once, finding it so distasteful she never returned. She didn't want to get dirty, and there was no one there to impress. It was a bore, especially with no shopping. The local stores were too hick for her upper-class taste. She felt the people socially beneath her, and her behavior embarrassed him. He didn't think Abby would be like that.

"Maybe next summer if ya want. You'll be adjusted to motherhood by then. Maybe even be ready for a bit of a break. If you let her, my mama will just steal that baby. She loves little ones so much and never gets enough of holdin' one. Then we could go out ridin' whenever ya wanted, or you could come to the stables to be there for the foalin' if ya'd like."

She pictured a baby just learning to toddle about, *oohing* and *aahing* at the animals. She imagined Chris on a horse, holding the baby on the saddle in front of him. The image was so vivid she could see it as easily as if she was watching a movie.

"A video camera," she blurted out.

"Well that comment came from nowhere. What's it supposed to mean?"

"Oops! Sorry. Thinking out loud I guess. I was just thinking that I should get a video camera before the baby comes. I'm imagining him at the ranch and how fun it will be watching him. Then I realized I want movies of it. Of everything in his life."

"Sounds like a good idea to me. Say, what are you gonna name this little buckaroo? Seems we oughta call him somethin' other than 'he'."

"I don't know. I'm thinking of Andrew, after his father, but I haven't made a final decision yet."

"Well, do me a favor. Don't call him Elmer. We wouldn't want him to grow up and run off with his best friend's wife, his truck and his dog now, would we?"

She giggled, unable to believe he remembered. He had such a natural way of making her laugh spontaneously.

"I could name him after you. I think Mozart Lockner sounds pretty good."

"Sass-mouthed girl! You remind me of Julie. You two would get along like a house on fire. I think I'll make certain you never meet. I wouldn't stand a chance with both of ya around! I'd have to pack up my saddle bags and go out on a cattle drive."

37

"I think Julie and I should definitely get together. Think of all the women we could save. After all, if you're out on a drive you can't be breakin' girls' hearts all over Tennessee. Good lookin' fella like you, I'll bet they just drop like flies wherever you go, don't they?"

"Yeah, right." He tried to sound sarcastic. She had no idea how close to the truth that was. Better get her away from this subject as quickly as possible. "Anyway, what about this baby's name? You could call him Andy to distinguish between him and Drew. And what if it's a little girl? Have you thought of that?"

"I think I might just go with Andy either way. Andrew for a boy, Andrea for a girl. That makes it a pretty simple decision, doesn't it? It seems the right thing to name it after him. It's like a gift. He left a piece of himself to be with me so I wouldn't feel empty."

"I think you're right. Someday you'll have other kids you can name whatever you want."

"No, this is the only baby I'll ever have. I'll never marry again. My life was with Drew."

"Abby, I know you feel like that now. Shoot, I've been goin' through these same emotions myself. But you will get through this. Look at you. You're beautiful, you're charmin', and funny. You're sensitive and compassionate. You're only twenty-five years old. You've got a lot of years ahead of you to be alone. Heck, I must know a hundred guys lookin' for a gal like you. I know you're hurtin' bad now, but don't close the door forever. Leave it open to possibilities. You deserve to be happy."

"Does that mean you think you could get involved with another woman after what Tansey put you through?" she countered.

He straightened and shook his head. "No way. But we're talkin' about two completely different situations. You and Drew were happy together. Marriage was a good experience for you. My marriage, on the other hand, was a disaster. I've lost faith in findin' happiness with a woman. You're another story. You've got the things a man wants in a woman. And a daddy for that baby wouldn't be a such a bad idea, either."

"Maybe somewhere down the road I'll feel differently. Right now time is playing with my head. One minute it feels like he's been gone so long, then it seems it's only been a day. I do have times when I think about him without crying, and I suppose that's an improvement. It's taken a long time to get to this point." She stared off into the distance, and her hand circled over her stomach. "I just can't imagine sharing my life with someone else like I did with Drew. He always seemed to know what I was thinking before I did."

He nodded in understanding. "That comes from a lot of time spent together. When I started bein' able to read Tansey's thoughts, I found I didn't like the way her mind worked. You know what you said before, about not missin' her, but missin' the dream? It's really pushed me along in healin'. I wish I could find a way to help you through your hurt."

Abby felt her stomach starting to roll. "I hate to be a rude guest, but I need to eat something quickly, or I'm going to be sick again."

Noticing her sudden pallor, he took the few steps to the kitchen and dropped two slices of raisin bread into the toaster.

The smell of the cinnamon made her mouth water. She smiled in gratitude when he handed her the plate. "Thanks. This is perfect."

"I live to please. Are you feelin' any better? Do you need to rest awhile?"

"That might be a good idea. Will you play for me? I want to hear what you've been working on."

"Sure thing." He retrieved his guitar from the games room and turned off the stereo.

"You're an inspiration, ya know. Wait until you hear the piece I did the other day. It still needs a bit of work, but it's pretty much there."

"What do you mean *I'm* an inspiration?" She readjusted herself onto her side and tucked a throw pillow under her stomach to support it.

Sitting across from her so she could see him easily, he set the guitar on his knee. "I named it *Vamoose*. It's about a man who's tired of his woman's cheatin' ways so he tells her to pack her bags."

She laughed until it woke the baby. It seemed like every time she lay down, he woke up.

Chris played the song and followed it with more. The music relaxed her, and she felt a peace settle in her soul as she closed her eyes. He continued to quietly strum while he watched her sleep. If Tansey was more like Abby, they would have been so happy together. He blamed himself, thinking he hadn't given her enough attention. It was a long road to realizing she never did love him. She was incapable of loving anyone but herself. The recognition gave him freedom.

Setting the guitar aside he went to the kitchen to fix lunch. He knew it was easier for her to eat smaller meals more often, so he adjusted his cooking accordingly. He'd discovered, oddly enough, tuna was something she craved, so he stuffed tomatoes with tuna salad.

He glanced at her on the couch. She was so beautiful when she slept. He couldn't believe how easy things were with her. He came here because he thought he needed to be away from everyone, especially women. Two weeks ago she showed up, and it seemed everything changed. He found it hard to believe he could spend time with a woman who didn't want something from him. Of course, she was the exception to the rule. He refused to change his opinion of women in general.

After putting the tomatoes back into the fridge, he sat in the chair and studied her. She liked him for himself, the man inside. He knew he should tell

39

her the truth, but he feared the changes that would occur. It was clear she was unimpressed by celebrity and money, never getting excited when he mentioned other big names he knew. She listened only to learn about him and his interests, not to hear about the famous people.

He would tell her the truth, but not until he felt more secure.

•

Maisie and Daisy holed up in their motel room for the fourth day of rain. Maisie wanted to go do surveillance in spite of the rain, but Daisy adamantly refused. And so, they again sat playing gin rummy.

Daisy noticed Kip and the woman getting closer. They spent increasingly more time together as the days went by, but always returned to their own homes at night, giving her the encouragement she needed to believe she still had a chance with him. Besides, what interest could he have in a pregnant woman?

Maisie started getting antsy, having more than one reason for keeping an eye on Kip Adams. Daisy thought she was only here as an avid fan. She had no idea there was much more at stake. Maisie needed to get rid of the woman on the island somehow. Her interference could become trouble for Maisie's plans. She knew he would go to Fan Fair in Nashville in June. She would also be there, but before she left she would set a plan in motion to get rid of that woman.

•

"Hey, where'd the music go?" Abby muttered, her eyes still shut. The first thing she realized when waking was that Chris had stopped playing.

"My audience deserted me. Lunch is ready whenever you are, Sleepin' Beauty." He set his book down and leaned forward in his chair. His hands hung loosely as his elbows rested on his knees. Reaching out, he brushed the hair from her face.

She stretched as she became more awake. "Sorry I crashed on you. I seem to sleep a lot these days, but this afternoon I promise you will have my full attention." She pushed the blanket aside and dropped her feet to the floor. "Can you help me up?"

He helped her to her feet and led her to the bar stool at the counter. He took the lunch from the fridge and sat next to her.

"Wow, this looks great. You must enjoy being in the kitchen. You always come up with something creative. Drew only knew how to microwave Chef Boyardee and popcorn, so I totally appreciate your skills."

"I used to spend time with my mama in the kitchen when I was younger.

Besides, I've been lookin' after myself for quite a while now. It's learn to cook or starve. A person can only eat out so long before it starts gettin' old." He cut into his tomato and watched her eat like she'd not seen food for a week. "Whoa, girl! Take it easy. That food ain't goin' nowhere. I can always fix more, ya know."

She giggled, then choked and reached for her milk to wash it down. "Sorry. I didn't mean to be rude. I'm so hungry I can't believe it. Maybe we should start into that cake soon."

"After you finish the healthy stuff, I'll let you enjoy the sinful stuff. Little Andy in there must be packin' on the pounds. He's gonna come out a full size bronc buster. I'll have him trained with a lasso by his first birthday. You just wait, Abs. He'll be ridin' in the rodeos by the time he's three."

"Ouch! Don't know if a little girl like me can get a full-size anything out of there. Maybe I'd better slow down eating. I'll have to pay full fare on the plane for him if he grows as fast as you predict. But I think to be good enough for a rodeo, he'd have to spend a lot more than a few weeks in Wyoming."

"You could be right about that. Man, I remember when we were kids, Jeff and I decided we were big enough to start practicin' for some events my daddy specifically told me I was too young for. We waited 'til he wasn't around, and we snuck into the corral with a young stallion that hadn't been broke yet."

He laughed at the memory. "I took his bridle and led him over to the railin' where Jeff was waitin'. He threw his leg over that horse's back. Talk about bronc ridin'! That stallion reared up on his hind legs and threw Jeff a'flyin'. The lead rope ripped out o' my hands. The stallion's front legs were kickin', an' I got it right in the mouth. Knocked my front teeth out. I was hollerin', an' blood everywhere. There was Jeff layin' on the ground with a broken arm, and Julie sittin' up on that fence just laughin' herself silly until she saw the blood. Then she switched to screamin', certain I was gonna die. Mama heard the ruckus and came runnin'. We had a long drive to the hospital, and you can bet by the time we got there our ears were as sore as the rest of us."

Abby looked at him horrified, and he noticed her protectively wrapping her arm around her stomach. "I can't believe you're laughing about it. You got your teeth knocked out?"

"Yessirree. Thank goodness for dentists. But you can bet as soon as Jeff had that cast off we were right back to mischief. Heck, I think it's probably lucky I was an only child. I gave Mama enough trouble for ten kids. Can't tell ya how many times I got taken out behind the barn for a lickin' by my daddy. Did me plenty o' good too. I never got in trouble for the same thing twice. I managed to come up with new ideas every time. Never a dull moment at the Adams ranch."

CHRISTOPHER

They carried their plates to the sink and settled back in the living room.

"Your poor mother. Does she live in an asylum now? You obviously drove her crazy."

"She's a pretty tough gal. Gotta be for ranch life."

"That's so different from my childhood. You were definitely a boy. I only had a sister, and we were both conventionally feminine. We liked to play dress up and have tea parties and play hopscotch. Dolls and strollers and lots of pink. Ruffles and lace, and experimenting with hair-dos. I have a cousin, Trent, who used to come to play. He was our exposure to the world of boys. When Trent was there we climbed trees and did a lot of active things. Tag, hide and seek, army, secret agent, that kind of stuff. He never sat down for long."

"Sounds like my kinda guy. Good imagination, lots of action. Probably did you a world of good to be subjected to that kinda stuff."

"No broken bones, but I sure lost a lot of blood to cuts and scrapes. Got stitches on my hand. We were digging a hole, and I hit a piece of buried glass." She paused and studied what remained of the little white line on the side of her right hand. "Yeah, I think you'd like him. He's coming up next week to spend the weekend with me. Checking up on me, I guess. Trent's different than me, though. He's into your country music. He's actually in a band that plays a lot of the clubs. They're apparently pretty good. His big dream is to move to Nashville some day and record. Music is his life." She reached for the fruit bowl on the coffee table and picked up a bunch of green grapes.

Chris tried not to show his disappointment. He should have known. Women always had ulterior motives, and Abby was no different after all. This was hers. Get her cousin connected. Trying to keep his voice neutral, he said, "I suppose you're wantin' me to meet him and give him some professional pointers."

She popped a grape in her mouth and answered, "No, not at all. You didn't come up here for that. You came to get away. I respect you and your need for privacy, you know."

He tried to read her. She looked totally sincere. "You really don't want me to?"

"Of course not. I don't even plan on introducing you two. I only mentioned him because we were talking about our childhoods, and he was a big part of mine. He'll probably take the boat out and do some fishing, for which I won't be joining him, then we'll hang out and catch up."

"Don't like fishin'?"

"Love it. Just can't handle the motion of the boat at anchor or drifting right now. Little Andy doesn't much care for it either. Oh, and he's going to bring my karaoke machine from home. We always sing when we get together. It's a family thing."

"You're gonna do karaoke and not invite me? Now I'm hurt."

"Yeah, right."

"Seriously! I can't believe you wouldn't ask me to come for that!"

"Hey, if it means that much to you, you're invited. Just remember, Mozart, it's amateur hour. I'm sure you'll be bored to tears."

"Not possible. Man, you've never heard my friend, Jeff, sing. If I can tolerate that, I can handle anythin'. He's enough to make your ears bleed." Actually, Jeff could carry his own quite nicely, but Chris wanted to be included.

Was she nuts? She had him sitting right here, and she didn't want to take advantage of it? Of course, she didn't know who he really was, but she knew he had all kinds of connections in Nashville. He switched from being ticked off, thinking she was an opportunist, to being ticked off because she didn't ask him. "You know, about your cousin, well, I'd be willin' to spend some time with him. Talk to him about Nashville. Just say the word."

"I wouldn't feel right about it. I try not to take advantage of friends. I'd rather not have you do it and us stay friends than ask you to do something you're uncomfortable with."

"You're not askin'. I'm offerin'. It's no trouble. In fact I could probably be a better resource to him here than in Nashville. I'm relaxed with free time here. There, I'm always on the run." What a change. He was actually offering. If the cousin was anything like Abby, Chris could trust him with his secret.

"If you want to, go ahead. Don't let me stand in the way of a man and his career. Let's just wait and see how it goes. I won't tell him you're here. Maybe you want to drop over for dinner Friday so you can meet."

That wouldn't work. As soon as Trent saw him the cat would be out of the bag, and he did not want that critter out one minute before he was ready. He needed to think of a way around it. He wanted to do something nice for Abby, just because she was a decent person. Giving her cousin some advice would be easy enough.

"Listen, let me know when he's supposed to arrive. I'll take the boat to the marina to pick him up. I can grab whatever you need from the store while I'm there." That would give him the chance to talk to Trent first and bargain with him.

"You don't have to do that."

"I know I don't have to. I'm offerin'. In fact, I'm set on it. Done deal."

"I think you have something up your sleeve, but if you want to it's all right with me."

"Great. How 'bout some of that cake now?" He cut the cake and poured them each a glass of milk. "I noticed you have a lot of novels at the cabin. You enjoy readin'?"

"Love it. Especially mystery and suspense novels. When I was young my mother would say, 'clean your room and don't come out until it's finished'. It took years for her to realize that was simply no punishment for me. I'd go up and sit down with a book. I could be happy for weeks up there. Luckily, I finally learned to clean in spite of the library."

He laughed, easily picturing her as a ten-year-old with her nose in a book, twirling a ponytail around her finger.

The rain continued to fall on the windowed wall of the cottage, but the people inside were oblivious. They continued talking for the rest of the afternoon. At seven thirty the rain suddenly stopped. Abby stared out the window and pointed at the sunset. He turned to see what captured her attention. Taking her by the hand, they went out on the deck and found themselves enveloped in a kaleidoscope with the pinks and oranges of the sunset in the west, and the brilliant colors of a rainbow painting the eastern sky. Hopefully a portent of things good to come.

CHAPTER 6

May became warmer as each day passed. They began a routine of meeting each afternoon at two o'clock and either going for a walk or sitting outside to enjoy the spring weather. Happiness enhanced each and every day.

The Friday Chris thought of as *Trent Day* arrived. He spent the day online answering email from fans, and on the phone with Nashville. His agent wanted to start booking for the fall and winter. He spoke with Darla, the president of his fan club; Donna, his publicist; Tim, the merchandising manager; and Cree, his financial manager. A call from Glen at the marina informed him Trent had arrived.

When he pulled in to the marina slip, he honked the boat's horn and saw a young man emerge from the store with a duffle bag. Trent waved and stopped to retrieve something from the back seat of his car. Chris pulled his ball cap low over his eyes, stepping to the side of the boat to welcome Trent.

Trent grabbed hold of his hand and pulled himself on board. With his footing secure, he started to introduce himself but never got past opening his mouth. "Holy Dinah! You're–"

"Chris Adams. Howdy." He stuck out his hand to shake, cutting Trent off quickly.

"Huh?"

"Drop your gear."

"Yeah, sure." Star struck, Trent was willing to go along with whatever his hero said.

CHRISTOPHER

Chris backed the boat out onto the lake and headed for the cottage. Five minutes into the journey, he pulled into a small inlet on the mainland side of the lake and cut the engine. Turning to the good-looking young man in his early twenties, he sized him up.

"I'm sure you have a million questions right about now. Yes, I am Kip Adams. Abby said you were a fan of country music, so I knew you'd recognize me. That's why I offered to pick you up. It's like this. I'm on vacation, and I'm just Chris Adams. She doesn't have any idea who I really am, and for now I'd like to keep it that way."

He turned his gaze and looked out across the water, swatting pointlessly at a swirling mass of no-see-ums. "You see, it's not often I get treated like a regular guy, but that's what I am to her. Just a songwriter who lives in Nashville. She likes me, the person. Not the name, not the money, not the career. I haven't told her any lies, I just haven't been totally forthcomin' with all the details. I'll tell her, just not yet. So, I'd appreciate it if you'd go along with me on this. Call me Chris. In return, well, she tells me you play. I'll be happy to listen to you. You can spend time at my cottage, and I'll be glad to answer any questions you have regardin' the music business. But you don't tell anyone else I'm here. I don't want the papers to find me. Word of celebrity sightin's tend to spread like wildfire. Is it a deal?"

"Sure...Chris. You'll have to give me a minute to catch my breath though. Man, I love your stuff so much, but I gotta tell you, you're the last person I expected to run into today. Sure man, I'll go along with you. It must be hell to live in a fishbowl all the time. And if you don't mind me saying so, you've certainly had more than your share of publicity this past year. I can only imagine what privacy must mean to you. I don't blame you a bit." He held his hand out once again. "I'm pleased to meet you, Chris. You don't need to buy my co-operation."

Chris smiled and shook his hand. "I think we'll get along just fine."

"I can't believe that Abby...well, yes I can. That girl lives in her own dimension. The rest of the world could come and go, and it wouldn't bother her a bit to miss it. I'll bet you probably thought you'd have to go all the way to Nepal or someplace like that to find someone who didn't recognize you." Trent shook his head and laughed. "Yes, the more I think about it, the more I like it. Our little Abigail making friends with the top name in country music, and she doesn't even know it. You can count on me. This is the best thing I've helped pull on her in years."

"Thanks. If you didn't agree I was gonna have to throw ya overboard and report ya lost at sea or somethin'."

Chris re-started the engine and continued to the island, docking at his cottage. He helped Trent tote his things to Abby's.

"She's been cookin' all afternoon. You must eat enough for ten people by the amount of food she's got goin'.'"

Trent laughed. "Well, I do like my cousin's cooking. She knows my heart lies in my stomach. Hey, how's she doin' anyway?"

"Better, I think. She had a real bad spell when she first got here, but since then she hasn't fallen apart too much. I think she's startin' to get used to the idea that he's gone. He must've been a great guy."

"Yeah, Drew was a lot of fun. She adored him. He loved her, too, but I never thought it was the same somehow. A lot of times it seemed he treated her like one of the guys. Sometimes I wanted to knock him in the head and remind him what a special gal he had."

They stepped onto the porch, and Trent opened the front door. "Honey, I'm home."

Abby came from the kitchen, and he scooped her up in his arms.

"Hey, what is this? You're getting bigger every day, girl. Are you sure there's only one in there?"

"Thank you for your compliments, kind sir, but yes there's only one. I'm down to eight weeks now. It won't be long before you can practice changing diapers for the day you have your own." She loved teasing him. He was determined to stay a bachelor and play the field until he was old and gray.

"Not on your life, girl. I brought the things you asked for." He set a bag down on the arm of the sofa. "How are you feeling?"

"Still being sick every day, but happier. I've been concentrating on what's best for the baby, and getting pretty excited. Nervous about labor, but Claire will be there with me. I hope you're hungry. Dinner is just about ready. You can wash up."

Chris set the karaoke machine just inside the front door. Going to the kitchen, he helped her put the food on the table without realizing he was falling into the role of husband and host. It was a natural response with him and Abby spending so much time together the last few weeks. They worked well together. He failed to understand Trent's odd expression when he set the potatoes and the bread basket on the table. Abby brought the last dish in, and he pushed her chair in for her when she sat. He returned to the fridge and retrieved two bottles of sparkling juice.

"Abby, would you like the white grape or the cherry?"

"I'll have the grape to start, thanks. Oh, I forgot the relish tray in the fridge."

"Sit tight." He dropped a hand on her shoulder in passing as he doubled back to the kitchen.

Trent observed the activity, fascinated. It amazed him to see her behaving as a couple with a man who wasn't Drew. Maybe when he awoke in the morning he would discover this was all a bizarre dream.

Chris resumed pouring the juice. "Trent, which would you prefer? We drink sparklin' juice instead of wine because of the baby."

Trent picked up on the "we." We? When did this man adapt his ways to suit Abby, and when did they become "we"? He sat back with interest to watch the evening play out.

"I'll have the same as Abby, if that's all right."

Chris poured for all of them, then lifted his glass in a toast. "To Abby, who worked all day to make this a wonderful evenin' for all of us. A woman with class, beauty, and talent."

Trent lifted his glass in tribute to his cousin. He beheld her eyes twinkling, and was stunned by her remarkable transformation over the past month. Her cheeks regained color, and her eyes lacked the vacancy that had taken residence there. He wondered if she would have come this far if Kip, er, Chris, hadn't been here.

When the meal was finished they continued to sit and chat. After an hour she finally complained of discomfort. Chris walked her to the couch. "You put your feet up and rest. You've been on them too long today. We'll take care of the dishes."

Trent started clearing the table, and Chris joined him in the small kitchen where they washed the dishes and put away leftovers. When they finished, they found her laying on her side, cringing.

"What's wrong? Is it your back again?" Chris asked.

She squeaked out a yes.

"Come on then. You should have said somethin'." He pulled the coffee table closer to the couch and sat on it. She rolled as far as she could toward him, and he began to massage her lumbar. She moaned with relief. "I knew you were doin' too much. Tomorrow you're stayin' down with your feet up. That's an order. You're probably gonna have swollen feet from standin' so long today."

Trent couldn't believe his ears. Abby didn't take orders from anybody, including Drew. She excelled at giving them, but certainly not at taking them. He was about to laugh out loud when to his astonishment he heard her say, "All right. Thanks."

He walked to the front door, opened it, and looked outside.

"Trent, what are you doing?"

"Just trying to figure out at what point I entered the twilight zone."

"Shut up, and close the door." She gave him a scolding look while trying to hide her grin. She knew he was amazed by her acquiescence. If not for the pain, she might have objected to being ordered. However, it was nice being looked after now that she was growing bigger.

He picked up the karaoke machine and set it by the television, making the necessary connections. From his duffle bag he pulled out a cardboard box and placed it on the cabinet shelf.

"There you go. It's all set up whenever you want it." He dropped into an overstuffed chair, watching in disbelief as his cousin interacted with the mega star, totally oblivious, and stifled a giggle. In all his twenty-two years, it was the best thing he'd ever witnessed. He had pulled a lot of practical jokes in his life, and was a pretty good sport when people got their revenge. However, this superceded any prank he'd ever masterminded, laying the groundwork for one heck of an interesting weekend.

"The famous karaoke machine? Abby mentioned you were bringin' it up. Can you believe she wasn't even gonna invite me? I had to beg to be included."

"Abby! I can't believe you'd try to leave Chris out of this. Afraid are you, Abby? Think someone might out do you?"

"Don't be ridiculous. I simply never thought he'd be interested in our nonsense. He's a very busy man, even though he's on vacation. Did he tell you he writes country music? He also works in a recording studio. If you behave, he might be willing to listen to you and give you pointers. Right, Chris?"

"Sure. My door's open."

"Besides, just because Mozart here writes songs doesn't mean he sings them. You don't need to do one to be able to do the other. Maybe he doesn't like to sing."

Trent erupted in laughter. Chris glared warningly, but it did no good. Trent clutched his stomach as he fell forward out of the chair, landing in a gasping heap on the floor.

Abby saw the tears streaming down his cheeks. "What is so funny? Are you sure you didn't have a few drinks before you got here? You sound like you're three sheets to the wind."

He tried to pick himself up off the floor. "I don't know. Why don't we just ask him? "Say, Chris, do you ever sing? You know, just for fun?" Laughter rang out as he fell back down.

She grew irritated with her cousin. "Trent, if something is that funny, why don't you let us all in on it?"

He sought to compose himself, honestly not wanting to give Chris away. With a furrowed brow, he tried unsuccessfully to look serious. "Sorry. Boy, I just don't know what got into me. So, Chris, do you sing?"

"I've been known to on occasion." Chris tried to keep a straight face, but it was hard with Trent laughing so hysterically.

Abby grabbed a throw pillow and tossed it at her cousin. "Get your act together, idiot. You're up first."

He stood and wiped away his tears, took a gulp of juice, and went to the cardboard box. "Hmm. Let's see. What will I do first? This looks good." He opened a CD case and dropped the disc into the player. Music started, and he did an imitation of Shania Twain as he sang *Man, I Feel Like a Woman*. The other two laughed and applauded when he finished.

"Hey, I thought the point of karaoke was to have the words run on the screen while you sang." Chris noted that Trent hadn't turned the television on.

"Ah, in most cases that is true. But we play for points. You get extra if you do it without the words being run," he answered.

"Wait a minute. Abby said this was amateur night. She never said nothin' about points."

"Yeah, well, don't worry, cowboy. I'm sure you'll manage." Trent gave him another stupid grin.

"Okay, then I'm up next. Let me have the box." Chris flipped through the collection, surprised to see it covered just about every type of music. He decided to show her he could do more than country. With the mike in his hand, he sang the *Bohemian Rhapsody* by Queen. Without the television. Impressed he knew all the words, she stood to applaud when he finished.

"That was fabulous. Maybe I do have some competition here." She changed the CD and took the microphone. Chris sat and watched as the tiny woman with the huge belly did a very sexy rendition of *Some Kind of Wonderful*.

Trent took another turn, selecting *Open Arms* by Journey. Chris sat back listening and decided it was worth hearing more. If he mastered a variety of styles with this quality, he had talent.

"Very nice, Trent. Very nice indeed."

Chris selected another track from the same CD, singing *Private Eyes* by Hall and Oates. It was apparently a favorite of Abby's, and she found it hard to sit still, moving with the music from her perch on the couch.

"My turn." She glanced at Trent and winked. She put her music in and took her place. Chris recognized the prelude notes of Andrew Lloyd Webber's *Music of the Night* from the *Phantom of the Opera*. Not an easy piece to sing and definitely not a joking-around kind of song.

She opened her mouth, and Chris stared in wonder as he listened to the most beautiful, clear soprano voice he'd ever heard. Without a doubt, a trained voice. She did the piece as beautifully as Sarah Brightman ever had. He sat back and smiled.

When she finished he continued staring at her. "You are such a brat. You never even hinted. That was magnificent. Why didn't you say somethin'?"

"Well, Mozart, you're the big man from Nashville. I didn't want to steal your thunder."

"Trent, if I strangle her here and now, will you testify to justifiable homicide?"

"Well, I don't know. You know what they say, what's good for the goose—"

"Point taken," Chris answered surreptitiously.

"Well, I didn't get it. What's that supposed to mean?" She turned from one to the other, expectantly.

"Nothin', Abby," Chris assured her.

"Yeah, nothing at all, Abby. Guy stuff, you know."

"No, I don't know, but I'll take your word for it. You two must have done a lot of male bonding between here and the marina."

Chris reverted the subject back to her. "Seriously, why aren't you in Carnegie Hall, or on Broadway? A voice like yours is a gift too great to be hidden. Where did you train?"

She settled back on the sofa and took a drink. "Did I fail to mention that while I was at university learning to be an accountant, I studied voice? That's what my scholarship was for."

"You know darn well you never mentioned it. It's okay though. I think it's nice to be pleasantly surprised every now and again. Don't you think so?"

"Uh, Chris, she's not real big on surprises."

"Well, maybe she could learn to be if they were *good* surprises."

"You guys are talking about me like I'm not even here. I won't have it. *Ouch!*"

Chris was at her side in an instant. "You okay, darlin'? What is it?"

"Andy's wiggled his foot up into my rib cage. It hurts like a son-of-a-gun."

"Here, lay down and stretch out."

When she was fully reclined, he massaged her stomach, encouraging the baby to change positions.

"Ouch. He's really stretching. It hurts."

The baby rolled over, and they all watched as her abdomen rolled with it.

"Thanks."

Trent looked stunned. "That is too weird. It's like a scene out of the *X-Files* or something. Come to think of it, this whole day has been like an episode of that show. Definitely surreal."

She laughed at him. He always made her laugh. It was the best thing about having him around.

●

Maisie watched from the shadows as Kip massaged the pregnant woman's stomach. Such an intimate gesture caused her anger to smolder. Their relationship seemed to be progressing further than Maisie was willing to let it. She enjoyed the evening to this point, watching them sing. Certainly more entertaining than watching them read a book. The new guy was a pretty good singer. And he was cute too, but a bit too young. The woman had a great voice, but Maisie would have her revenge soon enough. She didn't want Kip touching anyone with that kind of familiarity but her.

Turning, she figured she may as well take the trail to the house. It was a lot easier than tromping through the woods at this time of night.

Once inside Kip's house, the west window proved to be an architectural feature she appreciated only from the outside point of view. She made a bee-line for the office and closed the door. Turning on the flashlight, she quickly went through the drawers. She had promised to fax something by the end of next week, and her time away from Daisy was limited. She needed to take advantage of every moment she could to search. Nothing in the drawers. As she cast the light around the room she found what she sought on top of the keyboard.

CHAPTER 7

Jeff handed Julie a fresh cup of hot coffee. She sat in her robe and slippers, glad to be in her own apartment. The past month at home had been a lot less hectic, but being Kip Adam's personal assistant was a big job with a heavy workload, even when he wasn't around.

"Chris called last night. Actually it was more like this mornin'. About one thirty I think." He blew the steam from his drink before taking a gulp.

"How did he sound?" She ran her fingers through her wavy blonde hair, untangling it.

"He sounded great. Excited even. Seems he's not alone on his deserted island after all. There's a young widow sharin' it with him, and she's almost eight months pregnant. She's the same age as you. For a guy tryin' desperately to get away from women, he sure talked about this one. Nonstop. Says they see each other every day and are friends. How many women have you ever seen Chris be friends with, other than you?"

"I can count them on one hand." Wide-awake now and listening attentively, she forgot about the coffee.

"Anyway, he met her cousin who's also into music. He said the kid sounds promisin'. You know he only praises things worthy of it. He's goin' to meet with him again today to get a better idea of what the kid is about."

"You keep sayin' kid. Just how old is he, and does he have a name?"

"Didn't catch a name yet. I think he's about twenty-three. He plays in a band up there."

"What about this widow, does she have a name?"

"Now, that one I can answer. Her name is Abigail Lockner. Goes by Abby. You wouldn't believe it to listen to him. He sounds like Chris again. Laughs and jokes, sounds like the fella we know and love. He even said he'll definitely be here for Fan Fair."

"Wow! That is somethin'." She stared at her brother thoughtfully. "How does he feel about this woman? Does he say?"

"Says they're just friends. I think he's in love. Talkin' about feelin' her baby movin' around and the things they do to pass time. Here's the good part. She doesn't know who he is!"

"Oh, come off it. She's playin' him. Everyone knows who he is. She's just jerkin' his chain. He's smarter than that."

"No, really. She doesn't follow country music at all. Doesn't even like it apparently. He told her he's just a songwriter, and she believed him."

"Sure. That's why she brought in her country singin' cousin."

"Nope. He says she wasn't even gonna introduce them. He had to ask her."

"Oh, this girl's good. Let me get my hands on her, and we'll just see how genuine she is. I don't like it. Not one bit."

"Julie, he's happy. He's lookin' forward to life again. He still says he'll never get married, but he's so much better. There was somethin' in his voice that's been missin' for too long. In fact, you want to know who he compared her to?"

"Well, let's hear it."

"You. Said she reminds him of you. That he can trust her to be honest. She tells him what she really thinks, not what he wants to hear. Also, said she feels the same as him about marriage. Doesn't ever plan on gettin' married again. Loved her husband so much that she can't imagine ever lovin' anyone else. She's havin' a hard time dealin' with his death. They're sort of helpin' each other."

"He certainly must be in some kind of mood for you to get all that. He hasn't talked that much in the last six months let alone in one conversation." The changes Jeff spoke of were remarkable. She hoped this Abby woman was genuine. If she was toying with Chris, she would have Julie to deal with. For as much as she was the little sister to these two men, she became a mother bear defending her cubs when anyone tried to harm them. She wouldn't let an outsider tamper with her world or those in it.

●

As Trent followed the trail out of the woods Saturday morning, he spied Chris through the window with a mug of coffee in his hand. Chris noticed him and waved him in. He leaped up the steps and opened the front door.

"Howdy. Coffee's in the kitchen. Help yourself."

"Thanks. I didn't get any at Abby's. She's still sleeping, and I didn't want to make any noise. She said it's getting harder to get any decent sleep now with the baby."

"I know. The further along she gets, the more uncomfortable she is. I try to get her to lay down for a while every day. She says she'll only do it if I read to her. We're on our third book."

Trent's knowing grin told him they both knew she finagled him into it, but the fact was, he enjoyed it as much as she did.

"So, tell me, what instruments do you play?"

"Lead guitar. I'm afraid that's it, but I'm pretty good with it. I guess you could say that putting all my concentration into one instrument paid off."

"Let me grab mine." Chris went into the other room and returned with his Gibson acoustic. Trent took it reluctantly. He knew guitars, and this one cost more than he could ever dream of affording. He lovingly ran his hands over the craftsmanship in appreciation.

"Play me somethin'," Chris said, sitting down.

"Sure." His fingers easily found the chords needed to play a rather difficult Kip Adams piece. Chris was duly impressed. Trent was no strummer. He knew his instrument and how to make it sing. He went on to play a few more, covering a variety of styles, so Chris could get an idea of his range of abilities.

"Have you written any of your own, or do you rely on other songwriters?"

"I've done a few, but I always need a collaborator. I'm no good with the words."

"Listen, the way your fingers work, you don't need to be good with lyrics. You're as good as Paisley. Sing me one of your own." Chris had been in the business long enough to put on a persona of reserve as he listened through the next three pieces. "Tell me, what are your aspirations musically? Is it just somethin' to kick back on weekends, or is it somethin' more?"

Trent lounged back and continued to play quietly. "I've been playing since I was eight. It's all I ever wanted to do. I never bothered much with school sports. I wanted to be home playing my guitar. I've managed to put a band together. It's hard to find fellas who have enough talent and are interested in the same kind of music. I don't exactly live in a musical metropolis, you know. It's only Picton."

"Nashville part of your dreams?"

"Nashville is the whole cake. It's the ultimate dream."

"What are you doin' for a livin' right now?"

"I'm with a retail corporation in the marketing division. I finished my business degree last year, but even with that they still make you start close to the bottom. Not the mailroom or anything, but still pretty low on the ladder. I get to handle things I learned in grade eleven."

"Sounds like somethin' you'd really miss, huh?"

"Yeah, right. I could drop it in a minute and never look back."

"Gee, it always makes me happy to hear a man loves his job." Both men laughed. "You're quite talented." Trent beamed at the compliment. "Listen, I'm goin' to make some phone calls. Could you give me a few minutes?"

"Sure. Can I play your guitar some more?" He wanted to hold this one as long as he could, like someone with a beat up old piano being given the chance to play a Steinway Grand.

"Sure, buddy, go for it."

Chris went into his office and started dialing his phone. "Tug, Kip here…Yeah, I'm doin' great. Best vacation I've ever taken. Listen, I've got a kid here who has it…The big *it*, talent comin' out the wazoo. I want to send him down there to you. I promise you'll listen to him for about five minutes before you want him signin' a contract namin' you as his manager. He's got a real career ahead of him…You know I've never done this before. I'm willing to put myself out on a limb here. That's how much I believe in him. This guy is definitely a headliner in the not too distant future. He just needs good management and a band to back him up. Make sure Mitch gets him booked into some nightclubs down there."

Tug listened, but he couldn't believe it. This was so out of character for Kip. "This kid have a name?"

"Right. It's Trent. Trent Roblin. The kid's good lookin' to boot. I'll send him down Monday mornin'."

"Okay. I'll clear my calendar for a few hours in the afternoon. And, Kip, you're sounding good."

"Yeah, and I'm doin' even better. Thanks, Tug. I know I'm askin' a lot, but I believe he's worth it. Talk to ya later."

After hanging up he called Julie. She told him Jeff was with her, and Chris told her to put him on the speakerphone. This was the kind of call he liked. He could handle two things at once.

"I'm sendin' someone down there. Write this down. His name is Trent Roblin. I want you to arrange a flight for him for Monday mornin'. Have his ticket waitin' at the Toronto airport. I want you to pick him up from Nashville International. Put him up at my penthouse. I'm not usin' it right now, so he might as well. I'm financin' all his expenses, so see that Cree knows that.

"Jeff, I want you to hold auditions for a new band. Put a group together to play his backup. He could probably use a new guitar, too. And, Julie, take him shoppin'. Let him get some clothes he's gonna feel good performin' in, right on down to his boots. See that he has anythin' else he needs and a monthly draw for livin' expenses."

"Got it. Anythin' else?"

"If I've forgotten anythin', I know you'll deal with it. I trust your judgment. This kid is worth every penny I invest in him. He's got solid talent, and he's a good guy."

"Consider it done. I'll call you back with his flight information. You're soundin' good by the way. Canadian air must agree with you."

"Yeah, a lot o' Canadian things agree with me, which reminds me, you'll need to check with immigration regardin' the regulations for him to work and live in the States."

"Right. Well, I'll get busy on this end. Kip, does this have anythin' to do with that woman Jeff was tellin' me about?" She couldn't help asking. She didn't want to see him tangled up in another mess before recovering from the last one.

"'That woman' is Abby, and other than the fact that they're related, not a single thing. I'm sendin' Trent on his own merits. Abby's a friend but that's as far as it goes. I'm not about to put my reputation on the line for someone I don't believe is worth it. This fella has what it takes. Once you've heard him play, you'll know what I mean. All I want to do is give him a leg up, just like somebody once did for me."

"Well, I'll go ahead and do the things you asked, but there is one more thing."

"What's that?"

"When we got you that penthouse, we moved your boxes in and left it. You don't own a stick of furniture. We left on tour almost as soon as you separated. Remember?"

"Right. I'd forgotten. Well, go buy me some furniture."

"Okay, then. Talk to you soon."

He returned to the living room. Trent looked up and stopped playing. Chris studied him for a moment, then broke the news.

"Well, if it's okay with you, you're movin' to Nashville Monday mornin'. I thought ya might want a chance to pack some things to take along. You can live at my penthouse. My personal assistant, Julie, is bookin' your flight as we speak. My friend, Jeff–"

"You mean Jeff Clayton?" he asked in awe.

"Yeah. He's puttin' out the word regardin' auditions for your band. You're not just part of a band any more. You're the reason they are a band, and when you get rollin', they'll be on your payroll."

"Listen, Kip, uh, Chris. I really appreciate all this, but it's sounding pretty expensive. I mean, I have some money put away, but I don't think—"

"Don't worry about money. My production company is backin' you. You'll be managed by Tug Whitley. He's my manager, and he'll be waitin' for ya Monday afternoon. If ya find you aren't comfortable with him, or with any of my people for that matter, just say so. I don't have a problem with ya choosin' other people you feel ya can relate to. I've made arrangements, but nothin' is so solid it can't be changed to accommodate you. After all, this is your career. I already have my own. But for as long as ya need, I'll be happy to work with ya."

Trent waited for the bubble to pop. "I don't know what to say. How can I ever thank you? This is the greatest thing anyone has ever done for me. If this is a dream, please don't wake me."

"I'm not sayin' everythin' is just gonna fall into your lap. You've got a lot of work ahead. I'll be glad to take ya out on the road with me as an openin' act...next year. And you won't be recordin' yet. You need to be there with Jefferson when he holds the auditions. Get a feel for the kind of people ya want to work with on a long-term basis. Trust his judgment, because Jeff is the best, but don't be afraid to give him your thoughts and opinions. He'll respect that. You'll have to play the nightclubs for a while. Gel with your band, and develop a style that's yours. Learn to read your audience. That's crucial. Think ya can handle that?"

"Chris, I'm going to work my butt off for you. You can bet this is an opportunity I'm not going to take for granted or throw away. I know it would take years for me to develop these kinds of connections on my own. Thanks."

"Well then, I guess you'll be wantin' to go tell Abby. Write your phone number down so Julie can call your flight information to ya." He shoved a pen and paper across the coffee table.

"You're the best person I've ever met. Man, this weekend turned out to be a whole lot better than just hanging out with Abby would have been. I mean, I love Abby and all, but this is spectacular."

Trent stood, pumping Chris' hand until he thought he would get tennis elbow.

Smiling, he watched Trent take off running through the trees and wondered what Abby would have to say about all this. Not helping Trent would have been a major mistake. He could hardly wait to see her face. She would be so thrilled for her cousin and so grateful to him. It was just a ribbon on the package.

●

The cabin was quiet in the morning hours, and Abby enjoyed the cool breeze blowing in through the bedroom window. She hadn't gotten nearly enough sleep last night, waking every time she wanted to turn over. It took maneuvering and a sequence of movements now. Her hand slid to the empty space beside her, and she thought of Drew. Her husband. Her heart ached with missing him. Although doing better through the days, in private moments she still felt the agony, and the depth of her loss came rushing back. She allowed herself the tears that flooded her eyes.

When Trent came back to the cottage, he heard the shower running and decided if Abby was unavailable, he would call Claire. The excitement exploded inside him.

Abby turned off the water and heard Trent's voice in the other room. Figuring he must be talking to Chris, she used the door connecting to her bedroom and got dressed. She towel-dried her hair and gave it a quick brushing. The curls fluffed around her face. In the living room she found no one but Trent. "I thought I heard you talking to someone. Is Chris here?"

"No. I was on the phone with Claire. Sit down. I've got news you won't believe."

"Can't it wait until I get something to eat? I'm starting to feel queasy."

"You sit. I'll get it." He leaped to the kitchen and threw a few slices of bread into the toaster. He just finished pouring juice when the toaster popped up.

"Here you go." He shoved the juice and a plate into her hands. "Guess what? Just guess. You'll never guess. Guess what?"

"Well, apparently I'll never guess, so why don't you just tell me."

"I went up to the house to see Chris this morning."

"This early? That's nice. Why are you dancing around the room? You're making me nauseous. Sit down." She continued to nibble on her toast.

"Sure." He sat for about half a minute before he was up again. "Abby, this is the biggest thing that has ever happened to me."

"Trent, you started having sex when you were seventeen, so I hardly think this is the biggest thing. You assured me that would never be surpassed as the ultimate."

"I'm serious. This is huge."

"You got his autograph. It's not like he's a celebrity or something you know. He's just a writer and producer."

"Right, Abby. I'm telling you, this is the most exciting thing to ever happen in my entire life."

She sat looking bored. "I suppose he wants to be your friend. You're excited because it's hard for you to find a friend who will listen to the same garbage music as you."

"Will you smarten up? I'm going to Nashville!"

"Well, you take vacations every year. So what?"

"No. I'm moving to Nashville."

"Now you're being ridiculous. You can't move to Nashville. You have a job and your band and other things here." She had fallen for too many of his pranks in the past and refused to believe him.

"He listened to me play, and he thinks I'm good. He wants to produce me. He's already arranged for me to have a manager, and they're hiring a band for me and everything. I leave Monday morning."

Stunned, she sat motionless for a moment, then burst out laughing. "You almost had me, but I know you. This is another one of your jokes, isn't it? Give it up, buddy. I'm not buying."

"I'm so totally serious. I just talked to Claire. She's going to help me get my things packed. This is for real. I can't believe it. I've been discovered!"

"Do you mean it?" She saw how genuinely excited he was, and fear formed in her stomach. "You're really going to Nashville?"

"Yes!" he shouted. "I'm going to Nashville. He says I can't record until I've done the clubs down there for a year but he's getting me booked into them. He thinks I've got what it takes to make it big. I'm going to work so hard at this. It's everything I've ever wanted."

"Well, you're right. This is huge." She tried to be excited for him. "I'm really happy for you. I know you've wanted this forever."

"Thanks. Hey, I know I was supposed to stay the weekend, but in light of this new development, would you mind if I went home today? I have a lot of things to take care of."

"Sure. I can take you back to the marina right now if you want."

"You won't be mad, will you? I mean, I was looking forward to the weekend too, but this is a rather extraordinary situation."

"Yes, it is." She reached her hand out, and he helped pull her to her feet. She put her arms around him and tried to hold him tightly. Readjusting, she turned herself to the side and tried more successfully to embrace her cousin. "I love you, Trent. I'm glad this has happened for you. I know you'll succeed. You always have."

"Thank you, Abby. I'm gonna really work hard. You'll be so proud of me."

"I always have been. You don't need to be a star for that. Get your stuff together. By the time I've waddled down to the boat, you'll probably beat me there." She grabbed the keys from the kitchen.

When they arrived at the marina they said their goodbyes, knowing they couldn't predict when they would see each other again. Except for being away at school, they'd never been more than a few blocks from each other. Abby found goodbye much harder than Trent. He was embarking on a new journey. She was being left behind. Again.

CHAPTER 8

Chris didn't hear a word from Abby all day. Unable to take it any longer, he threw on his jacket and headed down the trail. The cabin lights were out. Looking in through the screen door, he saw her curled up on the sofa in the dark.

Quietly, he opened the door and asked, "Can I come in?"

She didn't reply, and he heard a sniffle. He crossed the room to her, uncertain. "Where's Trent?"

"He went home this morning."

"Are you all right?"

"I hate you for this," she whispered.

"Pardon me?"

"I said I hate you." She looked up at him, her eyes swollen with grief.

He took a step back. "For what? What have I done?" This was so far from the Abby he'd anticipated that he was taken aback, unsure how to respond.

"You took Trent away. Another person I've depended on my whole life who's no longer going to be there for me. My parents live in Arizona, and Drew's are out in Calgary. My baby isn't going to have grandparents to grow up with, and now the only other man in my life is gone. Who do you think is going to teach Andy to play baseball and hockey, and take him fishing, and talk to him about girls and things? A child needs a father figure, and you took him away. It's just too much to bear." She seemed to collapse in on herself and sobbed.

"Oh, Abby. Oh, baby, I'm so sorry." He knelt beside her and wrapped his arms around her. "I'm sorry, darlin'." He held her head against his shoulder as she sobbed out her pain, then moved to sit beside her on the couch and hold her. "It didn't even occur to me. I'm sorry, sweetheart. I would never do anythin' I thought might hurt you. You know that, don't ya?"

She continued weeping, and he felt like his own heart would break. He berated himself over and over for not having the foresight to realize the effect his actions would have on her. He held her close and stroked her curly head. She lay against him and cried until there were no tears left, then gulped and sniffled for what seemed forever. He rocked her and kissed the top of her head.

The darkness of the night settled in around them. Still he held her until she lay slumbering in his arms. He continued to caress her and hold her to his heart, wishing he could undo all the hurt in her life. He knew it was impossible, but emotions are rarely rational things.

He carried the sleeping mother-to-be to the bedroom. Laying her on the bed, he kissed her as though she were a small child he was tucking in.

As he left the bedroom, she spoke, "Please don't go, Chris. I can't bear to be alone."

He turned and looked at her. The moonlight shone on her face, and he could see her eyes watching him. He came back and sat on the bed's edge, looking down at her. "What is it you want, Abby?"

"I need you to be my safe place. I know that sounds lame. When you were holding me out there, it was so good. It seems like forever since I've felt that safe and protected. Would you please stay and hold me tonight? I know it's a lot to ask."

"No, it's not. You could never ask anythin' I wouldn't do for you, Abs. I'm sorry I hurt you so badly. Will ya forgive me?" His hand rested on hers, and she folded her fingers around it.

"I know you wanted to help Trent. I'm happy for him, and tomorrow I'll thank you. I just haven't progressed that far yet. I know I'm being selfish, but it hurts so much to have him leave. Will you stay?"

"Of course. I'll be your safe place whenever you need one." He walked around to the far side, took his boots off, and stretched out next to her, pulling her to his chest. She wiggled around to find a comfortable position, then settled against him and relaxed.

He thought about all the lonely nights he longed to hold his wife like this. Just another reminder of the things she cheated him of, and he realized he no longer hurt. Abby was right. Tansey was none of the things he wanted in a companion. He found his relationship with Abby Lockner far more fulfilling than his marriage to Tansey ever was. Friendship satisfied him. His fingers tangled in her hair, and he felt the soft down curling around them. Her scent filled his mind as he drifted off to sleep.

She woke twice in the night to use the washroom, and each time he wakened when she got up. His shirt pulled at his shoulders as he slept, so he removed it and got back into bed with his jeans on. She returned, rubbing her back. He knelt behind her to rub it for her, and she moaned with pleasure. She wanted to lay on her other side, so he curled up behind her with his arms still holding her safely.

Dreams came and went as he slept with her curled up next to him. He felt something moving against his hand and wakened just enough to realize the baby was gently nudging it. He caressed it through the wall of its mother and felt a kind of love and protectiveness for it. He went back to sleep and dreamed of the ranch, of Abby and the baby in Wyoming with him, of showing them all the things he loved most about his home, of watching the baby grow up.

His subconscious became aware of his fingertips being gently sucked on. With a warm body pressed up against him, his instinct responded. He began to kiss the back of her neck, and her head turned to his mouth. Dreams of her consumed him. His hands roamed over her body and held her tightly to him as his mouth took hers.

Abby felt desire rushing through her. It had been so long. She pressed herself to him, running her hands over his chest and shoulders, wanting him. "Oh, Drew. I love you, honey," she breathed.

Feeling as though a bucket of ice water had just been dumped in his face, Chris pulled himself away and got up, heading to the front porch to cool down. What had he been thinking? That was Abby in there. She was his friend, not his lover, and it was going to stay that way.

He breathed deeply of the night air, waiting for the rest of his body to catch up with his mind. Thank goodness she said Drew's name, or he would have made love to her. He leaned forward with his arms braced on the porch railing. The screen door opened behind him.

"Something wrong, Chris?"

"What do you think?"

Hearing the edge in his voice confused her. "If I knew I wouldn't be asking."

He heard her bewilderment and closed his eyes as he let out a deep breath. "Never mind, Abby girl. I'll be fine. I just needed a bit of fresh air. Let's get you back inside. We only have a few hours left until mornin'."

They got back into bed, but it took him a lot longer to fall asleep. Too many thoughts ran through his mind. He knew it was Abby beside him, even in his sleep, and he'd wanted her. He'd never thought about her in that way before, but now he acknowledged the attraction. She was beautiful, strong, but

63

feminine, and sexy as anything he'd ever seen, even pregnant. The problem remained; he didn't want that from her, nor she from him. Time to rein those hormones in. She needed a friend, a brother, not someone to hop into bed with.

Abby lay next to him wondering what happened. He suddenly seemed tense, and she couldn't understand why. She'd been having a wonderful dream about Drew. They were together, and she wanted him to make love to her. She cringed as the possibility hit home. Surely, Chris couldn't be attracted to her in that way. After all, she was huge. Knowing it would be embarrassing for both of them to discuss it, she chose to keep quiet and stay ignorant.

She lay, not snuggled against him any longer, but holding his hand. She hoped she hadn't hurt their friendship. What would she do if she lost Chris, too? She knew he wouldn't be staying forever. Only a few more weeks, a month or two at the most. Then he would be gone. She refused to deal with that right now. She knew their friendship got her through each and every day. It was important to have him here.

He wondered how soon he could leave the island without hurting her. He needed to return to Nashville in two weeks for Fan Fair. A graceful exit. With plenty of things there to keep him busy, he wouldn't be able to come back. It sounded perfect. Say goodbye, and see her next summer if she still wanted to come out to the ranch then. They could talk on the phone or email one another. A year away ought to cool him down enough to spend time with her again.

Finally, both fell asleep, and the morning sun found her once again in his arms with her head on his chest and a hand on his stomach. They peacefully slept until noon.

He woke first and looked down at the woman lying with him. In the light of day, he no longer felt afraid. There was no reason not to carry on as they had before. She still loved her dead husband, and he was still not interested in that type of relationship, so really nothing changed. It was selfish to think of leaving her now when she needed him. He smiled and ran his hand over her hair. Her sleeping mouth curved in contentment.

Maisie arrived in time to see Kip and Abby sitting down for brunch. She was losing patience with just watching him. She wanted to act, to be the one he shared his vacation with. Envy filled her, and she vowed to devise a plan and put it into action instead of just dreaming of the outcome. Hopefully he would be returning to Nashville, and she would be able to make her move for him there.

•

Maisie faxed the pages he'd been waiting for. He sat at the piano and played each one. They were good, very good. These songs would sell, possibly even be recorded, before Adams could do anything about it. Then let him try to prove ownership. Maisie promised to destroy the originals. Adams wouldn't have a leg to stand on in court, and that meant big money in the bank for this company. He took the music to his desk and picked up the phone. Demos would be recorded by tomorrow afternoon, then sent to various artists for consideration. Good fortune abounded.

•

In the afternoon, Chris took Abby to the house. While she baked butter tarts he took care of email, then sat at his piano keyboard to work. He couldn't stop thinking about the night, and the music filled him, requiring only a few hours to smooth out the kinks until the flow was perfect.

Hearing her in the other room seemed natural, as though she belonged there, creating a feeling of home as he worked and smelled her baking.

When the tarts were out of the oven, she visited the bathroom for the twentieth time, then settled in her favorite chair to read. He finished his song, then joined her in the living room, dropping a CD in the player and stretching out on the couch.

She listened to the music in the background for a few minutes before giving up reading. "I like this music. Who is it?"

"Kenny Hampton."

"Well, I like Kenny Hampton. Can I see the CD case?"

He got up and handed it to her.

She examined it, taking the booklet out of the case to read. "He's pretty hot."

He rolled his eyes without reply.

"Do you know him?"

"Uh-huh."

"Good. Maybe you can introduce me. He's got a great backside. Man, is he cute."

"He's short." He felt his irritation barometer steadily rising.

"So am I. Does Julie know him? Maybe she'll tell me all about him. Can I call her?"

"No, you can't call her." He realized how abrupt he sounded and modified it. "She's not home today. She's out shoppin' for furniture."

"Oh. So, are you friends with him?"

"I was 'til now," he muttered as he got up and went to the kitchen for a drink. Maybe he could change the subject. "Want somethin' to drink, Abs?"

"No, thanks anyway. How long have you known him?"

"About ten years. What are you readin' now?"

"The booklet from the CD."

"I meant what book are you readin'." His speech became more punctuated. "What is the hardcover on your lap?"

"Oh, nothing that's holding my interest today. Hey, these pictures look like they're taken someplace like Cancun. Wouldn't that be such a romantic vacation? Lying in the sun and snorkeling and diving. I wonder if he had a girl down there with him?"

"Kenny always has a girl."

"It must be hard though, you know, being famous and all. Everyone wants to know you, but very few really do. And how would you know who to get close to? How could you tell who only wanted you for the fame and the money? He needs to find a woman who couldn't care less what he does for a living. Someone to whom he could say 'I'm giving up the music, and I want to be a butcher or a mailman, and she'd say 'If that'll make you happy, then do it'. It's going to be hard to find a girl like that. Someone that genuine who sees beyond all the hype and the glitz to find the man inside. Poor guy."

"Been there, done that," he murmured to himself. "Story of my life."

"Of course, you never know, I could be that girl of his dreams."

He sat back down and glared at her. "Want to play Scrabble?"

"No, thanks. Man, he is really nicely built. He must work out a lot."

"Uh-huh."

"Oh, look, he wrote this song for his mother. That's so beautiful. He must be a really sensitive man."

"That's it." Chris strode across the room and snatched the CD out of the player, stashed it back in the case, and slammed it down on the shelf. He replaced it with Coby Kansas.

"Why did you do that? I was enjoying it." Abby looked up at him perplexed.

"Yes, I noticed. I think you were enjoyin' it entirely too much." His clipped speech was lost on her. She was still engrossed in the booklet.

"Can I borrow it to take back to the cabin? Have you got anything else by him?"

"This is Coby Kansas playin' now. You'll like him. He's a friend of mine. Has a terrific sense of humor. He's married with five kids and a ranch in Oklahoma. Horses. Would you like to meet him? How about a trip to Oklahoma? I'd be glad to take ya to Oklahoma if you'd like to go."

"I'll think about it. I sure want to meet Kenny, though. He's got the greatest butt."

"Guy doesn't have a butt! There's nothin' wrong with Oklahoma. It's a very nice place."

"Did you see this guy's bottom lip? The way it just sits there like that invites all kinds of fantasies. Makes you just want to play with it, suck on it, nibble on it."

"Oklahoma's a great place!" Chris thumped his drink down and stomped upstairs to his room. Standing in front of his mirror, he turned to check out his own butt. He thought it not bad at all. Then again, he wasn't a woman. But plenty of women commented on it, and they always showed pictures of it on CMT when promoting their 'Boys of Summer' week. So, how come Abby preferred a picture of Hampton's to his real thing?

He tugged his shirt off and checked his overall physique. It was firm, and those muscles were built by hard work and the sweat of his brow, not just weight training. She had lain with him last night and touched his chest. His strong arms lifted and carried her, pregnant and all. She never commented on how nicely built he was. Enough was enough. One more word, and he would explode.

He went back downstairs and found Abby still looking at the CD book. "Gimme that." He snatched it from her hands.

"Hey, I was reading that."

"Now, you're done. Let's go outside for awhile."

"What is wrong with you?" She couldn't understand his strange behavior.

"That is the question exactly. What is wrong with me?" He stood in front of her, his hands on his hips, glowering at her.

"I don't understand."

He took a step back and held his arms out. "Look at me, Abby. What's wrong with me?"

She looked at him, puzzled. "There's nothing wrong with you. I still don't un…" A light bulb clicked on in her brain, and her face lit up. "You're jealous. I think Kenny Hampton is a hot babe, and you're jealous." Smirking, she stood and sashayed closer, staring into his blue eyes.

He put his hands back on his hips and turned his head away. "I'm not jealous."

She smiled and thought of all sorts of ways to torture him. "Is this big man feeling a teensy bit insecure because little Abby thinks another man is sexy?" She ran her hands up and down his chest. He glared at her. Curling her arms around him, she put her hands on his derriere, caressed it, then gave it a squeeze. "Are you afraid I don't like your butt, Mozart? Afraid it doesn't measure up to Kenny Hampton's?"

"Stop it, Abby."

"No, no. It's quite clear now. The big stud-muffin is upset because he thinks the pregnant lady isn't turned on by his bod."

Chris gripped her arms and held them down at her sides, pulling her against him and staring hard into her eyes. She felt the burn in his gaze and swallowed her smile. Leaning into him with her face raised, her eyes drifted closed. He frowned, distressed by the changes his body was experiencing. Sliding his hands to her shoulders, he pushed her back a step and marched out the front door.

Abby stood in the center of the room in a daze. What just happened? She tried to sort through her reeling thoughts, unable to believe how breathless she was. The way he'd looked into her eyes made her heart pound. She felt disappointed he hadn't kissed her, and what was that about? Why would she even want him to? True, sex had been missing from her life, but she'd never kissed anyone but Drew in her entire life. That must be it. Just a hormonal surge. But why was he acting so strange? That was the question.

Chris stood on the dock gazing out over the water. Damn that girl. For the first time in his life, he wanted to grab a woman and have sex just to get it over with. Once this tension was gone, he could treat her normally again. That's all it was, just mounting frustration. A week in Tennessee with the Tansey-witch looked perpetually more appealing as the hours ticked by. Maybe he would run into Hampton and slug him. That might be satisfying right about now.

Walking back, he jumped to grab a branch for some chin-ups. That ought to consume some energy. When his arms were exhausted, and his muscles burned, he ran along the shoreline. By the time he circled the island, he might possibly feel better.

An hour later, showered and wearing fresh clothes, he went downstairs and put on *Martina McBride's Greatest Hits*. That should be safe. Maybe he would listen to more female artists in the coming weeks. Out on the back deck, he sat down and watched Abby at the barbecue turning the meat.

"Want me to take over?"

"No, thanks. I'm doing all right. I think about ten minutes should do it."

"Sounds great."

She slapped at her leg. "I think we should eat indoors. The mosquitoes are getting bad."

"I'll set the table."

After laying the place settings, he went out to Gilda's garden and cut a variety of flowers. Finding a vase in the cupboard, he set about arranging them. So, they looked like they were just shoved in. What did he know? He was a guy. At least it would add color, and the fragrance was nice, too.

Seeing her coming in with the tray, he leaped across the room to open the door. He carried the meal to the table, while Abby headed off to the bathroom again. She certainly did need it a lot.

When they sat down to eat he chose a safe topic. "I had a really good time with you and Trent the other night. I couldn't believe you. That was incredible. I mean, when you sang the other songs you sounded great, but it was nothing like when you sang Webber. How do you manage to make it so different, the trained voice from the normal voice?"

"It's actually quite easy for me. A lot of people, once trained, always sound that way, and it can come out pretty stilted when they do contemporary. For me, it's a different key register, different demands on the diaphragm. You don't have as many long tones and the musical phrasing is generally a lot shorter. Of course, it's more difficult now that Andy takes up so much room, but I still like to practice."

"Will you sing for me again tonight?"

"I could be coaxed into it. I guess I owe you, don't I? After what you did for me, you know staying with me and all. Want to play with the machine? We could make it interesting."

"What have you got cookin' in that pretty little head now?"

"Let me give it some thought, and I'll let you know."

After the dishes were washed and put away, he walked her back to her cabin. While she visited the bathroom again, he plugged in the karaoke machine.

"Now for my idea," she said. "Do you remember the *Donny and Marie Show*?"

"I have a vague memory."

"Well, they used to do a segment each week where she'd sing a country song, and Donny sang rock. I was thinking that it's kind of like us. You're country, and I'm rock. So, wouldn't it be interesting to challenge one another in the other one's category? I'll be Marie, and you be Donny. I'll sing a country song, and you sing rock. The challenge is you can't repeat a song."

"Okay, that sounds interestin'." He felt certain he could win hands down. She presumed country music was his exclusive interest, and he never bothered to disavow that presumption. In truth, his collection was as widely varied as her own. She needed to work a lot harder if she wanted to succeed at this game. "Wait a minute. I thought you said you don't know any country music."

"Well, my mother listened to John Denver and Kenny Rogers a lot when I was growing up, so I know a few." She got out a notebook to list the songs they sang, so there was no chance of repetition. With the country segment coming first, she selected *Rocky Mountain High* by Denver. He followed with *School's Out* by Alice Cooper. The evening continued until they each had seven songs, and she was amazed by his versatility. He suggested they sing some of Kenny Rogers' duets and Abby agreed enthusiastically. They started with her favorite, *Don't Fall In Love With A Dreamer*, followed by *Islands in The Stream* and *Every Time Two Fools Collide*.

"Abby, you still have to sing one for me. You promised."

"And so I shall. But first there's one I'd love you to do for me, if you would. I love it so much."

CHRISTOPHER

"If I know it, I will. What's your pleasure, milady?"

"*She Believes In Me*. If a woman really loves a man, she believes in him and his dreams. The fact that she sacrifices for his dreams, and he knows and loves her for it, is beautiful."

"I suppose in some people's worlds it happens like that. Personally, I've never experienced it. But heck, I'll sing it for you. I'm going to do a different version than the one you're familiar with, though. A guy named Ronan Keating released this one. The lyrics are amazing."

Her face took on a dreamy expression as she listened.

"Wow. You're right. Those lyrics are much deeper, more poetic. I used to wish Drew would realize how much I believed in him. I think he just took it for granted that I'd always support him."

"I've never known such faith and love, except for my mother. Whenever I played when I was young, Mama would turn off the radio or television and listen to me. She'd cry when it was a sad song, laugh when it was a funny one, and always, always applaud. She made me believe in myself. She's the reason I'm successful today. But from a woman, a companion, I've never had the privilege of a woman believin' in me and my dreams. It isn't the same thing. A mother's love and faith comes unconditionally. A woman's is a gift."

"That was beautiful about your mom. She must be an incredibly wonderful woman. You always speak of her with so much love and respect. Hey, did you ever write a song for your mother? Kenny Hampton did you know."

"So you said. Sing for me, Abby."

"What would you like me to sing? Do you have a favorite?"

"How about *I Will Always Love You*. Dolly Parton wrote it, but it's been recorded by a few different artists."

"I have it by Whitney Houston, and I have the music here. An excellent choice." She put the music in and stood straight but relaxed in front of the fireplace, not using the microphone. As the music started she opened her mouth and let the sweet melody pour out.

"What a gift," he said, admiration glowing in his eyes. "I'm quite serious. With a voice like that you should be on the stage. Concert halls would be packed to hear you. Have you ever thought about pursuin' music professionally? The world deserves to hear such an incredible talent."

"Getting into music as an artist is a big commitment. It just hasn't been my biggest dream. I may be old-fashioned, but I didn't want my kids raised by nannies where I'm just a face that pops in for a visit now and again."

"It's true. A career can be time consumin'. Once you're established of course, you have more control. You get to work fewer days, but you accomplish more. With greater flexibility in schedulin', you have a lot more time to spend with family and other things that are important."

"My most important job now will be raising Andy."

"He's gonna be one very lucky little fella," Chris smiled. "Well, it's gettin' late, and you need to get some sleep. I'm gonna head on home."

"I've enjoyed my day, Chris. Thanks."

"Well, except for a few minutes this afternoon, I had a good day, too. I'm glad we found each other on this little island, Abigail Lockner. I expected to sit in the depths of despair, feelin' sorry for myself. Instead, I'm goin' to bed each night a content man. I have you to thank for that."

She smiled at him. "Happiness often comes in a door you didn't know you'd left open."

He caressed her cheek with his fingertips before turning to go.

Thoughts of Abby comforted him through the night. He woke in the wee hours and realized Tansey hadn't haunted his dreams for weeks. Abby was there instead, and the dreams were pleasant. Smiling, he rolled over and went back to sleep.

•

Tansey slid the straps of her teddy down and let it fall to the floor. Lifting the sheet, she climbed into bed and stretched luxuriously. He raised himself on one arm to lean over her, kissing and fondling her. An hour later he lay amazed at the things she did. He didn't know where she learned it all, but she would have a best seller if she ever put it in a book. He wondered for the umpteenth time how Kip could let go of such talent. Even though she spread herself around, she was worth holding on to. Kip must be out of his mind. The man knew how to make a lot of money, but he obviously knew nothing about women. Tansey purred with pleasure, and the sound drove him wild.

"I think it's time for some more money. I've decided to have a party. I always have to feature some charity, so of course, I'll have to spend some money to make money. I've got it figured to get back all my expenditures as a charitable write-off."

"I have never known a woman who could spend money as quickly as you."

"It's a talent."

"Yes, ma'am. Talent is somethin' you have plenty of. There's no denyin' that. Have you actually used up the entire divorce settlement? That was a sizable amount to get through, even for you. One thing you can say about Kip, he was generous with you."

"Not nearly generous enough, or I wouldn't be needing more of it. Anyway, I don't want to talk about him. I haven't spent it all. It's invested. How else is it going to make me more money? I don't want to delve too deeply into it. It's my nest egg."

"Well, that's one heck of a nest egg, m'dear."

71

"You'll get me more?"

"How much this time? You've got to stretch it longer. We've set up a good scheme, but if we play it too frequently, we chance gettin' caught. You're gonna have to learn to wear an outfit more than once, is all. Now, don't pout. The door isn't closin'. We just have to learn to go in and out wisely. I'm thinkin' once a month could work well. Can you live with that, darlin'?" He brushed her hair out of her eyes.

She rolled over and sat up, straddling him. He was surprised to find himself getting aroused again, certain she'd completely sapped him already.

"I suppose I can learn to live with it once a month." She started to run her fingers through his chest hair. "Tell me, darling, can you live with getting it just once a month?"

"Okay, okay. I'll think of somethin'. Give me time. It'll take a great deal of creativity. Remember, if we get caught, we both go to jail."

"You're one of the smartest men I've ever met. That's why we're so good together. I just know you'll come up with a foolproof scheme for us."

CHAPTER 9

Chris spent the last week of May concentrating on his music. He completed what he determined would be the title track, called *Island of Dreams,* and had almost enough for a full album. Some pieces were upbeat while others more melancholy. Each evening he faxed the music to Jeff. When he returned to Nashville, the band would congregate and flesh out the rest, adding percussion, keyboards, and other strings.

Tuesday morning, thoughts of Abby and the baby formulated an idea in his mind. He knew she had an obstetrics appointment in Peterborough that afternoon. Maybe he could tag along. Making sure he had his wallet and keys, he headed down the trail to the cabin.

"Mornin', Abs. How you feelin' today?"

"Pretty good. I'm just writing in the baby's diary. Give me a minute to finish up."

He went to the fridge for a bottle of juice. She closed the book and put it away.

"What's up, Mozart? You seem to have something on your mind."

"Yup. You're goin' to town today, right?"

"Yes. I have an appointment."

"Right. So I was thinkin', I'd like to come along."

"Sure."

"Don't you want to know why?"

"Only if you want to tell me."

CHRISTOPHER

"I thought we could do some shoppin'. It's about time you got some things for little Andy there, don't ya think? Like a place to sleep. Some clothes to put on him. Some diapers. You know."

"I'd love that. You actually want to come? It doesn't sound like a guy thing to do."

"Well, I'm gettin' kinda excited about the little cowpoke. Can't have him comin' into the world without a buckskin to cover his little hide now can we?"

She laughed at his westernology. "When do you want to leave out? My appointment's at one-thirty."

"Let's take care of that first. Then, we'll have the rest of the afternoon to shop. Maybe we can have dinner in a nice restaurant. Where's a good place?

"I don't know. I don't go to Peterborough all that often."

"Okay, I'll ask around when we get there. Have you got somethin' to wear? I realize you planned on goin' to a cottage to be alone when you packed."

"I brought two dresses because they're comfortable. But they're very casual."

"Well, we'll just add that to the shoppin' list. My treat."

"I can't let you do that."

"Don't argue, or I'll deduct points from your karaoke score."

She frowned facetiously. "Now you're playing hard ball. With that kind of penalty you've got me between a rock and a hard place. I guess I'll have to let you buy me a dress."

"That's better."

She looked at her watch. "We should probably leave in about half an hour. I'll get ready."

He drove the Lexus, and she appreciated the comfort of the luxury car. When they reached Peterborough she directed him to the medical building on Charlotte Street. "Do you want me to come with you or come back for you?"

"Come up if you don't mind."

He put on his sunglasses and went into the office with her, chatting with her as she waited.

"Mrs. Lockner, you and your husband can come in now."

He was about to protest, when Abby surprised him by taking his hand. They stopped at the scale and she was weighed, then shown into an examination room. She handed the nurse a small bottle from her purse, and the nurse left them alone.

"Are you sure you want me in here? I mean, what's he gonna do?"

"Nothing to be embarrassed about, and it's a she. She'll measure my stomach and listen to the baby's heart. I thought you might like to hear it."

He was about to reply when the nurse returned and took Abby's blood

74

pressure. "Much better, Abby." She left the room as the doctor came in.

"Hello, Abby."

"Hi. Dr. Chambers, this is my friend, Chris Adams."

Chris took off his sunglasses and smiled.

The doctor turned to him and recognized him immediately. "It's very nice to meet you. I listen to your stuff all the time."

"Thanks. That's nice to hear."

Abby gave him a puzzled expression. "You know Chris' music?" she asked the doctor.

"Of course."

Abby shrugged. "We're going out shopping for the baby this afternoon."

"Sounds like fun." She covered Abby with a small sheet as she lifted the dress and measured Abby's bared stomach. "Good size. No problems there. I notice you're finally putting a few pounds on, too. Keep it up."

"I'm still being sick, but not as often, and Chris makes sure I eat and rest."

"I'm glad to hear it. I've been worried about you, young lady." She took a tube of jelly from the counter and squirted some on Abby's stomach.

Abby reached her hand out. "Come here, Chris."

The doctor ran the fetal stethoscope over the stomach until she located the heart. The Doppler changed from crackling to a steady swishing sound.

Abby watched his face and smiled. "That's the baby's heartbeat."

His face filled with wonder, his eyes tearing as he squeezed her hand. "That's amazin', Abs."

"Well, it won't be much longer. Only five weeks to go. I want to see you again in two weeks. Things are fine. Keep it up." The doctor squeezed Chris' arm as she opened the door. "Look after her."

"I will."

He helped Abby to her feet and hugged her. "Thank you. That meant a lot to me." He held the door for her and took hold of her hand as they crossed the street to the parking lot.

When they arrived at the mall, he automatically headed for the exclusive stores, and she automatically headed for Wal-Mart.

"Wait a minute. Where are you going?"

"To shop for the baby. That's why we came, isn't it?"

"At Wal-Mart?"

"Why not? I don't mind getting a few expensive things, but the baby will outgrow them so quickly, it seems silly to waste money like that. I don't believe in spending foolishly. Wal-Mart will have everything we want, anyway. Come on."

He felt totally disoriented. A woman not wanting to spend extravagantly? Was he in Trent's *Twilight Zone*? He followed her to the baby department.

She was right. They had everything.

She chose a crib, a car seat, a swing, a baby bath, blankets, sheets, a lamp, diapers, and lots of sleepers in colors that she could put a boy or girl into. She selected two little boy outfits and two little girl's dresses, just to be prepared either way.

He had his own cart filled with a stroller, a Diaper Genie, a dozen Fisher-Price toys for infants, a nightlight, a Snugli, bottles, more diapers, baby socks, a Pooh Bear with a nose that wiggled, and a nursery monitor.

At the cashier he checked out and insisted the sales girl put Abby's purchases on his card as well, in spite of her loud objections. They pushed their full carts to the car. As he tried to stuff the purchases into the trunk and back seat, he was glad he had arranged to pick up the crib in two weeks when he brought Abby back to town for her next obstetrics appointment.

She got in and buckled her seatbelt. With heavy breathing through her nose and a lot of body language, she made it apparent she was giving him the silent treatment.

"What's the matter?"

"I'm very angry with you."

"I got that much on my own, thanks. Now do ya wanna tell me why?"

"Well, if you don't know, I'm not going to tell you!"

"Hey, I'm Mozart, not Kreskin. I don't read minds."

"You humiliated me in there."

He stared at her, astonished. "How in blazes do you figure that?"

She turned away, tears burning her eyes as she stared out the window, refusing to acknowledge him.

"Well, fine then." He pulled out his cell phone and pushed a button.

A phone rang in Nashville, and Julie answered.

"Hey, Julie. Listen, she's not talkin' to me, and she won't tell me why."

"What happened?"

"We came out shoppin' for the baby. We got some great stuff, and now she isn't speakin'. I can't figure it out."

"Who paid?"

"I did."

"Uh-huh. And did you discuss that before you went? That you would pay for everythin'?"

"Well...no."

"Uh-huh. And when you tried to pay for it, did she argue with you?"

"Yeah, but—"

"But nothin'. She's havin' a baby, and she wants to be responsible for it. Especially now that she's on her own. Gifts are nice, but she gets a sense of security knowin' she can provide for her child. You took that from her and probably made her feel like a charity case at the same time. As though ya don't believe she's capable on her own."

"Oh. Well, I didn't know all that."

"Tell her you're sorry, and find a way to make it up. Remember, not every one in the world expects to ride on your coat tails. Not every woman is Tansey."

"So you keep tellin' me."

"Goodbye, Kip."

He turned the phone off and returned it to his pocket. "I'm sorry, Abby. I've been a jerk. I just got so excited. Especially after hearin' the little guy's heartbeat in there. I guess I got carried away 'cause I love him. I never meant to hurt you."

She continued to stare out the window.

"Hey." He reached over and tucked her hair back behind her ear. "I am sorry."

"It's not your baby."

He pulled back, stung by her bitter words. "I know it isn't. I guess I let myself get too involved. I won't make that mistake again." He knew full-well he wasn't the father, but somewhere along the line he started feeling like one, like he was a part of this little family. He would be certain to keep his distance in the future. "You can pay me back if that'll make you feel better. Now, if you'll excuse me, I have somethin' else I need to do while I'm here."

He got out of the car and stalked back to the mall, unable to believe he'd fallen into caring about the woman and her baby so easily. When would he learn?

He took out his cell phone and pushed the button again. "Julie, have my plane up here tomorrow afternoon. I'm comin' home early." He disconnected without giving her a chance to reply or ask questions he did not want to answer.

Weaving through the parking lot, he returned to the car. Starting the engine, he told her, "I've just had a call from Nashville. I have to go home tomorrow. I'm sure you don't mind if we skip dinner. I have a lot of things to pack before I go."

The drive was long and silent.

They arrived at the island in the early evening. Each went to their respective homes without another word spoken.

As soon as she stepped in her front door she broke down. It had been so hard to not let him see how upset she was. She knew as soon as she said those harsh words that she went too far. He hadn't fathered this child, but he'd looked after and helped her, physically and emotionally, and he wanted to do something wonderful for her. He didn't deserve what she did. She felt the words slice through him.

When he said he was leaving, devastation ripped through her. She knew it was coming, but she put it off as something to deal with later, not ready to lose him yet. He was going. How could she ever make it right, now?

Chris slammed the door and went to the office to pack his things. Once he had all his music together, he headed up the stairs and threw his suitcase on the bed. Pulling things out of the drawers, he tossed them in the bag haphazardly. It amazed him how two months of good could go down the drain in one afternoon.

He cursed himself for caring. He came to get away from women, and he should have steered clear of this one. He carried the bag downstairs to the front door and found Abby standing there. He dropped the suitcase and walked away. She opened the door and came in wearing a white Battenburg trimmed gown and robe. "You gonna leave me outside to get eaten alive by the 'skitos?" she asked in a small voice.

Ignoring her, he dropped in a chair and picked up a book, pretending to concentrate on it. Abby knelt on the floor in front of him, took the book from his hands, and set it aside.

"Chris, I'm on my knees asking you to forgive me."

He picked up the book and opened it.

She took the book away and closed it again. "What I said was harsh and cold, and if I could take it back I would. I was so upset that I didn't care I was hurting you. You didn't deserve such cruelty."

He stood and stepped around her.

She noticed his cell phone on the table behind the sofa. She snatched it and looked through the directory. He stood in the kitchen, clearing out cupboards. Abby pushed the button.

A phone rang in Nashville, and Julie answered.

"Hi, Julie? This is Abby Lockner. I'm—"

"I know who you are."

"I said something to Chris, and even though I apologized, on my knees, he won't talk to me."

"Uh-huh. How long ago?"

"About three hours now."

"Uh-huh. That sounds about right. Do you mind me askin', just what did you say?"

"I pointed out that he isn't the baby's father."

"Uh-huh. Well, he's not. You got him there."

"He was just trying to be kind buying all those things for the baby. I wasn't understanding."

"You probably still aren't. Has he told you anythin' about his ex?"

"A bit. He doesn't talk a lot about it. Just that it was bad."

"We're talkin' about a woman who doesn't think twice about droppin' fifteen thousand dollars on a dress that she'll wear once. Money was the only thing he ever gave her that pleased her, so now he thinks he has to spend money to make people happy. I've explained that not everyone is so selfishly self-centered, but it's hard for him to reconcile."

"If money is that big a deal to her, why didn't she marry a big name celebrity who had money to burn instead of a songwriter?"

Julie didn't know what to say to that. "I ask myself that same question all the time."

Aghast, Chris stared at Abby, unable to believe she'd called Julie. What a nervy broad. His glare grew blacker by the minute.

"How do I make him talk to me?"

"I'm afraid you're gonna have to talk to his mama on that one. She's the only one who can sort him out. Do you want her number?"

"No, it's here. I'm on his cell. Thanks for the insight. Next time I'll be more sensitive. If there is a next time."

She turned away from him and whispered conspiratorially into the phone. "Want to hear something funny before I hang up? Listen to this." She walked to the counter stool and sat down. "So, Julie, I understand you know Kenny Hampton. He's such a hot babe isn't he?"

"Yeah, I know him. What's all that bangin'? Is that Chris slammin' doors?" Julie couldn't discern what was happening on the other end of the phone.

"It sure is. Chris put on a CD the other day, and I liked it, and he said it was Kenny Hampton. I looked at the pictures with it, and I couldn't believe how sexy he is."

"Did I just hear glass breakin'?"

"You sure did. So tell me, is Kenny's butt as great in person as it is in the pictures?"

A loud snarling noise echoed through the phone. "Was that an actual growl I heard?"

"That's right. Anyway, he tells me how much alike you and I are, and that we'd be such great friends, so I was thinking maybe I could come down there for a visit, and you could introduce me to that sex god."

"Okay, now I'm not hearin' a thing. What's he doin'?"

"Looks to me like he just threw Kenny's CD—yes, there was the splash—into the lake."

"Oh, my Glory! He's jealous?"

"You know, it's interesting. That's the same conclusion I came to. But apparently not. The green-eyed monster emphatically denies it."

Julie burst out laughing. There was no way she would let him walk out on this. He obviously cared more than he admitted, even to himself, and Abby was good for him.

"Listen, here's somethin' to help you. Tell him I couldn't get him on a flight tomorrow. All the seats are booked. He's gonna have to come next Sunday, as planned. And thank you, Abby. He's changed dramatically since he got there, and it's all been positive. Even today."

"Let's just hope I can repair the damages. Bye"

He was about to say, *I can't believe you called Julie,* when she called someone else.

She saw the black storm cloud floating over his head and retreated a few steps.

"Hi. My name is Abby Lockner, and I'm calling from Ontario, Canada…Oh, you have? Well you obviously haven't spoken with him today. We had a misunderstanding, and he won't speak to me…Really? That's all I have to do?…Thank you…Yes, it was nice talking to you too…I'm looking forward to coming…That's very kind of you. I'd like that, too…Okay, I'll talk to you later, Maddie."

"My mother? You called my mother?" he bellowed.

"Gonna talk to me now?" She set the phone down on the table and stood with her arms folded. He folded his arms and turned his back on her.

"Well, that's fine, then. By the way, Julie says she couldn't get you a plane ticket, so you're stuck here until Sunday."

What was that supposed to mean? It was his plane! He put Julie on his list of women to murder. He looked over his shoulder to see Abby casually pick up his guitar. Opening the door, she walked out and headed home.

"Ah, dang it, Mom. Not my guitar." He dashed across the living room to the door. "Go ahead and take it. I have nineteen more at home," he shouted. She kept on walking. He stood fuming on the front step. "Man, I hate it when they take my guitar," he muttered. Jumping off the front porch he took up the chase.

She heard him shout her name, and she started to run. She made it to the cabin and shoved the guitar under the bed.

Chris bounded up on the front steps to find her perched on the sofa looking as though she didn't have a care in the world. Yanking the door open, he glowered at her.

CHAPTER 10

"Hi. Nice of you to drop by for a visit."

"My guitar, please."

"Won't you sit down? Can I get you something? Some juice, cookies, dinner maybe?"

"My guitar would be good."

"I'm sure you're not worried about that. After all, you have nineteen more at home." She went to the kitchen to root around in the fridge.

"Where is it?"

"Nope."

"That wasn't a yes or no question."

"We are going to sit and talk. When that reaches a satisfactory conclusion, you can have it back."

"I don't want to talk. Just give it to me, and let me get out of here."

"Nope."

"Fine. Let's get it over with."

"Sit down, then." She came back with cheese and crackers. "Excuse me for eating. I didn't get dinner this evening, and I'm rather hungry."

He slumped in the chair and glared. "There's nothin' to discuss. You simply pointed out the truth. I am not the baby's father."

She pulled the heavy stuffed ottoman in front of him and sat. "Chris, the thing is, you've given me everything important. You gave my life back to me. I was stuck in a tunnel of darkness, and you were the light that found me and showed me the way out. In return, I have done nothing but be selfish and demanding. You deserve so much more. I love you a great deal."

He turned his face away, and she lifted a hand to his cheek, turning it back. "I wanted you to feel the baby moving and hear that little heartbeat. This afternoon, I loved us picking things out together, because I needed to share these things. I love that you love the baby and want to share your ranch with us. You see, up here in our isolated world, I've grown so comfortable that I tend to forget there's a world out there we have to go back to. The truth is, I dream about you being in Andy's future. I don't want you to leave us. I need you, and he's going to need you.

She clasped her hands around his, and encouraged that he didn't pull away, she continued. "About today, I'm sorry. I've been so worried about him not having a father that I let you fall into it. I think subconsciously I wanted you to. Biologically, he isn't yours, but I want you to be the father in his life. I was cruel, and I'm so sorry." She wiped away the tears and blew her nose. "My heart is breaking to know I've hurt you like this" She dropped her head and cried. "You're such an important part of my life. Please, please don't stop caring."

He thought he was immune to tears. Apparently, it was only Tansey's tears that didn't affect him any more. He pulled her to him and settled her on his lap.

"Come on, Abby girl. I'm here. I won't leave ya." He held her to his chest, running his fingers through her lustrous curls, and saw tears glistening like diamonds on her eyelashes.

"I'm sorry, Chris. You didn't deserve it. It's all my fault."

"I'm sorry, too. You and the baby are both precious to me. I don't wanna lose either of you. I have dreams of my own, you know."

"You do?"

"Sure, I mean, I know I won't be his father, but I'd like to be part of his life. I'm gonna miss you somethin' fierce when I go home. I've even thought of bringin' you down to Nashville. I've gotten used to havin' you around, ya know?"

"Really?" Sniffle.

"You betcha. And holdin' you like this? I'm really gonna miss this. It's the most right feelin' I've ever known, Abs. It makes me believe in goodness. I'm sorry I'm so stubborn. Man, I can't believe you called Julie and my mama. Don't ever tell me you're not gutsy. That was a move I never saw comin'."

She giggled through her tears. He kissed her nose and gave her a tight squeeze. "How 'bout we find somethin' a little more substantial for you to eat." He kissed her forehead, then slid from beneath her and went to the kitchen.

●

Friday afternoon Chris pulled the boat around to the west end dock. He found Abby reading under the tree. "Hey, Abs. You know, I still owe you dinner and a dress, and I'm determined to take care of it before I head down to Nashville next week. How 'bout it?"

"You mean now?"

"Yup. Let's go to Peterborough, and do it right this time."

A smile swept across her face, and she reached for help getting up. "Let me wash my face and brush my hair." She bounced off into the cottage. He smiled as he watched her go, amazed at how happy it made him to be the source of her joy.

She returned a few minutes later, and they walked down to the boat. He told her about the song he worked on that morning and the lyrics he had trouble with, glad to be able to talk with someone who understood meters and phrasings. "I've got what comes before and after, but I can't get these two lines to say what I want."

"Explain the essence of what you're thinking, and if it needs to rhyme."

He gave her the four lines preceeding and the two after. Within minutes she recited two lines that flowed smoothly and articulated his concept.

"And I won't even charge you for that, Mr. Adams."

"You're amazin'." He tied the boat at the marina and helped her onto the dock. "I might have to get you a pair of new shoes for that. Man, I wrestled with that for two days, and you did it in two minutes. I may have to step aside as a writer and leave it to the master."

"Get serious, Mozart. You're a wizard, and you know it."

They chatted happily all the way to the city. When they arrived at Lansdowne Place she let him lead her to the exclusive stores, sure they wouldn't carry the kind of price tags Julie mentioned. Finding a maternity store, they went in. She was amazed by the large selection of evening dresses. Midnight blue chiffon caught her eye, and she pulled it out to take a better look at the graceful flowing lines.

"That's it, Abby. It's the prettiest one we've seen. Go try it on."

She checked the price tag on the sleeve and choked. "No, I don't think so."

"I do." He called the sales woman to assist, and before she could object further, she was being swept away. In the change room she slipped it over her head and loved the way it fluttered down. The style was flattering and the color perfect. She went out in her stocking feet to show him.

He glimpsed her coming and was instantly captivated. He watched as the twinkle in her eyes spread until she sparkled all over. "Abigail, you look positively breathtakin'.''

The appreciation in his eyes made her feel beautiful. As they gazed at one another, the sales women sighed, thinking it wonderful to see young couples so much in love and expecting a baby.

"We have hosiery in that same shade if you're interested."

He murmured, "We'll take it. And that pretty evenin' bag up by the front counter if she likes it."

"Yes, sir."

Abby smiled, feeling as though she would burst. She hadn't been treated so special since, well, forever. She padded over to the counter and loved the purse he'd chosen. She beamed her approval before escaping to the change room.

When she returned he had his credit card out, and she turned away not wanting to know the cost of this expedition.

"Listen, darlin', why don't you go ahead to the shoe store and start lookin'. By the time you've tried on everythin' I'll be there." He spoke in a quiet voice so the woman at the till couldn't overhear. "Make sure you get somethin' comfortable. Remember how your feet can swell."

When she was gone he asked for a restaurant referral. The saleswoman told him Roland's was the place he wanted and let him use the store phone to make a reservation. With that taken care of, he made one more stop on his way to the shoe store.

Abby was unable to decide between two pairs. She liked them both, so she called on him to make the final decision. He thought about buying both, but knew she had a limit to what she would go along with, and he wasn't about to push those buttons again. Besides, they still had the dinner ahead. She would be shocked enough then. He chose the black leather with the cut out toe and the court heel. She was pleased with the choice, and they left the store.

He carried her things to the car and drove to the Quality Inn.

"What are we here for?"

"Because you need to nap before we go out tonight, and you should have some decent space to get ready in. I'm not havin' you get all gussied up in some restroom cubicle."

She smiled, touched by his thoughtfulness. He checked her into a room and took her things up for her. "Anythin' you need, call room service. Don't worry about it, okay?"

"All right, thanks. You really do think of everything."

"Come on, get on over here to the bed, and lay down. I'll take your shoes off."

Half an hour later she was fast asleep.

At six thirty a knock sounded at the door, and there stood her date for the night. No, it was her friend. This was not a date.

"You look stunnin', Abby. I'm so proud to be seen with you tonight." He bent and kissed her cheek.

She blushed and smiled. "I don't know about going out for dinner. You look good enough to eat. Smell pretty good too. Maybe I'll just have my dinner right here."

"Don't tempt me, girl, or we won't get out of here."

"Yeah, right. As if anyone would be attracted to a horse like me."

"Whoa! I have known plenty o' horses in my day, and I never met a one that looked as ravishin' as you. Now, I'll not have you talkin' like that, or I'll put ya over my knee and tan your hide, and don't think I won't. You look fabulous, and we have reservations."

Pulling up to Roland's, her excitement escalated. He opened her door and helped her out of the car. Inside, they were shown to a quiet table in the corner.

They took a few minutes to peruse the menu while the waiter poured the sparkling juice Chris ordered when he made the reservation.

"I think you must be more famous than you let on."

He felt his heart stop, then quickly composed himself before lifting his eyes to meet hers. "Why do you say that?"

"The waiter knew who you were. He called you 'Mr. Adams'."

"That's because I gave my name when I made reservations, silly."

"Aha! But when we came in you didn't tell them who you were."

Uh-oh. Think fast, and make it credible. "I didn't have to. I told them I'd be bringin' the most beautiful woman here tonight. They took one look at you and knew." He smiled at her blush.

"You're lying, Mr. Adams, but you're so charming we'll overlook it."

She reached into her purse and brought out a velvet box, laying it next to his plate. His eyebrows raised, and he looked at her questioningly.

"I wanted to give you something to remember me, and our island. It's all meant so much to me, and I wanted to show you. I don't want you to forget me. I hope you like it." Holding her breath, she watched him open it.

He was taken aback. He received gifts from fans all the time, and he appreciated them. But he couldn't remember being given something personal like this. Tansey thought gifts were a one-way street that stopped at her door.

He took the box and felt his hands tremble. Lifting the lid, he found a gold bracelet with large polished links. He took it from the box and put it on his right wrist.

"Abby, it's beautiful. Thank you."

His pleasure seemed genuine, and she was moved to see his eyes watering. She remembered just a few days before when he'd been prepared to leave and was grateful things had been resolved. Leaning over, he kissed her cheek.

CHRISTOPHER

He'd planned to wait, but this was the moment. He reached into his jacket pocket and retrieved a similar velvet box, setting it on the table in front of her. "You and I had the same idea for the same reason. I didn't want you to forget either."

"You didn't need to buy me anything. You've already given me so much these last two months."

"Likewise, darlin'. Open it. I thought it would go nicely with the dress." He bit his bottom lip in anticipation.

She opened the lid and gasped. "Oh, Christopher, it's beautiful."

"You like it?"

"It's perfect. I've never dreamed of owning something so exquisite." The box held an oval blue sapphire surrounded by two layers of diamonds that caught the flame of the candlelight, giving off a warm brilliance. "Will you please put it on me?"

He stood and took the necklace from her. She lifted her hair from her neck while he did the clasp. Reaching around, she took his hand in hers, and he crouched beside her. Tears spilled over her lashes as she wrapped her arms around his neck. After holding him tightly for a few minutes, she gave him a chaste, sweet kiss on his mouth.

"Thank you."

Chris sat back down, wanting the moment to never end.

"I haven't heard from Trent since he left. I wonder how he's doing?"

"Julie's lookin' after him. He's got his band together, and tonight is their first gig. They're playin' at the Wildhorse Saloon, which generally has the better-class bands. After that, we'll see. But things are movin' along for him. He seems real happy and lovin' Nashville. He keeps havin' Julie pinch him, so he knows it isn't a dream. She's mighty glad to oblige. She loves to pick on a guy every chance she gets."

"Where's he staying?"

"My place. Julie says he keeps her on her toes. Apparently your cousin is quite the practical joker."

"Oh. Sorry, I should have warned you. He can be so infuriating. But you sometimes have to admire the genius of his mind. He's come up with some brilliant schemes in his day."

"So I hear. Anyway, he's doin' well, and he has a promisin' future ahead of him."

"Well, quite frankly, that's part of what worries me. I think he's got a good sense of who he is and all, but believing all the hype can be tempting. And the money—I guess I don't have to tell you, some of those people make a vulgar amount of money. And it's never enough, you know? They always want more, need more. I've always believed money and fame carry responsibility. Unfortunately, most who have it don't see it that way."

"What exactly do you mean by responsibility?"

"Say you make three million dollars from one song if it hits big. That's more than most people see in a lifetime. What are you going to do with it? No one honestly *needs* that kind of money. It's nice to have, but there's a big difference between want and need, isn't there? I think the line gets foggy, and suddenly frivolous desires become needs. I'm not saying they shouldn't enjoy their money. So much could be done with the excess, but people get their heads turned by success. I don't want that to happen to Trent." She took a drink from her goblet before continuing.

"A perfect example was the other day. You thought we needed specialty shops for the baby's things. I chose Wal-mart. Do you know how much money we saved? Sometimes, it's nice to treat yourself with the finer things, but day-to-day, it's a waste of money. Believe me, being an accountant I see people who struggle just to pay the mortgage. Always living on the next paycheck before they even get it. Time off sick could mean no food in the house for a week or so, living on oatmeal or rice or Kraft Dinner if they're lucky enough to have it."

He reveled in the differences between Abby and Tansey. Smiling, he let her carry on.

"I've also seen the other side. In university, I worked as a sales clerk in a golf store. Do you know, one day I sold a man a putter for two thousand dollars? One stupid club! That's down right indecent. Some people obviously have far more than they need or know what to do with. It boggles my mind when a high percentage of children in this prosperous first-world country are malnourished, that someone can spend that kind of money for a stick. I mean really, he's just going to hit a ball with it. Roger Maris never spent that kind of money for a bat, and he still managed to hold the world record of sixty-one home runs for thirty-seven years."

"Wow, and she knows baseball too. Anythin' you don't know about, Abby?"

She gave him a sly look from the corner of her eye. "Country music, but I'm learning."

He laughed, then sobered. "I know the kind of people you're talkin' about. I was married to one. I like the way you think. You're so well-grounded and sure of yourself."

The late night drive back to the marina was peaceful. They talked a bit, but they'd also learned to enjoy comfortable silence.

He took the boat to the west dock, so she wouldn't have to walk the trail in her new dress and shoes. As they disembarked, he held her hand and didn't let go. At the front door of the cabin, the only beacon in the darkness shone from the stars and moon above. He took her other hand and gazed down into her eyes. They sparkled in the moonlight, and he felt the romance of the moment. He desperately wanted to lean down and kiss her, to take her breath away.

"I think you're the most incredible woman I've ever met in my whole life."

She smiled up at him, as though she too felt the magic.

A mosquito landed on the back of his neck, and he felt the bite. He slapped it, and his feet came thudding back to earth.

"Goodnight, Abby. Sleep well."

He headed back to the boat with his hands shoved in his front pockets. "Dang mosquitoes. Now I know why I've always hated 'em."

●

Early Sunday morning, he went to the cabin to say goodbye. "What time is Claire comin'?"

"I'm supposed to meet her Tuesday afternoon at the marina. Don't worry. I'll be fine."

"I know you can look after yourself, but I'll feel better with Claire here. Otherwise I'd be worried the whole time. It's only a month 'til the baby gets here."

"I'm glad she's coming, too. I thought when I came that I wanted to be alone all these months. Now, I'm afraid of getting lonely. Strange how things can change so quickly, isn't it? When will you be coming back?"

"Tuesday next week, prob'ly early evenin'. I'd like to be sooner, but I have a lot to take care of while I'm there, so I'll have more time to spend with you when the baby comes."

"Okay. I know you have to get to Toronto to catch a plane, so you should probably be on your way. I'll miss you."

"I'll miss you, too. I'll be back as soon as I can."

"Listen to us. We sound like an old married couple, don't we?"

He laughed as he took her in his arms to hug her goodbye. "Look, you have my cell number, right? If you need me for anythin', call and I'll be here."

She smiled up at him. "Thanks, but I think I can get through a week. It's not like I haven't been on my own before."

"Okay. I'm gonna go now. You look after yourself and Andy." He headed for the door and turned back one last time. "See you soon, Abby girl."

She smiled as he walked out the door, waiting until she heard the boat heading down the lake before she let the dam burst. She cried until there were no more tears and told herself how foolish she was being. This waterfall was purely hormonal. Silly to cry just because a friend was going away for a while. But it was a sign of a world out there, and one day she would have to rejoin it, leaving her island summer behind. It wasn't a day she looked forward to.

That afternoon she drove the speedboat to the marina to pick up fresh milk and eggs. She knew she and Claire would sit up late with milk and cookies, both talking a mile-a-minute, especially since they hadn't seen each other for several weeks.

Glen handed her a parcel that arrived in the mail for her. Unable to imagine what it could be, she noted the return address. Hmm. Julie Clayton in Nashville. She thanked him and took it along with her purchases.

Back at the cabin, she cut through the tape and opened the box. A note sat on top.

Dear Abby,

Kenny is an excellent swimmer, but I fear his CD doesn't have the same ability. I ran into him the other day, and he sent you these. There's a copy of every CD he's released. I've also included a video of his Greatest Hits. Hope it will keep you busy while Chris is in Nashville. Enjoy it, and then hide it or it may suffer a similar fate to the last CD.

Thanks for all you've accomplished with Chris. You're a miracle worker, girl. Trent says to send you his love. He's doing real well down here. He'll be a star—if I don't kill him first.

Your friend,
Julie

Abby looked inside and instantly recognized the CD Chris had his tantrum over. She giggled as she took it out to investigate the rest of the contents. Every CD had been opened and signed, "To Abby, Love Kenny Hampton."

She slid the video into the VCR and sat mesmerized for the next hour. He was everything she'd expected and more. She particularly liked that little thing he did with his tongue. Yessirree, that Kenny Hampton was a fine male specimen. No wonder Chris felt threatened. She could see this man must have a large female following. Poor Chris. It must be hard being the friend of a sex symbol. Although he was a very attractive and sexy man in his own right, she felt certain if he was with Kenny he would be overlooked because of Kenny's star status. She'd just have to boost him up a little more often so he'd know he was good looking, too, and could have any woman he wanted.

On the other hand, maybe she wouldn't. Then he'd get involved with someone and be too occupied to spend time with her and the baby. It wasn't that she didn't want him to be happy, she just didn't want to give up the friendship they'd built.

•

Maisie and Daisy watched Kip leave for Nashville on his private plane from the small airport in Peterborough. They had to drive back to Toronto to catch an international flight. Fan Fair unofficially started Tuesday beginning with his fan club luncheon. They had purchased their tickets for that event six months ago.

Maisie planned to get rid of the pregnant one, "Abby" he called her, before they left. She had to arrange it so it wouldn't happen until she and Daisy were safely in Nashville. Tonight, she would rig up a surprise. Then it was just a matter of waiting.

CHAPTER 11

Even though it was Sunday, there remained only a few days before Fan Fair, and there was no such thing as a day off in Nashville this week. He touched base with Donna, and she emailed his schedule to him. He wouldn't have too many minutes to himself for the next seven days, but they were days important to his career. He would meet and greet the people he played his music for. He would have his picture taken a few thousand times and get writer's cramp signing autographs. The result would be huge sales of records, concert tickets, and merchandise.

Jeff popped in to tell him about Trent's band, and the conversation naturally progressed to the songs Kip had faxed from Ontario. The band had a few of them ready and wanted to get together to jam. Kip suggested they hang out that evening.

"Um, can't do that, buddy."

"Why? What's up tonight?"

Jeff looked decidedly uncomfortable, and Kip knew the answer.

"Okay, I get it. She's havin' a big party tonight, and everyone is sucked into goin' whether they want to or not because it's for charity, right?"

"Yeah. Sorry, Kipper. You know we won't even speak to her. Just put in an appearance and skedaddle on out again."

"Black tie or BBQ?"

"Barbecue at the mansion. Starts at five-thirty."

"Well, hey, let's go. There'll be a lot of people there I haven't seen for a

91

long time. Be nice to catch up with a few of 'em before this whirlwind starts."

"You've got to be kiddin' me."

"No. Let's do it. Things have changed. I can handle the Tansey-witch. She can't push my buttons any more, because they're all disconnected. I know she'll still try, and not succeedin' will drive her nuts."

Jeff took a closer look at his lifelong friend, and noticed the tension had been erased from his features. He seemed perfectly at ease about the whole thing. He really had changed.

"Okay, let's do it. Want to go on your own or with the band?"

"I think I'll just bring Trent along. I'll hang out with you when I get there, but the arrival is gonna be significant. I hate a woman who plays games. Man, that's why I'm never gettin' married again. I've learned. Never waste your time on a woman who isn't willin' to waste her time on you."

"When did you become the philosopher?"

"I don't know. I just seem to see things a lot clearer these days."

"Okay, where's the Kip Adams we all know and love, and just who is this imposter? You go away for two months and come home a different person? You're gonna be lucky if Julie ever lets ya out of her sight again. She won't recognize ya."

"I think she'll be pleased. And by the way, where is she? You've just re-minded me, her murder's on my to-do list."

Jeff stuck his head out in the corridor and shouted for her. She popped out of her office across the hall and two doors down. He pointed to her, then drew his finger across his throat indicating she was in trouble. She came to Kip's office.

"What's up?"

"Julie. Dear, sweet, Julie. It's only because I have great love and respect for...your brother, that I'm not gonna fire you. This time. But the next time I tell you to do somethin' and you purposely go against me, I swear, you'll be out of here."

Julie stared at him totally perplexed. "Am I even supposed to have a clue what you're talkin' about?"

"Do you remember me askin' you to send my plane?"

"Oh, that."

"Did my plane come when I said I wanted it?"

"No, but I sent you a message."

"Yeah, and that was so cute, wasn't it? Thing is, Jul, I wasn't amused. When I ask you to do somethin', I expect it done."

"Well, didn't you and Abby make up?"

"Yes, but that's not the point."

"And didn't you enjoy those extra few days there?"

"Yes, but that's not the point."

"That's exactly the point, Kip. My job is to look after you. Somethin' I've been doin' for about two decades now. I know my job. I also know she's the best thing that's ever happened to you. Career aside of course."

"It's not up to you to decide what does or doesn't make me happy."

"Well, pardon me for carin', but we've watched you suffer for too many years, now. I did the right thing, and you know it. You can stop my salary, but you'll never stop me from carin' and tryin' to do what's in your best interest. I don't get paid for that."

He stood with his hands on his hips. "Well, I think I made myself clear."

She mimicked his stance. "Well, I think I made myself clear, too."

"Right then. Are you comin' to the Beauty Queen's barbecue tonight?"

"Do not tell me you plan on goin'. I'm not gonna believe it even if I see it with my own eyes. Why would you do that?"

Jeff interjected, "No, I think it's a good thing. A lot has changed. I think it's gonna be a rather interestin' evenin'. Don't you, Kip?"

"Just might be. Julie, call Cree and have him cut me a check for fifty thousand for whatever charity she's sponsorin' tonight."

"No bloody way! You've got to be jokin' me."

"Didn't I just tell you to follow my orders in the future?"

"Yeah, but you've never given anythin' that size to one of her functions, even when you were tryin' to hold on to her."

"That's right."

"Then what gives?"

"I've come to realize that bein' a celebrity comes with a responsibility. I need to start usin' it to benefit others." His head tilted and he gazed into the distance, smiling. "You know, there are so many things out there I could be doin' to make a difference, and I haven't actively pursued that enough. Do you know how many people out there are starvin' while I've got all this money sittin' in the bank, just makin' more?

"I know, I work hard for my money. My daddy worked a lot harder for his, and he never had money like this. There are people with serious problems, and I pull in a million bucks in two weekends of concerts. That's more than they'll see in a lifetime. Well, enough is enough. I'm not gonna just sit on my duff and collect praise while the bank account grows. I'm sure that whatever the cause is, those people need it more than I do."

Julie and Jeff stood gaping at him. She found her voice first. "Listen, you've always been generous with time and money for charities. I don't see what's changed."

He sat back down in his desk chair. "A lot of things have changed. Like I said, I can enjoy it, but they need it. Besides, it'll irritate the heck out of the Beauty Queen. I like that aspect of it."

"Okay, I'll do it, I guess." She looked at her brother for a reaction. He gave her a grin that said, *So there!*

She went to her office and placed the call while ruminating over the scene she'd just witnessed. He wasn't the same man she'd watched for the last three years. It was a new, self-assured, stronger-than-ever-before Kip. He carried a sense of peace within himself that now allowed him to deal with the witch. It was a phenomenal amount of healing to achieve in such a short time. Just who was this Abby Lockner, a guardian angel, or something? She'd certainly worked a miracle with Kip.

Grabbing a cab to his apartment at the end of the day, Kip took the elevator to the penthouse. He found Trent in the kitchen putting together a sandwich of multiple layers.

"Trent, my fine young lad. Good to see you, buddy."

"Glad to see you're back. Man, I have so much to tell you. This has been the most fabulous few weeks of my life. And that Julie, she's some girl, isn't she?"

Kip raised an eyebrow. "Julie? Yeah, she's great."

"Boy, she sure is. She's a real good sport, too. We get along great."

"Is that right?"

"You gonna be sticking around for awhile? Want me to make you a sandwich, too?

"No, thanks, and I suggest you might want to wrap that up for later. Tonight we're goin' to a barbecue. I think you'll enjoy it.

"Terrific. Where is it?"

"It's bein' given by the Beauty Queen of Ice. My ex-wife in my ex-house. But it's for charity, so we put in an appearance and make our donation. It's expected. I'll take you along and introduce you to some people you might like to meet. Just about everyone will be there. I'd kind of like to steer clear of Kenny Hampton, though."

"Okay. You guys don't like each other?"

"Actually, we've always been good friends."

"Then what gives, if you don't mind my asking?"

Trent noticed a muscle in Kip's jaw start to twitch. "Your cousin thinks he's sexy. She likes his butt."

"And you find that irritating?" He wasn't surprised by the news. Having seen the two in action, he secretly hoped this fellow would one day become family.

"I just don't even want to talk about it. I'm gonna shower and get dressed."

Once in the shower, he let the hot water spill over him, draining out the tension. He couldn't understand why he suddenly felt stressed-out. He hadn't been when he came home.

Summer days were growing longer, with the sun still hovering overhead when they arrived at the mansion. Searching the large gathering strewn across the side and back yards, Trent quickly spotted Julie and sprinted off to join her.

Kip casually strolled across the lawn, smiling and saying howdy to shocked but friendly faces. With his hands casually tucked into the pockets of his khakis, he looked cool and collected. Wending his way through the throng, he found Tansey. She wore her waist length hair down, a halter top of white eyelet lace and matching slacks.

"Howdy, Tansey. Nice party. Good turnout."

She visibly stiffened at the sound of his voice. She was startled by his unexpected presence, well aware that he generally attempted to avoid her. "Hello, Kip. Surprised to see you here."

"Don't be. I have a check here for your cause." He slipped it out of his pocket and handed it to her. She quickly skimmed it, then stopped and looked again, closer. She had never seen him give away such a large amount of money in one shot before. "This is a joke, right?"

"Nope. It's as serious as cancer is to those kids."

"You can't just go around giving money away like this. It's not right."

"Funny, I was under the impression that's why you've got everyone corralled here tonight. You want to suck money out of them. Quit complainin' when you get it."

"No. I won't accept it." She held it out to him, expecting him to take it back.

"Yes, you will. You've gotten all you're gonna get out of my pockets, girl, so don't feel like I'm drainin' your resources. Take the money for the kids. They should get some enjoyment out of life while they still have one." He watched her seethe, knowing she would never have allowed it when they were married. She could go shopping with an amount like this.

"Nice seein' ya." He spotted a friend close by and left her to fume. "Howdy, Coby. How's it hangin', buddy?"

"Well, if it isn't the man! What the heck are you doin' here? You're about the last person I expected see tonight." Coby guzzled the beer in his hand. "You oughta get yourself one o' these babies. Help get ya' through the evenin'."

"No, thanks. We're not drinkin' anythin' alcoholic right now."

"Who the heck is we? I don't see nobody with ya."

"Did I say we? Sorry, I meant I."

"You got somethin' you want to share with ole Coby?"

"Nope. I've just been gettin' my life together, you know? I'm puttin' out the garbage and makin' room for things that are gonna make me happy. No woman is worth your tears, and the one who is, won't make you cry."

"Where the heck have you been? I mean, this all sounds good, but it don't sound like you at all. When did you become the philosopher?"

"I dunno. I just see things a lot clearer these days. Things I never understood suddenly make sense."

Kip was thrust forward as someone jumped on his back, yelling, "Kip Adams Bronc Ride!"

He bent forward and twisted to throw the rider off. "Hampton, ya didn't stay on long enough. Hope you're gonna do better on Saturday, or you'll be stomped on, you wannabe cowboy." He reached a hand down and helped Kenny up off the ground.

"Hey, Bubba, how's it goin'?" Coby asked.

"Life is good. So has the Kipper here been tellin' ya 'bout his new woman?" Kenny stood grinning, hands on his hips, what there was of them, and waited expectantly.

"No, matter of fact. This is news. Sure explains a lot, too. Kip, you ole dog, you got a woman? Where is she?"

"I don't have a woman. Kenny's just spoutin' off about nothin'."

"Are ya tryin' to keep her a secret or somethin'?" Kenny grinned.

"Well, let's hear about it, Kenny. Kip's holdin' out on me," Coby encouraged.

"Her name's Abby. She's 25 and a widow. Lost her husband last fall to heart disease. She's also quite pregnant." Kenny watched Kip's blur of emotions as he spewed forth the information.

"How in the hell do you know about Abby?"

Coby took a step back obviously enjoying it. "So, it is true!"

Kenny continued, "She's a pretty thing too. Got all those soft, shiny brunette curls. It's easy to see why he's keepin' her locked up in Canada."

"Hampton, you have about ten seconds before I smash the daylights out of you. You don't want that sweet little face all bruised up for the weekend, now do ya?"

"Hey, what'd I do? I'm just sayin' she's a real looker. You shouldn't be gittin' all twisted outta joint when a fella compliments yer woman." He wisely took a step back.

"You prefer blondes, and who told you about Abby?"

"Listen, buddy, if you don't want her–"

"That's it." Kip's anger boiled over.

Coby stepped in and grabbed Kip's arm as it started its journey towards Kenny's face. "Ho, ho, easy now boys. Now let's calm down here. Obviously, this Abby is a sensitive subject for the Kipper here, so I'm assumin' it must be pretty serious stuff. Now we won't be teasin' him about his new woman any more."

Kip's face hardened as he looked at them, his jaw muscle twitching. He spoke through clenched teeth, "She is *not* my woman."

"Okay, then why ya gittin' so uptight? If you don't want her, I'm just sayin' I might like to meet her. Maybe she could come down and visit sometime. She's a real fine lookin' woman. Smart, too."

Kip looked more incredulous by the moment. "Listen, if I have anythin' to say about it, she'll never meet you."

"So, what's the story then? If she's not your woman, what is she?"

"We are friends. Just friends."

"Yeah, well, you and me are friends, too, but I never seen ya throw a *woman's* CD into the lake just cause I thought she was sexy. It's pretty clear to me, buddy. You're in love."

"I am not." He didn't need this kind of rumor spreading.

"Then why are ya so jealous?"

"I'm *not* jealous. Why do people keep sayin' that?" He threw his hands in the air and shook his head.

"Looks like jealous to me, buddy," Coby tossed in.

"Forget it. I'm just not even goin' there with you guys. You're both full of it. Just...shove it up yer giggy with a hayrake."

Coby folded one arm across his chest and used the opposite hand to stroke his beard and cover his laughter. "Kip, are you sure you don't want a beer? I can just mosey on over there and get ya one."

"No, thanks."

"Oh, right, I forgot, *we're* not drinking right now. Is that because *we're* havin' a little buckaroo soon?"

"Now don't you start with me, too. Heck, I even offered to introduce her to you and Liza. She likes your stuff," he told Coby, who looked pleased with himself. Kip turned his irritated attention back to Kenny. "And now that I think about it, how in the heck did you know I threw your CD into the lake? You got a spy camera watchin' me or somethin'? Nobody else was there."

"I'm omniscient. Didn't ya know?"

Exasperated, Kip had enough. "Right. Oh, look. There's Jeff over there. If you fools will excuse me?" He stormed off in Jeff's direction, leaving the other two erupting into gales of laughter.

"*Woooo-hoooo.* I've never seen him so bad...or so mad," Coby laughed.

Kenny imitated Kip, "'No, I'm not jealous. I'm not in love. She's not my woman'. That guy's a sunk ship, and he don't even know it. Julie goes, 'He's totally gone over this woman', she goes, 'all's he talks about is this Abby, Abby, Abby', but man I couldn't believe it 'til I saw it for myself."

"Did you see his face when you started given out the stats on her? Man, he looked like he was kicked in the gut by a stallion." Coby laughed so hard he was wiping away tears. "Wanna place odds on how long before she gets him to the altar?"

"By the end of this year, for certain," Kenny bet.

"I'm bettin' he won't make it past September. That gives him three months to wake up and take the dive."

"You're on." The friends shook hands and broke into laughter again. "We just gotta git the idea planted in his head. This could turn out to be an interestin' evenin' after all."

"So, you saw her picture?"

"Yeah, he sent her cousin down here a coupla weeks ago. Julie's been totin' him everywhere. Me 'n McGarrett went an' heard his new band. They played the Wildhorse last week. Hey, I seen 'im here tonight. Let's go look for him. He's got a coupla pictures in his wallet. She's a beauty."

"What's Tom and Hope say about this?"

"They're havin' a real good chuckle, 'specially after these past six months constantly tellin' the press he ain't never gettin' hitched again. Tom came up with some great ideas of ways we can torture the Kipper all week long. You know what? Tom'll want in on this bet. Let's put some money on it. A hundred bucks."

"You got it. This is worth it. What was that about a CD gettin' thrown in the lake?"

"You're gonna love this one. Let's look for Trent and Julie. I'll tell ya on the way."

After ten minutes of hunting through the ever-burgeoning crowd, Kenny spotted Trent. He dragged him to the wall beside the French doors, which opened into the library.

"Hey, Trent. How's it goin?"

"I'm enjoying myself. Thanks for dropping in at the Wildhorse with Mr. McGarrett last week. I appreciated you coming by."

"Well, I gotta say, you were soundin' pretty good up there. Got a good stage presence, too. Man, you had everybody up and dancin' and havin' a good time. That's what it's all about. Listen, here's what I want to talk to you about. You got those pictures of Abby with ya?"

"Sure. I keep them right here in my wallet."

"Good. Give 'em to me."

"Why? What's up?"

"Coby and I were just talkin' with Kip, and he is a real piece of work. I never saw a guy so out of sorts over a woman. He's gonna be part o' the family before you know it. We just thought we'd give him a little push in that direction."

"Man, you oughta see them together. He's always rubbing her back and waiting on her hand and foot. She's got him under her thumb, and he doesn't even know what hit him."

"Yeah, well just the fact that he's here tonight and not the least bit worked up about the Ice Queen says a whole lot. You see Coby anyplace?"

"Saw him just a minute ago with Mr. McGarrett over by the pool."

"Okay, you go get 'em and tell 'em to bring you inside to the office. I got a plan."

"Whatever you say, Mr. Hampton."

Kenny reached out and smacked him in the back of the head. "Would ya drop the mister thing? Yer makin' me feel like I'm seven'y years old. Git goin'."

Kenny let himself in the French door and headed for the office. He knew Kip would be furious, but it was for his own good. Sometimes friends had to take things into hand and help a guy along, whether he liked it or not. Kenny's laughter echoed through the hall of the east wing.

●

Early Monday morning, Kip arrived at his office building where he'd converted two large offices into a soundproof practice room for the band. He was one artist who insisted his road band also be his studio band, guaranteeing the recordings captured the excitement of what they did on tour. Jeff and the boys were already there.

He was impressed with the arrangements they created for their individual instruments. It came together quickly, and the boys felt ready to hit the studio to lay down tracks.

Finishing at about seven o'clock, they went their separate ways, agreeing to meet the next morning for a sound check an hour before the doors at the luncheon opened.

Before leaving, Kip stopped at Cree's office. "Hey, Cree. How ya been doin'?"

"Can't complain." Cree dropped his pen and sat back in his chair. "You're lookin' good. Gettin' a lot of sun, huh?"

"Yeah, I spend a lot of time outdoors these days. Gettin' a lot of writin' done. So, wanna hang out for an hour or two?"

"Sure. Let me finish this up, and I'll be ready in five minutes."

"No problem." He dropped in a comfortable chair near the window and looked out over the city.

Cree went back to work and soon dropped files into a cabinet, punching the lock shut. He stretched and picked up his car keys. "Where do ya wanna go?"

"Trent's playin' up at Denim and Diamonds. He'll come on about nine."

"I've heard the kid. I think you made a solid investment. He'll be lucrative by this time next year. He's only been here a few weeks, and I hear clubs are already callin' askin' for him. That don't happen everyday in this town."

They found the club already crowded, signifying the arrival of the crowds for Fan Fair. Cree tossed back a few whiskey sours, while Chris stuck with ginger ale. When Trent came on they stayed for the first set before calling it a night and heading home.

When Kip got home he took off his boots at the door in true Canadian fashion. He picked up the phone and dialed as he stretched out on his new couch. He heard it ring, making him tingle with the anticipation of hearing her voice.

"Hello?"

"Howdy, Abby girl. How ya doin?"

"Chris." She felt a bud of pleasure blossom inside. "It's good to hear your voice. You got there all right?"

"Yeah, easy flight. Julie picked me up at the airport. Spent yesterday and today at the office. Got as much done as I could in two days so I can get back to you. What have you been doin'?"

"Not much of anything. Baked some cookies for when Claire comes. That's about it really. Been reading." She wandered into the living room and sat on the sofa resting her feet on the coffee table.

"That's good. Get lots of rest. Not much longer, and you won't be gettin' any sleep."

"Anything interesting going on in Music City since your arrival?"

"This ought to surprise you. Guess where I went last night?"

"The Opry."

"Nope. I went to a barbecue. Guess whose house?"

"Kenny Hampton?" she asked hopefully.

"No, but he was there. It was at Tansey's place."

"Are you kidding me?" Her mouth dropped open.

"Seriously. I just walked in, handed her a check for the charity, and had a good time. It didn't bug me a bit, her bein' there. In fact, I completely forgot about her. I did it, Abby. I'm over it. There was no hurt, no hankerin', nothin'. I couldn't even remember what it felt like to have loved her. This was a real milestone for me, Abs. I mean, it's one thing to think you're over somebody, then you run into them and it smacks you right between the eyes. But it didn't."

"Oh, Chris. That's great. Wish I could've been there to see it."

"And you know what? It really bugged her. That was the best part."

She laughed. "Nice to be in the driver's seat for a change, huh?"

"Boy, you bet. Hey, how come Hampton knows about you?"

"Excuse me?"

"Yeah, he started talkin' about you like y'all were best friends or somethin'. Even knows what you look like. What's that about? You been carryin' on behind my back or somethin'?" he taunted.

"Really? He knows about me? It would have to be Trent, but where would

Trent ever meet Kenny Hampton? So, tell me what he said," she prodded. She certainly wasn't going to tell him about the package Julie sent.

"He thinks you're pretty."

"Really? He thinks I'm pretty?" The excitement was evident in her voice.

"Abby, you're enjoyin' this a little too much." His arm dropped over his head.

"Sorry. I forgot for a minute. You're not jealous."

"No, I'm not," Chris declared.

"Well, that's good then. Maybe we'll invite you to the wedding."

"Ya know, Abs, I'm gettin' real sorry I called you."

"It's okay. I'm not jealous that you left me and ran straight back to Tansey, either."

"Darlin', you got nothin' to worry about there. She's got nothin' on you."

"Okay, I'll quit."

"Thank you. Listen, startin' tomorrow I'll be runnin' nonstop, so I don't know when I'll call again. I'll try, but I can't promise. It's hectic, but it's only once a year. This is one huge convention, ya know. About a hundred and thirty thousand last year."

"You're kidding me. If I'd known I wouldn't have let you go. You might get lost in all that and find yourself in California or something."

"No chance o' that, darlin'. Nothin's gonna stop me from bein' back with you next week."

"I miss you, Christopher," she whispered.

He heard it in her voice. The ache was there for her, too. "I know, Abby girl. I wish I could have brought you along. I promise I'll be back soon. Claire's comin' tomorrow afternoon, right? That'll keep you busy, and before you know it, I'll be right there singin' with ya again. You'd better go on up to the house and borrow some of my CD's, cause I think you've just about exhausted the Denver and Rogers repertoire. Then what are you gonna do?"

She gave a small laugh. "Okay, I will."

"I'm gonna go for now." He paused a moment, his voice dropping to a quiet, serious tone. "And hey, Abby? Me too. A lot." He clicked the phone off and lay thinking. It would be a long week. This was the world he belonged in, but it seemed empty without that little brunette around, teasing and laughing and singing. What would life be when summer came to an end?

Early the next morning he wanted to call Abby to check on her, but the limousine arrived when he started dialing, so he disconnected. When the limo pulled up to the banquet hall, hundreds were already lined up. The band's bus was already there, and it was time to start the day.

Kip entertained the fan club members for an hour, then allowed them an hour for questions and answers. Finally, he stood and had his picture taken with all 1,272 attendees and gave each an autograph. His face hurt from smiling for the camera. His fingers cramped until the last hundred or so fans got chicken scratches.

•

Tuesday afternoon, Abby headed down to the boat to pick Claire up at the marina. They were supposed to meet at three o'clock. It was already two forty-five. She was eager to see her sister.

Chris had only been gone two days, but they seemed long, lonely days knowing she was on the island alone. Finally, she would have company and a distraction to help her pass the time until he came back.

With a bounce in her step, she wound her way along the trail to the water's edge. A loud honking drew her gaze upward to a flock of Canadian geese flying overhead in their V-formation. At the top of the steps that led down to the dock, she tripped. Catapulting through the air, her head cracked on the pilings, and she landed hard on her stomach. She lay unconscious on the dock as the blood flowed, slowly dripping into the water below.

CHAPTER 12

At two o'clock Chris sensed something was terribly wrong. At five o'clock he saw his publicist, Donna, answering his cell phone. She usually kept it for him while he performed or did meet and greets. He watched her speak for only a moment before putting it back in her purse. He wanted to ask who called, but if he stopped now, he would be here all night. The camera flashed again. Another autograph, another few words, another camera flash, and soon he forgot about the phone call.

Maisie was almost at the front of the line. Her mind drifted to the little island in Canada. She laid the trip line late yesterday afternoon just before leaving for Nashville. Abby was certain to hit her head on the pilings when she fell. It was unavoidable the way the dock was constructed. Then, she could either fall in the lake and drown, or maybe have brain damage, or bleed to death. If she wasn't already dead, she would be soon. She hoped Abby's corpse would be half eaten by birds and wild animals by the time Kip returned to the island. Sunday afternoon she would return and remove the evidence of her tampering before his arrival.

The fan club luncheon was exciting. She hated stealing his music, but a girl needed to make a living in order to dog her idol's footsteps. It was maddening to be so close and so far at the same time. Watching him laugh and sing with the witch had been painful.

CHRISTOPHER

•

Claire waited for Abby at the marina. "Glen, do you mind if I call the cabin? She should have been here more than ten minutes ago. I know it doesn't sound like much, but she's such a punctual person. I just want to be sure nothing's wrong."

"Phone's right over there on the counter. Help yourself. She's gonna have that baby pretty soon, eh?"

"Yes, only a few weeks to go." She dialed the cabin and got no answer. "Well, I suppose she must be on her way. She's not at the cabin." Hanging up the phone, she stood scrutinizing the lake out the window. Everything looked calm and peaceful, but her gut instinct whispered it was a facade.

"Listen, Glen, I hate to trouble you further, but if she isn't here in the next five minutes, do you think you could take me up there?"

"Sure. I'll just call Marge to mind the shop, and we'll go."

"I appreciate it. I just feel something's wrong."

When they came within view of the island's west end, they saw the boat still tied up. Claire felt panic rise in her throat.

As they closed the distance, they spotted Abby's inert form. Drawing alongside the dock, Claire noted the sharp contrast of Abby's pallid complexion against the bright red pool around her and felt sick. A large puddle circled her head, and evidence of pelvic hemorrhaging was unmistakable as the blood flowed freely, staining the wooden slabs on which she lay.

Glen radioed Marge, telling her to alert the hospital in Peterborough. Claire jumped out of the boat and cradled her sister's head in her lap.

"She's still alive, thank God. We've got to get her to the hospital."

Glen awkwardly lifted her, well-aware he wasn't a young man any more. "You'd better run up to the cabin and get her purse. They'll need her health card at the hospital."

Claire dashed up the staircase. Upon reaching the top, her foot caught on something, causing her to fall to the ground. Wincing as she got to her feet, she glanced back to see what had tripped her.

Startled by her discovery, she shouted down to the dock, "Glen, look at this. It must be why she fell. Why would someone tie fishing line across the dock steps like this? It doesn't make sense."

Glen scuttled up the steps and took a quick look. "Maybe when she comes around she can tell us why it's there. Hurry on now. We've gotta get rolling, eh."

Taking the porch steps in one bound, she was inside and found Abby's purse on the kitchen counter. On her way out she noticed a piece of paper stuck on the fridge with a magnet. A quick glance told her whose phone number it was, and she snatched it.

Glen had Abby in the boat with the engine revved up. Claire leaped aboard, and they raced back to the marina at full throttle.

Marge met them with the van pulled up to the dock, the back door open and a mattress of blankets spread on the floor. Beside it sat a pile of towels and face cloths, as well as a case of bottled water.

Glen lay Abby on the makeshift bed. The women climbed in with her while he ran around to the driver's seat. He barely had the door shut before the van pulled out on the highway.

Claire's fear left her muddled. Marge took charge, instructing her to tend to the head, cleaning away the excessive blood so they could get an idea of the location and extent of the injury, and apply direct pressure to the wound.

Marge removed the blood-soaked clothing and attempted to staunch the flow. She knew Abby wouldn't survive if she continued losing blood at this rate. She grabbed another two blankets and covered her, trying to preserve her body heat so she wouldn't go into further shock.

Attendants rushed out with the gurney when at last they arrived at Civics Hospital in Peterborough forty minutes later. Claire stood at the back of the van, trembling.

Seeing her waver, Marge clutched her. "It's all right, dear. They'll look after her, now."

"Okay. I'll be fine. I'll be fine." She ran her trembling hands over her face, trying to wipe away the tears, wanting to erase the lost and helpless feeling with them. Blood from her hands smeared across her cheeks.

Marge led her inside to a public washroom where they used soap and water to wash before joining Glen in the waiting room.

A doctor came out of an examination room, and observing the fresh blood covering his scrubs, Claire knew he'd been with Abby. With fear in her heart, she went to speak with him.

"She's lost a lot of blood, and that's not good. Her biggest problem right now is that her fall caused placenta abruptio. That means the placenta is torn away from the uterus. That's what's causing all the blood loss. She's gone into labor, and we're going to try to get her through that as quickly as we can. I believe there's no harm at this point in a vaginal delivery, so that's what we'll try." He paused, scanning over his notes on the chart.

"If conditions change, we'll do a C-section. We're giving her a drug to hasten the labor. I don't feel good about giving her an epidural—too many unknown factors. Now, about her head injury, we'll do a brain scan and an MRI to determine if any damage has been done. Right now, the important thing is to get that baby out, or we'll lose them both." He placed a hand on Claire's arm to steady her. "I'm sorry, the baby didn't survive. There was nothing we could do. Our job now is to save your sister. Any questions?"

"Is she in a coma?"

"Not at this point. The sooner she delivers, the sooner we can get more testing done. It may be a concussion, or it could be a more serious head trauma. We'll just have to wait and see."

"Can I see her?"

"Not yet. We're still trying to stabilize her. After the delivery we'll let you in for a few minutes before we take her upstairs."

"Thank you."

She went to rejoin the others, her legs ready to crumble as the shock washed through her. "We lost the baby. How am I ever going to tell her?" Her throat choked, and a sob engulfed her.

Marge embraced her tightly. "There, there. We did the best we could. Things will all work out in time. I know it doesn't seem like it now, but we have to trust that the Lord in his wisdom has a purpose in this."

"What purpose can there be in making her suffer more? She's already been through so much this year. I don't know how she'll get through this. It's just too much," she sobbed while Marge rocked her.

A nurse arrived and sat next to her. "I'm sorry to have to bother you at a time like this, but we need to know where to send the body."

Alarm gripped her heart. "Body?"

"Yes, the baby. We have to know which funeral home you want contacted to pick it up."

"Oh. Yes, I see." She pressed her fingertips to her temples trying to assemble a coherent thought out of the swirling jumble in her mind. "That would be the Burley Home in Picton." It was such a short time ago that they'd been there for Drew.

The nurse wrote down the name and gave Claire's hand a squeeze before leaving them.

Another nurse arrived a few minutes later. "Claire. She's awake and asking for you. She's still in labor, and she'll need your emotional support through this. She hasn't been told the baby is deceased."

"Has she had anything for pain?"

"Yes, it can't hurt the baby now. We aren't going to give her the epidural, although it's standard practice for a stillbirth. Her condition just doesn't merit it."

Claire used a tissue to dry her face and blow her nose. "Okay, I'm ready. Let's go in."

When she saw her little sister hooked up to tubes and monitors, she felt helpless, but she couldn't break down now. She had to be Abby's strength.

She brushed Abby's hair away from her face, trying not to touch the wounded area. "How are you feeling, sweetie?"

"I've got a headache, but they gave me something for the pain. What happened?" The next labor pain started, and Abby gasped at the suddenness of it.

"Breathe, Abby. Breathe through it. Remember what we learned? Long, deep breaths."

She tried to follow the instructions, and soon the pain subsided.

"The baby can't come yet. It isn't time." Her panicked expression tore at Claire.

"Abby, something happened back at the dock. You fell. Do you remember that?"

She searched her memory. "Vaguely. I think I tripped, and that's the last thing I remember."

Another pain swept through her, and once more they breathed together with Claire massaging the abdomen until it was over.

"Oh, my head hurts so badly."

"You banged it pretty hard. I found you lying on the dock. The Miners helped bring you here."

Abby's own obstetrician came into the room as another pain hit hard. She couldn't manage the deep breathing any more. Dr. Chambers gave her a sympathetic smile, waiting until the contraction was over before she spoke. "How are you feeling?"

"I'm not supposed to have the baby for another month."

"I know, but we can't stop it now. Let me check to see how far along you are." She examined her patient, and Abby cried out with discomfort.

"That really hurts."

"I'm sorry. You're four centimeters. Almost halfway. A few more hours, and it'll be over. I'll be back in a while to check on you."

"Thank you, Dr. Chambers." The doctor left, concern marring her features.

Claire stroked her sister's cheek lovingly. "Honey, the reason you're in labor is because when you fell you hurt yourself. When I found you, you were hemorrhaging." She felt herself choking on the words, and paused, trying to swallow the lump in her throat. With a catch in her voice, she carried on. "You see, it was the fall, Abby. We got you here as quickly as possible. We did our best." Her eyes watered.

The next pain came stronger, causing Abby to arch her back off the bed.

"I think we'll try rolling you onto your side when this one's over."

"Aaaagh! Chris, where are you when I need you?" she cried out.

Claire stood stunned. She wouldn't have been surprised to hear Abby call for Drew. But Chris? She thought they were just casual acquaintances. Trent had explained who he really was.

The contraction subsided, and she helped roll her sister onto her side. "Here, now you can grip the bars if that makes you feel better. Aren't the drugs helping at all?"

"They're making me woozy, but believe me, I'm still feeling it."

"Honey, there's something you need to know." She sat on the edge of the bed so she could rub Abby's back and be in a position of comfort. "It's about the baby."

"What?" Abby looked stricken, as the horror of possibilities flew through her mind. "The baby's all right. It is, isn't it?"

"I'm sorry, Abby. No. It couldn't get oxygen when the placenta tore away. It stopped the blood circulation from getting to it. I'm so sorry, darling." Tears spilled down her cheeks as she held her sister.

"No, Claire, no," she begged. "Please say it's all right. Don't let God take my baby, too. I need this baby."

Another pain came ripping through and consumed her. "No! Oh, Christopher, please help me. I need him here. Please, Claire. Get Chris for me. I can't get through this without him." A sob broke, and she wept inconsolably. Her hand reached to her throat and clasped her necklace.

"I'll call him now." Claire gave her an extra hug and left the room.

The nurse saw her coming. "She knows?" Sounds of grief were clearly audible.

"Yes. I need to make a call for her. Can she have a sedative or something?"

"I think so. We're not worried about the baby, so I'm pretty sure it's all right. I'll check and see. Maybe I can give her some more Demerol. That should help."

"Thanks." Claire found her way back to the waiting room where Marge rose to meet her. "I just told her. She's devastated of course. There's no easy way to tell a person a thing like this. Losing her husband, and now the baby, all in such a short period of time. I'm afraid she'll give up, feeling she has no reason to go on."

"I'm so sorry, dear. This is a terrible thing, and it never should have happened, especially to someone as wonderful as your sister. Listen, we're going to go out and get you something to eat. You have to keep up your strength. Abby needs you." Marge hugged her, and they left.

Claire searched her purse for the paper she'd taken from the fridge. She tried to compose herself to make the call. To her surprise, a woman answered.

"Is Chris there please?"

"I'm sorry. He's not accessible at the moment."

"Do you know how long he'll be?"

"At least a good few hours."

"Oh, no." Distressed, Claire pressed her fingers to her temples. "Well, please tell him Claire called, and it's important I speak with him as soon as possible. We have an emergency situation here, and he's needed. Ask him to please call the marina. Please, it's very urgent," she begged.

"Okay, I'll give him the message."

"Thanks." Claire hung up. When Marge returned with barbecued chicken, she asked them to go home and wait for Chris' call. Hopefully he could catch a plane tonight.

Setting the food aside, she returned to Abby's room to find her in a semi-conscious state, crying out with two different kinds of pain. The most Claire could do was be there, keep cold cloths on her brow, and hold her hand. This she did, as Abby continued crying out for Chris over the next four hours, never once stopping the tears that streamed down her own face.

She called twice to see if Glen heard from Chris. He hadn't. She considered calling Nashville again but heard Abby crying from the other room, so she returned to her vigil.

Two hours later, it was over. The nurse placed the swaddled bundle in Abby's arms, then left the sisters alone together. She looked down at the tiny face of her five-pound daughter, wearing a small pink hat over her dark curly hair and a little pink sweater over a nightie. Her tiny feet were snuggled in little pink booties.

Silently, Abby counted every finger and every toe. There were ten of each. Every miniature feature of her face was perfect. She looked like Drew. There was no doubt she was his daughter.

"She's beautiful, Abby."

"Yes, she is. Perfect in every way. Too perfect for this world."

Claire couldn't understand Abby's sudden change of emotion. She appeared completely calm and serene. No tears, no grief.

Abby held her baby for half an hour. The nurse came and asked if she would like a picture taken. She nodded yes. The nurse brought the camera and Claire asked to take the pictures. She took a few shots of Abby holding her baby, then a few good, clear close-ups of the petite face with a tiny hand poking up out of the blanket, the delicate fingers curled into a fist.

When Claire was through, Abby rocked the baby, sang her a lullaby, and kissed her diminutive mouth. She told the nurse, "She's asleep now." She held her bundle out, and the nurse took it away.

They were the last words she spoke. When the baby was gone from her arms, she turned inside herself. She had to find a safe place to be alone. Darkness surrounded her, and her spirit curled up in a corner. She was in a haven now. Safe from the world, safe from the hurt. Alone with the knowledge that she killed her baby.

CHAPTER 13

When the limousine pulled up to the Gaylord Auditorium at six forty-five Wednesday morning, fans were already there, including Maisie and Daisy, waiting to see the celebrities.

Kip spent a few minutes talking and signing autographs while cameras flashed. It was rough having people expect you to look good so early in the morning.

Once inside, he made the rounds through interviews. He was nominated for five Flameworthy Awards that night. The fans were responsible for choosing both the nominees and the winners by voting online. He was nominated for Best Male Video, Hottest Male Performance, Best Video of the Year, Concept Video, and Fashion Plate Video.

Bands worked in rotation to set up their equipment and rehearse for the evening's performance. Others came and left, rehearsing for presentations. He fell into both categories and ended up spending most of the day there.

Tonight would be his first time attending an awards show on his own. Jeff and Julie had tickets to sit with him. Jeff would sit strategically in the middle to keep people from thinking Julie was his "new woman."

At seven o'clock it was time to walk the red carpet. He stopped a few times along the way to give an autograph. Camera's flashed from every direction as he approached the gauntlet. Reporters from various television stations were set up, and he was expected to stop and share a few words with each one.

The first microphone he came to was from Country Music Television. "We have Kip Adams here with us. Kip, you're up for five awards tonight. How are you feeling?"

"Well, it'd be nice to take at least one of them home, but I'm not gonna worry about it. Me and the band are gonna play and have fun, and hopefully the crowd'll have a good time, too."

"We've been hearing you're engaged to be married. A lovely young woman from Canada named Abby. Can you tell us a bit about that?"

He was startled, and his expression showed it briefly before he let the public mask fall back into place. It was one thing to be teased by friends, but how did the press get wind of it? He determined to kill Hampton. It had to be him behind it. Best to set it straight, and put the issue to bed. Okay, not to bed. Just be done with it. That's what he meant.

With a good-natured chuckle, he assured her, "Abby and I are friends. Nothin' more. I have stated before and will say it again for the record. I am never gettin' married again. The way I see it, marriage is an expensive way to get your laundry done for free."

"Okay, well you heard it yourselves, ladies. He's staying single. Thanks, Kip, and good luck tonight."

The camera stopped rolling, and he became serious. "Katie, who told you I was engaged?" He wanted it confirmed before he drop-kicked Kenny through the goal posts.

"Alan Jackson told me on his way in earlier."

"Alan?" Not at all what he expected.

"Yeah."

"Okay, thanks."

Where would Alan hear that? He puzzled over it as he moved farther down the carpet. The next interview was with Entertainment Tonight. "Hi, Jan. How are you tonight? You're lookin' lovely."

"Thanks, Kip. Talk to us about your nominations. You have more than any other artist here tonight."

"Well, I didn't have anythin' to do with that. The fans are the ones who did the nominatin' and the votin'. It's pretty darn flatterin', though."

"Listen, word has reached us that you're newly engaged to a woman you met while vacationing in Canada. I notice she's not here with you tonight. Have you got a date set yet?"

"Well, Jan, those rumors have reached me too, but I can tell you that's all they are. Just rumors. The lady in question is nothin' more than a friend. I see it like this: A fella has two choices in life. He can stay single and be miserable, or get married and wish he was dead. I prefer simple misery."

"Okay. He's staying a bachelor. Thanks, Kip. Good luck tonight."

"Thanks, Jan." The camera switched off, and he asked who her source was.

"Travis Tritt told me earlier today. Maybe he just misunderstood."

He moved on, encountering four more similar interviews. Who had given out the news of his impending nuptials? Richie McDonald, Chris Cagle, Shania Twain, and Brad Paisley. The list grew as the evening wore on. Not a single person said Kenny Hampton or Coby Kansas. Everyone gave him silly smiles and hugs, congratulating him and saying they couldn't wait to meet Abby.

Abby. He only had to blink and those chestnut curls filled his mind. Stepping into the men's room in search of a modicum of privacy, he took out his cell phone and dialed the cabin, but there was no answer. Disappointed, he joined Jeff and Julie, and they found their seats.

The evening got under way, and he was on early as a presenter. He arrived back at his seat in time to hear them announce a category he was nominated in. Sara Evans read the names of the nominees before opening the placard. "And the winner is…" Sara broke into a huge smile "the soon to be married, Kip Adams." The crowd divided in its response. Many cheered, happy he'd won. Others gasped in surprise at the news of his engagement.

When he took the stage he hugged Sara. Standing at the podium, he clutched his trophy and said, "You know, last night I overheard my ex-wife tellin' her friend it was thanks to her I was a millionaire. Her friend asked, 'What was he before you married him?' and I just had to cut in and tell her, 'A billionaire.'" The audience laughed and applauded. His divorce settlement of seventeen million had been highly publicized. "Sara here was just teasin' about me gettin' married. That's a walk I'm not ever takin' again. I never knew what real happiness was until I got married, by then it was too late." He thanked the fans who had given him such a great career. He thanked his band. He thanked Julie for his survival.

Later in the program, Kip's band performed, and the crowd was on its feet, dancing and singing along. The applause nearly brought the roof down. By the end of the evening he had three awards in his hands and faced a multitude of interviews, all confronting him about his engagement.

Thursday morning, the headline immediately caught his eye.

BIG WINNER AT
FLAMEWORTHY'S ENGAGED!!

He tossed it straight into the garbage, but curiosity won. Pulling it back out, he saw a photo of himself at the podium accepting one of his awards and beside it a portrait picture of Abby. Even though he denied it repeatedly, the news was confirmed by several members of the country music world, many of them his close friends.

He drove to the Convention Center to spend the morning at the Meet and Greet booth for the recording studio. He stayed only two hours, but in that time he endured countless comments about his fiancée.

In the afternoon, he played in the charity baseball game at Greer Stadium. The event sponsored a local hospital, and the stars loved the chance to have some fun instead of work. The celebrities joked and played tricks on each other to make it fun for the fans too.

He stepped up to the plate, bat in hand. As the ball was pitched, catcher, Shelby Clarkson said, "Abby sure is pretty. You're a lucky guy."

He swung and missed. Rolling his eyes, he leaned on the bat with his other hand on his hip.

"It's not true."

"Yeah, I heard you'd say that. I'd like to add that I approve of you choosing a fellow Canadian."

He recognized the futility of denying it and stared at the ground, shaking his head. "Okay, so it is true. She's the love of my life." He started wildly gesticulating, and Shelby had to duck more than once not to be hit by the bat. "I bought her a ten-carat diamond ring, because she just wouldn't accept anythin' smaller. We're gettin' married in October when all the maples are turnin' glorious colors, and then to top it off, we plan on havin' twelve kids. Does that make you happy?"

Shelby cupped her hands around her mouth and hollered to the pitcher, "He admits it. Wedding's in October."

The entire ball field and those in the dugout clapped and cheered. He frowned and shook his head. It was hopeless.

On the next pitch he belted the ball into the stands. He took the bases at a nice jog and was welcomed at home plate by the other two runners who had been on base.

Back in the dugout he felt a hand rest on his shoulder. "Good to hear you're getting married, Kip. When's your baby due?"

He turned to see Shauna Wright standing next to him. "It's not my baby, Shauna. It's her husband's. He passed away a few months ago."

Shauna sobered at the news. "Well, then she's lucky to have found you. You're gonna be a super daddy. Good luck to ya. You know we all wish you the best." She gave him a quick embrace.

"Uh-huh."

Thursday night a large crowd gathered for the RCA label concert at the Adelphia Coliseum. The stage was divided in half and set up so acts alternated between the left and right sides of the stage. Each performer or band played for half an hour. He was scheduled second from last. Navigating the corridor, he tried to find an empty room to be by himself for a few minutes. The Abby thing was starting to wear on him. He enjoyed ten minutes of solitude before Jeff discovered him.

"Oh, good, found ya."

"Yeah, I'm found all right," he sighed.

"Hey, I heard you're admittin' to bein' engaged. Is this a new development I should know about?" He came in and dropped on the bench perpendicular to his best friend.

"No. I've just learned it's easier to let a cat out of the bag than it is to put it back in."

"Okay, so we're back to Chinese proverbs again. Now what's it supposed to mean?"

"We haven't had much time since I got back, have we?"

"Not really. Somethin' on your mind?" Jeff leaned forward, resting his elbows on his knees and clasped his hands loosely.

"Abby. Jefferson, I have no plans to marry her or anybody else, but no one wants to believe me. No matter how often I deny it, people carry on like I haven't even spoken."

"How do you feel about her?"

He sat up straighter, stretched his shoulders, and leaned his head back against the wall. "I don't know. She's a good friend. That's honestly all there is to it."

"Okay. Julie's a good friend. Is it the same thing?"

"Yup. Exactly the same." Drawing his brows together, he modified his claim. "Well, not really. I've never given Julie expensive jewelry before."

"There was that birthstone ring you gave her on her sixteenth birthday. She still wears it. What kind of rocks are we talkin' about here?"

He refused to meet Jeff's eye, almost embarrassed to admit what he'd done. "I bought her a sapphire and diamond necklace. I didn't want her to forget our summer together."

"Geez, Chris. Summer doesn't even start for another two weeks. That's kinda premature isn't it? What are you thinkin', boy? It's gonna be tough explainin' that one in the context of friendship." Jefferson shook his head in amazement. The only other jewelry he'd ever known Chris to buy was Tansey's wedding rings.

Chris winced as he glimpsed at his friend's astonished face. "Ya think?"

"Well, duh!" Jeff gaped at him as though he was the village idiot. He dropped his head into his hand, knowing he was in for it now. Jeff's eye caught the gold on his wrist. "That's a pretty nice bracelet you're wearin'."

He automatically reached for it and fingered the links. "Yeah, fourteen carat nice. She gave it to me the same night. We surprised each other for the same reason."

"Right, so you can both remember the summer that hasn't even started yet. Certainly makes sense to me. You like being with her. A lot. You talk about her endlessly."

"What else do I have to talk about? She's with me most of the time. If I'm talkin' about what I've been up to, she's obviously got to be part of the story." He tried to explain himself but knew he was sinking deeper.

"The thought's never crossed your mind to take it to the next level?"

"Well, it's certainly crossed my libido's mind. She's sexy as anythin', even pregnant. But it's not just her body. It's the way she smiles and teases, the way she walks, the way she cries. Geez, when she cries I just want to hold her in my arms and get rid of every bad thing that's ever happened to her, to be her protector. On the other hand," he paused, "she makes me laugh. I feel happy just havin' her around, and when we talk she really listens. She never makes fun of me like the Beauty Queen did. She takes things seriously and cares about what I'm sayin'."

He looked at Jeff and ran his hand through his dark hair. "Honestly? The fact is, I'm goin' crazy missin' her, and we haven't even been apart for a week. I can't even begin to imagine what it's gonna be like when we go back to our own lives full time."

"Is it strictly hands off?"

"Sometimes I hold her hand. I've held her in my arms and consoled her. Heck, I even spent the night at her place just holdin' her when she hit a rough patch. We're really comfortable that way, you know? Like it's not a big deal. We know there's a lot of carin' both ways. But nothin' intimate. Certainly nothin' sexual. It's more like helpin' each other through a difficult time. That's all it can ever be with Abby. She's not the kind you casually mess around with for awhile. She's the kind you take home to mother, because she's special that way."

"And you're never gonna get married again."

"Not a chance in Hades. I've learned my lesson on that score. I'm not gettin' burned again."

"Well, I'll leave that to Julie. What about Abby? Where is she in all of this?"

"Her husband was everythin' to her. Only guy she ever went out with, and that isn't cuz there were no other options. She's still in love with him. Always will be. So you see, there's really no point in pursuin' this idea, even if I wanted to. "

"Do you think she's missin' you?"

Chris shoved himself off the bench and paced a few steps with his hands on his hips. He stopped and stared at the toe of his cowboy boot. "I know it," he said quietly.

"As much as you're missin' her?"

"Uh-huh. She said it first. Sounded like she was gonna cry. I don't know Jeff, she's been through so much this last year. Somethin', I don't know, I just always want to protect her, and yet at the same time I've seen her do some real gutsy things. I admire her spirit. She's strong and weak, and feminine and fun, and, well, she's Abby."

"But you're not in love with her. You're just friends," Jeff affirmed.

"That's right."

"Then why are you in here broodin'?" Jeff sat back, and stretched his legs out, crossing his ankles. "Remember in high school when you flunked physics because Marissa Larke was in that class, and you couldn't concentrate on anythin' else? You're back in physics class, my friend. Think about it. The reason your friends are doin' this, and I promise you I'm not a part of it, is that they've seen a change in you this week. Heck, look at the way you paraded around at Tansey's. There wasn't an eye there that wasn't glued to you all night, and you were comfortable with the whole thing. The way you talk is different. Even the way you walk is different. You don't look so beaten any more. It's like you've matured and gained some kind of inner strength. They know you've been on that island with her, so what else are they supposed to think?"

Jeff stood and clapped a hand on his friend's shoulder. "It's obvious you're happy. Think about a serious relationship with her, and if it stays this good, why not make it forever? You're lucky to have found her. Don't let it go."

"I'll think about it."

"Promise?"

"It's not like I can think about anythin' else."

"That's the plan. So instead of plottin' murder against the majority of Nashville's moneymakers, maybe you should thank 'em for carin'." Jeff looked at his watch. "Let's go see the rest of the guys. We're on in fifteen minutes."

CHAPTER 14

Friday morning Chris was at his booth signing autographs at nine, sharp. The tee shirts sold as well as anticipated, as well as ball caps, CDs, key chains, mugs, and 8x10 glossies. He stayed talking with the fans until the early afternoon. Most had seen the newspapers and congratulated him, hoping he would find happiness this time. Many commented they thought Abby pretty and asked questions about her. He smiled, said thank you, and moved the line along.

Deciding to spend the afternoon at the office making a dent in the stack of paperwork waiting for him, he retrieved his cell phone from Donna and suddenly recalled seeing her answer it a few days before.

"Hey, Donna, I noticed you answerin' my cell at the luncheon. I don't remember gettin' the message though. Can you remember who it was?

"Sorry, I guess I forgot all about it. Let me think. I believe it was someone named Carly Messina. She wanted you to call her back, but she didn't leave a number."

He racked his brain but couldn't think of anyone by that name. Flicking the phone in his hand open, he checked the callers list to see if the number was still in the memory. Unfortunately his phone only stored the last 20 calls, and he'd had so many from Julie and his band members in the past few days there remained no record of the unknown caller. Letting the issue drop, he headed to the office and worked for the remainder of the day.

CHRISTOPHER

At seven-thirty he tried to call Abby. There was no answer at the cabin. He clicked off, disappointed. It wasn't as though he could easily forget her when everywhere he went he was faced with news of his upcoming marriage. He called again at eight. There was still no answer. She and Claire probably went to a show or shopping.

At ten-thirty he cleared his desk and went home, falling into bed. His body was tired, but his mind was back in Ontario. Let down that she wasn't there to talk to, he wished he could tell her about winning the awards the other night, and about his friends sabotaging him. She would laugh. He missed her laughter. Only four days to go. He would simply have to stay busy to keep his mind distracted until then.

Saturday morning dawned bright and early. Jeff picked him up at the penthouse, and they headed to the Nashville Municipal Auditorium. Today was the bronc ride he was hosting with twenty-four celebrities entered. This event would separate the real cowboys from the ones who wore the hats and never set foot on a ranch in their life. People started arriving at one o'clock, and by two the stands were full.

Each rider got three chances. The one who stayed on the horse with the most points for style would be the winner. Some of the celebrities owned horse farms and would provide stiff competition.

Kenny Hampton bravely approached Kip before his ride. "Any last minute advice, Adams?"

"Hah, Hampton in chaps. Better get some shots taken in this outfit. Drive your lady fans crazy. And yes, I do have some advice. First, never squat down with your spurs on, and second, never, and I mean never, kick a cow chip on a hot day."

"Well, thanks. I'm sure with advice like that I'll be takin' home the trophy. Hope ya already gots my name on it."

"Yeah, I gots it on there all right. Ordered it made up that way."

"That was some pretty smart thinkin' on your part."

"I always think smart. Oh, and I just thought of one more thing, Bubba."

"Whazzat?"

"When you're layin' out there in the arena like a bag o' broken bones, don't frown, cuz ya never know who's waitin' to fall in love with yer smile."

"Good to see you in such fine spirits today, Kipper."

"As always."

"Hey, I heard you say at the ball game that you're gettin' married after all."

"Why, yes, as a matter of fact I am. Do you by any chance have anythin' to do with my upcomin' nuptials, cuz if ya do, I'd like to thank ya."

Kenny grinned. "My lips are sealed. Good to hear you've had a change of heart about the whole thing."

"Well, one thing I've learned is when ya find yourself in a hole, quit diggin'.

"Man, you're just full of one liner wisdom these days. When did you become the philosopher?"

"I dunno. I just see things more clearly these days. Whoa! I just had a major moment of *deja vu.*"

"I hear them callin' my name. I gotta get out there."

"Thanks for bein' part of it, just in case I don't ever get to see ya alive again."

Kip left the stable and ran into Jeff. "Hey, Jeff, I just sent Kenny off to his death. Let's go watch."

The two men jogged to the edge of the corral and waited with anticipation.

The voice on the loudspeaker burst out overhead. "That was Joe Nichols. He's stayed on for the full eight seconds and qualifies for the next round. Next up, Kenny Hampton."

Kenny climbed into position in the chute, ready to lower himself onto the horse on signal. Kip grinned. The gate opened, and the horse took off, jumping and bucking and twisting. Kenny held on for dear life. "That's it for Kenny Hampton. He qualifies to continue."

Kip turned away, amazed and disappointed. As Jeff walked with him toward the chutes to prepare for his own ride, Kenny approached with a big smile.

"I couldn't believe my eyes, Hampton. How the heck did you manage to stay on?"

"Did ya think I was stupid enough to come without takin' a few lessons first? I spent a coupla weeks at Coby's ranch."

"Well, I gotta admit, I was impressed."

"Thanks. Maybe next year Abby and the baby'll be here watchin', huh?"

"Boy, ya never know, do ya?" Kip felt Jeff tugging at him, and they continued on their way.

At the end of the day, the trophy went to Kix Brooks. It had been an exciting day for the crowd and for the riders. The event was hailed a success, and Julie delivered a check from the proceeds to the Nashville food bank.

Sunday afternoon the fans headed home. Martina McBride's auction officially ended the week. The guitar Kip donated sold for $3,000. He bought an autographed pair of Hampton's jeans for Abby. Even though he hated the idea, he knew she would get a kick out of it. She wouldn't get a kick out of the price tag, though. In fact, if she knew how much he paid, she would probably give him a good kick. Julie did the bidding for him. He thought it too embarrassing to bid on another guy's jeans, imagining the fun the headlines would have with that one.

CHRISTOPHER

ADAMS WANTS TO GET
INTO HAMPTON'S PANTS

Stopping at his office, he grabbed another pile of paper work to take home. After braving the crowds for the past week, he was in the mood to be a hermit for a few hours. He found a newspaper waiting on his desk. The headlines screamed out:

ADAMS SAYS, NOT MY BABY,
BUT I'LL MARRY HER ANYWAY

Again, pictures of him and Abby ran with a story about Abby cheating on him and getting pregnant. Apparently he was so crazy about her that he took her back and insisted on marrying her to give the baby his name.

The newspaper went home with him, just because it had Abby's picture, and he wanted to look at her. He should take a camera when he went back to the island to take a lot of pictures of her. Relying on newspaper photos was for the birds. He wanted to see her in living color.

Picking up the phone, he called the cabin. Still no answer. Maybe she and Claire decided to take a few days and go somewhere. As long as Claire was with her, he wouldn't worry.

Two hours into his work, Julie arrived, using her key to the elevator panel that allowed her access to the penthouse.

"Kip, are you home?"

He pushed away from the desk and ambled out to the living room. "Yeah, I'm here." He passed through the kitchen for a drink and brought it with him to the sofa. "Hey, Jul, do ya mind? Take your shoes off when ya come in. You're gonna mess up my carpet."

She gawked at him like he'd just arrived from Saturn, but complied with his request. "I talked to Jeff earlier."

"That's good. Nice to hear you're keepin' up with your family."

"Shut up, you goof. Now listen. He says the only reason you have for not gettin' married is Tansey. Now, I'll admit, she was hell to be with from the word go. However, that was just a brief period of your life, although I know it seemed like forever. Now, I think you're overlookin' somethin' real important."

"And what would that be?"

"Your daddy and your mama."

"What about 'em?"

"They were married for almost thirty years when your daddy passed on, and in all that time I never saw a couple happier together, unless it was my own parents. They set you the perfect example of what marriage is supposed to be. You've overlooked the best example that was right in front of your eyes your whole life. Uncle Greer would turn over in his grave if he heard the way you've been talkin'.".

She took his soda can out of his hand, drank, and handed it back before continuing. "Abby is different. I didn't want to believe it at first, but I can see it. She fought to hang on to your friendship and keep you from walkin' out when you were bein' so bullheaded. Think how hard she'd fight to keep a marriage goin'. And remember, hers was a good experience. She knows what it's supposed to be like, that it takes two people to make it work. She knows how to be a partner, not a spoiled brat. In fact, I think she's about the most unspoiled person you've ever met."

"Yeah, she is different. But regardless, why are you all tryin' to get me married off? Abby and I are just friends."

"Don't ya see how much in love ya are? She's everythin' to you. Ya talk about her all the time. I know you're missin' her bad. There is a difference between the way ya feel about your friends and the way ya feel about her. She's the one. Tansey was just a mistake that happened on your way to findin' Abby. Don't let the witch stop ya from bein' happy the rest of your life. In fact, you could even thank her. After all, if it wasn't for Tansey, ya wouldn't have taken that trip to Ontario in the first place. Ya never would have met your Abby."

"My Abby?"

"Definitely your Abby. You've plunged off the cliff and right into the Wind River, my friend. I'm afraid there's no climbin' back up now. You've gotta accept the current and swim along with it."

"Hey, that was a good analogy."

"Glad you appreciated it."

Tired of being relentlessly confronted with the issue over the past week, he set the banter aside. "You've forgotten one crucial thing, Jul. A relationship involves two people, and Abby is so much in love with her husband, she'll need years to get over losin' him. She can't handle anythin' more than a friend, so please drop it, will ya?"

She turned sideways and sat on her foot to face him. "I think you're already more than that. She turns to you with her hurt because you're her safe place."

He sat quietly, trying to digest her words. "Those are exactly the words she used. Her safe place. She said I was her safe place. The day I arranged for Trent to come down here, she was so distraught she asked me to stay and hold her through the night."

"Well, that says somethin' about her progress. Women who've lost a husband sure don't want to be held by another man. Wanting you to hold her is an important step. But I think it goes both ways. She's your safe place, too."

"She's so darned easy to be with. I'm not afraid to talk to her. There's definitely a feelin' of security, like I can trust her with the things I tell her. We're comfortable together. That's what friendship is."

"No, it's because she's your soul-mate."

He twirled the idea around in his mind for a few minutes. "Julie, we're just good friends. Yeah, we get along great, but that's it. I don't know how many times I need to keep repeatin' myself before somebody listens to what I'm sayin'." He got up and stood at the window with his back to her.

"Give her some time. You've got your whole lives to be together. A few more months won't hurt. She's got some pretty strong feelin's by the look of that bracelet, especially for such a frugal gal. You're right. She probably isn't ready to move on yet. But when she is, you'll be ready."

"I'm not gonna be ready. I don't want this figment of your imagination"

"When are ya gonna tell her the truth about who you really are? She deserves it, ya know."

"I know. I'm just scared. It's the best thing I've felt in a long time, not havin' to wonder what she ultimately wants from me. I don't want to lose it yet. I think she holds a bit of contempt for celebrities. She certainly isn't impressed by it."

"Well, don't leave it too long, or it could all blow up in your face. I don't wanna see that happen, dear friend. So, can Trent come home now?"

"What are you talkin' about?"

"He's been stayin' at my place all week. Afraid ya'd murder 'im in his sleep."

"Because of leakin' the information about Abby and the pictures?"

"Yeah, but you should know, it wasn't his idea. They convinced him it would be the best thing to get you two together. He's all for that idea. He says ya both carry on like you're already married."

"So, he didn't want to give me up, but he did anyway. Good to know."

"You have some pretty persuasive friends, ya know. Don't lay all the blame at his door."

"Yeah, he can come home. I thought he was the quietest roommate I ever had. That explains it. Thanks, Julie."

●

Tansey stormed into the bedroom, slamming the door behind her. The sound penetrated his sleep, and he lifted his head a small fraction, dragging one eyelid open. Identifying the intruder, he put his head back down. "What time is it? It's still dark out."

"It's almost five-thirty."

"Right. I only have a few hours left, Tansey. What do you want?"

Tansey blustered around the room, unable to settle. "Have you seen the press the last few days? Every single headline is about him and his new bride-to-be. What's the story?"

He knew any further sleep wouldn't be forthcoming, so he rolled onto his back and sat up, stuffing the pillows up behind him. "That's why you're here this early? Because of him? That's not exactly flatterin' you know."

She stopped pacing and glared at him. "We can do that after. Right now, I want information. This is throwing a serious wrench in my plans."

"And what do you think I know?"

"Well, is it true? Is he getting remarried or not?"

"Talk is that it's true."

"Well, that's great. Just great. Now what?"

"What's the problem?"

"First of all, it means someone else is going to have an expense account that he's financing. He'll probably spend about ten million to build her a house. That tends to deplete what's available to me. Does he think he's just got money to throw around? This nonsense has got to stop! He's a spending fool!"

"Tansey, it's not exactly bleedin' him dry. There is plenty more where that comes from, and he's hot. He's got a lot of years of big money still to come. Beyond that, his investments will continue to pay large dividends, probably until he's in his grave. I really don't think we need to worry. There will always be an inordinate amount for you to keep yourself in luxury, my darlin'." He reached over and pulled back the covers beside him in invitation, patting the mattress to beckon her. She pouted and went to sit on the side of the bed. He pulled the sweater over her head, delighted she wore nothing under it. He lay her down and continued removing the rest of her clothing.

She carried on, as though oblivious to his actions. "And did you see the way he acted at the mansion? I mean, what was that about anyway? He walked around as though I wasn't even there! And those pictures in the paper. Did you see her? How could he possibly find her attractive? She's nothing next to me!"

"No one is, dear. Now then, enough about Kip. You're in my bed, not his. No more talkin'." He ended her tirade by covering her mouth with his own.

CHAPTER 15

Tuesday morning dawned bright. Claire took Abby from the hospital back to the island. She knew Abby wanted Chris, and he was due back that day. If he didn't show up by tomorrow, they would drive home to Picton. And even if he did come back, Abby needed full-time care. She hadn't spoken for a week.

Claire led her into the house and sat her on a chair. After laying clean sheets and pillows on the sofa, Claire dressed her in a nightgown and positioned her to look out the window, uncertain what Abby actually saw, if anything. She moved when led and acknowledged nothing. She'd been fed intravenously for the past week. The doctors hoped returning to a happy environment might help.

If only she would cry. She cried after Drew. At least that was something Claire could understand and deal with. The total absence scared her.

At five-thirty she finally heard the engine. She left Abby and headed to the house.

Chris finished tying up the boat, then collected his armload of boxes before stepping onto the dock. An auburn haired woman with Abby's face stood on the walkway waiting.

"You must be Claire." He gave her an award winning smile. "Gee, it's really good to meet ya. Abby's talked a lot about you."

"Likewise." Her jumbled emotions left her uncertain how to react. She grieved over Abby's situation and hated being the bearer of such sad news. On the other hand, she was angry he hadn't bothered to return her call.

"Come on up to the house. I'll put these things down first, then I'll greet ya properly. You should see what I got for the baby. I found these cool little cowboy boots and a baby Stetson. Oughta fit when they come to Wyoming next summer. Did she tell you they were comin' out? And I got her a video camera. She wanted to take movies of the baby growin' up," he enthused.

He unlocked the door and went in, unloading the things on the coffee table. "Hey, where is she?" Stopping abruptly, he studied her more closely. It was then he noticed how pale and drawn she appeared. "What is it Claire? Somethin's wrong, or Abby would be here."

"There's no easy way to say it." She fiddled with her hands and stared at the floor. "Abby lost the baby, Chris. And we almost lost Abby as well."

He felt a wall of bricks collapse upon him. His legs gave out under him, and he dropped on the sofa.

"This just can't be. Not Abby. Where is she? Is she all right? Oh, dear God. Not our baby. I have to go to her." He started to rise. "Abby..." A sob burned its way out of his throat, choking off his words as his concern for her escalated.

Stunned by his possessive referral to the baby, Claire reached for his arm and stopped him. "She's at the cabin, but she isn't all right. That's why I came to meet you here. It's important you understand the situation, and be prepared before you see her. Abby needs you now. She needs to be able to draw on your strength to get her through. If you go dashing in there and fall apart like this, it's only going to make it worse. It's essential you get yourself together first."

Reluctantly, he sat back down on the edge of the sofa. "Tell me what happened. Damn it, she can't deal with more. She's still fragile over losin' Drew." The agony ripped his heart open. His hand fell to his chest to cover the pain.

Claire sat on the arm of Abby's favorite chair and wiped at the tears threatening to mist her vision. "You're right, and that's the problem. After the baby came, she held her for a while, then said, 'She's sleeping now'. They took the baby away, and Abby hasn't spoken since. In fact, she hasn't responded to anything. It's sort of like a coma, but she's awake. The doctor said she's shut down emotionally. She's inside somewhere, but we can't find her. I'm not even sure if she knows I'm there. She just sits and stares into space. It's frightening to see."

"Poor Abby! It's too much. Too much loss, too much pain. No wonder she's tryin' to escape." He didn't even try to stop the tears. His heart was breaking.

125

"Something else I need to tell you. The police have been here investigating. It wasn't an accident. Someone intentionally tried to hurt her. We don't know who, or why, but someone set a tripwire at the top of the dock steps so she'd fall. She hit her head hard and was unconscious for more than two hours. We found her lying on the dock. There was so much blood." She cringed, choking as the memory flashed so clearly in her mind. Her last words came out a gentle whisper. "If I hadn't gotten here when I did, she would have bled to death."

Chris struggled to digest the information. None of it made sense. "Why would someone want to hurt Abby? She's so good."

"I wish we had an answer. We don't have much to go on."

"I need to see her. What can I do to help?"

"I honestly don't know. I thought maybe just you being there. When she was in labor she didn't call Drew's name once. Only yours, which quite frankly was a bit of a shock for me. She said she couldn't get through it without you. I don't know what the connection is between you two, but I'm hoping maybe you can reach her somehow. If not, I'll take her back to Picton with me. I'll have to hire a nurse to help look after her."

"I'd do anythin' in the world for that woman. I'll take care of her."

"I have to get back to her. Give yourself a few minutes to compose yourself. As I said, she's not even aware of what goes on around her right now. She doesn't recognize who is and isn't with her, so it's not like she's desperately awaiting your arrival. Take the time you need."

"Thanks, Claire. I promise, I won't be long."

Claire let herself out, and he was alone. He opened the box with the tiny tooled leather boots in it, taking them out and caressing them. All his visions of being with the baby through the years flashed through his mind. Tears streamed down his cheeks, and he mourned the loss of the child he never got to know. He cried for Abby and her pain

He needed to talk to someone, if only to hear himself saying the words. Maybe that would make it seem more real. What he wanted most was to wake up from this nightmare. He called Jeff but there was no answer. He called Julie and got her machine so he hung up. This wasn't the sort of news to leave on a machine. He thought about it and tried one more number.

"Hello?"

"Hope," he paused, trying to swallow the lump that had taken up residence in his throat. "It's Kip."

Hope Hilton could hear the anguish in his voice. "Kip, what's wrong?" She motioned anxiously for her husband, Tom McGarrett, and their friend and neighbor, Kenny Hampton, who were sitting at the kitchen table to pick up extensions. "Just a minute, Kip. Kenny and Tom are coming on the line."

Kip heard his friends pick up, and he fought for control. "Abby…"

"What's happened with Abby?"

"The…" He had trouble formulating the words between sobs, "it's the baby."

Hope asked, "Oh, no, what's wrong with the baby?"

"We lost the baby. I just heard its little heart beatin' two weeks ago. It was so healthy and strong. Abby wanted me to be a father to it."

"Oh, Kip. Geez, I'm so sorry." Kenny was the first to speak. "I know we gave you a hard time an' all last week, but we never wished nothin' bad for ya. Man, I'm really sorry."

"Kip, are you gonna be okay? Do you want us to come up there?"

"No, I'll be fine, I think. I have to be. It's Abby. She's taken it hard. She's catatonic. Been this way for a week now. It's just too much for her to lose her husband and now her baby in such a short space of time." He hunted for a tissue to blow his nose.

Tom shook his head with sorrow. It hurt them all to hear their close friend suffering. Kip had already been through enough grief of his own, first losing his father, then the mess with Tansey.

"I have to go to her, but how can I? I can't let her see me like this, if she can see me at all. They're hopin' I'll be able to get her to respond somehow. I have to be strong for her. I don't know how I'll manage it. Just seein' her like this is gonna kill me. And what if she doesn't come back? What if I've lost both of them?" The crying would not, could not, stop.

Hope spoke through her own tears, "Kip, listen, if anything ever happened to one of our little girls, I'd want Tom to cry with me. I'd be hurt if he didn't. I'd feel he didn't care as deeply as I did and resentment would build. I wouldn't know he was keeping it hidden from me. And you know him well enough to know that sharing it with me is exactly what he'd do. It's that kind of sharing that makes a relationship. If you only share the good times and not the things that hurt the most, then what's the point?"

"You think so, Hope? I should do that?"

Tom pitched in. "It sounds right to me. She's retreated inside where she's alone with her grief. Maybe it would help her to know she's not alone. Maybe she needs you to share it with her so she can let it out."

"God help me, I'm just so devastated. I can't even begin to tell you."

"I'm sorry, honey. I wish we were there with you, even just to give you a hug."

"Thanks, Hope. I appreciate y'all bein' there for me."

"Hey, buddy. You call anytime you need to talk, day or night. Understand? We'll be here for you," Kenny offered.

"Thanks. I better get over to her. She needs me." He felt a little calmer, a little stronger, a little more ready to be there for Abby.

"Call when you can. We're worried for you both."

CHRISTOPHER

He turned his phone off and set it down. Folding his hands, he prayed aloud. "Dear God, I need help. I need the strength to help her bear this grief. I'm countin' on you to get me through this one. And what's more, to help Abby through it. I can't do it alone."

He retrieved his guitar to take along, knowing the music soothed her as it did him. The moment he felt the smooth wood beneath his hand, inspiration swept through him, and he battled with himself over whether or not to succumb to it. He needed to get to Abby. He didn't have time for this. Yet, intuition told him it was right. Struggling against his better judgment, he sat with his instrument and poured his heart out. Soon there was a song. A song just for Abby. It would be hers alone, forever.

With guitar and suitcase in hand, he sought courage with each footstep along the trail to the cabin.

Abby remained in the same semi-reclined position Claire had placed her that afternoon. He pulled the ottoman alongside her so he could sit close.

"Abby, I'm here, darlin'. I'm sorry I didn't get here sooner. I'm sorry, Abby." He stroked her cheek and kissed it.

She didn't move, didn't twitch a muscle. Uncertain if she could even hear him, he picked up his guitar, played the opening chords, and began to sing:

I know you're feelin' empty
The babe within is gone.
You felt its life being torn away
Your world of two, now one.
With grief so strong
You feel that you've died too
I beg you please,

Put your heart into my hands
Let me hold it, keep it warm
Let me mend the broken pieces
And protect you from this storm.
And when you feel
There's no light comin' through,
I'll be a warm and glowing candle
Burning bright for you.

I know that you've been plannin'
For the nursery down the hall
With pink and blue dancin' in your mind
And teddy bears up on the wall

Carrie Chesney

The dream is gone
The rain is comin' down,
I beg you please

Put your heart into my hands . . .

If I could take this pain away,
You know I'd do it
But I will be your safe place,
Hold you tight,
And I will love you through it.
Put your heart into my hands
Let me hold it, keep it warm,
Let me mend the broken pieces
And protect you through this storm
And when you feel
There's no light comin' through
I'll be a warm and glowing candle,
Burnin' bright for you.
I'll always shine for you.

In the deep recesses, curled up in her own dark corner, Abby thought she heard music. It seeped in, starting to fill her. Was it safe to come out? She strained harder to listen. It was Chris. He had come for her at last. He hadn't forgotten. Would he blame her? Would he forgive her?

He saw tears forming in her eyes. He played the song through again, without the singing. Tears started to drop. One…two…three.

He looked at Claire, wanting to know that she saw it, too. Her hands flew to her mouth as she witnessed the first signs of Abby responding.

Abby could almost see. The music was getting louder. She was almost there. She crept a little bit closer to the edge of the tunnel. A light shone near the entrance, but she was still frightened, timid of leaving the darkness to go to it.

He sang the bridge and chorus again. With effort, she turned her head, and slowly his face came into focus. He put the guitar down and clutched her to him.

"Oh my, Abby. I'm here now, darlin'. I'm right here with you, and I'm not gonna leave you. Not for anythin'."

She felt his warmth surrounding her. It was her best safe place. She allowed the tears to run freely as he held her. He lifted her to slide beneath her and cuddle her on his lap. They clung together, both of them crying. Abby

129

came out of the dark place altogether. "Oh, Christopher. I need you," she gasped.

"I know, honey, I'm here with you. I've got you now. We'll do this together, okay?"

She nodded and burrowed her head into his shoulder.

Claire headed outside, grateful for the miracle of her sister's return. She was exhausted from the constant care she had been providing for the past week, and welcomed the break, happy to let them have some time alone.

Chris held Abby until she quieted. She looked up and for the first time noticed his face was wet.

"Oh, Chris." She wiped his cheeks with her hands and looked into his teary eyes. "You're crying, too."

"Of course I am. I loved our baby, Abby. I feel so guilty for not bein' here for both of you. Maybe if I hadn't gone, maybe I could have saved it, or prevented the whole thing from happenin'. It's my fault. I never should have gone. I'm sorry I left. I'm so sorry."

It was just like him, she thought. Always feeling responsible for what went on around him. Always wanting to right the wrongs. "Oh, sweetie, it's not your fault. It's my fault. I wasn't watching." She turned her face away, unable to bear the accusation in his eyes when she confessed her guilt. "I'm sorry, Chris. I killed our baby. It's more than I can bear."

"You're not at all responsible for this. Someone did this to you, and I don't know who or why, but you can bet we'll find out. Abby girl, you loved that baby more than your own life. There's no way you would ever do anythin' to harm it." He ran his hand over her hair, smoothing it out. "Listen to us, both feelin' like it's our fault. The reality is neither of us could have prevented this from happenin'. Somehow, I think we have to work at puttin' our guilt aside. It won't bring the baby back."

"It was a little girl. Andrea Claire. I don't know anything more. I don't know where they took her or anything."

"It's okay. We'll ask Claire later. Tell me everythin' about her."

"She's so perfect. I counted her fingers and toes. She has lots of dark curls and the prettiest little face. She looks so much like Drew. Now, she's left me to be with him. My last piece of him is gone. All I have left are memories." She stopped and gulped a sob. "Oh, Chris. My baby, I want my baby."

"I know, honey. I do, too. I wish I could give her to you. I'm gonna stay here with you at the cabin. You won't be alone. I'm here now, and I'm not leavin' again."

He squeezed her tighter, and she snuggled in closer. "Wait a minute." Her head popped up, and she looked at him. "I just remembered. Claire took pictures. They must be here somewhere."

"You stay here. I'll look for them." He shifted her so he could get up. He started rummaging around the house and went into the bedroom. A few things sat on top of the dresser, but no photographs. He opened the top drawer and there he found them, along with a pink sweater and hat, a small pair of booties, and a small pink crocheted blanket. He took them out of the drawer with the photographs.

"I've got them, Abs." He stood as though glued to the spot. She was right. It was a beautiful little girl. Pain shot through his heart, and his legs felt weak. He turned to the next one and saw Abby holding her. She looked so drained with the huge gash on her head held together with small Steri-Strip tapes. He ached at not having been there.

Returning to the living room, he went to sit on the ottoman next to her, but she wanted to be back on his lap. Clinging together, they looked at the photos. "I wish I'd been here. I wish I could have held her." His voice broke, and she reached out from her own grief to comfort him.

"I know you do. I know you loved her. I can't believe we don't have her here with us. It just isn't right."

"No, it isn't. We both had such plans for her. I wanted so much to watch her grow up. To give her dancin' classes and music lessons, or whatever she wanted. To have her get all dressed up and take her out on little dates, you know, out for dinner and to the theater, or a musical, or her first rock concert. To teach her how to sit a horse properly, and when she got older to give her one for her birthday. I can just see her face, all excited and throwin' her arms around me. And maybe one day watchin' her graduate from college and then walkin' her down the aisle in a beautiful white gown. Yeah, I'm gonna miss her every day for the rest of my life. I love her so much, as though she is mine." He buried his head in her shoulder and allowed her to console him.

It was good to have someone who felt the exact things that were in her heart and understood. He knew her grief, because it was his too. It made it different this time, having someone to share it with, making her feel needed, and for that she was grateful. Now, she had to go beyond her own grief to help him with his.

"Will you sing for me? I want to hear it again. Please?"

He lifted his head and looked into her eyes. For her, he would move heaven and earth if he could. He dried his eyes with his shirtsleeve and sang the song for her again. This time she was here with him and heard the words his heart had written for her. The lyrics made her cry again. She was grateful to have a friend like this, who understood the pain in her heart and cared.

"I love it."

"I wrote it this afternoon. It's yours. No one else will ever have it. It's just between us. I meant every word for you. I want to be your safe place and look after you and that heart of yours."

"It will be our sacred secret. Something no one else will ever share. I want you to put it on a tape for me. Then I'll be able to listen to it all the time and remember my little girl, and you." She paused, lost in thought for a moment. "I didn't know what to do when they took her away. You weren't there, and I was so scared and alone. I had to find a haven to go to so I could protect myself. It was so dark, and I was alone with the horror of my guilt and the anguish of my heart. Then I heard the music, and I knew you'd come back for me."

"I'm sorry, Abby girl. You know I would have been here if I'd known. I kept callin' you here at the cabin every time I got a minute, but there was no answer. I figured you two were off doin' somethin'. We've got each other now, though. We'll make it through this together."

She tucked her head on his shoulder and nodded. Together they would do it.

"I'm gonna get you somethin' to eat. Claire left some soup on the stove. Do you want to get up for the bathroom first?"

"Yes, please."

He helped her up and let her lean on him to walk. He took her to the bathroom and asked if there was anything she needed.

"I don't think so. Maybe later I'd like a shower, though."

"Sure thing. Don't try walkin' on your own. Call when you're ready."

"Thank you."

In kitchen he ladled a bowl of soup for her and sliced some cheddar from the fridge. She stood against the doorframe waiting for him. He saw her legs trembling and scooped her up in his arms, carrying her back to the sofa where he commenced to spoon the soup for her. She ate as much as she could handle, then he took the tray back to the kitchen.

He returned to find her asleep, displaying a countenance of peace. Silently, he prayed she would get a solid restful sleep and not be bothered by nightmares. He brushed his knuckles over her cheek and stroked her hair, wishing he could protect her from the pain.

The things Claire told him played heavily in his mind as he stepped outside, and he went to check out the dock. He found her standing on the hill at the top of the staircase, staring down at it, her emotions jumbled.

She remembered the day last winter when Abby first told her about the baby. She remembered how sick Abby had been through the entire pregnancy. She remembered finding Abby lying in her own blood, so much blood. She remembered her sister holding her dead niece and singing her a lullaby. She remembered Abby as she'd been for the past week. She mourned for her sister and the baby. She rejoiced Abby had finally come back to them.

The prominent bloodstains on the wood made Chris nauseous, and he averted his eyes. He knew no matter how hard he scrubbed they would never come out. Kneeling by the trees where the line had been tied, he observed where the pressure from her trip caused the nylon line to bite into the wood. Unable to fathom why anyone would do this to Abby, his eyes misted over, and he rubbed the back of his arm across them to clear them.

"When did all this happen, Claire?"

"Last Tuesday."

After a few moments he asked, "Why didn't she call me? I would have been here for her. I told her to call if she needed me."

"I did call you, Chris. She cried out for you all through the labor, and I called you."

Numb, he shook his head in disbelief. "I never got a message."

"I called your cell. I figured that was my best chance of reaching you."

"Last Tuesday? The Luncheon." He felt a sinking in his stomach as he remembered his premonition. "Oh, no. Did you call around five or six o'clock?"

"Yes, it was at six. Some woman answered and said you couldn't come to the phone and that it would be hours before you'd get the message. I told her it was an emergency."

"The message I got was somethin' about a Carly Messina wanted me to call back. I didn't have a clue what she was talkin' about, and I didn't get that much until Thursday."

"Carly Messina? I said it was Claire, and please call the marina. I repeatedly stressed to her that it was urgent. Glen waited to hear from you so he could fill you in. He was with me when I found her."

Rage consumed him. It didn't matter what the circumstances surrounding the phone call were. If Claire told Donna it was an emergency, she should have given him the phone, or made damn sure she got the message right and not waited two days to deliver it.

"Hang on one minute." He pulled out his cell phone and pushed a few buttons. "Hi, Donna, Kip. Listen that message that you took for me last week at the luncheon?... Do you remember her tellin' you the message was important, because as I understand it, you were told more than once it was an emergency, that they were desperate to reach me...That was my family callin'. Someone very close to me was dyin', and I was needed. Now, it's too late. I pay you to do my publicity, not keep me from my family. You're fired." He clicked the phone off.

Claire was surprised by his swift action, yet it pleased her. A small recompense for all the suffering Abby went through while waiting for him.

"I'm sorry, Claire. I would have left in a minute." Staring intently at the bloodstain his emotions caught up with him, and his voice trembled. "Dear heavens, Abby girl."

"You've returned, and she's back with us now. You performed a miracle. That's what matters the most," she comforted.

CHRISTOPHER

He helped her carry the baby's things to the Miz Gilda. They agreed it would be better for Abby not to have them sitting under her nose all the time. He stood on the dock and waved goodbye as she left the island. His phone rang, and he sat on the top step of the staircase to answer it.

Tom McGarrett said hello and asked how Abby was doing. Kip heard Faith and Kenny on the line with them.

"Better. She's come back to us, thank God. We talked about the baby, and I did like you said. I'm grievin' with her. She's sleepin' now."

"Is there anything at all we can do down here for you," Tom offered.

"I couldn't reach Jeff or Julie. Julie needs to be told as soon as possible so she can break the news to Trent. He'll take it hard, too."

Kenny spoke quietly. "I'll call Julie for ya. Are ya sure you don't want me to fly up? It's no problem."

"No, there's nothin' you can do here. I just want to be with her. But thanks, Kenny. I appreciate that you'd do that for me."

"Kip, what happened? I mean, she was pretty far along wasn't she?" As the mother of three little girls, Hope Hilton knew it didn't even occur that something could go wrong this far along.

"We only had four weeks to go. Someone set a tripwire, causing her to fall. Abby would have bled to death if her sister hadn't found her in time. The police are investigatin'. And get this, Claire called me when Abby was in labor. She told Donna it was an emergency, but Donna didn't even tell me about it. Here was poor Abs, thinkin' I didn't care and sufferin' through it without me. I just fired Donna." Chris ran his free hand through his dark hair.

His voice broke as the guilt ate at him. "What if Abby died, and I missed being there for her. Geez, I feel so guilty. There I was, the Big Star, signin' autographs, and winnin' trophies, and gettin' my picture taken like I was somebody important, all the while denyin' any feelin's for her to anyone who'd listen. And here she was goin' through all this without me. You know, I'd give the whole thing up in a minute for her." The constriction in his throat was painful. He felt himself choking on his tears.

"You can't help what you didn't know. If you'd gotten the message, you would have gone to her. As for the rest of it, you were doin' your job." Tom tried to reassure him, yet knew he would feel the same if the roles were reversed.

"But I think I did know. I remember havin' a feelin' that afternoon that somethin' was terribly wrong. When I saw Donna answer the phone I should have followed my gut instinct and stopped what I was doin' to take the call. Claire said Abigail cried out for me all through the labor. She probably believed I deserted her."

A moment of silence passed between them.

"I'll call the papers to let them know, and tell them to downplay it. If I tell them quietly now, they won't be houndin' you next month to find out about the baby."

"Thanks, Tom."

"Kip, will you tell her that our thoughts and hearts are with her? We're so sorry this happened. We'll all pray for the both of you. Give her our love." Sorrowfully, Hope hung up the phone.

Wandering back to the cabin, he sat down on the porch swing with his guitar. He told it of his pain, and it sang its solace in return. That's what he loved most about this old guitar. It always made his heart feel better.

CHAPTER 16

Maisie watched, dismayed. The scheme had not gone as planned. When she returned from Nashville Sunday night, she came straight to the dock hoping to find a dead Abby and to remove the evidence of tampering. There was no victim to be found, but she thrilled at the sight of bloodstains on the dock. The tripwire was gone and the island deserted.

She stayed hidden in the brush regardless. Someone knew foul play was involved and may be watching. Kip should return in a few days. She would listen in when he got here and hopefully learn more then. The newspapers in Nashville teemed with news of Kip and Abby's engagement. She didn't believe it. Having watched the entire relationship take shape, she'd never seen them kiss, and she knew they didn't have "sleepovers." Yet, by the time the week ended, he admitted it was true. So was it or not? If her plan succeeded, and Abby died, then it was a moot point. She decided not to worry until she needed to.

A woman she had never seen before arrived at the island Tuesday morning, bringing Abby with her. So, she didn't die, but her behavior was peculiar. Maisie determined they must be sisters; different hair color, but a strong similarity in features. It pleased her to see Abby was no longer pregnant, and they brought no baby with them.

Tuesday evening Kip returned. She watched as he and Abby clung together and wept. The sister left the island, and the two were on their own. It appeared the tragedy brought them closer together rather than driving them apart. Not at all the way she planned it.

•

Chris laid the guitar back in its case and took his travel bag into the bedroom. With Abby sleeping peacefully, he decided to take a quick shower.

He leaned his arm on the shower wall and rested his head against it as the water pelted him, wishing he could wash the events of the day down the drain and start it over again. Not wanting to be away from her any longer than necessary, he turned the shower off and got out. After putting on pajama bottoms and a tee shirt, he went into the bedroom.

He turned down the covers to move Abby into the bed where she would be more comfortable, and his memory flooded with the night he almost made love to her. Shaking the reminiscence aside, he carried her into the bedroom. Sitting on the edge of the bed, he brushed her curls aside and lay his hand on her cheek, grateful for the sweet repose on her face. He kissed her temple and left her to dream of castles and unicorns and rainbows.

Back in the living room, he claimed her spot on the sofa. He smelled her scent on the pillows, and sleep soon settled on his mind. In his dreams, Maisie and Daisy waited in line for his autograph, and he relived the moment he knew something was wrong. For the remainder of the night, no matter where he went or what he did, those two fans were always there, plaguing him.

Morning sun shone in his eyes through the east windows, waking him. He lay for a few minutes, enjoying the quiet of the paradise island. Abby slept through the night, and he thought that was a good sign. He poured a glass of juice and stepped out onto the front verandah. The leaves of the aspens quaked and trembled and flashed silver, and he heard the occasional splash of fish jumping in the lake.

He sat on the porch swing and let the blessings of morning seep into his system. Another day faced them, and somewhere in it, it would hit him that the baby was gone. Right now he was numb. He hoped she would be for a while, too. It was almost an hour before he heard sounds from inside. He grabbed an old, vinyl-covered kitchen chair and put it into the tub so Abby could sit in the shower, knowing she wasn't yet strong enough to stand on her own for long.

Standing in the bedroom doorway, he smiled at her. "Mornin' Sunshine."

"Morning. I don't know about the sunshine part. I'm not feeling particularly sunny." She attempted to smile but didn't quite make it.

"It's a beautiful day outside. First, I thought you might want to have that shower you missed out on last night." He sat on the bed beside her, running his finger along her cheek.

"Yes. I don't even know when the last one was."

"Well, it doesn't matter now. Let's get you in there." He pulled the covers back, helped her out of the bed, and walked her to the bathroom. "Are you gonna be all right on your own? I mean, I don't know how to ask without soundin' like a guy, but you know, if you need help washin' your hair or gettin' in and out of the tub, well, I'll help you and I promise not to ogle your body. Do you know what I'm tryin' to say?" How was it he could write great lyrics, but couldn't find the appropriate words in his own life? He felt like a stammering idiot.

"Yes, I do. You're saying you're here to help me, and I shouldn't feel embarrassed about being naked in front of you, because you'll treat me with dignity and respect." She looked into his eyes and showed him she believed he meant it.

He let out a deep breath. "Exactly. I mean, I'll help you without seein' you in a sexual way."

"That's certainly no surprise. This poor body of mine couldn't attract a man who had just been rescued after twenty years alone on a deserted island."

"Abs, you know that's not what I meant. Listen, girl, if you want to take your clothes off, I'd be right happy to tell you how absolutely gorgeous you are. You'll always be beautiful, no matter what your body goes through. Cut it out. You know exactly what I meant."

"Yeah, I do. Thanks." She stood on tiptoe to kiss his cheek. "I promise I'll call if I need you."

"That's better. I put in a chair so you don't get dizzy and fall. You take your time, and enjoy it. Do you need anythin' that isn't here?"

"Umm, just my chenille robe. I think it's hanging in the closet. And maybe if you could bring me some fresh underwear and leave me a clean nightie on the bed. Would you mind?"

"Of course not." He kissed her forehead and left her. Going to her dresser, he took out the things she needed and went to the closet for her robe. He heard the water turn on and gave a small knock. She told him the door was open so he put her fresh panties on the vanity and hung the powder blue robe on the back of the door.

He picked up her soiled clothes and put them in the laundry. He was about to lay her fresh nightie on the bed, when he saw the bed sheets also needed changing. Knowing she would be embarrassed, he quickly stripped the bed and put clean sheets on, then added the soiled laundry to the washer. When he returned to the living room he heard her crying in the shower. He considered going in to check on her, but decided to allow her privacy to mourn.

Abby sat beneath the water's spray not sure of anything in her life. Her hand rested on her stomach finding it considerably smaller than it had been a week before. The knowledge cut into her heart, and she closed her eyes, wanting to deny it. As the heated water ran over her breasts, she felt a pressure building inside. Looking down, she watched as her milk ran freely. Her arms ached with the emptiness of not having a babe to hold to her breasts for nourishment. Her womb ached with the emptiness of not having a babe within. Everything was wrong, and nothing was right. Succumbing to the grief, she wept.

When the water finally shut off, he figured the hot water tank must have run out. A few minutes later she opened the bathroom door, leaning against the frame with her robe wrapped around her. He helped steady her as he walked her to the bed, then grabbed a towel from the rack in the bathroom and dried her hair until it was fluffy. Giving her time to put on her clean nightie, he went to the kitchen and poured her juice. She joined him a few moments later.

Sitting on the ottoman, he looked into her eyes. "Abby, you don't ever need to go back inside again. I'm here now, and we're a team. You don't have to carry this on your own."

She stared at the glass in her hands and felt the tears well in her eyes. She relied on his strength and gained a sense of security from him. Maybe she could get through this if he stayed and helped her along the way. "I owe you so much. How can I ever repay you?"

He wiped at her tears with his thumb and chucked her under the chin. "Listen, sweetie, there is no payin' back between us. Of course, if you insist, I'm sure I'll think of somethin'." He gave her a lascivious grin and wiggled his eyebrows, and she gave a half-hearted giggle. "Now about breakfast, what does your heart desire?"

"I'm not really hungry."

"I know you aren't, but you have to eat somethin'." He rummaged in the kitchen for a few minutes and returned with a bowl of granola.

After breakfast he took her out to the porch swing and stretched her out with pillows behind her back, draping a lightweight blue and white crocheted afghan over her legs.

"You know something we've never talked about, Abs? Art. Who do you like?" He sought to keep her mind engaged, knowing if he could occasionally get her mind off the baby, things would gradually become easier.

"I like Trisha Romance, and that's her real name. She's from down at Niagara-on-the-Lake. Pretty little town. We should drive down there sometime. Have you ever been to the falls?"

"Niagara Falls? No, I haven't. I'd like to go. How far is it from here?"

"About four hours."

"I've noticed that about Canadians. You ask how far somethin' is, and they always reply in time instead of mileage."

"I never noticed, but I guess you're right. We always talk about distance that way."

"Hey, Jeff and Julie are comin' up next month. Why don't we make some hotel reservations and all go down together? It could be a lot of fun. How 'bout it Abs?"

Despondency dwelled close at hand. "Oh, I don't know. You'd have a lot more fun without me. I'll just depress everyone."

"First of all, I'm not gonna listen to that kind of negative talk. Secondly, we wouldn't even think of goin' without you. They're both so anxious to get to know ya."

"Maybe." A few minutes later she asked, "When in July?"

"Third week."

She thought about it, trying to calculate how many weeks away that would be. "Okay. Let's do it."

"Great. I'll book us a couple of rooms. Do you want to share with Julie or have a room of your own?"

"If she doesn't mind, sharing is fine."

"Are you kiddin'? She'll think it's a pajama party." He went inside and came back with cold drinks. She took the glass from him and after taking a drink, set it on the small table he placed beside her.

"Looks like we're gonna have a warm day."

"Yup. The sun is bein' good to us. Unfortunately, the humidity will get worse soon." She attempted a grin as she put on a snobbish English accent, "Of course being a lady, I never sweat. I just glow a lot."

"Abby girl, that beautiful smile of yours makes you glow all year round."

She giggled. Then the guilt hit. How could she laugh when her baby was gone? Solemnity fell on her spirit, and she was appalled by her behavior.

He immediately noticed the change. "What's goin' through that head of yours?"

"I was laughing. How can I possibly find anything humorous when I don't have my little girl?"

"Listen, findin' somethin' that makes you happy for a moment's reprieve doesn't mean for one minute that you're not in pain. I know how bad your heart's hurtin', and I know goin' on without her is gonna be one of the hardest things you've ever done, almost as bad as losing Drew. The thing is, life keeps goin' on around us and sooner or later, and we have to become part of it again. It doesn't seem fair, though. I know that."

Teary eyes blinked at him. "No, it sure doesn't."

He knelt beside her and placed his hand on her arm. "But we have to keep goin' on. We aren't the ones who died, so we must still be here for a reason. I don't know how the Lord decides who he takes back home, or why he chooses the times he does, but I know that as long as we're still here, we have many more trials as well as blessin's ahead of us. I really believe that, Abby girl."

She broke the eye contact and gazed out at the trees. A breeze was blowing through the new green leaves, and they danced and rustled in response.

"You and I are gonna keep talkin'. We'll talk about the baby, and we'll talk about other things. We'll cry together, and we'll laugh together, and we'll survive together. I'm not gonna let you go back into that dark place again. Do you understand what I'm sayin'?"

She continued to stare out over his shoulder. "I understand. It just feels so wrong to laugh when inside it hurts so deeply." Tears finally tipped over the edge, rolling down her pale cheek.

"Of course, it does. But you need it. You need laughter as much as you need the air you breathe. It's part of who you are. It's part of carryin' on. She's with Drew, honey. He's probably watchin' you and wonderin' where you're hidin' that spirit that makes you Abby. He wants you to find happiness in your life."

"You're probably right. I can imagine him telling me to 'get over it and move on'. When are you going to?"

"When am I gonna what?"

"Move on. You were going to stay close and be part of my life because of Andy. Andy's not part of the equation any more, so I assume that changes things. You can go back to your life now."

"Abs, I said I wanted Andy and you. I went nuts missin' you when I was away. That doesn't change. I need you in my life, honey. I told you I won't leave you, and I meant it. We'll work somethin' out, but I'm not sayin' goodbye. I think we need each other. Unless you want me to go."

His words comforted her. "No, I don't want you to go. I do need you. I'm scared of being without you. Things aren't right when you're not here."

"Ditto. So when we're feelin' better, we'll talk and make some decisions." He ran his fingers through her hair and held her to his chest for a moment. "Hey, guess who wanted me to give you their condolences and tell you they're prayin' for us?"

"I don't know. Julie? Trent?" She wiped away the tears from her eyes before they could start to fall.

"Nope. The McGarretts. Kenny too."

"Who are the McGarretts? Is that somebody I'm supposed to know?"

He looked at her in amazement. Then he remembered, she didn't know who he was either, so instead of making fun of her, he answered her simply. "Tom and Hope."

"I don't think I've ever heard of them. Should I have?"

"Tom McGarrett? Hope Hilton?"

"Hope Hilton? I know who she is. Wait, you're just kidding me. She doesn't know who I am."

"They're close friends of mine, and I called them last night. They were real upset when I told them about Andy. They even offered to fly up here to be with us."

"You're just teasing to try to make me laugh, Mozart."

She must be feeling better if she called him that. Climbing from the depths of anguish that held her captive to communicating and making attempts at humor was a remarkable transformation in an incredibly short time. He knew she would have many more hours of grief, but she was almost functional again, and for that he said a silent prayer of thanksgiving.

"No joke. Cross my heart." He hated to bring her down, but something plagued him, and he needed to talk about it. "Hey, Abs, I've been wonderin' why someone would do that thing with the fishin' line. I mean you can't possibly have enemies. So why? That's what's botherin' me." He leaned back against the railing with his arms braced on the ledge.

"How would anyone find me? Only Trent, Claire, and the Masterson's know I'm here. Obviously it wasn't personal."

"We lost our daughter. That's real personal to me." His anger surfaced rapidly. "Damn."

She reached out to him, tears blurring her vision, and he took her hand. "Like you said, though, we can't go back and change it, no matter how badly we want to."

"No, we can't change it, but I'd sure like to know why. Why did it happen? You know, maybe it isn't such a good idea for us to spend the rest of the summer here after all."

"That's a bit extreme, isn't it?"

"I don't want to take any chances. If this wasn't a random act of stupidity by a coupla kids or somethin', I don't want you here like a sittin' duck waitin' for the next time." He pulled a chair beside the swing so he could sit close and look at her straight on, keeping hold of her hand.

"I can't believe it was aimed specifically for me. What possible reason could there be? Let's just try to put our lives back together."

"I don't like it, Abby. I'm scared. I almost lost you along with the baby this time. I don't want there to be a next time. If stayin' here is what you really want, then okay for now. If anythin' else happens, though, we're packin' up, and you're comin' back to Nashville with me."

"I understand your concern, but what makes you think I need to go all the way to Tennessee? If I'm not safe here, I can always go back to Picton."

He tensed noticeably and looked her in the eye, his voice deadly calm and serious, "There's no way I'm lettin' you outta my sight. Whither I goest, thou goest, too, and I'll brook no arguments."

"Chris, you're my friend, not my owner, and misquoting scripture isn't going to change that."

She watched his blue eyes turn navy. "Abigail, I mean it. If I leave and somethin' happens to you, I won't be able to live with myself. You're just too important to me. You stay with me. Please."

It was obvious he wasn't doing this as a matter of controlling her. His concern, no, his fear dictated his actions. It made her feel special to have someone care that much about her.

"All right. That's *if* something else happens. I just don't believe it will."

"I hope you're right."

"It might be all right going to Tennessee. Maybe Kenny wants to meet me.

"Well, I think we're goin' when he's away on tour."

"You don't even know when we're going, so how do you know he'll be out of town?"

"Cause if he isn't already, I'll send him."

"Are you afraid he might like me? You said before he thinks I'm pretty."

"I don't think you'd be happy with him. Besides, you're not blonde."

"Only likes blondes, does he?"

"It seems to be his preference."

"What about you, Mr. Adams? What's your preference?"

"Well, right about now I'd say I'm real partial to chestnut curls." He reached out and twirled a lock around his finger.

She looked at him and sighed. "You must think I'm beyond hope of recovery to say something that silly. I'm sad, not gullible. Chestnut curls, my eye. What kind of hair does Tansey have?"

"She's blonde. Long blonde hair past her waist."

"It must be beautiful."

"Not my cup of tea. I told you, I'm likin' chestnut curls, and I'm stickin' by that. I've gotta hang the laundry out on the line," he said to escape.

He took the load from the washer to the back yard and went about mechanically pegging things on the line. When he was finished, he sagged against the cabin with one foot braced on the wall behind him and rubbed the back of his neck with his hand. She was right, and he knew it. He had no right to boss her around and insist she go anywhere. He had crossed the line, but even though he knew it, he couldn't stop himself. The thought of anything taking her from him overwhelmed him with fear. He wanted to keep her close by as long as he could. He needed to protect her.

He was accustomed to being the boss. He ran a multi-million dollar business. He spoke, and people jumped to do his bidding. But Abby didn't work for him, and she certainly didn't take orders. He would have to watch himself in the future.

CHAPTER 17

Kip had been back on the island for three weeks, and Maisie couldn't be more upset. Instead of drifting apart, the couple seemed closer than before. He spent his nights at the cabin since his return, so maybe the engagement stories were true. She searched his cottage, finding the gifts he brought for the baby. What she needed to get her hands on wasn't there. The last batch of music brought in ten thousand dollars. That should be enough to get by for a while, especially with no concert tickets to buy and not much in traveling expenses.

It was clear she needed a new plan. Abby must be eliminated so he could get on with his work and be available to fall in love with her. She obviously needed to put some more thought into it.

Daisy stayed behind in Nashville this time. It was just as well. They had grown tired of each other, but she missed having her sidekick to toss ideas around with.

Maisie watched as each day the couple sat on the porch talking. Kip would sometimes bring his guitar out and play. After the first few days Abby got dressed, and they took walks. Each afternoon he sat under the large sugar maple in the side yard with her nestled between his legs, reclining against his chest. They took turns reading to one another. Sometimes they put the book down and talked. Sometimes he held her while she cried or slept. Sometimes they just sat in silence.

Maisie wanted to be the one under the tree with him, reading and laughing and talking. It should be her, not that Abby woman.

Each day her jealousy and hatred grew deeper as she watched the woman stealing her life. Each night she slept in the main cottage in his bed. The bedding still carried his essence and brought her many erotic dreams. She determined to make them a reality. She knew she would be far more pleasing in bed than Abby could ever be. When his scent began to fade she splashed some of his cologne from the bathroom cabinet onto the pillows.

●

Abby and Chris sat under the maple tree. They'd been reading the Janet Evanovich series together over the past week and a half. It provided them the incentive to laugh, and laughter for even a little while each day was healthy. They found the same things funny and enjoyed predicting what the heroine, Stephanie Plum, would do next.

He wore a pair of jeans and a cotton shirt with the sleeves casually rolled to his elbows, and sat with both knees bent and his feet pulled up alongside her. She leaned back against him and rested her hands on his knees. He placed his hands on top of hers, and she lifted her fingers to entwine with his. He made her feel warm and secure and happy.

"Sing me my song."

She turned to look up at him, and he swallowed. She gazed into his blue eyes and smiled, and he was lost, struggling not to lower his mouth to hers. It would be so easy and natural. Restraint grew harder each day, and when she looked up at him like this, this close, it took every ounce of discipline not to go spinning into a world of self-indulgent folly.

He turned away from her face, focusing on their linked hands, and sang her the song that was hers.

She relaxed against him and listened. When he finished, she said, "I did, you know."

"Did what, darlin'?"

"Put my heart into your hands. I knew you would protect it."

"And have I?"

"You did more. You saved my life. Your light brought me out of the darkness, and your gentleness made me feel safe. If you hadn't come, I might never have come back. The words so perfectly describe what I felt. It's amazing how you saw right inside my heart and knew everything there. The emptiness, the darkness, the wrenching pain, and then to know exactly what I needed from you and verbalize it so accurately—it truly is our song. I think it's the most personal thing anyone has ever given me. Well, except for my wedding night," she blushed.

She reached up and placed her palm on his cheek. He turned his lips into her hand and kissed it. "I'd do anythin' for you, Abs. I wish I could protect you from all the bad things in this world."

"I know you do, and just knowing that means so much. How did I get by all these years without you?"

"You didn't need me. You had Drew lookin' after ya."

"I suppose you're right. But this is different, somehow. I never had this same sense of security. Maybe I didn't need to before. I suppose I never needed him in the same way I've needed you. I never really had anything bad happen in all the years we were together. But you, well, I know I can trust you to catch me if I fall. Did you ever have this kind of relationship with anyone before?"

"You mean this feelin' of closeness?" He reflected back on his life. "I shared my entire life with Jeff and Julie, so they probably know me better than I know myself, but I'd say it's not like this. I mean, I never held Jeff on my lap and cuddled him."

Abby laughed at him.

"And with Julie, it was more like she was always watchin' out for us and takin' care of us. Besides, even though she's a girl, she's really just another guy with us. And Tansey never needed anythin' from me but money. She can't let anybody inside, because there is no inside. You've honestly never met anyone so shallow or self involved in your entire life."

"Well, I don't want your money. Just your friendship."

"That you'll always have," he assured her.

"I'm glad." They sat quietly, each in their own thoughts. "Did you make my cassette yet?"

"No, I have to go up to the house to do it. All the equipment is there."

"Maybe this afternoon? I'm getting tired and need to lay down for a nap anyway."

"All right. While you sleep, I'll go to the house and record it. Deal?"

"Deal. And in return, I'll make dinner tonight."

"If that's the case, I promise it'll be in your hands when you wake up."

She stood and held her hand out to pull him to his feet. "I'll bring the clothes in off the line."

He went inside and made sandwiches for lunch while she folded the laundry. When everything was in its drawer or hanging in the closet, she joined him at the table.

"You know, I was sure my peach blouse was in that load, but it isn't there. I can't find it in the closet either. There's a few items I can't find. I've heard of washers eating socks before, but not shorts and blouses."

"I hung it on the line this mornin', darlin'. Strange it's not there now. I'll have a look around after lunch. Maybe the wind blew it off the line or some-thin'."

"I'm glad it isn't a figment of my imagination. I was getting worried. How come it's only my clothes that go missing? Your things are always accounted for."

"It's obvious the laundry Bogart is a girl, so she doesn't need my clothes." He made light of it, but she had a valid question.

She chewed her BLT and sighed. "This is good."

He sat back and grinned. "This may be the only restaurant on the island, but in spite of our monopoly, we aim to please."

"You always please." She finished the last bite and drank her milk.

"Gee, I wish my wife had felt that way." He took her empty plate to the kitchen. "Would you like somethin' else? Some ice-cream or yogurt?"

"No. I'm going lie down now. I'm so tired. I can't wait until I have more energy."

"All in good time. It hasn't been that long you know. You get all the sleep you need."

He led her from the table to the bedroom. She lay down on the bed and took his hand.

"Chris, if the money was all she saw when she looked at you, she totally missed out on the real treasure." She closed her eyes, curled up, and was asleep within minutes.

His heart tripped at her words. He watched her sleep and appreciating how incredible she was, bent, and kissed her head.

Pulling himself back to the moment, he headed off to the house to make her tape. At the keyboard he set a percussion rhythm, then grabbed his guitar and turned on the cassette recorder.

"Abby, this is our song, so we never forget Andrea Claire and how much she's loved."

His fingers played over the strings of his guitar as he sang the song, and when he listened to the playback, he was pleased. He pulled another blank cassette from the shelf and made a duplicate for himself.

With an eye on the clock, he took the time to make some calls to Nashville and answer email. An hour and a half later, he turned things off and strolled back to the cabin. She would probably be waking soon.

He searched the yard surrounding the back of the cabin to see if he could find the Abby's blouse, but found no sign it. Laundry didn't get up and walk away by itself. It had to be somewhere.

He approached the back door, and the smell of gas assailed him. Holding his breath, he ran inside to find Abby. She lay on the bed asleep, just as he left her. As he bent to lift her, the cassette fell from his shirt pocket unnoticed. Frantic, he scooped her up and ran back outside.

Carrying her to the maple in the side yard, he lay her on the grass. Her breathing was shallow, and he was scared. He shook her and called her name, over and over. Taking her face in his hands, he tried to jar her awake, but she remained unconscious. Sliding his hand up the back of her blouse he undid her bra to lessen the restriction on her chest and hoped the fresh air would help revive her. He pulled out his cell phone and dialed 911, trembling as he continued to hover over her. The Poison Control Center in Toronto assured him he had done everything possible for her, and as she was an hour from the nearest hospital, they recommended he let her rest and get plenty of fresh air. There wasn't much more the health care providers could do other than monitor her anyway.

Reluctantly, he accepted their suggestion, and left her to sleep it off in the shade. Searching through the shed behind the cabin, he found a large wrench to turn off the main gas supply. He propped both the front and back doors open, allowing the breeze to blow directly through. Glancing inside, he saw the missing peach blouse on the couch, cut to shreds.

His mind was troubled by the possibilities confronting him. Was it an accidental leak, or had she tried to kill herself? Maybe she wasn't doing as well as he thought. He knew she was still battling post-partum depression on top of grieving the loss of the baby. Maybe she'd been putting on an act to convince him it was all right to leave her on her own. The only reason he'd gone to the house was because she'd asked him to. Now, he was plagued with worry about her, both her physical condition and her mental state. Lifting her in his arms, he carried her to the house as quickly as his feet could take them. As he lay her on the bed in the second bedroom, she began to waken. He stepped to the window and opened it, along with the skylights, to let fresh air waft in.

●

Maisie stayed hidden in the woods, watching as Kip raced to the house with the woman in his arms. It was obvious he was scared, and Maisie felt excitement percolate in her stomach. The woman remained as lifeless as – the dead, Maisie smiled at the comparison, ever since he'd brought her out of the cabin, giving Maisie hope she'd succeeded. She knew she should be off the island, but some compulsion made her stay. She felt a rush watching it play out.

Once Kip was out of sight, she went back into the cabin. Seeing a cassette tape on the bed, she snatched it and tucked it in the leg pocket of her pants.

●

Abby couldn't understand why her head hurt her so viciously. She tried to open her eyes, but it was too painful. She heard a faint mewling sound, not realizing it emanated from her. Someone sat on the bed and took her hand.

She wanted to talk, but her throat hurt, causing her to moan.

"Abby, are you okay?"

She winced with pain, moving her hand from her head to her throat. He brought her a glass of water, supporting her shoulders while she drank. The motion made the headache so intense she wanted to scream. After guzzling down the whole glass, she lay back down. Her throat felt a bit better, but her head still throbbed.

"My head. It hurts so bad. I feel sick."

Her words were slurred, but Chris understood. He went to his own bedroom to snatch his Tylenol. Refilling her water glass, he sat her up again, so she could swallow the pills.

She whimpered.

"Just lie still and rest, Abby girl. You should start to feel better in a while. I'll be right here if you need me." He lifted her hand to his cheek and held it there as he watched over her. Her thumb felt wetness, and she moved her fingers to investigate.

"Are you crying?"

"Yeah." His voice was so tender it soothed her.

"Why? I'm the one with the killer headache." Her words drifted off as she fell back to sleep.

His kissed her palm and whispered, "Don't leave me, Abby. Please, don't leave me. I need you."

Letting her sleep, he sat in a chair by the open window and studied her, his fingers steepled to rest his chin on. There was much to think about, and the longer he thought, the clearer things seemed. Abby's accident. Someone sabotaged her then. What if this were another attempt to hurt, or kill her? It made sense. Certainly a lot more sense than her doing this to herself. He recalled his glimpse of the slashed blouse and knew it wasn't her handiwork. He should have realized the truth right away.

Going downstairs to the office, he called the Ontario Provincial Police and filed a report. Next he called the marina to tell Glen of the episode. Glen offered to bring the police to the island, so Chris wouldn't have to leave Abby. With that arranged, he called Claire, knowing there would be hell to pay if he didn't. She insisted on returning to the island to be with Abby. Finally, he called Jefferson and brought him up to date before returning to Abby's bedside.

An hour later her eyes drifted open again. Her head still pounded, but the pain wasn't as extreme as it had been earlier. She saw pale green walls and felt lost. She remembered going to sleep in the cabin, and this definitely wasn't the cabin. Confusion converged with pain, and she closed her eyes again. A moan slipped out, followed by a small cry.

He knelt beside the bed and stroked her cheek. "Abby?"

"Hmm?"

"Are you all right, darlin'?"

Her eyes fluttered open, and she saw him looking down at her, his brow creased with worry. "Chris?"

"I'm right here."

"Where am I?"

"I brought you up to the house with me. I'll bet you've still got a headache, don't ya?" His fingers continued to stroke her warm, soft cheek.

"Mm-hmm."

"Does anythin' else hurt?"

"My chest feels like a ton of bricks is on it. It hurts to breathe. My throat hurts."

"Would you like some more water?"

"Mm-hmm."

He took the glass back into the bathroom to get fresh cold water for her and helped support her again, so she could drink.

"Thank you," she whispered. He kissed her forehead before laying her back down. Setting the glass on the night table, he took hold of her hand again.

"Honey, I know you're in a lot of pain right now, but I need to talk to you. Do you think you can concentrate for a minute?"

"I'll try. I'm still sleepy." Her other hand settled on the top of her head as though trying to keep it in place.

"Darlin', did you turn on the stove or the oven?"

"I don't know, wait, no. You made lunch, we ate, and I went to bed for a nap. Isn't that right?" She squinted an eye open to look at him.

"Yeah, that's right, sweetie. You don't remember anythin' after that?"

"No, just waking up with this horrid headache. I've never had one this bad in my life. I feel sick to my stomach."

"I'm sorry. I can't give you anythin' more for another few hours. How 'bout you get some more sleep."

"Okay." She turned onto her side and went back to sleep.

Half-an-hour later, Glen was at the door. "Hey there, Chris. I got the police down at the cabin, eh? The air is pretty much cleared out there now. They're probably gonna be there for a few hours, collecting evidence and whatever else they do. I guess we're just lucky you got there when you did, or it would be a homicide, eh?"

"Yeah, that's the way it looks. Thank goodness I got her out in time. She was barely breathin' when I got to her. All I could think of was gettin' her into the fresh air so she could re-oxygenate. Man, I was scared."

"Yeah, eh? And so soon after that thing down on the dock. Seems like somebody out there wants Abby out of the picture. Can't figure it though.

She's always been such a sweet kid."

Chris lifted his eyes and stared at Glen as a new understanding dawned. "Wait a minute. You just said somethin'. Somebody wants Abby out of the picture. That perspective opens a whole new avenue of possibilities."

Glen looked puzzled. "How do you mean?"

"Well, maybe whoever's doin' this isn't out to get Abby, per se. You know what I'm sayin'? It isn't Abby, personally. Maybe they see her as an obstacle, standin' in the way of somethin' they want. They need to remove the obstacle, whatever or whoever it happens to be."

"Well, I see what you're sayin' young fella, but I can't imagine what it is they're after."

Chris chose not to explain, but he had a pretty good idea. He had some great fans, but apparently he had some crazy ones too. It seemed he now had one with an unhealthy obsession. It was the first and only thing that made any sense to him. The attacker always waited until he wasn't around to be certain it was Abby, and not he, who suffered the consequences. Someone must be stalking him, watching them together.

A huge wave of guilt crashed into him, dropping him onto the leather sofa. If it was true, then it was because of him she lost her baby, and almost lost her life. Twice. How could he face her knowing this? Maybe he should leave as soon as Claire arrived. Maybe then Abby would be safe.

Glen walked back to the front door. "I need to be getting on back to the cabin. I'll show the officers the pathway to get here, then head on back to the store. Don't like to leave Marge too long on her own. Listen, you take care o' that little girl."

"Thanks for all your help, Glen. You and Marge have been great to us."

"That's no problem at all, son. Just call when the police are done, and I'll come back up for them."

"Actually, Claire's on her way up here, so why don't you just have the police take Abby's boat back to the marina, and Claire can bring it back when she arrives. "

"I'll do that." He waved farewell as he headed down the trail towards the cabin.

Chris went into his office and picked up the phone again, guilt gnawing at him. He needed a sounding board, and more than anyone else, Jeff would understand.

"Jefferson, I think I've made some sense of this. Hear me out, and give me some feedback."

"Shoot."

Pacing nervously back and forth, he told Jeff his theory.

Jeff ruminated over it for a few minutes, then straightened in his chair . "Geez, I think you've got somethin' there. Anybody particular come to mind in regards to obsession, cause I can think of a few?"

"Maisie and Daisy? It doesn't take a genius to spot a sheep in a herd of cattle."

"They're the first ones who pop into my mind. We've had groupies before, but those two are beyond that. The amount of money they spend to follow us around is phenomenal. Then again, it could be somebody we don't even know. It's gonna be hard to pin this down."

"Remember our last concert in Toronto? Guess who was at the hotel with me?"

"No way!"

"I kid you not! The elevator doors opened, and there they were, large as life. I couldn't believe it. I didn't let on to them. I acted as though it was normal they would show up in the same hotel on the other side of the city, in an area overflowin' with four-star accommodations. A little too much coincidence for my likin'."

"I concur, Sherlock. They get my nomination in the category of known fruitcakes."

"Thanks, Watson." Though banter between the friends came naturally, the tone of voice was deadly serious, and his expression remained grim. "I thought by talkin' about it out loud I'd figure out whether I was makin' sense or bein' egotistical. I wonder if those newspapers postin' Abby's pictures and sayin' we were engaged had anythin' to do with this."

"I think you need to lasso that idea, and bring it into the open corral. It's perfectly logical."

"Hey, wait a minute. Maisie and Daisy were in Nashville with us. They were there at the luncheon when Abby was hurt." He heaved a sigh of disappointment, and his shoulders slumped. "I guess that gives them an alibi. Looks like we're back at square one."

"Chris, one word of advice. Get her off that island, and go someplace you can be sure she's safe."

He hung up the phone, knowing Jeff was right. He needed to take Abby away from here. Somewhere she couldn't be followed. The safest way would be on his jet. They wouldn't be traceable that way. He just needed to get her to agree, and that wasn't going to be easy. She would argue about going anywhere, as she did a few weeks ago when they first discussed it. Then she would view using a private jet as pretentious, and she despised that.

As he stared unseeing at the view out the west windowed wall, he realized privacy was no longer a luxury afforded by the island. For the first time since his arrival, he hurriedly dropped the blinds and curtains on all of the windows on the main floor and made sure all the doors were securely locked. The house suddenly seemed eerily quiet. Unnerved by it, he mounted the stairs to be with Abby and found her awake.

"How you feelin now, darlin'? Any better?"

"My head is still pounding, but not as bad as before. At least this time I knew where I was when I woke up."

He sat on the side of the bed gingerly, careful not to cause an excess of motion that would send flashes of pain through her head. "Want some more Tylenol?"

"If I can have some answers with it."

"Be kind, pretty lady, and a tall, dark, mysterious man will reveal all to you."

She attempted to play along. "Will you read my palm, too?"

He looked at her, lying weakly in pain and thought how very like her it was to attempt humor when he knew how awful she felt. He gave her the Tylenol and water.

"Think you can handle being downstairs?"

"Sure. I can handle anything, Mozart." She made a lame attempt at a smile.

He carried her down the stairs as though she weighed nothing at all.

"I'm a little too big for you to be carrying me around like this. I haven't even lost all the weight from the baby yet."

"Honey, you're not as heavy as a heifer, so don't worry about it."

She smiled and lay her head against his shoulder. He set her on the sofa, then perched himself on the coffee table beside her so they could talk, taking her hand in both of his.

"Abby girl, there's no easy way to tell you this. See, the thing is, remember when somebody tried to hurt you with that tripwire?"

"Rather hard to forget, given the outcome." Her eyes dropped along with her voice.

He clasped her small hand in his. She knew she didn't like the expression on his face, worry, and concern written in every line. Her own face started to reflect his.

"What is it? What do you want to tell me?"

"Abs, somebody was at the cabin."

"What do you mean? Who? I didn't hear anything."

He hesitated before answering. She saw the horror in his eyes. "You weren't supposed to. Whoever it was tried to kill you again."

Abby nearly leaped off the couch. He caught hold of her shoulders and urged her back down. "They turned on the gas oven and blew out the pilot light. When I got there, you were barely breathin', honey. That's why your head and your chest are hurtin' so much and why you slept so long. If I'd been any longer..."

"I can't believe this. Nobody's bothered me my entire life. And now in the last few weeks, I've had two murder attempts." She felt her brain spinning. Suddenly the room was spinning too. Leaning back, she closed her eyes and fought against the nausea.

"I'm not tryin' to upset you, but you deserve to know what's happened. I called the police, and they're down at the cabin now doin' their stuff. They'll be up here in a while to talk to us. They'll probably want our fingerprints so they can eliminate any evidence left by us and isolate that of the attacker."

Abby sat as though transfixed, her gaze unwavering. "This is beyond comprehension. It just can't be real."

"I'm sorry, Abs."

"Why? You aren't the one who tried to kill me."

"Of course not, but I said I would look after you and protect you. I guess I did a lousy job of it."

"Well, Mozart, as long as you've been with me, I've always been safe, haven't I?"

"Yes, but—"

"There is no but. You can't stick to me like glue. Maybe it's time for me to go home. Maybe stay with Claire for awhile."

Chris felt the bottom falling out of his world. "Please, honey. I don't want this to change our lives. We have plans, and I missed you so much when I was in Nashville. I don't want us to say goodbye. I wanna be with you." He paused and studied his feet for a moment, then took hold of her hands and raised his eyes to hers. "Please, Abby. I need you."

Closing her eyes, she thought about it. "I'm not ready yet either, although I'm not sure why you need me. I'm the one who's spent all this time leaning on you. You're still my safe place. I'm scared, Mozart. I need you, too." She saw the anxiety in his eyes. "I don't think I'm ready to face the world yet. Not without you beside me."

He wrapped his arms around her and held her tight as her head nestled into his shoulder. He kissed the top of her curly mop, then lay his cheek against it. The chestnut curls were magically weaving their way around his heart and into the little crevices, filling it and making it whole. He only knew he had her safe in his arms, and he didn't want to ever let go.

CHAPTER 18

The police questioned Chris and Abby separately.

Sergeant Cavendish, who had responded to the call when the tripwire was discovered, handled the interrogating. He easily detected the panic in her demeanor but knew it was the result of fear and not an attempt to conceal facts. Scared, Abby offered up more questions than answers.

"I really don't understand any of this, officer. I can't think of a single person who hates me so much they would want to hurt me. I don't have any enemies that I'm aware of."

"This is the second attack, Mrs. Lockner. You're sure there was never anything before you came to this island?"

Abby looked perplexed. "No, nothing. Do you really think I'm being singled out, or could these be random acts by some itinerant person who wants us off the island?"

"I really don't know at this point."

When Chris sat in the games room, Sgt. Cavendish prepared to start again from the top. Before he got the chance, Chris blurted out his belief that he was the reason for the attacks on Abby. Surprised by what seemed a confession of sorts, Cavendish could see he was wracked with guilt.

"How do you figure that?"

Chris confided his theory of being stalked by a fan and his reasons for thinking so.

"Do you have any proof of this?"

"No, the two attacks on Abby are the only signs of it."

"No previous encounters or incidents?"

"No, there were no problems in Tennessee. Only here on the island."

Cavendish appeared interested and made notes.

Rejoining the others, the sergeant told them, "We couldn't prove intent with the tripwire incident, but this time there's no doubt. We'll treat both as attempted homicides."

Officer Austin asked how long the two intended to remain on the island. "If you were on the mainland, we could provide regular drive-bys. It's a little harder to guarantee your safety here on the island."

"I think only about a week and a half," Chris responded. "We won't be stayin' the entire summer as we initially planned, but I can assure you, Mrs. Lockner will not be left on her own for any reason. We'll both stay in this house until we've had time to make further plans."

She assured the officers she didn't fear for her life as long as Chris was with her. They said they would patrol the lake for anyone who didn't belong and search the island for evidence of a third party.

Later in the afternoon, Chris had dinner cooking on the stove when a loud pounding on the front door echoed through the cottage. He twitched the corner of the curtain to peek out. Seeing Claire, he unbolted the door, and she flew in, crossing the room to gather Abby in her arms, needing to ascertain for herself that her little sister was safe. They embraced tightly, and Claire was reluctant to let go.

Chris brought them all cold drinks, and they sat in the living room. Claire was filled with questions, and the other two gave her a play-by-play run down of the afternoon. There was no sense even trying to talk about anything else at this point. The murder attempts consumed all of their thoughts.

Guilt dug its claws in when he denied having any ideas of the reasons behind the attacks. He knew if Claire suspected his role in it, she would whisk Abby away, and he would be left alone. With that in mind, he manipulated the conversation to protect his secrets.

When dinner was over he tried to change the subject, wanting Abby to relax. He encouraged Claire to tell him stories of the girls' childhood, and Abby soon joined in with her memories. They told of youthful pranks, embarrassments, holidays, and joyful moments, but in spite of their efforts, there were long pauses of thoughtful silence, and although no one said anything, they all knew what they were thinking. It was a challenge for Chris to continually try to steer things to happier thoughts.

Shortly past eleven, he suggested Abby needed her rest, knowing in spite of the lightheartedness, her head still hurt. After she went upstairs to bed, Chris and Claire sat at the counter on the stools and talked.

"You worry me, Claire."

"Me? Why?"

"Except for the red hair, you and Abby look too much alike. I don't want you to be victimized."

Claire's eyes grew large at the possibilty. She hadn't considered that she could become the focus of the danger. Trying to keep a cool head, she said, "I think part of the problem is that the attacks were unexpected. They're going to have a much harder time pulling something off now. I don't know if that will make them more determined, or frustrated enough to give up. Hopefully the latter."

"I hope so, too. I want her sense of security restored, so she's free to be Abby again. I want things as normal for her as possible this week."

"I agree. We'll make it a week of fun memories for her. She doesn't need to know we're constantly on the lookout."

"I'm glad you could come up, Claire. It will do Abby good to have you here for a few days." He stood and stretched his neck and shoulders. "Listen, I'm goin' down to the cabin to pick up some clothes for her." He picked up a flashlight and headed to the front door. "Lock the door behind me."

"Are you sure it's a good idea to go now? It's late. Maybe you should wait until morning."

"I won't be long. The police have checked the island. We'll be fine," he assured her.

He slipped out the front door, and Claire quickly fastened the deadbolt behind him. Turning out the lights, she pushed the blind aside to watch him go.

•

Maisie lay on the bed listening to the tape play for the eighth time. She had a copy of the song packaged and neatly addressed to Tennessee, ready to drop in tomorrow's mail. Tonight, she wanted to stay in and listen to Kip sing to her. She felt certain it would bring in a lot of money. The music played on,

*"Put your heart into my hands,
Let me hold it, Keep it warm..."*

•

Claire and Abby each grabbed a pool cue, while Chris transferred the numbered balls to the pool table. Playing had been his idea. They each had a can of root beer, and a bowl of chips sat on the side table. He asked what they wanted to play, and they looked at each other with a knowing grin.

"There is only one game. At least in the annals of our growing up," Claire

157

told him.

"Okay, what is it?"

They smiled and declared in unison, "Beaver Billiards."

He gave his head a shake and looked at them perplexed. "Okay, girls, you've lost me."

Abby sashayed around the table and poked at him with her stick, teasing, "Do you mean to tell me you've never heard of Beaver Billiards? I guess you're not as educated as I thought."

He made a study of their faces and speculated, "Trent, right? It's somethin' he made up."

"When we were young, we always wanted to play, but we were no good and didn't know the rules anyway, so Trent made up Beaver Billiards," Abby told him. Claire stood at the blackboard drawing a chart with names and numbers.

"What's she doin'?"

"Drawing the scoreboard. Here's the rules. It's really easy. The first person to sink every ball five times wins. As soon as you sink one, it's recorded and goes back on the table. It comes off only when everyone has sunk it five times."

"Abby, that's gonna take seventy five balls to win!"

"Yes, and we're so bad it could take days," she stated proudly.

"Remind me to get you billiard lessons."

"Oh, no, that would never do. You see, we're quite pleased with being lousy players."

He looked at the two of them with his hands on his hips and shook his head. Girls! He had a feeling a week with the two of them would leave him totally nonplussed, and they were only getting started.

"Should I even ask about the name of the game?"

"Well, you could ask, but it should be rather obvious. Beaver, great Canadian icon. Game invented in Canada. Get it?"

"Absolutely. It makes perfect sense. After all, what else would it be called?" he agreed with mock sarcasm.

"Right."

He rolled his eyes and racked up the balls as Abby peaked out the blinds, frowning. He reached out a hand and pulled her away from the window, settling his arm comfortably around her shoulders and giving her a gentle squeeze.

On her fourth turn, she once again had every ball on the table rolling, but sunk not a thing.

"Abby, that's awful. You're terrible at this."

She beamed with pride. "I told ya so."

"Are you this bad at other things?"

They both answered together. "Bowling!"

"Last time we went, Abby's ball hit the score keeper."

"How in the heck…never mind. I don't want to know. And what about horse back ridin'?"

"Well, I've never been before, but I'm optimistic. I don't want one of those English saddles, though. I want the cowboy kind with the knobby thing on it to hang onto."

He sat on the sofa and chuckled.

"Did I say something funny, buckaroo?"

"Abby, the knobby thing is a horn, and you're not supposed to hang on to it."

"Well, then why bother having it? Seems silly to put a perfectly good handle on the thing and not hang on to it."

"You're supposed to use it for carryin' your rope or tyin' it on."

"I thought they were called reins. Now you tell me it's just rope."

"No, Abby. Reins are reins. I mean rope for catchin' the cattle with."

"Well, if I don't have a rope, then I don't see a problem with hanging onto it."

"Promise me somethin'."

"Sure, what is it?"

"Remind me of this conversation if I ever think of puttin' you on a piece of good horseflesh."

Chris led by twenty-seven balls at the end of the evening. He could plainly see why the game had been invented for them. It could take weeks if they had to sink them in any order.

The day had provided the much needed break from the tension that had taken up residence with them. He knew Abby was ready to fall apart from the strain, so he made it his goal to provide fun and take her mind to happier places, allowing her the freedom to breathe without fear, even if only for awhile. He noticed that as the day wore on, her peeking out the blinds became less frequent until she forgot about it altogether.

Abby once again preceded the other two to bed. When Chris came back downstairs from saying good night, Claire was making raisin toast.

"Want some?"

"Sure. Hey, I have an idea for you. I won't be insulted if you don't like it."

She buttered the toast. "Okay, what is it?"

"You're a photojournalist, right? I'll bet *Country Weekly* would pay good money for a photo spread on Kip Adam's summer getaway. By the time it hit the stands, Abby and I will be out of here anyway. If you're gonna be here, ya might as well take advantage of it."

She looked at him incredulously. "Are you kidding me? It's an opportunity of a lifetime. I would never have asked you. I don't want to take advantage of your friendship with my sister."

"Just don't put Abby's picture in it." Chris got two glasses out of the cupboard and filled them with milk. "If you want, I'll tell the magazine you have exclusive rights to this. That, along with some direct quotes, could help boost your askin' price."

"My sister's right about you. You really are a gracious, caring, wonderful man."

"She said all those things about me?"

"That's just a few of the appellations she's attributed to you. You're very good to her. This has been hands down the worst year of her life, and you've helped her survive it. I don't know what I can ever do for you, but I owe you so much."

"Claire, friends don't keep track. Your sister helped me through a pretty rough time too, you know. She's taught me a lot."

"Yeah, she's special."

"Yes, she is."

Chris went down to the cabin early the next morning to pack everything that belonged to either Abby or himself and move it to the house. He was surprised to discover a box tucked under the bed with familiar handwriting on the label. Inside, he found a collection of Hampton's CDs and a note from Julie. Frowning, he packed it with the rest of their belongings. It took a few trips, but when he was sure he had it all, he shut everything off and closed the cabin for the season.

With his final journey completed, he found the girls taking things to the cabin cruiser. "What's up, Claire? Where you going?"

"Abby packed a cooler, and we thought we'd spend the day out on the lake. I really think it's a good idea just to get her off the island for a while. Maybe she won't be so concerned about being watched all the time."

"Excellent idea. Anything to get it off her mind is great. Have you got the fishin' equipment?" he asked.

"It's already on board. You just have to go potty, grab anything you want to bring along, and we'll be off."

"Okay, give me five minutes, and I'll be with you."

He was glad Claire had come. Between the two of them, they kept Abby in an upbeat frame of mind. A picnic lunch and an afternoon of fishing and laughter was the best medicine he could offer.

As Abby toted the empty Styrofoam cooler for storing fish down to the boat, she stopped dead in her tracks the minute her foot stepped on the wooden planking. A memory flashed before her of the last time she headed for a dock, and she felt a fluttering in her abdomen, much like a baby kicking. Dropping the cooler, she settled her hands over the phantom feeling, and the name came out as a plaintive cry. "Andy."

Only a few steps behind, Claire reached her sister and enfolded her in her arms. "You okay, Abby?"

Her voice trembled as she answered. "I'll be fine. I was just remembering the last time I was on a dock."

"Oh, Abby, honey. I'm sorry. Maybe this isn't such a good idea after all."

"No, we're going to do this. I've never run away from my fears in the past, and I'm not about to start now." Picking up the cooler, she stepped onto the boat and got ready to cast off.

The boat sliced a furrow through the glistening water, and the wind blew through the girls' curls. After traveling a few miles through the lake system while keeping an eye on the water behind them to make certain they weren't being followed, Chris cut the engine and dropped the anchor. Claire got out the fishing rods, and Abby retrieved the bait.

Chris and Claire settled in deck chairs with their lines cast over the stern. Abby walked around and around and around the boat, staying quiet.

Chris watched her, admiring the way her wind-tossed hair shone in the bright sunlight. Unable to determine exactly what she was doing, he finally relented and asked. "Abby, what are you doin'?"

She didn't take her eyes off the water. "Looking for something."

"For what?"

"I'll let you know if I find it."

"Claire, do you have any idea what she's doin'?"

Claire tried to hide a grin. "Yeah, but if I told you, you'd never believe me. Just leave her to it. She's fishing Abby style."

Chris nodded in understanding. Doing anything Abby style meant it was pointless to ask further. "Enough said." Truth be told, he was just happy to see Abby focus on something other than fear.

Claire pulled out her camera and took pictures of Chris casting, and relaxing with his fishing pole in one hand and a can of pop in the other. He kept an eye on Abby, watching as she came back along the side, rod in hand, suddenly stopping and casting her line. Moments later she reeled in the first fish of the day.

Chris gawked at her, his brows drawn together and his mouth open. "What the heck? How did you catch a fish that fast?"

"I'll never tell." She winked at her sister as she took the wriggling bass off her line and dropped it into the fish cooler. After baiting her hook, she started circling the boat again. Minutes later, she dropped her line in off the bow. Another beautiful large bass joined its brother in the cooler. She rebaited the hook and started around again.

He scratched his head and turned to Claire for an explanation.

She just shrugged her shoulders and told him, "Abby always catches the most."

The grin she tried unsuccessfully to hide told him there was another sister secret going on.

He sat back down and stared at his line. He slowly reeled it in and cast again, a little farther to the right. Ten minutes later, his thoughts were disrupted with a squeal. Abby had a fighter on the line.

"Chris, help me. I think he's too strong for me."

He smiled proudly at Claire and boasted, "She needs me," before he bounded out of the chair and moved in behind Abby to help her land the fish. Reaching around her, his hands fell on top of hers as the pole doubled over from the strain. Releasing a bit of line, he let the fish play for a few minutes before finally bringing in a lake trout two-and-a-half feet long. Supper would be good tonight.

Abby baited her hook again and started to wander. Unable to take the suspense any longer, Chris hefted himself out of his chair and followed her. She walked slowly, studying the water.

"Whatcha doin', Abs?"

She nearly jumped out of her skin and gave a startled scream. "Geez, you scared me. Don't sneak up on a girl like that." Turning away, she started searching the water again without answering.

"Abigail?"

"Christopher?"

He spoke slowly and emphatically. "What are you doin'?"

"Fishing." She turned away from him, feeling her answer was adequate and not willing to give any more.

"Apparently, since you're the only one catchin' anythin'. Now I'll ask you again. What are you doin'?"

"I told you. I'm fishing."

"Is that your final answer?"

"Are you Regis Philbin?"

He took the rod from her hands and dropped it on the deck. "Abby girl, you're gettin' sass-mouthed again."

She saw the twinkle in his eyes and started backing up. "No, I'm telling you the truth. I'm fishing." She turned to make her getaway, but he was too fast for her. He grabbed her and clutched her against him with one arm, while tickling her with the other. She twisted and giggled, managing to turn herself around so she could tickle him back. They were both laughing and trying to attack each other while avoiding being tickled themselves. The sound of her mirth sent a thrill straight to his heart.

He grabbed hold of both of her arms and held them behind her. She stood pressed against him, looking up at him with laughter on her lips and a sparkle in her eyes, and he couldn't resist her. He bent and covered her mouth with his own. Her eyes drifted closed, and she felt her knees giving out beneath her. She opened her mouth to let him in, and he let go of her arms, moving his hands up to hold her head. Her freed hands ran up his chest and settled on his shoulders. He deepened the kiss, knowing he wanted to lay her down right here and now and make love to her.

The moment was broken when Claire's voice penetrated his brain, "What are you guys doing up there? I'm getting lonely back here."

Chris pulled his lips away, then ducked back for one quick nip before scooping Abby up in his arms and holding her out over the edge of the boat.

He shouted back to Claire, "I'm tryin' to get Abby to tell me what she's doin', and she's on her last chance."

She smiled at him, still feeling the wonder of his kiss. "Chris, put me down."

"Are you gonna tell me?"

"If you put me down, I'll consider it."

He gave her a skeptical look and released her so she was on her own two feet. "Okay, I've put you down. Spill it."

"I didn't say for sure that I'd tell you. I only said I'd think about it."

"Think fast."

"No, I think I'll just keep it a secret."

He gave her a shove, but before toppling overboard, she tucked her fingers into the waistband of his khaki shorts, pulling him in with her.

Claire heard a loud splash and ran to the bow to see the two of them treading water. They splashed at one another, both pretending to be outraged, both having the time of their lives.

"If you children can't learn to behave yourselves, I'm going to have to take the boat home and leave you here," she scolded playfully.

"Abby fell in, and I jumped in to save her."

"How's the water?"

Chris replied, "Well, I'd say it's cooled things down considerably."

●

The heat of the day became less oppressive as Claire did the dishes that evening after their delicious fish dinner.

Chris went into the games room and connected the karaoke machine to the sound system. He'd avoided Abby's eyes since the afternoon, and both of them carried on as though 'the moment' hadn't happened. He knew it wasn't just him. She responded completely. Were they just going to pretend it meant nothing to either of them, or was it going to be a turning point? He knew they wouldn't discuss it as long as Claire was visiting.

Abby saw the machine set up and went to retrieve the box of CDs for it.

To her delight, she found a collection of new ones stashed inside. "Where did these come from?"

"Oh, I picked up a few when I was in Nashville. I figured if we're gonna play Donny and Marie, we would need more."

"Good thinking." She called over her shoulder to the kitchen, "Claire, Chris got us a new batch of karaoke CDs. Wait 'til you see."

Claire wanted to be first. She put on Cyndi Lauper's, *Girls Just Wanna Have Fun*. Abby followed with Sara Evans', *Born to Fly*. Chris did the Monkees*, Last Train to Clarksville*. Claire tried Celine Dion's, *My Heart Will Go On*. Then to Chris's surprise, Abby sang a song by Lonestar. *Amazed*. The lyrics were so intimate. He wondered if she meant them0for him personally, or if it was a random choice. She looked into his eyes throughout the entire piece.

He decided to quickly diffuse the situation by singing Wings', *Band on the Run*. The evening carried on, and Claire won because she was free to pick from any category she wanted. At the end of the evening, she asked them to sing a duet together. They agreed and she dropped in *Endless Love*. They each knew their parts and harmonies, and it came out beautifully.

Claire clapped enthusiastically. "You two should record together. My gosh, it was perfect. What do you think, Chris?"

"I think you may be right. I've been tellin' Abby her talent is too good to hide. She should be recordin'."

Claire grew excited. "I really think you should consider doing it. Your two voices compliment each other, and it's a unique sound. It would be so great."

"I agree, at least one. You just have to help me to convince your sister."

"Come on, Abby. It would be wonderful. Just like when Hope and Tom sing together."

"Hey, I know who they are," she piped up, pleased with herself.

Claire scampered back to the discs on the table. "I think I saw one of theirs in here." She ran her hands through them, looking for the one she saw earlier. "Here it is." She popped it into the machine and turned the television on. "You need to learn this one, Abby. It would be perfect for you two to sing together."

Abby turned and looked at the screen. The song was called *Tonight, We'll Make Love*.

"Do you know this one, Chris?"

"Pretty much. I've never done it before."

"Let's learn it so we can sing it for Jeff and Julie when they come." Their enthusiasm was contagious, and Abby felt herself being swept up in it. "Please?"

"If you want to, we'll do it," he acquiesced, wishing they'd chosen a different song.

"Let's not tell them. We'll just surprise them with it, okay?"

"All right, Abby girl." He smiled, but his thoughts were elsewhere. He knew that when he sang the words, he would mean them. Now that he'd tasted her, he wanted more. So much more. She had no idea of the fire that kiss had ignited. It would take a lot of work on his part to keep the flames under control. As much as he wanted her, he knew he could never have her. Abby would require a commitment, and he couldn't give it. He would never suffer through a marriage again. Not ever.

•

Tansey slipped her hand under the pillow and touched a piece of paper. "What's this?"

"Oh, so you've found it." He laid back and raised an arm above his head. She pulled the paper out and looked at it; an airline ticket to Brazil. Her eyes lit up, and he smiled. "They have some great nude beaches in Rio. I thought you might enjoy a few weeks there."

"Who's funding this trip?" she asked.

"The one and only Kip Adams, of course. But don't go thankin' him. He doesn't know about it." He grinned at her, knowing this would make her as happy as anything could.

She laughed and kissed him. "I can't wait. Ooh, this is so delicious. But you naughty man, you've only left me a month to shop before we go."

"My dear, Tansey," he ran a finger across her breast, "this is the only wardrobe you're gonna need. I think you look perfect just the way you are."

"You have a one track mind."

"Hard to think of anythin' else with somethin' as beautiful as you beside me."

She settled back on the pillow. "Not that I want to change the subject, but somethin' has been playin' on my mind, and you might have the answer for me."

"What's that, darlin?"

"Am I still listed as the main beneficiary in my husband's will?"

"That's *ex*-husband, darlin, and as far as I know, yes you are."

"Hmm."

"What's that mean?"

"Nothing. Nothing at all." She pressed her body against his and kissed his neck.

CHAPTER 19

With Jeff and Julie due to arrive in the afternoon, Abby bustled through the house, cleaning. Chris decided Julie should have the sofa bed in the games room, and Jeff could have the living room couch.

When they left the island to go to Niagara Falls, they wouldn't be returning, and that meant closing the house for the season. The island had once meant privacy and isolation from the rest of the world, where they could pretend they were the only two people on earth. That all ended when danger found them and made its home there. What had once been the sweetest of escapes was now harsh and frightful. The sooner he could get her away from here, the better they would all sleep at night.

Once Abby finally agreed to go to Nashville, Chris faced the dilemma of where to keep her. He finally decided there was nothing at his penthouse identifying him as Kip Adams, so she could stay there with him.

At three o'clock his cell phone rang, letting him know Jeff and Julie were at the marina. He told them Claire had left the speedboat at the marina for them and to get the key from Glen in the store.

Ten minutes later they heard the engine of the approaching boat. "Come on, Abby. Let's go meet them."

"Are you sure you don't want to welcome them on your own first?"

"I'm positive. Come on." He took her hand, and they walked to the dock.

Jeff pulled the boat alongside, and Julie tossed the rope to Chris who dropped an efficient clove hitch over the piling. After a round of welcoming hugs, they gathered their luggage and headed for the house.

Abby gave them the grand tour and made them feel welcome. On the back deck she poured them each a glass of iced tea.

"Abby, you're even prettier than your pictures," Jeff told her.

She blushed gracefully. "Where did you see a picture of me? Oh, never mind. Trent, right?"

"He's awful proud of you. I think most of Nashville has seen your pictures."

"That's embarrassing. He hasn't been there that long. How could he possibly have met that many people?"

"He's been hangin' out with Julie. That means he's met just about everyone he could hope to meet. Besides, a pretty gal should never be embarrassed to have her picture shown."

Abby asked about their flight.

"It was very nice actually. We'll all fly back from Buffalo."

"Buffalo?" Chris questioned.

"Closest we could get to Niagara. The Gulfstream needs the runway length. It's not far anyway, is it, Abby?"

"No, it's about an hour from Niagara to the Buffalo Airport. I'm getting pretty excited. I've never flown before."

Julie assured her, "I think you'll enjoy it. We just flew out to Wyomin' a few weeks ago to visit the family. It was kinda strange though, bein' home without Chris," Julie smirked. "Nobody to get us in trouble."

Abby laughed. "Oh, he's trouble all right. My sister just spent a week with us, and we went out fishing. Someone got a little irritated I wouldn't tell him my fishing secrets and threw me overboard."

Julie reached over and smacked him playfully. "Shame on you, pickin' on a girl. I thought I taught you better than that."

Abby smiled and coyly added, "Of course, I made sure I didn't go in alone."

They laughed and applauded her ingenuity. Julie looked at Chris and told him, "I totally see why she reminds you of me. She's great."

"Oh, no," he moaned. "I knew it would be trouble to let these two women get together. I think we're in trouble now, Jefferson."

"Sounds like a good time to me," Julie quipped, and Abby nodded.

"Well, I think that's our cue. Against my better judgment, Jeff and I are gonna take a little walk and let you two get better acquainted." He gave Jeff a clap on the knee, and the men tramped down the deck steps and ambled off together.

He took Jeff to show him Abby's cabin, wanting him to see where she'd been sabotaged and lost the baby. He needed to say the things he couldn't say

167

to Abby about his fear and trepidation.

Jeff saw the bloodstains still marring the dock's surface and experienced some of the horror his friend must have suffered.

"Geez, Chris, it's amazin' she could lose that much blood and still be here to talk about it. The tripwire was here at the top of the stairs?"

"Yeah, see the marks here in the saplin's?"

"That's one heck of a fall. No wonder she lost the baby. I can see why you're so concerned." Jeff looked at the spot through squinted eyes for a few minutes. "You know, I've been thinkin' about it. We ruled out Maisie and Daisy, because they were in Tennessee at the luncheon that day, right?"

"Yeah."

"Well, this isn't somethin' they would have had to be here at the time of the accident. It's not like a direct assault. They could have set this days before, and Abby just never came down to the dock until then."

Chris abruptly lifted his head and stared at him. "You know, you're right. Maybe I shouldn't have been so quick to rule them out. Any idea what their real names are?"

"Nope. Never cared enough to ask or remember. I don't even think the guys who bedded 'em bothered to ask. Conversation wasn't heavy on their minds at the time."

They wandered back to the cabin and sat on the porch swing.

"Have you heard back from the police yet?"

"Yeah. I didn't say nothin' to Abby, though. No use gettin' her any more worried and scared than she already is. They found evidence farther up the island of a small boat being pulled up on the shore on more than one occasion. Two sets of footprints, and what looks like it may have been a campsite further inland. The whole thing appears to be fairly recent, so they're goin' on the assumption it's got somethin' to do with all this. They've collected bits of trace evidence all over the island. Still, not enough to identify anyone without a suspect to take samples from for comparison. Fingerprints, but no previous set on record that match.

"So it might never get solved?"

"Looks that way. Unless of course there's another attempt, and pray God that doesn't happen. I don't think she, or I, could take it."

"How's she been handlin' it?"

"We've tried to keep her focused on other things, but it's always there, hangin' over us like an albatross. The fear is never far from the surface. A couple of times she's broken down. She still has bouts of post-partum depression and mourns the baby. Add knowin' someone wants her dead to the equation, and she's carryin' a heavy load. I sometimes wonder how she even manages to get up in the mornin'. It's really hard on her, Jeff. And it's hard to watch her sufferin' through it. She's normally such a vivacious person. We just try to find ways to lighten the mood to give her some reprieve.

"Let's hope once we get you off this island, the problems end. There's no way they can follow the Gulfstream. Once we're in the air, you're free."

The men headed down to sit near the water's edge in front of the house.

"Oh, and let me warn you. Don't suggest the girls play pool with us."

"Okay. I noticed the pool table in the games room. Why don't we want to play?"

"Playin' any game with Abby can be disconcertin'."

"Like how?"

"Monopoly. She makes you buy raffle tickets to support charities. You have to spend at least five hundred bucks on charitable donations every time around the board or you get penalized when you pass go. When we played Risk, she had peacekeepers."

"Wait a minute. That's supposed to be a game of conquerin' until you have world domination."

"Not in Abby's rule book. She doesn't believe in dictatorships."

"Then how does anybody win?"

"The U.N. wins. She says it doesn't matter if you don't win as long as you play with honesty and a kind heart. Pretty much the way she lives her life. I thought, well, Scrabble's gotta be safe. Not much she could do to that one. But no, you can only use words that have no negative connotation. Suffice it to say, a game of pool lasts three days, minimum."

"Get serious." Jeff laughed, sure he was jesting.

"I kid you not, my friend. I only wish I was. In fact, Claire told me that on occasion a game has lasted more than a week. Trust me, if you agree to play with her, you've been forewarned. It won't be with rules you know."

Jeff chuckled. "She's certainly an interestin' girl," he observed. "Real pretty, too. Her pictures don't do her justice."

"I know. It's like there's a light inside that a camera just can't catch. There is a new development by the way, but I don't know what it means, if anythin' at all."

"What's that?"

"Remember when she said I threw her off the boat last week? There's a bit more to the story. Before that happened, we were teasin' each other, and that went on to ticklin'—"

"You son-of-a-gun! You kissed her! About time, my man."

Chris wore a lopsided grin, the kind that pops up whether you want it to or not and is always a dead giveaway.

"Well? Spill it."

"Do you hear us? We're talking about a single kiss like when we were in high school, back in the days when you had to work so hard just to get that far."

"Yeah, so? Spill it."

"It was good."

"Not enough information."

Chris laid back on the grassy slope, chewing on a piece of alfalfa grass. "Well, it was definitely two-way."

"Always a good sign."

"I was just gonna kiss her, you know, regular, but she was rather…invitational. I thought I was gonna die right then and there. Then she was pullin' me closer. I was ready to go all the way."

"What stopped ya?"

"Her sister. I guess we'd been quiet for too long, and Claire called to us." He blew out a long breath. "We both pulled away, and then I didn't know what to do so I went back to the jokin' and ended up throwin' her in."

"And since then?"

"Since then, we haven't discussed it. We've just sort of carried on as usual. I don't know how she feels about it. Did she like it? Does she regret it? Does she just want to pretend it didn't happen? I don't have the answers, and we haven't been alone to talk. Claire was always with us, so there wasn't really time. I don't want it to be uncomfortable for her, so I didn't bring it up."

"Wow. So it was really good, huh?"

"Geez, Jeff, is that all you can think of? Yeah, it was good. It was great. I felt the earth move beneath my feet!"

"That's cuz you were on a boat, cowboy."

"Oh, yeah. Let's just say, she has definitely left me hungry for more."

"When was the last time you felt that way just from a kiss?"

"Too long to remember."

"So, if we're back in high school, I suppose you want me to talk to Julie, so she can talk to Abby and find out for you how she feels."

"Don't be ridiculous. I'm twenty-eight. I think I'm old enough to handle my own love life."

"Of course you are. So, I'll talk to Julie when I get a chance."

"Thanks, buddy! Knew I could count on ya."

"Anytime."

They laid back on the slope, relaxing and looking up at the sun breaking through the leaves and listening to the sounds around them. Every now and then they heard feminine laughter sailing on the breeze from the back of the house.

Jeff broke their silence. "I can understand where the music came from. You can feel it in the air, can't ya?"

"Yup. It just flows. I wrote *Solitude* like my second or third day here. It's given me direction for the tone of the whole album."

"Tug got you this place?"

"Yeah, he's friends with the owner. Best vacation I ever had."

"Is that because of the location or the company you keep?"

"Both."

"Someday when I find a girl crazy enough to take me on, I might like to bring her here for a honeymoon. What a great atmosphere. A real sense of privacy."

"Well, do me a favor, and don't come until after the stalker is caught. I'd want your privacy to be real."

"Good point."

"Man, you know this time with you is the first time she and I have been apart, except for sleepin', for over a week. The neat thing is we don't irritate each other in spite of our prolonged confinement. We're always happy just bein' together. Really, it's been longer than that. Except for the day when I came here to the house for two hours, and Abby almost died, again, we've been together pretty much every minute since I got back from Nashville. Aside from enjoyin' each other, I just can't bear to let her out of my sight. If anythin' else happened to her, I couldn't live with the guilt."

"That's one big lot of time. Although I don't know if you can actually classify this as bein' apart. She's only a few hundred feet away."

"For us, this is apart. Talkin' her into comin' south with us was pretty easy, cuz we can't hardly bear to be apart."

"You know there's a word for this condition, don't you?"

"I know what you're gonna say, so don't bother. It's been plaguin' my mind ever since I got back here."

"Let me know when you finally get there. I'm tellin' ya. It's just like physics class."

"I know. You don't need to remind me."

"I suppose we should get back to them. I'm hungry after that long trip."

"Okay, Jeff, let's go and show them how to barbecue. We're gonna do it ranch style tonight. We'll give Abby a taste of Wyomin'. I got some nice thick steaks marinatin' as we speak." They could hear the women laughing even before they rounded the corner.

●

Abby put the last of the dishes away, and she and Julie joined the men in the games room. "You guys wanna play a game of pool?"

Both men looked panicked and in unison gave a resounding, *"No!"*

She raised her eyebrows in surprise, startled by their sudden reaction, and Julie studied them curiously.

"What are you guys up to now?"

"Nothing. It's just that, um," Chris searched for a quick excuse, "Abby and I have somethin' else planned. Remember, Abby?"

"Yeah, but we don't have to do it now." She couldn't fathom the reason behind his unusual behavior.

"Well, I don't know about Julie, but I'd sure like to know what it is." Jeff could always be relied on.

"Okay, you and Julie sit on the couch, and we'll get ready." He hustled to the kitchen, while Abby made sure the music was in the machine. Returning with two stools, Chris positioned them at center stage for Jeff and Julie's viewing pleasure.

"What are you doin'?" Julie asked.

"Watch, listen, and be amazed," he quipped. "Seriously, though, Abs and I have been workin' at this. I'd like to hear honest, professional opinions at the end. I know I can count on you for that, Julie."

Seated comfortably on their stools facing one another, Chris nodded, and Abby reached to hit the play button. The prelude notes of *Endless Love* started, and Chris led in with his lines. When Abby joined in, Jeff and Julie sat entranced. Her pure voice harmonized the blend to perfection.

Julie's eyes grew bigger, and her mouth started its journey to full gaping. Jeff leaned forward with absolute interest, his ears keenly tuned to what he was hearing. When *Endless Love* was over, they sang *Tonight, We'll Make Love,* gazing into each other's eyes as though that was exactly how they planned to spend the night. At one point Chris reached out his hand and held her cheek as he sang to her, and she leaned into it. She got off her stool and moved closer, standing between his legs. Leaving her microphone on her stool, they both used his, staring at each other and forgetting anyone else was in the room.

The words and music came without thought. Abby was lost in his eyes and couldn't think of anything but touching him. His face was so smooth, and her hand reached out of its own volition to stroke it.

Feeling her hand on his cheek, his arm curled around her waist and drew her closer. She smelled so good, and he knew it wasn't cologne, it was simply Abby. Dropping his gaze to her lips, he watched them, fascinated as they sang words of love to him.

Julie nudged Jeff's leg, wanting to know if he was seeing what she was. He gave a slight nod.

When the song was over the singers gave each other an intimate smile. Remembering his friends were in the room, he refrained from kissing her and looked to them for their reactions.

"Well, what do you think?"

"Well, that was…quite a show," Julie offered.

"I think he was talkin' about the music, Julie." Jeff spoke under his breath as he gently elbowed his sister, then addressed the performers. "I hope Chris talked you into recordin' with him. That was an incredible blend. Even better than a single cut, you should do an entire album of love songs. Sales would skyrocket. Money in the bank, before you even step into the studio. *Endless Love* was a great choice. Got any more?"

"Ooh, wait a minute." Abby leafed through the CD cases until she found the one she was looking for, remembering how good it sounded when they sang it back at her cabin. Smiling in reminiscence, she popped it into the machine. "We've done this one before."

Chris recognized the opening strains of *Don't Fall In Love With Dreamer* and sang his part on cue while she climbed back onto her stool, grinning. Abby simply loved to sing, whether she was alone or in front of two hundred people. When it was over, Jeff and Julie both applauded.

"I think Jeff's right. You two should definitely lay some tracks. What do you think, Chris?"

"I think the same thing. And you're right, we should cut an entire album. Her voice is too spectacular to spend the rest of her life in Ontario, unknown and unheard."

Abby slapped at his shoulder. "Don't talk about me like I'm not in the room. I'm happy being a nobody in Ontario, thank you very much. I'm not holding my breath, waiting to be discovered."

"That's not what I mean, Abs. I wanted their opinions, but they've just confirmed what I've thought all along. We have a unique blend, as though our voices were created to sing together. Will you think about it? Please?"

Thinking it was nothing more than talk, she decided to play along. "You didn't say pretty please with sugar on top."

"Pretty please with the whole dang candy store on top!" he grinned.

Abby laughed at him. "A request that eloquently phrased certainly deserves some consideration. I don't know much about your business, but surely people don't just decide to do an album and walk into a studio to cut it. There has to be a lot more involved than that." She looked at each of them, waiting for answers.

"It's that easy if you have connections, and Chris definitely has those connections. You just have to start pickin' songs, and it's a done deal." Julie made it all sound so uncomplicated.

Abby turned to Chris, a dubious look on her face. "Really? It's that easy?"

He reached out and tucked a curl around her ear. "You just say the word. It's up to you. Julie knows what she's talkin' about."

"This is going to take some thought. I've never considered something like this before."

"Great. In the meantime, why don't we take a turn with the karaoke machine," Julie suggested.

Abby's gaze slid to Jeff and then quickly away. "Oh, well maybe that's not such a good idea."

Jeff added, "Hey, I think it's a good idea. Go pick somethin', Julie."

Abby gave Chris a desperate look and hoped for support. He didn't have a clue what she was alluding to. "Really, Jeff, I'm sure we can find something else we can all enjoy."

"What's the problem, Abby?" Chris turned and addressed his friends, "Remember? I told you guys I had to beg before she'd let me play. I don't know why, but for some strange reason it's hard to get into her inner karaoke circle."

"All right. We'll do it," she conceded. "Far be it from me to keep people from having a good time." She and Chris sat together on the couch, and she made a face that said, "You're no help at all."

Julie chose Chelley Wright's *Jezebel*. Jeff dropped his CD in the machine next, and Abby tried not to cringe in anticipation. He sang the Eagles' *Desperado*. Abby sat forward gawking, not quite believing what she was hearing. When he finished she turned and glared at Chris.

His eyebrows lifted in surprise. "What?"

"You liar. You big fat liar." She started pummeling him. "You are in so much trouble."

Chris managed to get himself to his feet, but she kept coming at him. He backed up, trying to get out of her reach. "What did I do?" he laughed.

"You've been caught, Mr. Honesty." She dropped her voice to mimic him. "Honesty, Abby. We must have honesty in all things. We should never lie to one another." She punched him again. "Do you remember that conversation? Let me refresh your memory. It was the first day we met," hit, punch, "out on the back deck of this very house. And then you *lied*." He started running, and she was right behind him every step of the way. He laughed, and she got madder.

"What did I say? When did I lie?" He ran backwards around the living room, his hands out in front of him trying to fend off the attack.

"You lied about Jeff. You said he couldn't sing! In fact, I believe what you said was, his singing is so bad it would make my ears bleed."

Jeff folded his arms. "Okay, now I'm gonna take offense at that. Hey, Abby, want me to hold him for ya?"

"No, thanks, Jeff. I'll let you beat him up yourself when I'm done with him." Her eyes never strayed from Chris' face.

"Now, honey,"

"Don't you honey me, mister! You're in big trouble, and you know it."

He caught hold of her arms and pinned them to her sides so she couldn't move them. He looked down into her face and warned, "Abby, do you remember the last time I held you down like this?"

"Yes."

"Do you remember what happened next?"

"You threw me in the lake!"

"Before that."

"No, I don't remember anything of significance." Of course she remembered. She'd relived the moment a thousand times in memory. She could see the passion flaring in his eyes as he willed her to recall the kiss, but she refused to concede an inch.

"Looks like you need a reminder then."

"You wouldn't dare!"

Julie leaned to Jeff and asked, "Wouldn't dare what?"

"Hang tight, Jul, I think you're about to find out."

Abby saw the fire building in his eyes, but she wasn't that easy. He leaned forward and planted his lips on hers. She waited a moment, then softened, convincing him he was winning. She leaned into him, and when she opened her mouth he let go of her arms and wrapped his own around her. Now that she had him right where she wanted him, she slid her hands up his chest as though she were going to curl them around his neck. Clamping her teeth down on his tongue, she pounded on his shoulders, causing him to recoil. His holler was all the satisfaction she required.

"You bit me!" He tried to talk, his sore tongue hung out, throbbing.

Julie's eyes grew large, and she quickly slapped a hand over her mouth.

"That's right, Mozart. And you deserved it. Don't you ever, ever, lie to me again." She turned her back on him and looked at the other two. "He's all yours now, Jeff. Julie, would you like to join me in the games room?" She exited the room with dignity and poise.

"Geez, that really hurt. I think I'm bleeding."

"Good. Since she did such a fine job, I guess I don't have to beat you up now."

"Thanks, buddy."

"She's a little bundle, but she sure can stand up for herself can't she?"

"Uh-huh. Jeff, there are two ways to argue with a woman, and I promise you, neither of them works."

He went to the fridge and grabbed an ice cube to soothe his tongue before they rejoined the girls.

Now that Abby had vented her anger she was herself again, and the evening continued without further mishap until ten thirty. Julie unwittingly chose to do Darryl Worley's hit, *I Miss My Friend*, a song about someone who missed their deceased spouse.

Chris and Abby sat together on the couch with his arm draped around her. Abby hadn't heard the song before, and by the chorus the lyrics brought her a wave of grief. She turned her face into Chris' chest and softly cried. Julie started to put the microphone down when she realized her mistake, but Chris shook his head no.

"She doesn't want you to stop. These things happen," he said quietly, then whispered, "Come on, sweetheart." He gave her a small tug, and she slid onto his lap so he could hold her while she burrowed her head into his neck. He kissed her head and laid his cheek against it while he held her tightly, stroking her back.

When the song was over, she apologized to his chest. He put his finger under her chin and lifted her face. "It's all right, Abby girl." His voice was soft so only she could hear his words.

"But it's so embarrassing. Your friends—"

"They understand. They know what you've suffered this year. Why don't we go upstairs now?"

She nodded in agreement. He looked at the others and said, "We're gonna call it a night. That in no way means you should stop your fun. Do what ever you want, the sound won't bother us. I think she's had a big day."

They bade their company good night, then climbed the stairs with their arms around each other.

CHAPTER 20

Julie turned to her brother. "Well this has been a most enlightenin' day, wouldn't you say."

"I'd have to agree with you."

"Confirmed everythin' we thought didn't it?"

"Yup."

"He is so smitten it isn't even funny."

"Definitely smitten."

"I think it's mutual, in spite of her husband."

"It does look that way."

"So, what's our plan of action? You know we can't leave him to handle his own love life. He's simply not capable. Look at the way he messed up the last time we let him do it on his own. He ended up with the Beauty Queen, and we all know what a mistake that was."

"That was an all time doozey. No question about that."

"Spill your thoughts, brother dear. I'll put in some music so our voices don't carry. We don't want them to hear us arrangin' their lives for them, now do we?" She grabbed a CD and slipped it into the stereo, not caring what it was.

Upstairs, Chris lay with his eyes closed, trying to fall asleep. He had a lot of Abby running through his mind. Where would this all end? If he tried to kiss her again, would it ruin things between them? Would she want him to back off and become uncomfortable around him? Would they always stay just friends, or would she become his lover? He knew what he wanted, but trying to guess what went on in a woman's mind was something a many great men before him had puzzled over.

Startled, he felt a finger brush against his arm. He opened his eyes and saw her standing at the side of his bed in her powder blue, silk nightgown. "What's wrong, Abs?"

He heard the tears in her voice as she whispered, "I wondered if I could have my safe place."

He lifted the covers for her to slide in beside him. She lay against him to feel his warmth with her head on his shoulder. Her fingers tangled intimately into the hair on his chest, and he could feel her staggered breathing on his skin. He was grateful he had at least put on pajama bottoms tonight. His arms wound around her and held her close. After a while he felt her fingertip running up and down his arm.

"I'm sorry about earlier, Chris."

"For what?"

"Hurting you. I got carried away. I was just so startled to find that you hadn't been honest with me. I realize it's no big deal whether Jeff can sing or not. It just felt like a breach of our trust."

"I'm sorry, Abigail. You know I wasn't tryin' to hurt you. Heck, I didn't think you'd remember I said it. I didn't even remember."

"I remember everything you say. I know you wouldn't purposely hurt me. It's okay. I'm just trying to explain why I reacted so badly and embarrassed us in front of your friends. I'm ashamed of my behavior." She paused a few minutes before breaking the silence again. "Did it hurt much?"

"Yes. You have very sharp teeth, and you can bet I won't make that mistake again."

"Oh."

"Oh, what?"

"I was going to ask if you wanted me to kiss it better, but I guess I've pretty much scared you off now."

His voice deepened as he confided, "Oh, baby, I'm not that scared."

"You're not?"

"Nope."

She slid further up the bed and leaned over him. The stars outside gave enough light in the room for her to look into his eyes. "I'm sorry, Mozart," she whispered. Her fingers slid into his hair, and her mouth brushed his lips. She pulled back and looked at him again. "Enough?"

"Never." He wanted to pull her down onto him, to touch her and learn all her secrets, but he restrained himself, relinquishing control to her. He wouldn't go any further than she was willing. Her heart was still fragile, and that was more important than his needs.

"How about this then?" She set her lips back on his and gently started to nibble on his lower lip. Her tongue slid along his mouth requesting permission to enter, and he willingly gave it. He buried his fingers in her curls and marveled in the softness of them. She continued taking the initiative and lowered herself onto his chest. When she finally pulled back, he was about to take a deep breath to regain some equilibrium but she simply readjusted and came back for more. He wanted to roll her over and become the aggressor, but settled for running his fingers up and down her bare back. She kissed his eyelids, his cheeks, his neck, sucked on his earlobe, and drove him mad.

"Oh, Abby, baby."

She came back to his mouth and kissed him again. He was totally lost in her. Finally, she lay beside him, breathing heavily. A smile played about her mouth as she reveled in the moment. His scent, his taste, the pressure of his lips all left her senses reeling.

"Sweetheart, if that's makin' up, I think I'll let you beat up on me more often, cause it's definitely worth it." He took her hand while they each tried to catch their breath. As his mind floated back to earth he turned and gazed at her. "Abby, what does this mean?"

"I don't know."

"Shall we try to figure it out together?"

"Mm-hmm."

Holding her gaze, he raised her hand, still clasped in his and slowly drew each of her fingers, one at a time, into his mouth. He sucked on them, watching as her eyes fluttered closed, and she gave a small gasp. He slid his other hand across her stomach as he rolled closer to her.

He kissed her shoulders and across her neck as she tilted her head. His finger slid up her side, and he felt her shiver. He pressed his lips against hers and continued what she had started. She clutched him to her and held him as though she couldn't get close enough. She moaned into his mouth, and he couldn't take any more. He pulled away from her and flipped back to his own side of the bed.

"Chris?"

"I can't."

"I don't understand."

"Abigail, you make me crazy."

"Is that good or bad?"

"I'm not sure."

"Did I do something wrong?"

"Honey, you came to me lookin' for a safe place. But I'm just a man."

"I know that."

"No, I don't think you do. Darlin', I think you're about the most beautiful thing I've ever seen. Sometimes you just steal my breath away. I know we're comfortable bein' affectionate with each other. But this is different. This isn't just holdin' hands. I'm a man, and you're playin' with fire. I wanna make love to you, Abby."

His words began to fill a part of her heart. "Do you?"

"You know I do. But that isn't us. You're not anywhere near that. I'm not sure what to make of all this tonight."

She felt as though a bucket of cold water splashed over her, leaving her newly discovered desires, doused. Abby sat up and hugged her knees to her chin. "I don't know what to say. I'm so embarrassed." Tears burned her eyes, and she wanted to escape, saving any smidgen of pride she had left. She slipped out of the bed and started to flee to her own room.

Chris jumped out of the bed and caught her. He lifted her in his arms and carried her back to his bed, this time lying on top of her to pin her down. He saw the tears on her cheeks, glistening in the starlight. He gently kissed them away, tasting the salt on his lips. "Sweet, darlin' Abby. Please don't run away from me. You're supposed to run to me, not away from me."

She kept her eyes closed, feeling humiliated. He spread her hair out on the pillow around her. "Do you know how much I love your hair? I love how soft it is and the way it curls around my finger when I touch it. I love the way your eyes sparkle when you look at me. I love your smile because it makes me feel happy inside when I see it. Can't think of a single thing about you that doesn't excite me. I'm seduced just by bein' in the same room with you. I've been wantin' you for a long time now."

"Yeah, right. I'm so attractive you just threw me out of your bed. I know what I look like, Christopher. You don't need to lie about it. I haven't lost all the weight from the baby, and my skin isn't all firm and toned like the women you're used to."

"I didn't throw you out. I just didn't think you realized how much you had me turned on. And as for all the rest of the nonsense you're spoutin', my wife was a model, and it was like beddin' a skeleton. I don't care if you gain another fifty pounds, cuz you'll still be Abby, and you'll always be beautiful. I wanted to make love to you when you were eight months pregnant. It's the woman inside of you that attracts me. And what's that crack about the 'women I'm used to'? Do you think I just go around sleepin' with anybody? I'm not that kind of guy. I haven't been intimate with a woman for over four years, and believe me, I've had offers. The fact that I want you says a lot."

She still refused to look at him, certain he was only saying these things to assuage his guilt and bolster her self-esteem. "I'd like to go back to my own room now," she pleaded.

"You don't believe a word I'm sayin', do you?"

She shook her head no.

"Dang, honey. It wasn't three hours ago you were down there cryin' over your husband. If I made love to you now, I can promise you would regret it in the mornin', and I'd feel like hell for bein' the one who hurt you. I don't want to be a replacement for the one you really want."

"It wasn't Drew." The words came out barely more than a whisper.

He was sure he couldn't have heard correctly. "What?"

She opened her eyes, looking straight into his. "I said, it wasn't Drew."

"That's what I thought you said, but I don't understand."

"I was listening to the words, 'I miss my friend'. I was thinking of you, Mozart. I thought of how much I missed you when you were away in Nashville, how much I'll miss you when you go away again. How hard it's going to be without you there. That's why I cried. I'm going to miss you beyond anything you can imagine." Tears flooded her eyes again.

He looked down at her in wonder. "Baby, what would I ever do without you?" He rolled onto his side and pulled her with him, keeping her pressed tightly to his chest. "Darlin' Abby, my sweet girl." They stayed that way for a long time. "You okay?"

She nodded her head. "I should go back to my room and let you get some sleep."

"Please don't. I want you to stay here with me. I need you here with me. I did have another reason for sayin' no. I thought it might be painful for you. It was only a month ago you had the baby. I figured you needed more healin' time, besides which, I don't have any protection here with me. I don't want to hurt you. I'm afraid I'd get so carried away I wouldn't be as gentle with you as I'd need to be."

"Oh." She felt humbled by his caring. "Thank you."

"What about us?"

"Did you like kissing me?"

"Foolish question. I've been wantin' it forever. I never want to stop. I've told you how damned sexy you are."

"I loved kissing you. It felt right. It felt wonderful. You may be right, though. I'm probably not ready for anything more yet."

"Told ya so."

"Didn't your mama teach you that's rude to say?"

"My mama taught me a lot of things. But when I'm lookin' at somethin so beautiful, everythin' I've ever known goes out the window."

"I'm not beautiful. You're beautiful. I love looking at you. I can't believe you'd even give me the time of day."

"You really don't know, do you? Didn't he ever tell you?"

She shook her head. He flopped onto his back and stared out the skylight. "Unbelievable! I know you loved him, and I have no right to say anythin', but I could just slug the guy. How could he have somethin' as incredible as you and not be bowled over every time he looked at you? How could he not tell you every single day how exquisite you are?"

"I loved him a lot, but the fact that he's gone doesn't suddenly make him perfect or even a saint. He wasn't a romantic guy. He didn't say all the things I needed to hear, but that was Drew. He lived for sports. I can even remember one time when we were making love, and I caught him checking the hockey scores on the television. I'm not sure if one person can be everything you need. No one is perfect, and you accept that when you love someone."

Chris was shocked by her words. He turned his head to look at her. "I think you're wrong about one thing. You're more than any man could ever dream of havin'." He watched the smile that slowly spread across her face as she savored his words.

"What are you thinkin'?" He touched her. He needed to. His fingers traced along the curve of her face.

"I'm just trying to treasure this moment," she whispered. "I want to keep it in my heart forever, so I can pull it out when I'm lonely for you."

His lips were on hers, and she wrapped her arms around his neck to keep him close. They couldn't get enough of the intimacy. Somewhere in his head he heard the music the night played to him. Over and over it played on, like the kiss, on and on.

"Abby, stay with me."

"Yes."

"I don't just mean tonight. I want you to share my bed every night."

"And we won't…?"

"No. We'll stay like this, kissing and holding each other. We'll go slowly, until you're sure you're ready. I want to hold you and have you sleepin' next to me. I get so lonely for you at night."

"Not in Niagara when Jeff and Julie are with us. I'd like to be more discreet. It's one thing having people know, it's another to flaunt it in their faces."

"Tennessee?"

"Yes. Tennessee."

"I know it's too soon for you, but I'll be here when you're ready." He kissed her again, making his own commitment clear. "Things have changed tonight. I don't want to go back to last week when we were just friends. I care about you more than I ever dreamed possible, and I want you to be a part of my life every day."

"I'm going to need time."

"Take all the time you need. We'll take each day as it comes, let things progress naturally. It's worked great that way so far, and there's no rush. Just don't stop kissin' me."

She fell asleep as the first light of morning struggled to make its way into the night sky. He held her curled up next to him and knew a completeness that had escaped him for too long. He rejoiced that she'd come to him, taking the initiative to move their relationship forward–that he was free to hold her and kiss her whenever he wanted to. Kissing the back of her neck, he closed his eyes and held her snugly against him. Finding peace, he slept solidly. The Tansey nightmares were gone, never to return.

•

Jeff and Julie sat with their morning coffee on the back deck until shortly past ten o'clock, waiting in vain for their hosts to join them. Deciding to go for a walk, Jeff showed her Abby's cabin and the scene of the accident. She instantly fell in love with the little house, like Abby, preferring the cozy feeling to the larger cottage.

When they returned they heard the shower turning off upstairs, and soon Chris came downstairs, his face wearing that same giveaway smile.

Jeff looked at him speculatively. "You didn't look this happy when you went up to bed last night. So, either you're really glad to see us, or somethin' happened in the last twelve hours."

"Yes, and yes."

Julie spurred him on, "Are you gonna share?"

"Maybe."

"Forget maybe. What's happened?"

Chris grabbed a mug of coffee and stood at the counter grinning. "Want to go down and look at the cabin cruiser?"

"No."

"Yes, you do. Let's go." He led the way, and they followed down to the dock where they climbed aboard *Jim's Toy* and sat on deck chairs.

"Okay, now do we get to hear?"

"Julie, do you think I need to tell you every tiny detail of my life?"

"Yes, I manage your life."

"Very good point. Well, I guess it will be obvious that things are different."

"I'm gonna smack you if you don't quit playin' games."

"Okay. Abs came to my room last night. We talked for awhile, then we kissed for awhile, then we talked for awhile, then we kissed some more."

"Don't you dare tell me you took advantage of that poor girl."

"No, I did not! Julie, what do you take me for?"

She rolled her eyes at him. "A Lothario."

"Get off this boat. You're banned from the rest of the story."

"I'm sorry. I know you're one of the good guys in the white hats, even though you wear a black one."

"Thank you. I guess you can stay. I've told her I want us to be more than friends. She's gonna think about it, but things are definitely lookin' good. She wants us to be together too. I've asked her to sleep in my bed with me."

Julie looked at Jeff in amazement. "Well, Jeff, seems he doesn't need our help after all. He's actually gettin' it right on his own this time."

"Seems to be."

"So, you're gonna marry her."

"Whoa! I never said nothin' bout marryin' anybody. I said I want her to sleep in my bed. I told ya before. I ain't never getting' married again."

"Does she know that?"

"I never said a word about marriage. Heck, we both agreed it's gonna be awhile before she's even ready for sex. But in the meantime, she sure can kiss."

"Well, I guess it's one step at a time. At least you're admittin' you're in love."

"Quit puttin' words in my mouth, Jul. I never said that either. We just know that we're happier when we're together."

"Chris, dear brother, I feel I need to tell you somethin'."

"Yes, dear Julie?"

"You're just about the biggest jerk I've ever met. I hope she dumps you flat on your keister. That's what you deserve." She stood and left the boat, disgusted.

"Man, Jeff, what's with your sister?"

Jeff stood and frowned, "You really are an idiot." Climbing onto the dock, he left Chris alone to figure it out.

Abby came bouncing down the stairs, looking fresh in her navy Capri pants and her red and white pullover. She found Julie rinsing out a mug at the kitchen sink. "Sorry I slept so late. I don't normally do that. I seem to need more sleep since the baby, though. Guess my body's still trying to heal."

"Don't worry about it. That's what vacations are supposed to be about. Want some coffee? It's still hot."

Abby rummaged through the fridge. "No, thanks. I think I'll just have an orange." She pulled one out and started to peel it. The front door opened, and Jeff stormed in. "Morning, Jeff."

"Good mornin', Abby."

"I don't mean to pry, but is everything okay? You seem a little...agitated?"

"No problem. I'm just not talkin' to that moron."

"Neither am I," Julie added.

Abby frowned. "Oh, no. Is he in one of his irritating moods? I've seen those before."

"No, he's just a jackass," Jeff stated.

"Uh oh." Abby looked from one sibling to the other. "Is this one of those things where we have to take his guitar away again?"

Jeff and Julie burst out laughing, and Julie gave her a hug.

"What? What did I say?"

"You surely are a treasure, Abby." Jeff grinned and wrapped her in a bear hug.

CHAPTER 21

"I want to drive past the falls before we go to the hotel," Chris told her.

"Oh, Chris, the road is always jammed. Let's check into the hotel, which is a right turn…here. We can walk down to the falls. You'll see them better that way anyway. Trust me. I've done this before."

With a sigh of resignation, he bowed to her wisdom and turned into the driveway of the Radisson Hotel sitting atop of the Niagara Escarpment. A porter collected their luggage and escorted them to their room on the top floor. Using the card key, he unlocked the door for them, and they were greeted with a panoramic view of the Horseshoe Falls.

"Are you sure we're in the right room?"

"Yes, ma'am. This is Mr. Adams' room. Penthouse suite as requested."

She stared at Chris. He refused to meet her eye, so she stepped in front of him. "You ordered this room?"

"*Ssh*. Not now Abby." He thanked the porter and tipped him. The man left, and Chris turned around to find Abby standing under his nose again.

"Excuse me. Did I just see you give him a red bill?" She stood with her hands on her hips, a look of astonishment on her face.

"Abby," he tried.

"You gave him a fifty dollar tip for bringing our bags up? Let me explain the currency exchange rate to you. It's not nearly as extreme as you apparently think it is."

"Abby, you—" he tried again, but she cut him off.

"You requested this place? Not only is it the most expensive hotel in this city, but this is outrageous. Just how many rooms do we have here? This must be about a bazillion dollars a night. I thought we were getting two simple rooms."

Before he could try for a third time to answer her, Julie grabbed her by the arm and dragged her into one of the bedrooms, closing the door behind her. She sat Abby down on one of the matching wing chairs and pulled up the other to sit opposite her so their knees were almost touching.

"Abby, I'm afraid it's time you had an education. No, not a word until I'm finished. I understand your shock at seein' this place and at his tippin', but there are things you don't know."

She took Abby's hands in her own. "You've had a few wonderful months secluded on an island with a terrific man. He's been kind and gentle and basically a great guy. That's who he is. You got to meet the real man. Very few have ever gotten to know him as well as you do. He was as happy as I've ever seen him on that island, and he didn't want to leave. The fact is, he loved it because it was such a break from his real life, and he found someone genuine who treated him like a normal person.

"I just—"

Julie raised her hand to cut Abby off. "Listen, and don't talk."

Abby closed her mouth and pressed her lips tightly together between her teeth in obedience.

"Chris cares a great deal for you. He wants you to know him for the man he is, not the man everyone else wants him to be. The truth is, he's not just a songwriter. He's a very powerful man in Nashville. He's an extremely wealthy man. He's recognized everywhere he goes. It's places like this that offer him a few hours of privacy. He needs that for his sanity."

Abby tilted her head, trying to take in what Julie was telling her.

"Any other place he would probably be mobbed. He gets tired of all the publicity, but it's part of his job, so he's had to learn to cope with it. People know he's rich. What are they gonna say when it gets around that he only tipped the bellboy five bucks? It'll be in all the papers that he's a selfish skinflint.

"What he did for Trent is somethin' he's never done for anyone else before. He arranged a manager, a publicist, an agent, band auditions, a new wardrobe, new instruments, all with two phone calls, and he's payin' all the expenses for two or three years minimum. When he speaks, people listen."

Abby listened in amazement, feeling her eyes crossing as she tried to keep her attention focused on what Julie was telling her. She found it difficult to instantly assimilate all the new information. "I had no idea."

"I know. But, Abby, he's also here because he wants to give you the best.

Remember when we talked on the phone the day you two went shoppin' for the baby?"

"Yes."

"Do you remember what I told you about him only knowin' how to please people by spendin' money? It's all anyone's ever wanted from him."

"I don't want his money. I don't care if he's broke."

"That's one of the reasons you're so special to him. You've accepted him as he is and allow him a freedom he only gets with Jeff and me, and even then, we're still the business. It's going to take time, but give him a chance. In the mean time, he wants to please you the only way he knows. He wants to treat you like a princess, to give you things no one else has. It hurts him when you won't accept it."

"He's already given me the things I've wanted and needed."

"It's not enough for him."

"But—"

"If you're gonna be a part of his life, you have to accept the things that go along with it. If you don't, you'll be throwin' away a chance for happiness with the greatest guy out there."

Abby bit her lip, trying to understand. Finally, she nodded. "Thanks, Julie."

Julie began to unpack, leaving Abby to contemplate her words.

When the meaning sank in, Abby gave Julie a quick hug and went to the living room. Chris sat alone on the sofa, looking decidedly unhappy as he stared out the window at the falls. She straddled his lap so she could look him in the eye.

"I'm sorry, Christopher. I know I've embarrassed you, and I'm sorry. I didn't understand. I won't do it again, ever. I'm just not used to money. What I am used to is being happy with you. Please try to forgive me," she whispered as her lips touched his. It didn't take much encouragement for him to pull her closely against him and respond. Her arms curled over his shoulders, and she buried her head in his neck.

"I'm sorry too, honey. I should have prepared you. It's my own fault. You'll still be my Abby, won't you?"

"It's all I want. The rest doesn't matter, so long as we're together, and I have you. It's all I need."

He dipped his head and kissed her cheek. "You're my joy in this life, Abs."

"I don't ever want to hurt you. I don't want anything to come between us that would keep us apart."

In the late afternoon, they walked to the falls, stopping at the souvenir store in the Rock Table Building by the head of the falls. Julie bought herself a silver, maple leaf brooch and earrings. The men picked up tee shirts. As

Abby browsed on her own, she noticed Chris being approached by people wanting autographs. He was very pleasant and spoke with each a few minutes. She was proud of the way he treated the people who admired his work, although she was still uncertain how a songwriter became so well-known.

At the bottom of Clifton Hill the foursome found the entrance to the Maid-of-the-Mist, a boat taking people to the base of the falls. They slipped on the blue raincoats they were given, and Abby giggled, thinking they looked like a boatload of Girl Guides in all that blue. After the boat ride they walked back to the falls and decided to eat dinner at the Rock Table Restaurant where they were given a table by the window.

After placing their orders with the waitress, they talked about their plans for the following day.

"You'll be twenty-six, Abs. How do you want to spend it?" Chris asked her.

"I'd like to go to Niagara-on-the-Lake. It's a quaint little town north of here. That's where the Romance Art Gallery is."

"Sounds good to me," Julie agreed.

"Then that's what we'll do. And for your birthday dinner, I've made reservations at the Skylon Tower," Chris affirmed, admiring the sparkle in Abby's eyes.

Before leaving the restaurant, Jeff excused himself to go to the men's room and subtly nodded for Chris to accompany him.

"Julie spotted Maisie on the Maid-of-the-Mist with us today. She's here in Niagara. It's too much for coincidence. She's obviously followed us here from the island."

Alarm flashed in Chris' eyes. "I can't believe the gall of the woman. Does she really think she's gonna win me this way? She's insane." He leaned against the wall and shook his head, trying to comprehend such a personality. "Let's think on it and talk later, back at the hotel. Thanks for the heads up. I was actually startin' to relax. At this point that would be a huge mistake." He stared at the floor and rubbed his jaw as he contemplated the situation.

"No question. I think it also tends to confirm our suspicions about the identity of Abby's attacker. Looks like your theory was right."

"It sure does. Damn it, Jeff. I thought we left all this garbage behind when we left the island. Was I being naïve or just too hopeful?" His fist pounded against the wall behind him. "When I get back to the hotel, I'll call the OPP and talk to Sgt. Cavendish. I'm sure he'll be interested in this little tidbit."

"Sounds like a smart move. Listen, we're going out for the evening so you can have some time alone with Abby. Just keep your eyes open. Maisie's out there somewhere. She's watchin', she's dangerous, and she's unpredictable."

They left the restaurant, and Chris kept an alert eye on those around them.

He snugged his arm around Abby's shoulders while they walked to the railing by the falls. "I've missed bein' alone with you," he told her.

"We're hardly alone. There must be a few hundred people here."

"You know what I mean. It's been just us for so long that it's been hard havin' so little time to ourselves lately." They walked to the point where the water roared just before tumbling over the edge.

He leaned back against the railing, pulled her into his arms and kissed her passionately. "Your kisses are like a drug, darlin'. Now that I've had them, I can't get enough. I'm gonna miss you bein' beside me tonight."

"Me, too. But it's only for a few nights, and then we'll be in Nashville."

"And when we get there I'm gonna kiss you until my lips fall off," he declared.

"You're a very good planner." She smiled up at him and kissed him again, folding herself into him. When she finally pulled back, she looked into his eyes, her tone growing serious. "Chris, I want to talk to you."

"'Bout what, darlin?"

"Julie explained that you're a highly respected and very well-known man in Nashville." He looked away. With a hand on his cheek, she turned his face back to look at her. "Remember me? I'm the little nobody from Picton, Ontario, and I've always been happy with that. She told me how different your life there is from anything I've ever known. You know I don't care about all that, don't you?"

"Yeah, I do."

"I'm not saying I'll hate it. I'm saying I care about Chris, the man I met on a little island in the middle of nowhere. The rest isn't important to me." Her eyes started to tear, and she kissed him softly. "It's going to take me awhile to adjust. I'm a bit scared of it all, but I'd rather be scared and tackle it than to be without you. I'm hoping that I'll adjust well enough that you'll ask me to stay longer in Nashville."

"Stay forever. I don't want this to be a vacation. I want you to live with me. Abby, I'd give it all up if it meant keepin' you. If you can't hack it, then I don't care. We'll go spend the rest of our lives on that island or out at the ranch. Wherever you'll be happy."

"I'd give you up before I'd ever ask you to leave your music. It's a part of who you are, and you could no more give it up than you could give up breathing. I know that."

"I've done what I wanted to do. The rest is all just icin' on the cake now."

"Let's not talk about sacrifices. I'll never ask you. I only brought it up because I want you to be patient with me and guide me through, preparing me for things so I don't get scared and run. Help me understand what I'm facing."

He pulled her close and held her head against his heart. He didn't know how he got lucky enough to find her, but she was genuine, and he knew he wouldn't let her run. Her head bobbed up, and she smiled. "Hey, I've got a good idea!"

"What's that, darlin'?"

"Jeff and Julie are out of the room for awhile, so we could go back and do some serious necking," she grinned.

"I love the way your mind works, Abby girl." With her hand in his, they ran all the way back to the hotel.

Abby's birthday dawned with warm sunshine. The scenic drive to Niagara-on-the-Lake followed along the Niagara River, which flowed along at a quick pace into Lake Ontario from the bottom of a deep gorge.

Niagara-on-the-Lake was a charming little town. After they browsed through the shops on Main Street, they took their purchases back to the car and deposited them in the trunk. Then they strolled to Trisha Romance's gallery.

The gallery exceeded Abby's expectations. Many of the paintings illustrated local settings, and they recognized places they'd seen earlier that day. Abby found one in particular that she couldn't help gravitating to entitled *Bright Eyes*. It depicted a mother in her flowing nightgown in a nursery, looking out the multi-paned glass window with her baby resting on her shoulder. The little eyes were open, brightly looking around.

Abby felt the fluttering of a baby in her stomach just as Chris came up behind her and slipped his arms around her waist. Silently admitting there wasn't really a baby inside, her eyes moistened as she looked at the painting.

"I miss my Andy, Chris."

"I knew that's what you were thinkin'."

She leaned back against him and they looked at the picture together.

"Someday, Abby. Maybe we'll have one of our own."

"Maybe."

While the others rambled through the rooms admiring the artwork, he purchased *Bright Eyes,* arranging for delivery to his penthouse in Nashville to surprise her when they got home. Home. It had a new meaning now that Abby would be there.

Returning to the hotel in the early evening, Julie called the flower shop in the lobby to have rosebuds and baby's breath delivered to the room. Abby finished dressing in her new pink taffeta gown they'd bought on the way to Niagara.

Julie stood behind her as she sat in front of the mirror, and starting at Abby's forehead, twisted her hair into a French braid. Taking the flowers, she trimmed the stems short and tucked them into the braid. Little wisps of hair escaped and curled around Abby's face.

Julie wore a powder blue shift with an outer layer of chiffon that floated around her. Abby pulled her light blonde hair back into a French roll. When at last they opened the double doors of their bedroom, the men jumped to their feet.

Jeff took one look at Abby and swallowed hard. "Hey, Abby, if you have a clone, please, give me her number."

"As a matter of fact she does," Chris said. "Her name is Claire. They look alike, they walk alike, they talk alike, they think alike, and neither one can play pool. The only difference is the hair color. But I seem to recall you likin' redheads, so it works. Abby, set him up with your sister."

She laughed at the two of them.

Chris reached his hands out to take hold of hers, and his eyes opened wide in feigned astonishment. "Honey, I think you grew!"

"You've just never seen me with heels on before."

"Well, it sure makes you easier to kiss." He tried to pull her into his arms.

"Not on your life, Mr. Adams. I just put my lipstick on, and you are not going to ruin it." She leaned over and whispered in his ear, "Do I have any on my teeth?"

He laughed as she bared her teeth for approval, loving the artless candor of her personality. Taking her bare shoulders in his hands, he tipped his head to her ear and whispered back, "No."

"Good. Anyway, you can't kiss me until after dinner, and then it just all depends on what you got me for a present."

Chris looked at the others in shock. "Was I supposed to get her a present?"

She grabbed his ear and gave it a tug. "You'd better," she giggled.

When they arrived at the tower and took the elevator up, the maitre d' showed them to their table by the window. Chris sat beside Abby and took her hand in his. He wanted to touch her all the time, so proud to be with the most beautiful woman in the city that night. The pink dress emphasized the glow of her cheeks.

The waiter came to the table and explained that the restaurant revolved around the tower once an hour. It would be getting dark when they returned to this spot, and they would see the falls displayed by colored floodlights.

They started with French Onion Soup and happily bantered throughout the meal.

Before the dessert, the waiter arrived with wrapped gifts and set them in front of Abby. "How did these get here?"

"Chris had the concierge at the hotel send them over earlier."

She beamed at him. "Do you always think of everything?"

"Well, not always, but I do try."

First she opened the present from Julie. It contained volumes eight and nine of Janet Evanovich's series. "Wow, this is great. I love these books. I didn't even realize nine was out yet."

"Chris said you were both anxious to get hold of the next one in the series. While I was in the store, they were just taking number nine out of the box to stock the shelf, so I grabbed it too."

"It's wonderful, Julie. Thank you," she grinned, pleased with the gift.

Jeff's present was next. "Sorry, Abby, Chris wouldn't let me get you what I really wanted to."

"Damn right," he muttered as he rested his chin on his hand and turned away to look out the window.

"Now I'm curious. What did you want to get me?"

"Well, personally, I always like to venture into Victoria's Secret for a browse around."

"I just might have liked that."

"Over my dead body you would." Chris gave Abby a dark look.

Her eyes brightened. "Jeff, on second thought, it's probably a good thing you didn't buy me anything there."

"Damn right."

The women laughed at him. "Good thing he doesn't get jealous," Julie observed. He gave them both an irritated scowl.

Abby went ahead and opened the gift. It was a cell phone. She looked at Jeff with surprise.

"He said you don't have one, and I have a feelin' someone is gonna be wantin' to call you every five minutes when you're out of his sight."

She laughed at his reasoning and gave a sly look at the dark-haired man beside her. "Jeff, I love it. Thank you."

"Well, it was hard to pick somethin' that wasn't girl stuff."

"Victoria's Secret is girl stuff," she informed him.

"No, that's definitely guy stuff," he argued.

"Damn right, and you'd better never buy her anythin' there. And as for you, Miss Abigail, you're not supposed to like gettin' lingerie from a man unless you happen to be sleepin' with him. And if it's not me, it sure as hell better not be Jefferson."

"Do you think I should give you know who the number?" Her eyes slanted sideways toward Christopher, and the girls giggled again.

Abby read the card attached to the last package. She quickly recognized the handwriting that scrawled across the bottom, *This is as far as I'll go.* She took off the paper and opened the box. Inside was a pair of used blue jeans. She felt disappointed but tried to look pleased, thanked him for the gift, and started to put the lid back on the box.

"Abby, I think you might want to take them out of the box," Julie advised.

She set the lid back down and lifted them from the package. As she did, she saw writing in black marker on the leg. "What's this?" She could see it was a signature. She looked closer to try to read it. It looked like Kenny

Ham...

Julie filled her in, "They're Kenny Hampton's jeans. Chris bought them for you at Martina McBride's auction."

She stared at them, then she stared at him, her eyes lit with excitement. "You did this for me?" She threw her arms around his neck and kissed him. "Thank you. That is the most original present I have ever received, and I know it cost you a great deal of male pride to get it. And all of you, it was nice to get gifts that meant something to me. Each one is something I'll get a lot of pleasure from." She reached back in the box and picked the jeans up and clutched them to herself.

"Not too much I hope."

"Does that mean I can't sleep with them?" She bit her lip, knowing she was pushing his buttons. He turned away frowning and finished off his whiskey.

She tried not to laugh at his irritation and got in one last dig at his expense. "No, I won't enjoy them too much. I wouldn't want these to end up at the bottom of the lake."

CHAPTER 22

After Jeff dropped Chris and Abby off at the falls, he and Julie went back to the hotel. Chris arranged her wrap around Abby's shoulders, then stuck his hands in his pockets.

She tucked her hand in the crook of his arm as they ambled along.

"Abby, did I tell you how stunnin' you look tonight?"

"As a matter of fact, only Jeff commented on my appearance."

"I could hardly take my eyes off you all evenin'. I felt so proud, just bein' seen with you. I felt like everyone who looked at us thought 'wow that guy is so lucky to be with her'. Look around. Everyone here is pointin' at you and smilin' at how lovely you are." He leaned to kiss her forehead, letting the scent of her cologne stir his senses.

Happy that she pleased him, pleasure flowed through her. They walked in silence for a few minutes before she stopped him to ask, "Do you really want me to record something with you?"

"Yeah, I do, babe. I think we have somethin' great when we sing together."

"Okay, then. Let's do it."

His eyes searched hers. "Have you completely thought this through? I know Julie made it all sound easy, but you know there's more to it than goin' to the studio and singin'. We'll have to make guest appearances all over the place to promote it, Regis, Leno, the Today Show."

"Yes, I figured all that would be part of it. But I won't be alone, so there's no reason to be scared. I mean, you'd be with me, wouldn't you. I can't sing a duet by myself."

"All right. If you're sure it's what you want, I'll have Julie start makin' arrangements tomorrow. If you have any songs in particular you want us to do, say so, and we'll get the copyright permission." They walked a few more steps before he asked what was on his mind. "Honey, have you thought about what we spoke of last night? You know, livin' with me in Tennessee?"

"I've thought about it. I can hardly think of anything else. I think I'm still too scared to make a decision. Your life there is so different from anything I'm used to. I want to see what it's like first, before I make an absolute commitment to it. I've been through so much this year, and the changes you're suggesting are so radical for me. I'd be giving up so much. My home, my sister, my job, my friends, my whole life as I've known it."

"I realize it's askin' a lot. I just don't want you to turn around and walk back out of my life. You're too important to me."

She hugged his arm closer to her. Reaching the head of the falls they leaned against the railing to look over the edge. Now that it was getting dark the colored lights illuminated the falls.

"Well, Abby girl. I do have one more present for you."

"I think you already gave me more than enough."

"When you look at this I want you thinkin' of me, not Hampton. I just wanted to be alone with you when I gave it to you." He reached into the inside pocket of his jacket and pulled out a long, slender box.

She carefully lifted the lid and gasped. "Oh, Christopher. This is too beautiful."

"Can I put it on you?"

She handed him the box, and he lifted the diamond and sapphire tennis bracelet from it. She held out her wrist, and he put it on her. She held her arm up to the light to look at it. "It matches my necklace."

"Do you like it?"

She looked at it with tears sparkling in her eyes. "I love it. Thank you."

"You are very welcome."

"You know, you don't have to buy me things like this to keep me."

"I want to give you every beautiful thing in this world."

"This is me. Abby. You've already given me the thing I want most."

"The necklace or the bracelet?" he teased.

"Just being with you," she admitted. She lifted her eyes to see if he thought she was silly and instead found him melting at her words.

"Honey, you have me." He looked into her eyes and was blown away by the things he saw there. Emotions rose up in him, strong and overwhelming. He kissed her with all of it.

She stood still, keeping her eyes closed.

"You okay, Abs?"

"Yeah. I'm just treasuring the moment again. I know I never want to lose this one."

The next morning they packed their bags, ready to head to Nashville. Chris drove the rental car across the tarmac at the airport up to the stairs of the Gulfstream V and parked it. Needless to say, Abby was taken by surprise. She assumed they would travel on a commercial airline.

"You can't just park the car here and leave it."

"Don't worry about it, Abs." Chris tucked her small hand firmly in his and led her up the stairs into the plane.

It was beautiful inside, beyond anything she imagined. At the front of the airplane she saw a kitchen with seats for two flight attendants, one of whom was present. There was seating in the main cabin for twelve people along with a table that had large comfortable seats on either side, and a deep leather sofa that seated four. Chris towed Abby to the sofa while Jeff and Julie sat at the table beside them.

Abby looked out the window and watched the rental car pulling away from the plane. "Where's our luggage?"

"It's been stowed below. Don't worry about it. It'll get there when you do." Chris gave her hand a squeeze of assurance.

"Well, I must say this is a surprise. Looks like you went ahead and borrowed the McGarrett's plane after all, huh?"

Jeff and Julie stole furtive glances at each other, then turned away to look out the window.

Chris answered, "Somethin' like that. Do your seatbelt up, darlin'."

The plane took off on schedule with clear skies, and they expected a smooth flight. As Abby investigated all the nooks and crannies, she found a large bathroom which included a shower, and a bedroom with a queen-size bed. "Is there anything this plane doesn't have?" she asked in astonishment.

Julie piped up, "Apparently the only thing you can't get on a plane is a hot tub."

Abby's eyebrows lifted in surprise as she continued opening doors and cupboards. "That's amazing. I wonder how much something like this costs?"

"Got it second hand. Good deal. Only cost thirty-three." Julie spouted out the information without thinking.

"You mean the McGarretts spent thirty-three million on an airplane? I had no idea they had that kind of money. For that matter, I never knew airplanes cost so much. I guess people can make a lot of money in your business."

Jeff found the charade distasteful and relocated to a seat closer to the front of the plane. He flicked a switch, and the flat screen computer monitor lit up.

Abby snuggled closer to Chris on the sofa. He hooked his arm around her neck, and she lay her head on his shoulder.

"I'm glad you're with me, honey. You know, now that I'm gonna be back in Nashville there's gonna be things I should be doin', and I'm gonna resent like hell everythin' that takes me away from bein' with you."

"I don't expect you to babysit me. I'm sure I'll find things to do."

"I'm still gonna be with you as much as I can manage. I hate bein' apart."

She raised her lips to his and kissed him softly. "You're a very wonderful man, Christopher Adams. I'm not sure I deserve someone as special as you."

"You keep talkin' like that, and I might start to believe it. You wouldn't want me gettin' a big head now, would you?" He grinned, his eyes growing soft as they looked at her.

"No, I quite like it just the way it is." She lifted her hand to his head and ran her fingers through the strands, watching the way it fell into soft layers. "I love that you have enough hair for me to put my fingers in. I don't like those really short cuts that are so fashionable now."

"Are you sayin' I'm not fashionable?"

She smiled as she kissed him. "No. I'm sayin' you're pretty darn perfect. Except for the temper that goes with that little jealous streak you deny having, I still haven't found any faults."

He closed his eyes for a brief moment, and warned, "They're there, Abby. Just don't look too close."

Her hand rested on his cheek as she nestled her head back onto his shoulder. "I don't know. I think I've gotten to know you in our months together. I don't think you could carry on a charade of who you really are for all that time. The man I know is someone I like being with."

He knew the stakes were increasing, and it made him sweat inside. The closer they grew, the more she had the right to know the truth. What would she say if she knew it was his jet? What would she say if she saw him on stage with the crowds screaming? Everyone warned him he was playing a dangerous game. At first she was just a woman he might get to know for a few weeks, and he was protecting his privacy. He hadn't planned on caring so much or on taking her home with him. He hadn't planned on someone killing her baby and trying to kill her because of him. He owed her the truth, and the sooner the better.

But the more he cared, the more insecure he became. Afraid she would leave him, he wanted them bound more tightly so she wouldn't walk out.

Two limos waited at the Nashville airport. One drove Julie and Jeff to their respective homes while the other took Chris and Abby to his place.

"What's your place like?"

"I have a rather large apartment, the penthouse in fact. Nobody gets up without a key for the elevator, so it's secure. You won't have any reason to be afraid as long as you're there. The other thing is, well, it's pretty barren."

"I'm sure I'll manage. I'm rather adaptable you know, as long as people around me aren't trying to kill me."

"I was wonderin' if you'd like to help me pick out some furnishings?"

"Sure. I'll have to check my appointment book, but I'm sure I can rearrange my schedule to fit you in."

"Thanks, Abs."

"You know how it is. Sometimes I have to be kind to the little people."

He laughed and kissed her. "She's just arrived in town, and already she thinks she's a star."

"Deal with it, big boy."

The driver let them out in front of the building, and the doorman retrieved their luggage. When the elevator opened on the top floor, she stepped out onto the plushest carpet she'd ever felt. Without even thinking about it, they took their shoes off and left them with Trent's on a mat by the elevator door.

He led her into the living room, vacant except for a sofa and television. The expanse of windows covered with ivory sheers overlooked the city of Nashville. "It's a wonderful view, Chris."

"Wait 'til you see the city at night with all the city lights on." He kept hold of her hand as he showed her the other rooms.

She was surprised to see a large kitchen in what she erroneously thought of as an apartment. It led into a large dining room, easily able to seat twenty people. He showed her his office, the room Trent was using, the master suite, and the other four rooms. He planned to use one as a den, one was set up as a music room with numerous instruments stored in it. The other two still sat empty.

"I'm thinkin' one should be a guest room, and I haven't decided about the other one yet. Look, we've a laundry room right around the corner here."

"What about these two rooms next to it."

"Oh, those are the murmel-murmel." He covered his mouth with his hand trying to disguise the words.

"The what? I didn't understand you."

"Those are the servant's rooms," he admitted. "At least, that's what the floor plan calls them. Since I don't have any servants, they just sort of sit there. Do you like it?"

"This is bigger than most houses I've been in. You must have felt claustrophobic in my little cabin on the island."

"Abby, I loved that cabin. It had everythin' I needed, with the exception of a music room. I can't wait until you start thinkin' of decoratin' ideas for this place. I really want us to turn it into a home. A refuge from the world out there. Someplace I can come to and relax with you. I don't want glamorous. Just tasteful comfort."

"I think we can manage something."

"I'm thinkin' we should start with the master bedroom."

"You would."

She gave him a flirtatious smile and pulled him towards the office. "I'm going to need a notebook and a pen."

He opened a drawer in the desk to extract a pad of paper and grabbed a pen from the desktop. Taking her hand, he pulled her to his bedroom, backed her up against the bed, tossed the paper and pen over his shoulder, and leaned against her, kissing her until she fell backwards onto the bed. She giggled and kissed him back just as vigorously. They stayed a long time, investigating the interior of his room at a leisurely pace, most of the time with their eyes closed, not surfacing until they heard Trent come home.

"I can't let him see me like this!" she whispered.

"You look great to me."

"I look as though I've been tumbled. Look at my hair."

"Yeah, I love your hair."

"Christopher, would you be serious! My things are in my luggage, which is still by the elevator."

"Tell him we just woke up from a nap."

"I can't do that! He's my family!"

"Well, honey, he lives here. This is *our* room. I think he's gonna suspect somethin's up."

"Dang. I guess you're right. I just hate giving information to Trent. You never know when it's going come back to bite your butt."

"Dang?"

"Hmm. Must have picked that up from a cowboy I know."

He laughed and led her by the hand to the living room.

As soon as Trent saw her, he leaped across the room to scoop her up in his arms.

"Abby, my darling girl. It's so good to see you. It'll be great to have someone around who actually speaks the same language. These Tennesseans have a vernacular all their own, and it's hard to understand what they're saying most of the time." He pulled back and looked at her. "Hey, I don't want to insult you or anything, but you look like you just got rolled in the hay."

As her face turned beet-red, she gave Chris an *I told you so* look, and punched Trent in the arm. "Be nice to me. I'm having a bad hair day."

"Abigail, I have seen your bad hair days, and I'm telling you this isn't it. You look as though–"

"Just shut up."

He held his hands up in front of his chest defensively. "Doesn't matter to me if you're sleeping with him. I'm just glad to see you here."

She grew exasperated while Chris sat on the sofa watching it all play out and smiling at her discomfort. "I am not sleeping with him."

"Abby…" Chris warned.

"Okay, so I am sleeping with him. But it's not what you think. We aren't doing *that*. It's also none of your business for that matter." She folded her arms defiantly.

"Sure, Abby, whatever you say. You're sleeping with him, and it's totally platonic. Did I tell you about the fruit farm I just bought in Death Valley?"

She turned to Chris for help. "You could jump in any time you know."

"Sorry, Abs. I don't know too many guys who would admit they're goin' to bed with a woman and not touchin' her. It wouldn't be good for my reputation. People would start thinkin' I'm gay or somethin'." He gave her a beatific smile, and she threw a small pillow at him.

"Speak now, or I'll take the bedroom, and you'll be out here on the sofa!"

Trent grinned mockingly. "Gee, you're already being threatened with sleeping on the couch, and you're not even getting any. Seems to me like she's holding too many of the cards here. Stand up to her. We look to you as a man who knows how to handle the ladies. I'm just not seeing it here. You ought to take her back in that bedroom, and put the wench in her place."

Abby let out a squeal of indignation and took her suitcases to the bedroom.

Chris told Trent, "This is new. She's still not over Drew yet. I know she'll always love him, but he's not here with her. I am. She's tellin' the truth. We're still celibate. She's not ready yet. It's gonna be hard for her to be with a man that isn't him. In the meantime, I've made it to first base, and I'm just happy to hold there. No rush to steal second."

"You're an amazing guy. I don't know too many who could sleep with a woman every night and not even try for it. You have incredible will power."

"She's worth waitin' for."

"Yeah, I told you she was special."

Chris sat forward and spoke quietly. "Listen, don't mention all that nonsense about an engagement. She's had enough to deal with. I suppose Julie's kept you up to date."

"Yeah, Julie keeps me in the loop. She's quite a girl that Julie. I wish she'd get rid of the boyfriend. The guy is a total loser. I know he's cheating on her, but I have a feeling that with Julie, she'd kill the messenger. So I'm just minding my own business."

"Probably a smart move. Julie's a clever girl. She'll figure it out. And when she does, God help him."

Abby returned and flopped down next to Chris. "Well, Mozart, I'm unpacked, so I guess I'll stay a day or two. Trent, do you know what he did? He had the McGarretts send their plane to fly us down. He's always got something up his sleeve to surprise me."

Trent glanced at Chris. "Yeah, he's full of surprises. Hey, I think I'll go see Julie now that she's back. I was thinking Abby and I could spend some time together tomorrow so you can go into the office if you need to."

"That sounds good to me. Okay with you, Abs?"

"Sure."

"Okay. It's a date. Tomorrow we'll catch up with each other, and I'll show you around Nashville."

●

He picked up the phone. A voice on the other end asked the cost of having someone eliminated. He quoted the fee and agreed on a place to make the transaction. By that afternoon, he was ten-thousand dollars richer with another fifteen on the way upon completion. Surprised by the face in the dossier, he felt a brief moment of regret. He would be sorry to put this one down, but paid assassins didn't choose their victims. They merely carried out the assignment.

●

Trent was dressed when she emerged from the bedroom. "Come on, Abby. Lots going on in this town."

She grabbed her purse, and they set out to see the sights of Nashville. They spent a few hours in the heart of the city, and Chris only called her six times to say hello, with a few text messages in between. She pretended to be exasperated, but she was pleased.

It was five o'clock when they arrived back at the apartment. The security guard at the lobby desk stopped her. "A delivery just arrived for you a few minutes ago, Ms. Lockner."

Abby took the long slender box, thanking him with a smile. It was a flower box, obviously from Chris. When the elevator stopped at the penthouse, Trent realized he'd forgotten to pick up his newspaper and went down again.

Setting the box and her purse on the counter in the kitchen, she went to the bedroom to change her shirt, which now bore a ketchup stain from lunch, before hunting for a vase to put the flowers in. It would be just like Chris to send her flowers and not have anything to put them in. One more thing she'd probably need to put on their shopping list.

Standing in the dressing room between the closet and the powder room, she was suddenly thrown to the floor as a thunderous blast resounded. Her head banged against the counter top, and everything went black. Debris fell around her, covering her over, but she was oblivious in her world of subliminal darkness.

CHAPTER 23

Trent crossed the street to pick up a copy of Nashville's daily paper, *The Tennessean.* An explosive blast rent the air above his head, the impact throwing him off his feet and knocking him to the ground. As bricks and glass rained down around him, he looked back over his shoulder to see a gaping hole smoking in the sky where Kip's penthouse used to be.

Abby!

Terror filled his heart as he stumbled to his feet, seeking refuge from the burning rubble still falling. Searching for his cell phone, he finally managed to withdraw it from his pocket. Clutching it tightly, his shaky fingers pushed the buttons.

Sitting in his office, Kip reached across his desk and answered his phone. "Howdy."

Panic came through the line as Trent shouted to be heard above the chaos. "Kip, it's Trent. You've gotta come home." He tried to catch his breath as the horror invaded his soul. "There's been an explosion. It's a nightmare. You've gotta come."

Kip rose to his feet, feeling trepidation at Trent's words. "What exploded? Where are you? Trent, where's Abby?"

Trent couldn't hold his tears back. "The penthouse. We're at the penthouse. It's gone. It's all gone. Abby's...Abby's up there."

Kip felt his knees weaken, and he dropped back down into his chair. "Is she all right?" Please, God, let him say she's all right.

Trent's words came, stumbling and disjointed. "I don't know. Just happened. Stuff flying everywhere. All I can see is a huge hole where your place used to be. Smoke and fire. Doesn't look good."

"On my way," Kip shouted as he tossed the phone, not even bothering to hang it up. Running from his office, he hollered frantically for Julie. She stuck her head out the door, and he grabbed her as he passed by, dragging her behind him. The elevator doors were just opening as he got to them, and he shoved past people to get in, not bothering to apologize. His finger repeatedly punched the button to take them to the underground parking lot. Julie grabbed hold of his hand to stop him, demanding to know what was happening. He relayed his conversation with Trent as he frantically paced the small space

After what seemed ages, the doors finally opened again, and they spewed out into the garage, racing to get to his SUV. Kip gunned the engine, and they hurriedly navigated the streets of Nashville, running red lights, breaking city speed limits, narrowly missing several collisions, and a few times resorting to sidewalks to bypass traffic.

They could see black smoke curling in the sky, and it implanted deeper fear into both of them. Within minutes, they approached his neighborhood and found the roads blocked off by emergency personnel. He parked in the middle of the street, and the two got out and ran the rest of the way. The front of the building was a mass congestion of emergency vehicles and men in uniforms.

Kip pushed his way through the crowd, pulling Julie in his wake. A yellow police tape ran around the building to keep the curious and the press out of their way and safe from the detritus. Bits of brick and other farrago continued to fall randomly. He ducked under the tape and headed toward the officer who appeared to be in charge.

"I'm sorry, sir. You have to stay back. This area is off limits." The officer tried to shove him back to outside the roped-off area.

Kip pulled free of his grasp. "I'm not a spectator. That's my penthouse."

"I'm sorry about that, sir. But you still have to stay behind the tape."

"No. Listen to me. Someone was in my apartment when it exploded. I need to know if she's all right. Is she out? Is she safe?"

"We'll want to question you."

"I don't have any answers. I need to know if Abby's safe. Did someone get her out of there?" Frantic, his eyes searched the vicinity, continually drawing back to the burning building

"Can I have your name, sir?"

He needed answers, not stupid questions. Wasn't anyone around here thinking straight? Wasn't anyone going to save Abby? He tried to push past the officer but the man physically restrained him.

Julie pulled on Kip's arm and stepped in, taking over the role of the rational head in the midst of mass confusion, a role she was well familiar with. "This is Kip Adams. Please, we just need to know if the woman in his apartment has gotten out."

"Never mind, Julie. This guy's no help." He reached out and grabbed the arm of another officer, hoping to find someone willing to assist.

Trent saw Kip and ran to him. "Kip. I swear to God, I just left her for a few minutes."

"What the hell happened? Where is she? We've got to find her."

Trent's tears streaked down his dirt smeared cheeks. Blood made its own trail, dripping from a gash on his cheek. "We went up in the elevator, and I came back down to get a newspaper. I just got outside the front door when the explosion went off. There's been no word on Abby yet. If she dies up there, it's all my fault."

Kip stood as though rooted to the spot, aghast at the reality of what he was seeing and hearing. Finally, he came out of his stupor and spoke in a lifeless tone. "Nothin' you could do, Trent. I'm glad you weren't hurt." Spotting the fire chief, he ran to accost him for information on Abby.

Julie flew to Trent, tears clouding her vision. She threw her arms around his neck and kissed him on the mouth. "Oh, Trent, I'm so glad you're safe."

He held her tightly, shocked by her reaction. He'd never seen Julie behave as anything other than the bossy take-charge person she usually was, and certainly never with any affection for him.

"What about Abby? Have you heard anythin'?"

"Not yet. They're having difficulty accessing the penthouse. They're bringing a helicopter to let the rescue workers down from above. It's the only way they can get them in. Parts of the building are still on fire, and the walls aren't structurally safe to use ladders. They don't know the extent of the damage yet, but I don't think it would be wrong to assume I'm homeless."

"You know you can stay with me." She pulled the scarf from around her ponytail and started to mop at the blood on his face. "You're hurt."

"It's only a scratch, Jul. Don't worry." He took her in his arms and held her tightly, feeling she was the only thing real to hang onto in this tragic turn of events. She buried her face in his neck, thanking God he was still alive.

Kip joined them, grief stricken. "They don't know anythin' yet. Nobody's been able to reach her." Running his hands through his hair which was already tousled in every direction, he stared up at the building. "I can't figure what was up there that would go off like that. The place was practically empty. We didn't have anythin' that would cause somethin' of this magnitude. Did you and Abby buy anything today?"

"No, the only thing different was the flowers you sent her."

Kip turned his head sharply, his eyes seeking Trent's. "What flowers? What are you talkin' about?"

Trent returned a puzzled expression. "When we got back this afternoon a florist box had just been delivered for her. She took it up with her, assuming they were from you."

"I didn't send flowers. If the explosion was just minutes after she took possession of the box, that had to be what it was. Geez, I thought I'd gotten her away from this." Unable to bear the guilt, he balled his hands into fists and buried his face in anguish. "It's my fault. I left her again. I keep promisin' her and then lettin' her down." His shoulders shook with the sobs that wracked his chest. "What will I do if this time was successful? I love her so much. I just can't bear to lose her."

Julie hugged him in comfort, and Trent laid a supportive hand on his shoulder and squeezed.

"I love her, Julie. I never even told her, but it's true. I've loved her all along."

One of the firemen lumbered toward them. "One of you guys Adams?"

Kip leaped forward, eager for information. "I'm Adams."

"The helicopter just lowered two men down into the penthouse. They've been notified to look for your wife."

"She's not my wife. She's my…" What exactly was she? She wasn't just a friend any more, but nor was she his lover. "…girlfriend."

The man's somber expression said he didn't hold out much hope of finding her alive.

Like Kip, Trent found it impossible to maintain any semblance of composure, eaten by the very real possibility of losing her from their lives permanently. He held onto Julie tightly as memories of Abby flooded his mind. He remembered the little girl with her hair in ponytails, swinging from a tree, ice-skating on Hay Bay, and bike rides all the way to Belleville with a picnic. Abby had been a part of him his whole life, and he couldn't bear the thought of her not being there when he woke up tomorrow.

Reluctantly, they finally allowed an officer to shift them to the other side of the tape, realizing they were in the way. The policeman was kind enough to stay close by, allowing them to know immediately when any news of Abby was relayed over the radios.

The three huddled together, hoping and praying. Each radio transmission was preceded by a great deal of static They strained to listen carefully, willing the news to come, willing her to be safe. Twenty-six minutes later the suspense finally broke.

"We've located a woman on the upper floor. She's alive, but unconscious. We're airlifting her to Southern Hills."

The three clutched each other, joyful that she had been found, but didn't linger. Kip led the way as they dashed back to the SUV and fought traffic to the hospital.

After a thorough examination by a neurologist, Abby was assessed with a severe concussion, but amazingly nothing more serious. Another doctor stitched the laceration on her left arm. She was awake, but groggy and confused when Kip was finally permitted in to see her. He refused to leave her side when the Nashville PD questioned her.

As soon as the doctor released her, Kip carried her back onto the Gulfstream and headed for Wyoming.

●

In the morning Abby awakened to noises she couldn't identify outside her window and found herself in a room with pretty floral wallpaper she didn't recognize. The only thing familiar was the tall, dark-haired man sleeping in a chair next to the bed, looking haggard and uncomfortable. She reached out a hand and placed it on his leg. He startled awake instantly. Seeing her bright eyes looking at him, relief poured through him. He sat forward and took hold of her hand.

"How are you feelin', sweetheart?"

"I'm not sure. I have a headache but a couple of Tylenol should handle it. I'm pretty confused, though, about a few things. Do I have some kind of amnesia? The only thing I recognize here is you, and I don't have a clue how I came to be wherever this is. The last time I woke up like this, not knowing where I was, it was because someone tried to kill me."

She saw the sorrow in his eyes as he turned away, unable to face her. She wasn't certain why, but he seemed upset about something, and she was pretty sure she was at the center of it.

"We're in Wyomin' at the ranch. Mama helped me get you into bed last night."

Abby's glanced around the room again, wondering why and how she landed herself here. "I dreamt I was on a ride at an amusement park with colored lights flashing past."

He glanced at her briefly, then dropped his gaze again, refusing to meet her view. "You've had another head injury, but the doctor gave the okay for you to be moved, so I brought you here," he explained, holding her hand and stroking it lovingly. "I guess the colored lights you saw were on the runway."

"Okay. So that explains where I am, but I'm not certain how I got hurt again. Chris look at me. What's going on?"

He lifted his eyes to meet hers, and she saw the guilt and remorse that dwelt there. "Do you remember takin' a box of flowers up to the penthouse yesterday?"

She searched through the mists into her memory. "Vaguely. You sent me flowers, and I took them up when I got home with Trent."

"Only they weren't from me." Anger and hurt burst forth in his voice. "Dang it, Abby. I let you down again. I keep promisin' to keep you safe, and the minute I let my guard down, the minute I turn my back…"

Abby lay her hand on his cheek and turned his face toward her. "Christopher, whatever happened, I'm sure it's not your fault. Please, sweetie, talk to me."

"There was a bomb in the box, Abs." He watched the play of emotions that ran over her features and felt another wave of guilt crash over him. "I'd be so lost without you," he admitted. "I'm just glad ya weren't standin' next to it when it detonated."

"I feel like I was. Chris, I can't believe this is still happening to me." She closed her eyes and lay back into the pillows, making a valiant attempt at calm and courage. "I thought all this would end once we left the island. Who is after me? And why? Why would someone follow me all the way to Tennessee, and how did they find me there? None of this makes sense. Nothing has made sense since the day I lost Andy."

"I know, honey, and I wish I had the answers for you."

"Is there such a thing as a safe place? How can we escape when we don't even know who or what it is we're running from? I want this over, Chris. I want my life back."

"I've called my friend, Brody Ashton. He's a Deputy Sheriff here. I'm going over this afternoon to talk to him. I'll see that he gets in touch with the Nashville Police and the Provincial Police back in Ontario. We're gonna find whoever is doin' this, and put an end to it. I promise you, Abby. We won't stop until we've solved it."

Another thought occurred to her, bringing renewed panic. She leaped back up and clutched his hand tightly. "Trent! What about Trent? Is he hurt?"

"Honey, he's fine. He was outside when it went off. Got off with just a few scrapes. He's stayin' with Julie."

His reassurance made her visibly relax. "Did it do much damage to the apartment?"

He swept the hair from her forehead and let his fingers slide down her cheek. "Well, a big chunk of the penthouse isn't there any more. I'm thinkin' it's a good thing girls like to shop, because it seems you're without clothes. Maybe you and Mama wanna go into Lander and do some shoppin'. Or you could go up to Riverton. They have a Wal-Mart there. I know you like shoppin' at Wal-Mart, so I'm not even gonna suggest Bloomies or Saks."

"I'd rather give money to the people of Lander trying to make a living running a small town business. If I still need anything I can't find, I can go to Riverton for that. Maybe we can go this afternoon."

"Absolutely not. Today you are confined to bed rest. Plenty of time to shop tomorrow, if you're up to it."

"No, really, honey. I'm fine." She tried to sit too quickly, and the room started to spin. Lifting a hand to her head in an attempt to steady things, she added, "Or tomorrow might be better."

"That's what I thought. Okay, how about some breakfast? You haven't eaten for almost twenty four hours, so you must be gettin' hungry."

"Now that you mention it, I am. What must your mother think of me? She gets to see me naked before I even get a chance to say hello. You must admit, this is not the customary way to arrive as a houseguest. And I arrived a whole year early. She must have been charmed having to undress me," she groaned. "I may just pull the blankets over my head and hide. I'm so embarrassed."

"Don't be silly. She's downstairs waitin' to see how you're feelin' and welcome you. Now, enough worrying about silly things." He picked up the phone by his bed and called down to the kitchen to have breakfast brought upstairs for their patient.

Maddie arrived with a tray of pancakes and sausages. She stayed for a brief visit, but the young woman tired quickly and slept on and off most of the day.

The following morning, Abby insisted she felt much better and wanted to join them downstairs in the kitchen for breakfast.

"Mama left a robe for you. After you've had a shower you can come down for somethin' to eat." He stood and looked down at her. "Want me to help you up?" He hesitated to leave her.

"No, I'm getting used to losing my senses. It's getting to be a routine with me. The question is, how will I smack my head next week? You know the rules, no repeat performances. Seriously though, you don't need to hover. I'm sure you have better things to do."

"Nothin' as important as you. I'll be outside waitin' for ya." He bent to kiss her cheek and left the room, closing the door behind him. She went to the ensuite bathroom and looked in the mirror. The image that looked back resembled a ghost with gray hair, the dust having settled thickly on her. Luxuriating in the feel of the hot water, she lathered her head and rinsed it twice, just to be sure. Once she was dry, she put the robe on and found Chris waiting for her in the hall. Firmly gripping her hand in his, they went down the stairs.

"Mornin', Mama." He bent and kissed her, and she patted his cheek.

"Mornin', honey." She got up from her chair and opened her arms to embrace Abby. "Abby, it's nice to have you with us. I hope you're feelin' better today. You should probably just take it easy for a while. You must be hungry."

"Yes, I am."

"Make yourself at home. We don't stand on ceremony here. If you want somethin' you just help yourself."

"Thank you. It's nice of you to have me."

"You're very welcome. I've been waitin' to meet you for months."

"It was nice of the McGarrett's to let us use their plane to come out here. They've been very good to us."

"I'm sure they have." Maddie smiled, waiting until Abby turned away before giving her son a stern look of reprimand.

He led her to the table, and they sat down. Maddie brought them plates of eggs, bacon and home fries, and joined them with her cup of coffee.

"Mama, Abby needs to go shoppin'. She doesn't have any clothes."

"I'll take her into town. That's not a problem, unless she was wantin' to go to Denver to shop." Memories of Tansey lingered bitterly, but she kept her voice neutral.

"Denver? That's not even in the same state! I can't imagine wanting anything I can't get in town. I just need some basic things. Some jeans and a few shirts. That shouldn't be too difficult to find. Wait a minute. Do I have a purse? What am I going to use for money?"

"I'll give you one of my credit cards." He took her fingers in his and gave them a gentle squeeze.

Abby frowned and thought about it. "Only on the condition that I pay you back every penny."

Maddie looked pleased, and Chris winked at his mother. "She's different, Mama."

"You'll probably want a bathing suit, too, Abby. Chris built a pool out back, and on a hot day it's nice to have."

"Oh, I don't know. I don't think—"

"Mama, tell Abby how great she looks. She's worried she doesn't look good after the baby."

"Land sakes, you look just fine. And even if you don't feel it, it's just us in the back yard. Not like you'll be paradin' around in front of the whole town."

"I was thinkin' that if you ladies go on into town this morning, when you get back I could take Abs for a picnic up in the hills and show her our spread. Think you're up to it, Abby girl?"

"I would love that, if it fits in with your schedule, Maddie," she amended.

"It sounds fine to me. You kids go and have a good time. Somethin' you want us to pick up at the store while we're in town?"

"Yeah, maybe a helmet for Abby. She keeps gettin' her head knocked around. I'm afraid if she keeps it up, she'll do permanent damage."

"And I'd still be smarter than you, Mozart," she teased.

"Yes, you would. That's what worries me." He walked to the back door where he put his boots on. "I'm goin' out to the stables. Come here, Abs."

She got up from the table and went to him. He lifted her in his arms and kissed her tenderly, then leaned his forehead against hers. "You hurry back. I'll be missin' ya." Setting her back on her feet, he turned to his mother. "Later, Mama." He opened the door and left.

"Well, I've waited a lot of years for that!" Maddie exclaimed.

"For what?"

"To see my son kiss a woman like that. Never saw him kiss any of the girls he brought home in high school, and then there was...well never mind about her. She was just a pillar of ice, and thank goodness she's gone, and other than that he's never brought anyone home." Maddie started clearing the table. "That's just the way his daddy used to kiss me," she remembered fondly. "Keep it up. It brings a lovely color to your cheeks. Why don't you run upstairs and get dressed while I finish up here."

Half-an-hour later she sat in the truck on her way into town with Maddie. Abby enjoyed her first glimpses of Lander. She found it a pretty town, larger than she expected, but definitely western with wide streets from the days of oxen and Conestoga wagons passing through. Maddie parked on Main Street and let Abby choose where she wanted to shop.

"Hey, that looks good. The Neat Repeats Boutique. Let's start there."

"Well, dear, that's a second hand store."

"I figured that from the name. I'll bet we can find some great bargains there."

Maddie hid her surprise and went along. Abby skimmed through the racks, finding plenty of western wear. She chose a blue gingham shirt, a plaid shirt, and two tee shirts she liked. Next they went to Wear Agains across the street, and she found two pairs of jeans and a denim mini skirt. She didn't generally wear short skirts, but it would be fun for an evening out with Chris. She also found a crazy tropical cotton sun hat that struck her fancy and a few bandanas. Nipping into the Whippy Bird, she selected some casual silk skirts and pretty blouses. She also picked up two bathing suits, some baby doll pajamas, and a small purse with a shoulder strap.

A quick trip into Shirts N More got her a sweatshirt from the University of Wyoming and a Lander tee shirt. Maddie took her to the Mountain West Sporting Goods where she was able to get cowboy boots, and running shoes. They ended their trip at the department store where she picked up a pair of cargo pants, underwear, sunglasses, and all the toiletries she needed.

Maddie enjoyed her morning with Abby, impressed by the young woman's sense of practicality and her down to earth approach. She was easy to talk to with a similar sense of humor, and Maddie understood why Chris was so taken with her. Abby was everything Tansey wasn't, and that fact alone made Maddie instantly like her.

As they drove up the lane to the ranch house, Abby searched for Chris.

"He's comin' out of the west stable, Abby."

"Hmm?" Abby blushed at being caught.

"I said, Chris is right over there. He's comin' our way, don't worry."

Abby bit her lip as she smiled. As soon as Maddie put on the brakes, she was out the door and running across the yard. Chris smiled and quickened his step, holding his arms open for her. She flew into them, wrapping her arms around his neck as he caught her and spun her around. She giggled in his ear and wrapped her legs around his waist.

"I've missed you, Abigail."

"Me too, Mozart." She kissed him and hugged him again. "I have to take my things in the house."

"I'll help you. Did you get everythin' you wanted?" He put her down, and they walked to the car with their arms around one another.

"Mm-hmm. What a pretty town, Chris. It's got a lot of great stores, and the people are so pleasant. Your mother introduced me everywhere we went. Of course I'll remember who everyone is, but it was so friendly. I got a lot of nice things. Even a pair of cowboy boots. So what do you think of that?"

"My little Abby's gonna be a cowgirl, is she?" He stopped and kissed her again. "Thanks, Abs."

"For what?"

"For bein' you. For likin' my home. For bein' here with me."

She smiled up at him and saw something in his eyes; past hurts there that still haunted him. She wanted to erase them.

"Don't need to thank me for that. It's all just natural, isn't it?" She opened the truck door and retrieved her purchases.

Maddie stopped what she was doing and stared when they came in the kitchen door. "Why are you takin' your shoes off?"

"It's a Canadian thing, Mama. You've got better things to do than to spend all day sweepin' up and washin' floors."

She gave them an odd look as they passed by. Abby led the way as they took her things upstairs.

Chris reached out and grabbed hold of her arm. "My room is back this way. You passed it, sweetie."

She turned and looked at him in horror. "You can't possibly expect me to stay with you here in your mother's house."

"I can't?"

"Don't be ridiculous. She's your mother! She'll think that we're, you know."

"So?"

"So, no!"

"Are you ashamed to be with me?"

She dropped her bags on the bed and turned to him. "Of course I'm not ashamed. How could I be? You don't really believe that, do you?" Worry creased her brow as she searched his eyes. "I think we have somethin' very special between us. It's of the ultimate importance to me. But I also have a great deal of respect for your mother. This is her home, and I'm not comfortable marching in here as though I were your wife. Give me time, but know that you make me extremely happy."

His fingers smoothed out the lines on her forehead. "Sorry, honey. I'm just bein' overly sensitive. But don't be surprised if you get a midnight visitor. I don't like bein' away from you that long."

"Now that could be interesting. Having a man sneaking discreetly into my room in the midnight hour, searching for his secret paramour. It sounds so Regency. Oooh, Mozart! You've got fantasies dancing in my head now. This could prove to be quite exciting. I've never had clandestine meetings before."

"Want to have one right now?" he teased.

"I thought we were going on a picnic."

"You just love to build the anticipation, don't you? Okay. Show me what you bought." He sat on the bed as she displayed her purchases before putting them away in the dresser.

She shooed him out the door while she put on her new old jeans with the blue gingham shirt. She rolled the sleeves to a three quarter length and tied the bottom edges in a knot at her waist. With her new hat on her head and her cowboy boots in her hand, she went out in the hall and modeled for his approval.

"What do you call that?" He looked at the hat in a disturbed manner.

"It's my hat. You don't want me to get sunburned do you?"

"And you bought that today?"

"It's great isn't it?"

"Abby it's orange, lime green and pink."

"Yeah." She looked quite pleased with herself. "Well, I had to get a hat, didn't I?"

"Honey, that garish thing doesn't qualify as a hat. It's not exactly a Stetson, is it?"

"Of course it's a hat. I think you're jealous I didn't get you one just like it!"

"No, jealous isn't the first emotion that crossed my mind. Are you really gonna wear that thing? Maybe you could get a refund."

"I like my hat! If you don't like it I can always stay home. Maybe I'll find someone else who has good taste to take me out and show me around."

"Okay. Wear the silly thing if it makes you happy."

"Thank you. I will."

He smiled and dropped an arm around her shoulders as they went downstairs. In the kitchen he picked up the bags with the picnic food and took her out to the stable, where a chestnut stallion stood saddled and ready.

"Who's your friend?"

"His name is Nevada. I was going through a phase that year, naming all the new colts after Western States. We also have Montana, Colorado, Utah, Arizona and Idaho." He tied the bags on the back of the horse and led him into the sunlight. "I thought we could ride together this time. Later, after a few lessons, you can take your own horse." He gave her a foot up to the saddle before climbing up behind her. "You can hold onto his mane, but I have a feelin' you'll be happier with the horn, won't you?"

She grinned at him over her shoulder.

"That's what I thought," he said. "Now the nice thing about this is that I get to have my arms around you."

"I like that part. You're going to be my own knight in shining armor, aren't you?"

He kissed her neck and murmured in her ear, "Would you like that?"

She leaned back against him and nodded affirmatively. He directed the horse across the plains toward the mountains. Nevada broke into a smooth canter, and Chris nabbed Abby's hat, tossing it back over his shoulder. She loved the feeling of the wind whipping through her hair and the freedom of the run, and laughed out loud.

"I love this, but you owe me a new hat!"

He curved his arm around her waist a little more tightly.

CHAPTER 24

When they started climbing up the Wind River Mountains Chris slowed Nevada to a walk so he could pick his way over the rocky ledges. As they neared the top a whole new vista opened before Abby's eyes. He took her to a gently sloping grassy area overlooking the river running through the canyon below. She was so taken with the beauty of the area, she neglected to notice him bring the horse to a stand still. He dismounted and took the picnic bags off the back, then reached up and put his hands around Abby's waist, lifting her down beside him.

"It's just the way you said it would be. Back at the cottage I envisioned it to be like this."

"Do you like it?" He stood behind her and slid his arms around her waist. She rested her hands on his arms and leaned back into him.

"Oh, Chris, it's beautiful. It must be hard to leave it when you have to go away. It's easy to see why you love it so much. I'm glad you brought me."

"I'm glad you came."

"I'm not sure I had a whole lot of say in it this time, but I hope you'll bring me again someday. The mountains are so powerful. I'm definitely a mountain girl. I knew I would be. Just being here, it's so peaceful and relaxing, isn't it?"

His heart thumped wildly as he listened to her. She understood his home

215

and the things he loved. She was sharing them with him. Tansey never came up here. She refused to get near the dirty creature they'd ridden today. She criticized everything he loved and couldn't wait to leave. Abby was different.

She thought of the first time they discussed his home. How he talked of bringing her here one day, along with the baby. "There's just one thing missing."

"I know. We should have Andrea here with us."

"How did you know I was thinking of her?"

"Because I was. She was a part of our dream. Did you think I'd forget?" He tightened his hold on her. "I miss her, too."

They lingered a few moments more before he pulled away and took her hand. They unpacked the picnic lunch, and he uncorked a bottle of white wine. They talked and laughed as they ate. When she finished, Abby lay back in the grass and closed her eyes.

"Sleepy?"

"No. I just want to hear the sounds. You're right. It is different. The sights, the smells, everything."

"Could you be happy here, Abs?"

"I could be happy never leaving this spot. Just build me a house right here."

He smiled at her answer and lay down next to her, taking her hand in his. "If you stayed right here and never left, you'd miss the secrets of the other mountains. Each one is different in some way, each with its own personality. I want to introduce you to all of them. Well, at least the ones on my property." They felt the warmth of the sun on their faces as they spoke of things important to them. They talked of childhood dreams and aspirations, things that came true and things they were glad didn't. Love grew deeper as they explored each other's musings and desires.

After hours of serious discussion, teasing, and laughter, Chris rolled onto his stomach and looked down into her face, letting a finger glide through the strands of her hair. "You're so beautiful, Abby. Someday I want to bring you to this very spot and make love to you."

"I hope that's a promise." She lifted her hand to cup his cheek then curved it around through his hair, pulling him to her mouth. The kiss was tender and brief, like a butterfly landing for a moment, then softly fluttering away. She looked deeply into his eyes. She loved his long spiky lashes, the way they framed his topaz blue eyes.

He kissed her again, this time with a passion that made her body stir with desire. She knew that as much as she wanted to be his lover, she was still not quite ready. His kisses were long and slow and teasing. She found the scent of his cologne arousing. His fingers tangled in her curls, and she loved running her fingers through his hair just as much.

"I hope that day comes soon. You make me so happy."

He kissed her again, and she wanted to stay like this always, with his mouth on her, loving her. She felt it sliding down, kissing her chin on its way to her throat. She tipped her head back as he lavished her with his caressing mouth.

He thrilled when he heard a small moan escape her lips. "Oh, honey, you make me crazy." He couldn't get enough of her. He loved the little sounds she made when they were together like this. The whimpers of desire when he kissed her, the gasps when he sucked gently on her earlobe, the sighs when he held her face in his hands to kiss her, the way she held onto him while she tried to catch her breath. All of these private things were his. When he reached his limit, he flopped onto his back, and they both lay breathing heavily.

With heads turned toward each other, they gazed at one another but didn't smile. The moment was too deep. They felt the connection between them growing in new places. Feelings she thought she would never have again. She never wanted to be out of his sight.

Chris lay looking at her. He loved her and had for a long time. He wouldn't tell her yet in those words, afraid of scaring her away, but love her he did. She gave him all the things missing in his life. A driving need to always be with her, to always be touching her possessed him. He couldn't get enough of everything about her.

He thought about moving his entire operation to Wyoming so he and Abby would never have to leave this paradise they found together. He wanted to share the rest of his life with her and knew he couldn't have it any other way. He would marry her and devote himself to making her happy.

"Darlin', there's somethin' I need to tell you."

"Okay. What is it?" She prepared for a deep discussion about something of great importance to him.

He rolled back onto his stomach and looked into her eyes with all seriousness. "Abby, that was absolutely the ugliest hat I've ever seen." He continued as her laughter erupted. "I mean it, Abs. It was downright hideous. In fact I think I'll put a few hundred cattle in that pasture tomorrow so they can tromp all over it until there's nothin' left of it."

More peals of laughter filled the air. "But I need a hat."

"I'll buy you a hat. I'll buy you a hundred hats. But I won't have you walkin' around lookin' like a rejected Hawaiian tourist."

When she regained her composure she took his face in her hands and smiled at him. "I adore you, Christopher Adams."

●

CHRISTOPHER

True to his word, a few days later, Chris drove the truck into town and found a parking spot in front of the Mountain West Gifts and Sporting Goods. Taking Abby by the hand, he led her inside. "Now, this is where you buy a hat in this town. You didn't get that atrocity here, did ya?"

"No."

"Well, we're just gonna fix that little mistake."

"I liked my hat."

"I don't believe you. You always have such impeccable taste. You're with me, aren't ya?"

"Yeah, but you're not conceited are you?"

He stopped walking and turned to her. "You're gettin' sass-mouthed again. I know how to take care of that." He bent down and kissed her sweetly. "Now come on."

She followed in his wake as he took her to the hat section. The salesgirl measured her head, and while she sat on a stool in front of the mirror, Chris started plopping hats on her, trying various styles and colors.

"Tell me. When am I ever going to wear a hat like this in Picton? Are you anticipating they'll have a rodeo day sometime in the next forty years?"

He balanced a tan hat on her head and studied the reflection before shaking his head and taking it off again. "I'm anticipatin' you spendin' a lot of time at the ranch with me."

"You have some plans I don't know about?"

"Yup. Abs, what color do you like?" He studied the rows of Stetson's on the wall.

"What about that ivory colored one?"

He picked it up and placed it on her head. "That's it. That's the right one. Now, Abigail, this is a hat! Take a good look. I don't want to see one of those fruity things on your head again."

"I think you're getting to be a bossy britches."

"Kiss me."

"No."

"Kiss me."

"There are a dozen people watching us. I'm not going to kiss you here."

"Kiss me, Abby." He put his hands on her waist and lifted her until her face was level with his. She gave him a quick peck. "Kiss me, Abby." She saw the playfulness leave his eyes, so she took hold of his face and kissed him properly.

He set her back on the floor and took hold of her hand, tugging her to the front of the store.

"Wait a minute. We didn't even check the price tag."

"Doesn't matter. That's your hat."

"Of course, it matters." She pulled her hand from his grasp and took the hat off. Looking at the tag stopped her dead in her tracks. "Oh, no you don't. We are not buying this hat."

"Yes, we are. Let's go."

"No. I absolutely refuse to spend almost four hundred dollars, and that's in U.S. currency by the way, on a hat. That's almost full weeks' salary. I won't do it." She stood her ground with her arms folded across her chest.

"You aren't gonna do it, I am. Now come on."

"No. Would you stop and listen to me? Stop trying to railroad me. I'm not putting up with it."

He stopped and turned to her, hands on his hips. "What exactly is the problem?"

"It's an extraordinary amount of money for a hat. Now my hat, I got for fifty cents at the thrift shop. That was reasonable."

"No, reasonable would have been if they'd paid you to take it off their hands. Honey, this is how much these kinda hats cost. It's considered a necessity out here."

"But I don't live here. I don't need something this expensive."

"Please, honey. It's an investment in our future. I want us to spend a lot of time in Wyomin', darlin'."

"Are you always going to be this difficult?"

"Only when it's somethin' this important to me."

"All right then," she conceded.

"Thanks, Abs. I owe ya for this."

"You're a big ole' softie."

"Not when I'm kissin' you I'm not," he claimed, giving her a leering grin.

"Behave yourself, cowboy. Go pay the man."

He paid for the hat, and they headed back outside. "One more stop before we grab lunch."

"Fine with me. Where to?"

"Main Street Books. I want to replace those Evanovich novels Julie bought you. We lost them in the explosion, and I can't wait to find out what trouble that Stephanie Plum is going to get herself into next."

Abby grinned, happy he was enjoying the series as much as she was. After a lengthy browse at the bookstore, they stopped at the Breadboard to pick up some lunch which they took to the park. Choosing a large spreading cottonwood, they settled under it. "These are the best subs in the world," he told her as she bit into it.

"It is good. They put a lot of filling in it."

"Mm-hmm." When they finished eating, he took the wrappers to the garbage can.

"I love your town. So, do you know everyone?"

"No. Only about eighty-five percent."

"Gee, how lonely for you."

"You're the only one who makes me not lonely, Abby girl. Knowin' people doesn't take that away. It doesn't fill the empty space."

She scooted sideways and lay her head on his lap. "I know. I understand lonely too." She reached her hand to take hold of his and tangled their fingers together playfully. "Chris, I'm really happy."

"Then I'm happy. It's all I've ever wanted for you, Abs, to have you be happy."

"It's more that. There's a contentment that goes deeper and lasts longer than happiness."

He curved his hand around the top of her head, stroking her cheek and temple and running his finger around the curve of her ear. She studied his face and thought how very beautiful he was and wondered what he possibly saw in her. They stayed that way, totally comfortable with the silence.

Suddenly she sat up and looked him straight in the eye, her face all seriousness. "It's the bubbles."

"What bubbles?"

"The little air bubbles that come up to the surface. That's what I watch for. Then I just drop my line in at that spot. That's how I catch the fish!"

He spilled over sideways with laughter. "The bubbles. You're hilarious, Abs. The bubbles."

"Well it works, doesn't it?"

"I guess it does, but leave it to you to come up with that theory. I've never met a mind quite like yours."

"I know. Doesn't it make you feel sad for the rest of them?" she grinned, and he laughed more. She playfully slapped at him, and he hooked an arm around her neck and kissed her before plunking her hat on her head and pulling it down over her eyes.

Their playtime was interrupted. "Hello there, Christopher. Nice to see you back in town."

"Hi, Mrs. Beadermeier."

Abby felt him stiffen to attention and sat up beside him as he made the introductions.

"Abby, this is my fourth grade teacher, Mrs. Beadermeier."

"Hello, it's nice to meet you," she smiled.

"This is my friend, Abby. She's here visitin' from up near Toronto."

"Well, Chris, I see you still don't say what it is you mean. From what I saw she's more than just a friend, but you look happy, and that's what counts. By the way, the school is havin' it's fundraisin' carnival tonight. I'll expect to see you there."

"Yes, ma'am, we'll be there," he answered crisply.

"Good. The children need new text books. We're still usin' the same ones

we had when you went to school, so you can see how old they are. We're forever taping things back together."

Abby had mischief on her mind. "You know there have been so many
changes in geography over these last few years, I'll bet you could use some
new updated atlases, couldn't you, Mrs. Beadermeier?"

"Oh land sakes, that's somethin' on the wish list we won't see for another
ten years."

"Christopher, the children need new atlases at the school." Abby looked
at him with too much innocence. "You wouldn't want your kids to have to use
old outdated books, would you?"

"I don't have any kids."

"That's not the point. If you had them, you wouldn't want them using
outdated materials. Would you?"

"No, Abigail. I wouldn't want that."

"Mrs. Beadermeier, how many atlases do you think the school needs?"

"Oh, I'd say about two hundred and fifty."

"Well now, that doesn't seem like too much at all does it, Chris?"

"No, I guess it doesn't, Abigail." He gave her a brilliant smile and turned
to his former teacher. "Mrs. Beadermeier, how 'bout I just buy those atlases
for the school. You go ahead and order them. Let me know how much it's
gonna be, and I'll have a check for you."

"Thank you, young Christopher. You always were one of my favorites.
I'll be seein' you later tonight."

"I'll be looking forward to it," Abby told her. Mrs. Beadermeier continued on her way across the park, and Abby turned back to Chris. "That was a
very nice thing you just did."

"No, Abby girl, that was a very nice thing you just did."

"Did you mind terribly?"

"Course not. You know I'd do anythin' to make you happy. I just have a
funny feelin' that one day I'll live to regret tellin' you that." He tugged her
back down on his lap. "Boy, that Mrs. Beadermeier. She sure is a goin' concern. I don't think we ever got away with anythin' around her. She's a pretty
sharp tack. Well, it seems we're stuck goin' to the school carnival tonight. If I
don't show up, she'll never let me forget it."

"Oh, it sounds like fun."

"I love your optimism."

Abby twirled her new hat on her finger when the tag inside caught her
eye. She scrutinized it more closely. "So, Mozart, this is the real thing, huh?
An authentic western cowboy hat!"

"It sure is."

"Well, gee, I don't want to burst your bubble, but this was made in
Guelph, Ontario. Just a few hours from my home. Boy, you sure do know

221

your stuff. I sure can trust you for a taste of the real west all right."

The park rang with joyous laughter when he tickled her. They stayed for the rest of the afternoon while he pushed her on the swing and twirled her on the round about. When he noticed the evening traffic, if it could be called traffic, he suggested they go to the school.

A crowd was already gathering when they arrived. Holding hands, they immersed themselves in the fun and games. Cotton candy stuck to her fingers and chin. Chris laughed at her mess, as she tried to feed him a wad of pink fluff. "I think if we kissed now our lips could be stuck together forever," she giggled.

"Good! C'mere." He kissed her, then guided her toward to the ferris wheel. "Let's go on, Abs. I'll take you to the top of the world."

"I don't think so."

"Come on. We don't get a lot of rides at this thing, and this is the best one here."

"I can't."

"Why not?"

She dipped her head low and murmured.

Unable to decipher a single word, he crooked a finger under her chin and tipped her face back up. "What was that, Abby?"

"I said, I would be scared."

"Abigail Lockner. I don't believe it. You stood on the top of a mountain the other day. You weren't afraid of heights then."

"I didn't feel like I was going to fall off the mountain, now did I?"

"How would I know? You didn't tell me how you were feelin'." He leaned closer with words for her ears alone. "You made some real cute noises, though."

She bit her bottom lip as she elbowed him in the stomach. "You are being a naughty little cowboy, and I'm going to have to find Mrs. Beadermeier and tell on you."

"Okay, I'll quit. But I still want you to come on with me. How 'bout if I sing to you all the way around? Let's strike a deal."

"All right. If I go on the ferris wheel, you go back out, and find my hat you threw away."

"Come on. Make it something realistic. Heck, I think a bison saw that hat and puked all over it. You don't want it now." He felt an elbow digging into his side again.

"You are so mean. All right, if I go on with you, you have to invite Kenny Hampton to come out to meet me."

"Okay, we'll forget about the ferris wheel."

"But I thought you wanted to go on."

"Not that badly."

"Still not jealous though, right?"

"Don't be absurd. I don't get jealous." He took a few steps away to speak to some old friends and hopefully avoid the subject altogether. Abby stood behind him and started writing words on his back with her finger. It drove him crazy trying to figure out what she was doing and keep track of the conversation at the same time. Cutting his visit short, he reached behind and grabbed hold of her hand, tugging her in front of him. She gave him the most beguiling smile he'd ever seen.

"Want to go on the ferris wheel?" she offered.

"Maybe I do. What's it gonna cost me?" He set his hands on her waist and played along.

"I'll stay on it for as long as you want in return for a game of pool!"

"I suppose, of course, you're referring to your crazy Beaver Billiards." He made a face as though it was a tough decision. "I don't know. I think the pot needs sweetening. Every time I sink a ball, you have to kiss me." He grinned at the prospect that played in his mind. It provided great incentive to sink those seventy-five balls in two hours.

"Hmm. I don't know about that. Sounds like you're getting all the pleasure out of the deal."

He pulled her closer, still holding her. "Are you sayin' you don't enjoy my kisses, young lady?"

She looked thoughtful and answered slowly, "I don't know. I may have had better. Maybe I need reminding."

"I'd say you do. Of course, I wouldn't want to get any cotton candy in my hair. Then again, I could just take you into the shower with me to wash it out."

She thought he had the sexiest smile she'd ever seen, and at the moment his suggestions sounded pretty good. "Hmm. I guess we'll just have to take our chances, won't we?" She stood on tiptoe and reached her mouth up to his. He lifted his hand to cup the back of her head and pull her closer. His kiss was warm and sweet and gently inviting.

When she returned to her feet, she kept her eyes focused on his. "I think I'm dizzy."

"Good. Come on." He led her to the ferris wheel, and they got on. He promised not to rock it, and she leaned against him. "Sing with me."

They rode around and around, quietly singing together.

"I'm having a very good time, Mozart."

"You are a good time, Abby girl. You're the best time I've ever had."

She lay her head on his shoulder and sighed. The world kept spinning round and round, and she didn't care if she never got off. Life was bliss.

●

Maisie picked Daisy up from work and they headed to a nearby restaurant for dinner. "Hey, I read in the paper that she lost the baby. That was kind of sad. I mean I hate her and everything, but still, that's not something you wish on your enemy. Did you find out what happened?" Daisy asked.

"No. I have no idea. When I went back to the island after Fan Fair no one was there. Abby and her sister came two days later, and she wasn't prego any more."

"That must have been horrible for her. What about Kip? How did he take the news?"

"He put on a good show in front of her, but it really didn't bother him at all. Why would he care about someone else's kid? Hey, I got my quarterly deposit from my trust fund. Want to take off to Wyoming and see if he went to his ranch? We've never been out there yet."

"I could be talked into that. I'm dyin' to get some pictures of him on a horse. Just the sight of it could melt me into a puddle. I've missed looking at his body and that face that you could just die over. God knew what he was doing when that man was created. He's absolute perfection. You never know, Travolta's mother used to invite his fans to come in and spend the night. Wouldn't that be a hoot, being a guest at his ranch?"

●

Abby and Chris basked in the Wyoming summer. They spent the majority of their time on the ranch, with a side trip to see the Wind River Indian Reservation where Abby watched a pow-wow, ate dinner, and saw authentic Indian dances performed by the Arapaho and Shoshone people. They also backpacked mountain trails, went rock climbing, and rode the horses.

One hot and sunny afternoon, Maddie and her son sat in lounge chairs on the deck drinking iced tea while Abby swam.

"I've enjoyed her, Chris. She's a delightful surprise every day. I'll tell ya, I just about dropped over when she wanted to go clothes shoppin' at the second-hand store. She's everythin' Tansey wasn't. Don't you dare let this one get away."

"Mama, if I could keep her here on the ranch for the rest of her life, nothin' would make me happier. Just when I was sure I'd never love anyone again, there she was, thinkin' the same thing. And now look at us. I think we were meant to be together."

"So do I. I hope she's gonna be my daughter in the near future."

"It's crossed my mind."

"Don't let it cross. Grab it and hang on. If she goes, it'll be the biggest mistake you've ever made. And you'd better tell her the truth pretty soon, Mr.

Kipster, because I'm tired of your deception. It was one thing to have some-body on a vacation treat you normal. It's quite another to carry on considerin' the relationship you've got goin'. She deserves better. Do it soon." Reaching over and covering her son's hand, she gave it a squeeze. She hoped the situation didn't explode in his face. He'd suffered enough, and as for Abby, that poor child was enough to break her heart.

"I got a call from Brody Ashton this mornin', Mama."

"Brody? Was it a friendly call or business?" Brody was a deputy sheriff in Fremont County and had gone to school with Chris.

"I went to see him when we got here. Told him about the threats against Abby."

"So what did he have to say today?"

"I got some video from Julie that showed the two women at one of the concerts. Brody checked the National Crime Register and said one of the pho-tos matched up. A Stacey Fillion."

"Do I want to know why her photo was on file?"

"Brody talked to the arrestin' officer in Kentucky. Seems she was raised on a thoroughbred farm, big family money. She developed an obsession for the stable foreman, and when he got involved with another woman Stacey went ballistic. She invited the woman out for a ride one day, and only one came home. She was arrested on suspicion of murder, but they couldn't make it stick. Her father believed she was guilty though and disowned her. She lives on a trust fund her grandfather set up years ago."

"Let's hope she doesn't find her way to Lander. We'll have to keep a close eye on Abby." Maddie's brow furrowed with concern as she watched the young woman in the pool.

As the three sat around the dinner table that evening, conversation was in-terrupted when the phone rang. Chris answered it and listened briefly before addressing Abby.

"Hey, Abs, Dean says we've got a mare in labor. Wanna see a foal born?"

She was already at the door putting her boots on.

"I take it that's a yes."

She grabbed him by the hand and ran to the stable, dragging him along. "Who is it?"

"Tempest. She's the black mare."

He took her to Tempest's stall and found the mare lying on her side.

"Can I stroke her to comfort her?"

"Sure can."

She knelt alongside the horse's spine, patiently massaging its belly. An hour later two small hooves began to appear. Chris beheld the wonder on her face as she watched the birth. Soon a young colt with a coat as raven as his mothers' struggled to get on his feet.

Abby stepped closer to Chris to hug him. "That was so wonderful."

"Do you like him?"

"He's beautiful. He's perfect."

"He's yours."

"Really? He's mine?" Her eyes twinkled with delight.

"Yes, sweetheart, he's yours. What's his name?"

"Mr. Knightley."

"And this name is from…?"

"Jane Austen. I always loved Mr. Knightley."

"Well then, Mr. Knightley it is."

She hugged him tightly, then knelt to get a good look at her new baby.

"Hey, boss? Got another one on the way," Dean called.

"You've gotta be kiddin' me. Looks like this is your lucky night, Abs." He took her by the hand, and they left the new mother and babe on their own to get acquainted. Farther down the long aisle they spotted the stall door open and Dean's hat poking above the rail. The sign on the stall read *Panache*. Chris could see the mare had progressed considerably, yet two more hours of hard labor passed with no sign of birth. He knelt to check on the fetal positioning as another hard contraction came, and a nose pushed its way out.

"We've got trouble. It's not in the right position." He saw fear flash in Abby's eyes. "I'm gonna need your help with this one, Abs. Your arms are a lot smaller than mine."

"What do you want me to do?"

"Come down here to the end. See the nose comin' out first? That can't happen. You have to push the head back inside,"

"OUCH!" she flinched.

"Abby, listen to me! You have to push the head back inside, and then reach in and grab hold of the front hooves," he instructed.

"Okay, but as one who has given birth, I can't imagine anything more painful than having it shoved back in!"

Dean brought the lubricant, and Chris coated her hand and arm. With her hand wrapped around the protruding nose, she pushed it back into the birth canal, then reached deeper into the equine uterus, blindly searching for front hooves.

Another contraction hit, and she believed her arm would be squeezed off. She held her breath, wincing with pain until it let up.

"I've found one. They're tucked up under the belly. I have to get it unfurled." As she started to straighten the leg, the second began to follow. Another contraction hit, and she was once again left immobile. When it subsided she quickly yanked the hoof into place. She pulled them well into the birth canal, then withdrew her arm and left the rest to nature.

Minutes later a palomino colt joined the world. "Another boy?"

"Looks that way. What's this one's name."

"Indeed, I believe it's Mr. Darcy."

"Jane Austen again?"

"Pride and Prejudice." She knelt beside the new arrival, stroking its wet hair. "He shall be proud and noble with an aristocratic bearing, just like Mr. Darcy."

"Well, Dean, it seems we're about to start an English house of lords. Mr. Darcy, and Mr. Knightley."

"I'll get it recorded in the books." Dean told him.

"I'm gonna take Abby to the house and rub some liniment on her arm. I'll be out later to look in on them."

"Yes, sir."

Chris dropped his arm around her shoulders as they strolled back to the house, stopping to look at the stars on the way.

"I've never owned my own horse before."

"I sort of figured that, but thanks for clearin' it up." He looked down at her and smiled. She had performed brilliantly tonight.

"I love him already. He's quite grand, isn't he?"

"I suppose you'll be wantin' him eliminated from the geldin' process."

"I should think so!" she replied indignantly. "He and Mr. Darcy both are very masculine characters. Now, when Willoughby and Wickham make their appearance, you go right ahead and snip those fellas off. That will be poetic justice!"

He laughed at the sound of revenge in her voice. "I'm hopin' for a few new mares as well, ya know. They won't all be colts."

"That's fine. We'll just handle it as they come," she declared confidently.

"And what happens when we run out of Jane Austen?"

"Then we can start with Evanovich characters. Can you see naming a new baby Grandma Mazur?"

His laughter rang out in the night air.

A few days later, they drove into town to give Mrs. Beadermeier a check for the school atlases. She invited them in for lemonade and asked Abby questions about Ontario. Two hours sped quickly by, and Chris found Mrs. Beadermeier not nearly so formidable when he wasn't sitting in a little desk, and she didn't have a pointer in her hand. As they left, she and Abby embraced one other.

"I like this one, Chris. You bring her back again."

"Yes, ma'am."

He felt elated with the way she slipped into his world so easily. Everyone she met liked her immediately, and it was mutual. She fit in, both on the ranch and in Lander.

CHAPTER 25

The Shady Eagle was packed. No fliers advertised the evening's entertainment. Word of mouth effectively filled the bar to standing room only capacity, with the exception of the table directly in front of the stage. Julie sat there with her parents and two empty chairs. Jeff and Kip were on stage with the band. Wally, the bar's owner, gave their opening announce, and the hometown crowd thrilled to have their boys back. This was the bar they grew up in, where they first learned to read an audience.

Kip sat on his stool and nodded to the crowd. "It's good to be home, playin' for the people closest to my heart." Hoots and whistles cheered him on. Holding his hand up after a moment, he silenced them. "Listen, y'all know me. Most of ya watched me grow up. I'm gonna ask a favor tonight. My mama's gonna be bringin' a special friend of mine. Many of ya have already met her. Now, I know y'all are not gonna believe this, but she honestly doesn't know I'm Kip Adams. She just knows me as Chris, and I don't want her to find out quite yet. She's gettin' pretty fond of the cowboy who scribbles songs."

Smiles and giggles and a round of applause supported him. "The band is donatin' our cut from tonight to the buildin' fund for the new library addition, and I'll chip in as many new computers as they need." More applause filled the room. These were his people, and they loved him.

"We're gonna play a few that you know tonight and try a few new ones that we're lookin' at for the next CD. So sing along, have a few drinks, dance, and have fun tonight." He played the first few notes of a rousing number from their last CD, and they were on the way.

Back at the Adams' ranch, Madeline shouted down the stairs, "I'll be down in a minute, Abby. I'm almost ready." She continued to fill in the crossword, stretched out relaxed on her bed. She didn't approve of Christopher keeping his career a secret from Abigail, but after Tansey, she understood why he felt he needed to go this way. Her assignment tonight was to make sure they got to the bar late.

Forty-six down was a stumper. She checked her watch. Eight-ten. Time to go. It took exactly twenty five minutes to get to the Shady Eagle. She could hardly forget after having driven there three nights a week for four years. She never missed a single performance Chris played within a four hour driving radius.

Coming down the stairs, she noticed Abby pacing across the living room. "Shall we go now?" She picked up her purse from the table in the front hall. "Sorry, I'm not usually late, but we'll only miss the first fifteen minutes. Takes Christopher that long to get settled and over the stage fright anyway." She felt her nose growing as she spoke. Her son had never known a minute's stage fright in his life.

Abby had the grace to smile and hide her annoyance. Madeline was impressed with the young woman. She liked her. Really liked her. She just hoped her son knew what he was doing.

An excess of vehicles forced them to park three blocks from the Shady Eagle. Getting through the front door presented a challenge of its own. Maddie took Abby by the hand and squirmed through the crush to the table Julie kept reserved.

Abby leaned close to Julie and shouted in her ear, "Have we missed much?" Julie shook her head no. She pointed to the stage, then held up two fingers, indicating this was their second song.

Abby raised her eyes to the stage in front of her, and there sat Chris. His Wrangler's were much tighter than usual, and she swallowed. He smiled down at her and winked. She sat mesmerized. She knew he was good, but she'd never heard him with the full band backup except for the karaoke machine, and it was different. He was incredible.

Leaning closer to Maddie, she declared, "I think he should record for himself instead of writing songs for other people. He's too good."

Maddie smiled and nodded in agreement, suppressing the urge to throttle her son. Maybe she would have their foreman, Dean, take him out and horse whip him. She resented the position his deception put her in.

Eight more songs came and went. Abby recognized *Solitude* and clapped ecstatically. It was a wonderful evening, one of many since coming to Wyo-

229

ming. Chris' home and family provided everything he promised, making her feel welcome and instantly comfortable.

"I'd like y'all to meet a very special friend of mine. This is Abby Lockner. She's visitin' out at the ranch with us all the way from Ontario, Canada. Everybody, say howdy to Abby." Chris pointed to her and the whole place hollered howdy. She pasted a smile on her shocked face, half stood, and gave a general wave to the room with a resolve to shoot him when they got home. Her embarrassment evaporated as she realized he grew up with these people. A small town where everyone knew everyone. It was only natural that he wanted people to know her.

"We have a game we like to play. Come on up here with me, Abs."

She gawked at him, aghast, and shook her head no, in no uncertain terms.

"Hey, everybody, let's get her up here." Everyone clapped and urged her to the stage. Julie took her by the arm and pulled her from the chair.

"Go on up, Abby. It's just fun, not like it's gonna cost him a career or anythin'. Just do it like you did that night at the cottage."

Reluctantly, she stepped up onto the stage.

"See, as much as I'm country, Abby here is rock and pop, so we challenge each other. I do the rock, and she tries to come up with somethin' country." He turned to her and said, "Let's make it a round of four, okay? Give the band the names of your songs. Remember, no cheatin'. You can't have done them before."

She stood with her hands on her hips, smiling at the crowd and leaned closer to inform him, "You're gonna pay for this." She told Jeff what her four songs would be.

He put on a headset microphone, attaching the battery pack to the back of his jeans and handed her the mike from the stand. They sat on stools next to each other, her cheeks a bright pink.

The music started up behind them, and Abby led off with Kenny Hampton's *It Don't Come Easy*. It was a favorite, and soon most of the bar sang the chorus with her. Chris stood with his arms folded and frowning, to which she sweetly smiled. He followed with Rod Stewart's *Maggie May*. Abby did a very sassy Shania Twain's *Any Man of Mine*, and he came back with the Hollies' *Long Cool Woman*. Her voice showcased in Martina McBride's *Where Would You Be?*. Her strong clear soprano brought the crowd to their feet with an overwhelming applause, and she stuck her tongue out at him. He reciprocated by making everyone laugh as he did the falsetto required to sound like the Bee Gees in *Nights On Broadway*. Her final choice was *Lovin' You Like I Do* by Kip Adams.

Chris stood frozen to the spot, unable to twitch a muscle. Did she know? Where in the heck did she learn that song? She seemed perfectly at ease and not expecting any reaction from him. He gathered his wits and made a face at the audience which said, "Oops, I might be in trouble now!" Everyone went from shocked silence to giggles.

Abby didn't know understand why was everyone snickering, and her confidence faltered. Had she gotten the words wrong? Attempting to keep a small modicum of dignity, she finished her final number, and people clapped, but he didn't immediately follow this time. She looked at him questioningly.

"Y'all know I've had a pretty rough year." He dropped an arm around her shoulders and pulled her to his side. "Well, Abby not only helped me through it, she turned it into one of the greatest years of my life, even though she has a horrid habit of singin' Kenny Hampton songs all the time. I've been wrackin' my brain to find the words to write her a song tellin' her how I feel, and over time I'll probably write her a thousand of them, but I realized yesterday when I walked into the den and she was listenin' to music that the words have already been written better than I ever could. "Abby, this is for you."

The piano tinkled the opening notes as they sat back down on their stools, and he sang her favorite song, *Lady*.

So, he felt it too. And now it was here, out in the open. She felt tears burn her eyes and trickle down her cheeks. Unable to pull herself out of his eyes, he held her captive as his heart told hers he was scared too, but he couldn't deny his feelings for her any longer.

When the song ended, there was silence. No one applauded. No one breathed. Oblivious to the crowd around them, she stood and kissed him. His arms went around her and lifted her off her feet. She marveled in being held so tightly against him, and she took the initiative to deepen the kiss. When she finally came up for air, she leaned her forehead against his and tried to catch her breath. Then the crowd cheered. Jeff gave him a slap on the back, and Julie couldn't stop grinning.

Abby returned to her seat while the crowd continued applauding. A number of songs passed, but she didn't notice, deep in her own world of thought.

Julie spoke to her, but it was difficult to be heard over the volume of the crowd. "What did ya think of him doin' that song for ya?"

She still felt overwhelmed and said so. "If he wanted to knock me on my backside he could have just come down here and shoved me."

Julie laughed.

"I don't know how I'm feeling. Did he have to let me know in front of the whole town? It was a bit embarrassing."

"That's Chris. The deepest parts of his heart are revealed through the music. It's easier for him. And I can tell you, I've never heard him dedicate songs to anyone but his mama and daddy before. Not even when he was in love with Tansey. You're the first."

"Thanks, Julie. Make me feel more messed up. I don't know what I think. I love my friend, and I don't want to lose that."

"I think you passed friends a long time ago. He never kissed me like that."

Chris addressed the crowd. "Well, folks, what do you want to hear now?"

Mrs. Beadermeier called out, "Play that nice boy Gary Allan's song about bein' *The One*."

"Okay, Mrs. Beadermeier. That's a song I always wished I'd written. Clear the way for Abby to come up here. I want to dance with her." He picked up the headset microphone and put the battery pack on again. Abby went onstage, and he extended his hand to her, pulling her into his arms. She tried to look straight ahead at his chest, but when the band started to play, and he began to sing, she couldn't stop herself from looking into his eyes.

She was familiar with the song. It was one she'd heard at the cottage. He couldn't have chosen a more appropriate piece. She saw the love shining in his eyes as they begged her to believe in him, to trust him not to rush her. The room around them disappeared and so did the microphone. It was just the two of them, dancing alone while he sang to her the feelings of his heart. He loved her, and her heart thumped wildly.

Resting his head against hers, his cheek rubbed against her hair. Warmth flooded through his body being so close to her. Her perfume filled his senses, and he didn't want to let go of her. The last notes of the guitar played, and the room slowly came back into focus. He kissed her forehead tenderly before pulling away. The crowd went crazy around them. What a show they were getting tonight!

Maddie stood when the last set finished. "I'll see you back at the house. Probably not until tomorrow. I'm goin' to bed when I get in.'

Abby looked confused. "But I'm going home with you. We came together."

"Abigail, my son just told the whole town tonight he's in love. If I adiosed you out of here, I don't think he'd forgive me. I can promise you, he has every intention of drivin' you home himself, and heaven help anyone who thinks otherwise. But listen, come outside for a few minutes."

Collecting her purse, Abby followed. They walked down the street to the corner and stopped.

"Abby, I know what you've been goin' through. Remember, I lost my own husband just a few years ago. He was my only love from the time I was a young girl. And when I had Christopher, complications prevented me from having any more, so I know about mourning for children I couldn't have. But, honey, you've got a chance at a new life. One that could make you very happy. I think you love him, too, but you feel unfaithful to Drew. You have to realize that Drew is memories. He loved you, and what you had was wonderful, but he's not your future any more.

"You have to be strong enough to build a new one. I can also tell you that if Drew loved you as much as you believe he did, he would want you to be happy. I don't believe he'd want you to spend the rest of your life alone. Happiness and fulfillment are what we want most for the people we love. Think about it. Time can work miracles. Lovin' again doesn't mean you love Drew any less. Chris understands that. Now, you get back in there before he thinks he's been abandoned. He'll be finished packin' up, and he'll be lookin' for ya."

"Thank you. I understand what you're saying. I think I needed to hear someone other than Chris say it. I'll see you in the morning. Night, Maddie."

"Goodnight, honey." Maddie patted her on the shoulder and headed for her car. Turning back, she said, "And, Abby, things may not always be as they appear, but please try to remember–my son is a good man. He doesn't do things without a valid reason. His love for you is very real. If you ever want to talk, I'm a good listener."

"What's that supposed to mean, Maddie?" She'd never heard the woman speak so cryptically before.

"Just remember, honey. Please."

"Okay." Totally puzzled by the exchange, Abby walked back to the bar, arriving as Chris closed his guitar case. Julie saw her come in and told Chris. He said goodnight to his friends and the rest of the band, shook Wally's hand, and at last made his way to her.

As he approached she turned to the doorway, and he guided her with his hand on the small of her back. They walked silently together to the Blazer. He opened her door for her and put his guitar case in the back seat. Coming around the other side, he got in beside her and put his hand over hers. She turned to him and saw his blue eyes sparkling under the streetlight. He silently waited for her to speak, to give him some kind of response. She tried to smile, but it came awkwardly.

"Can we just drive for awhile? I need some quiet time to think, if that's okay."

"Whatever you want, Abby girl." He pulled out of the parking lot, and once they cleared the town limits, he increased his speed in the direction of the ranch.

She reclined her seat and stared out at the night sky lit with thousands of stars, wondering if Drew was out there somewhere watching over her. What would he tell her now? She still loved him. She always would. But how she felt about Chris was the question she needed to answer. Was it gratitude for helping her through such a hard time? No. Their friendship was one of the closest she'd ever experienced in her life. She knew she relied on him, but it was more than that. She cared what he thought and how he felt about things. She always looked forward to seeing him. They enjoyed each other's humor. He was handsome and sexy.

How would she feel without Chris in her life? That was an easy answer. It would be empty again. She realized that he filled the spaces in her life and in her heart. When he went to Nashville on business she missed him terribly. She remembered how he reached her when no one else could. Maybe this was love, after all.

In the final analysis, she knew she couldn't be happy just being casual friends. But to love him would mean so many changes in her life. He might be willing to give her time, but in the end he would want a commitment, giving up the life she had and moving to his world. She was happy with him at the ranch, and knew she could stay here forever. Nashville she could adjust to. She wondered how his time was divided between the two.

She talked to Drew in her mind. "Drew, are you watching me? Can you believe I'm doing this? I still love you, Drew. How can I love someone else as well?" There was no answer. Drew wasn't there to talk to any more. She felt a wash of pain as it hit her again that he wasn't coming back. Ever. She turned her head away so Chris wouldn't see the tears. Was she really ready to say goodbye?

Realistically, she knew that part was over and had been for some time. Chris already gave her so much. The things Maddie said to her earlier came back. Loving him wouldn't diminish what she shared with Drew.

He drove beyond the ranch house and up into the foothills west of Lander, parking on a plateau overlooking the valley. When she became aware the truck had stopped she got out, wandering about twenty feet away. Chris got out too, but respecting her need for privacy, he leaned back against the SUV with his arms folded.

The canopy of stars twinkled over the Wind Rivers, and she inhaled deeply, aware that this was a defining moment in her life. Her breath trembled, and so did she.

"I've come to say goodbye, Drew. I couldn't say it when you left. I wasn't ready. I'm scared. I'm so scared. I didn't want you to leave me, but you did, and now I have to go on with my life. I'm sorry. I don't want to do it on my own. Chris is so special, and I do love him. Please let me go. Let me start again. I need to know it's okay with you."

A bright star shot across the sky. Abby saw it through her tears; a bittersweet moment that would stay clear in her memory for the rest of her life. Saying goodbye to one man so she could say hello to another. Drew sent his approval.

"Thank you, Drew. I'll never stop loving you."

It was time. She clasped her hands tightly together and looked at the wedding rings on her hand. Lifting them to her mouth, she softly kissed them before sliding them off her finger and slipping them into her pocket. She wiped her eyes and turned to see Chris hanging back, giving her all the time in the world.

"Chris." It came out barely a squeak. "Christopher, I need you."

Chris was spreading a blanket from the back of the Blazer on the ground so they could sit and talk. Hearing her call to him, he walked to her, took her hand and pulled her into his arms. She lay her head on his chest and silently wept a few moments. His arms held her snugly, yet tenderly. She lifted her face to look into his eyes. He wiped her tears away with his thumbs. Her eyes drifted closed, and her lips parted as she leaned closer for his kiss.

Just seeing her like this was like a dream for him. It felt like it was the first time. Maybe because this time words of love had been spoken.

"I love you, Abby," he whispered and felt his heart pound as he covered her mouth with his own. When he tasted the sweetness of her tongue, shyly touching his, he thought he would lose it. He was kissing the woman his heart loved more than any other and knew she cared for him; the real man, not the image. It was better than a dream. He would tell her the truth soon. He just needed this.

Valiantly attempting to keep one toe in reality, he was careful to give her time and not demand any more than she was willing to give.

"Chris, you're the only guy I've ever kissed. Other than Drew I mean. He's the only boy I ever dated. He's the only one I've ever been intimate with."

"Honey, it means the world to me every time you let me kiss you. You're in my heart as deep as it goes, darlin'. I'm in love with you, and I have been for a long time."

He intended to say more, but she pulled his head back down to hers. Her arms curled around his neck, and she pressed her body against him as tightly as she could. Passion flooded through her, and her knees grew weak.

He pulled himself back and took her hands in his, kissing each one. "I think I'd better take you home now while the goin's still good. Another kiss like that, and I'll lose all sense of decency here."

"I don't want to go home, Mozart."

"Abby?" Could she mean what he thought she did?

"I think I'd like that kiss."

"Abby, I mean it. Darlin', I want you so bad, but I don't want you bein' sorry after. I need it to be right for you, too."

"I've already thought it through. Are we going to go through another four months of foreplay before you make love to me? You said you wanted to do it here." She slid her hands under his shirt, lifting it over his head and dropping it on the corner of the blanket. Her hands ran up and down his chest muscles, admiring his strength and firmness. He kissed her while he undid the buttons of her blouse. It soon joined his shirt on the ground. Her fingers swept down through the hair on his stomach, and she heard him suck in his breath as her hands grasped his belt buckle.

235

"Oh, Abby, you're drivin' me wild here, girl," he groaned.

"Tell me somethin', Mozart. Is it true cowboys do it with their boots on?" He felt the zipper on his Wrangler's sliding down.

"This cowboy will do it anyway you want it, if you don't waste me before I get the chance."

"I think maybe this time we'll go with boots off." She stopped attending to him long enough to tug her own boots off while Chris made short work of removing his. Returning his hands to her, he marveled at the softness of her flesh. As the last pieces of clothing fell to the pile, he pulled her back into his arms and kissed her deeply.

"Are you sure, sweetheart?"

She stood back to give him a full view of her body. "Christopher, I'm standing here naked in front of you, offering myself to you. I'm asking you to love me."

Taking her hands in his, he realized she'd removed her wedding rings, and understood the significance. He lifted her in his arms, laying her on the blanket and stretching out alongside her. He caressed and adored her. "You're the most beautiful woman I've ever known, Abby. I want you for my own."

"Yes." Her eyes shone in the moonlight as she gazed into his, and he couldn't wait any longer for her. Entwining his fingers with hers, he made love to her, their passion building like fire as he made her his.

Abby felt the desire culminating inside of her. "Christopher, oh, Christopher." She opened her eyes and saw the stars overhead flying in every direction at once.

It completed him. She cried out his name, not Drew's. She knew who she was with. She loved him. He stayed inside of her, laying his head beside hers. "I love you so much, Abs. I want you to be with me always," he whispered.

She ran her fingers through his hair with one hand, while her other hand slowly stroked up and down his back. They smiled into each other's eyes.

"Next time we'll go spurs and all, cowboy."

"Oh, Abby." He knew he didn't have the time to get his boots on before he loved her again.

The morning sunlight crept up on the horizon.

"Wake up, dream girl," he whispered in her ear and kissed her cheek. "There's somethin' I want to share with you, sweetheart." He sat up, and she nestled in front of him with his arms snugly around her. In a moment where words would be inappropriate, the Wyoming sunrise was glorious.

She felt an internal joy she thought would never be hers again. The way he had loved her left no doubt in her mind in regards to his feelings for her, and she loved him too. His arms felt warm and secure.

With the sun well on its way, they quickly dressed, and he drove straight to the ranch house, ignoring the highway. Parking by the back door, he jumped out and ran around to open her door for her. He bent and kissed her as he pulled her out. They stopped to take their boots off by the kitchen door, and he led her upstairs to his bedroom.

"What's your Mama gonna say about me being in your room?"

"I'm a grown man, Abby, not sixteen years old. She thinks you're the best thing that's ever happened to me."

"And what do you think?"

"A smart fella knows his mama's always right."

"But are you smart?"

"Must be. I'm with you, aren't I?" He started peeling her clothes off her again. It took only minutes before they were in his bed, cuddled together.

"This is where you belong, Abby girl. Right here in my arms. I love you."

"This is where I want to stay. It's right isn't it, Mozart? Us together?"

"It's the most right thing I've ever felt."

"Can it always be this wonderful for us?"

"I don't ever want anythin' to become more important than our relationship. I plan to keep you as my top priority for the rest of my life, Abigail."

"I never thought I could feel this way. Be this happy." Her fingers lazily ran up and down his chest and stomach. "I love touching you, being so close to you."

"I wish we never had to leave this room. Think you might get bored with me?"

"Nope. Sounds like heaven. Of course if we never left this room, we'd have a lot of children running around with no one looking after them."

He kissed her head and stroked her cheek. She was everything he dreamed of and thought he could never have. He was blessed. "I want that, Abby."

"Neglected children?"

"No, babies with you. I want you to be the mother of my children."

She lay her head on his chest as tears filled her eyes. He felt the wetness and tipped her face up to look at him. "What is it, darlin'?"

"I'm treasuring the beating of your heart. It's a sacred sound."

"You can lay with your head on my heart for the rest of our lives. It's beatin' for you."

She kissed him. "Chris, please don't ever leave me. I couldn't take it. I know I couldn't."

He knew being left alone again frightened her. He also knew he never wanted to be anywhere else. He felt his passion stirring and pulled her on top of him. "I'll never leave you, Abby girl. It would break my heart."

She held his face between her hands as she kissed him. Her hair fell around him, surrounding him, and he was in her world. She loved him until he trembled in her arms, and she smiled.

CHRISTOPHER

"You make me so deliriously happy. Are you happy, too?" She kissed his cheeks and his neck.

"I've never been so happy in my entire life, and it scares me to death." His voice was rough and choked.

"Why is that, babe?" She looked down into his eyes and ran her fingers through his hair.

"Darlin', this has been the most perfect night of my life. I totally belong to you, and I've never felt so complete. It's like my whole life led me to this moment. I don't want the world to intrude. I just want this night to last forever. I'm afraid if I go to sleep I'll wake up and find it was all just a dream, and I'll be without you again."

She kissed him with her heart and moved to lay curled beside him. "Oh, sweetheart, it's been everything to me too," she whispered. "I promise you, I'm not going anywhere. I'll be right here beside you. I'll always be yours."

He wrapped his arms tightly around her, and she smiled as she drifted off to slumber.

She never saw the tear that slipped down his cheek. For the first time in his life, he felt totally loved for the man he was. He kissed the top of her head and made a firm decision. Today he would tell her the truth about his career. He wanted to marry her and have her with him eternally. Hopefully, she loved him enough to forgive him.

CHAPTER 26

An overcast sky hung over the ranch when loud pounding on the door woke Chris. He slipped out of bed without disturbing Abby and threw on his robe, ready to tell his mother to leave them alone for the rest of the day, but it wasn't Maddie on the other side of door.

The foreman stood tapping his hat against his leg. "Sorry to bother you, Chris, but we've got a problem with two mares foalin' in the south range. We need your hands."

"I'll be down in ten minutes. Wait a minute, Dean. What were they doin' way out there so close to their time? We've never done that."

"We'll discuss it when you come down."

"Right." He closed the door, and after showering off the remnants of sleep and Abby's loving, he dressed and headed downstairs.

Dean waited outside the kitchen door. Chris grabbed a mug of coffee and took it with him.

"We'll have to take the pick-up and trailer so we can bring the foals back. I hope they're someplace easily accessible. Now, how did they get way down there?"

"Nobody seems to have an answer. All our hands have been here for years. They all know the way it works. It don't make no sense. Looks like somebody did it on purpose, but I cain't figure why. Ain't nobody in these parts got a grudge against this ranch."

CHRISTOPHER

Chris thought of all the strange things that happened since his arrival in Canada. Of course, this time it had nothing to do with Abby.

Slowly coming awake, Abby realized she was alone. Feeling well loved, she lay her head on his pillow and luxuriated in the scent of him. Could life really be this good? She stretched, wondering what time it was.

During a leisurely shower, the events of the night replayed in her mind. It had been a night to remember forever, causing her heart to overflow. She survived the darkest storms of her life and found the rainbow at the end.

After pulling on jeans and a navy polo shirt, she bounced down the stairs in search of food and human company. She poured herself some coffee and nabbed a blueberry muffin from the plate on the counter. Looking out the kitchen window, she noticed Maddie's car was gone. The SUV still sat parked by the back door, but Chris was nowhere to be seen. He must be in one of the barns. Seeing the black storm clouds hanging heavily over the mountains, she figured there was no sense venturing out in it.

Wandering into the family room, she noticed the mail on the desk. An envelope addressed to her sat on top of the pile. She expected a number of items to arrive over the next few weeks, as her replacement ID trickled in. Opening it, she was pleased to find a new Visa card. Finally, access to her own finances again. She hated using Chris' money, and kept track of every penny she owed him.

Remembering Maddie mentioning one of the cupboards in the wall unit held videos, she decided it was a good way to spend a rainy day. Pulling open the door on the right hand side, she didn't comprehend what she found. In front of her eyes were numerous trophies and stacks of 8 x 10 picture frames with pictures of Chris holding the awards.

She picked up the statues and read them. People's Choice Awards, three of them, all for country entertainer of the year, Kip Adams. That was a name even she recognized, but why were they here? Was he a relative? She'd never made the connection before, even when she learned that Kip Adams song. It wasn't an unusual surname. What a talented family! Funny they never mentioned it. Nine CMA awards, seven Flameworthy's, Six ACM's, Four Grammy's, an MEV award and last but not least, an Oscar Best Original Song. All of them belonging to Kip Adams. A row of videotapes were labeled with individual performances. 'Kip at the Academy's', 'Kip at the ACM's 1997, 1998, 1999', Kip and Tansey at Miss USA 1996', 'Kip's Christmas Special 2001, Flameworthy's 2002, 2003, and so on. Another shelf held a stack of Kip Adams CD's and scrapbooks full of mementos and newspaper articles.

Abby stuck the pageant film in the machine. Her mouth fell open when Miss Tennessee, with her long blonde hair and the body of a model, introduced herself as Tansey Aubrey. That was why Jeff and Julie referred to her as the Beauty Queen! At the time, Abby thought it nothing more than a sarcastic nomenclature, but it was true.

Her mind went on tilt when they announced Kip Adams. The crowd hooted and cheered and there was Chris, her Chris, taking the stage and making it his. He sang and worked the crowd as she watched, flabbergasted.

One by one, she worked her way through each and every video, clutching the remote as she fast-forwarded to his appearances in each one. The final one was marked as this year's Flameworthy's. She stuck it into the machine and watched as he arrived and walked the red carpet. He was met first by someone from a television station. "We have Kip Adams here with us. Kip, we've been hearing you're engaged to be married. A lovely young woman from Canada named Abby. Can you tell us a bit about that?" Abby was shocked to hear herself being talked about on television and felt violated.

"Abby and I are just friends. Nothing more. I have stated before and will say it again for the record. I am never gettin' married again. The way I see it, marriage is an expensive way to get your laundry done for free."

"Okay, well you heard it yourselves, ladies, he say's he staying single. Thanks, Kip, and good luck tonight."

The next interviewer was ready. "Hi, Jan. How are you tonight. You're lookin' lovely."

"Word has reached us that you're newly engaged to a woman you met while vacationing in Canada. I notice she's not here with you tonight. Have you got a date set yet?"

"Well, Jan, those rumors have reached me too, but I can tell you that's all they are. Just rumors. There is no truth in it. The lady in question is nothin' more than a friend. I see it like this: A fella has two choices in life. He can stay single and be miserable, or get married and wish he was dead. I prefer simple misery."

"Okay. He's staying a bachelor. Thanks, Kip. Good luck tonight."

"Thanks, Jan."

Four more interviews followed. Same questions asked, more smart one liners given.

The awards ceremony got under way, and Chris came on early as a presenter. Then it jumped to Sara Evans presenting. "And the winner is…the soon to be married, Kip Adams." The crowd's mixed reaction surprised Abby. Some cheered while others gasped, disappointed. Chris hugged Sara, then turned to the podium. "Sara here was just funnin' ya about me gettin' married. That's a walk I'm not ever takin' again." Now there was a lot of cheering from the fans. "I never knew what real happiness was until I got married, by then it was too late."

The tape was recorded the night after she lost Andy. No wonder he never came. A big star didn't have time for the problems of some silly woman he

241

met on vacation. He had *important* things to attend to.

Tears burned her eyes as so many things suddenly became clear. Last night. She made love to him believing he wanted to marry her. When he said, "be with me always," she presumed he meant marriage, even though he never used the word. What was she thinking? He told her enough times he wouldn't get married again. He made it abundantly clear to the nation. Why did she think things had changed? Because her own heart turned, and she wanted to be committed to him, she assumed the same was true for him. She gave him everything he could get from a wife, and all it cost him was a few pieces of jewelry. Much cheaper than alimony. She picked up the phone and called Trent.

"Hey, Abby, good to hear from you. How's life on the ranch?"

"Trent, did you know that Chris is really Kip Adams?"

"Of course. You're the only person in the world who didn't know. Glad he finally told you. Now we can all stop pretending."

"Trent, why didn't you tell me?" Her voice shook as she struggled to maintain control.

"You know me. Always ready for a good joke. You're not mad about it, are you?"

The pain raged through her heart. "Am I mad because you betrayed me? You allowed a complete stranger to make a fool of me in front of the world. You could have told me at any time, but your loyalties were to him, not me. Then again, he is buying you a career, isn't he? It's good to know you didn't sell me out too cheaply!"

"Come on, Abby, you're making too much of this."

"Well, Trent, it just figures you'd think so. You are no longer part of my family. What you did was unspeakable, and I'll never forgive you."

Dropping the phone back onto the receiver, she lay her head down and cried. There was only one person in the world she could always count on to be in her corner. She picked up the phone and dialed again.

"Hi, Claire."

"Abby, what's wrong?"

"I've just learned something about Chris, and I've slept with him. I've betrayed Drew."

"Honey, it isn't a betrayal. You and Chris are in love. You're doing the right thing. He'll give you a wonderful life."

"I don't want a life with him. He's lied to me."

"About what?"

"About who he really is. He's Kip Adams, the country singer. He's hugely famous. Every word out of his mouth from the moment we met has been a lie. I want to come home. I can't stay here any longer. I hate him for what he's done to me. Can you believe he actually mocked the idea of being married to me, on national television! I hate him. I have to leave here."

Silence loomed on the other end.

"Are, are you still there?"

"Yes, Abby. I'm still here." Claire's tone changed from sympathetic to somber.

"Claire, I…oh no! Don't tell me you knew, too. Please don't tell me that."

"I'm sorry, Abby."

"Who the heck is this guy? He has my own family lying to me! I have no one I can trust in this whole world. Goodbye, Claire."

She hung up the phone, lost and bewildered. She returned to the couch and leafed through one of the scrapbooks while trying to figure out what to do. Her shock only elevated when she saw familiar pictures; Chris on the island. Turning to the beginning of the article, she checked the byline. Claire Rose. Abby didn't know which was worse; the agony of the betrayal or the burning anger.

She could sit here and cry, or she could leave. Taking a piece of paper and a pen from the desk, she began to write. Her chest heaved with the sobs that wracked through her, but she needed to do this. Rain battered against the windows while her tears fell on the paper, leaving the stains of her agony. The more she wrote, the angrier she grew.

She carried the letter upstairs and left it on his pillow, along with the necklace she hadn't removed since he first put it on her and the bracelet. In her bedroom down the hall, she put her wedding rings back on where they belonged, dumped her clothing into plastic shopping bags, and ran back down the stairs. Grabbing his keys and her new credit card, she slipped her shoes on at the back door and bolted out to his SUV. Soaking wet before she could get in, she started up the engine and headed for Lander.

Finding an available parking spot at the intersection she'd specified in her letter, she left the truck as promised. Raindrops mingling with tears on her cheeks, she passed motels by, knowing they would be the first places he would hunt for her, if he cared to search at all. At the far end of town, she checked into the Pronghorn Lodge using her new Visa card and offered the man at the desk one hundred dollars to stay silent about it.

"My discretion doesn't require money. We'll respect your right to privacy. I'm givin' you one of the rooms lookin' out at the Wind Rivers. That oughta help whatever's ailin' ya. Mountains are always relaxin'."

"I appreciate it very much."

"I sure hope you decide to work things out with young Christopher, though. Never saw a young fella so much in love before."

Abby looked up in surprise.

"I was at the Eagle last night."

"It isn't going to happen. I promise you, he feels nothing for me. It was all just an act for the crowd."

"Well, I'm right sorry to hear that. That kid's had a real rough go of it. We were hopin' he'd finally found some happiness. You need anythin' at all, my name's Howard Wagner." He handed her the key and watched her walk away, defeat in her shoulders. She'd been so sparkling and happy when he saw them together. He hoped Chris would find her and put that sparkle back. He knew what he'd seen. A flame like that couldn't be fabricated, even in the best Hollywood movies.

Abby locked the door and headed for the bathroom. After throwing up, she turned on the water, stripped off her wet clothes, and sat in the bottom of the tub hugging her knees under her chin. The water spilled over her while her mind ran on, forgetting she was even in the shower. Without bothering to dry herself, she went into the bedroom leaving her wet clothes strewn on the bathroom floor.

Pulling the bedding down she lay naked with just the sheet pulled over her. She thought of all the things they'd talked about through the last few months. Of all the lies he told her. Of last night. How she so willingly opened herself, body, and soul, to give every part of herself to him. Of the way he must have laughed as he claimed his prize. The humiliation of her behavior washed over her. At least no one else knew of her shame, except him. And as she would never see him again, what he knew failed to matter.

She replayed all the moments she called her treasures; the moments of extreme happiness she wanted to keep in her heart forever. The moments that were all lies now. She felt as though the clock had struck midnight, turning them all into pumpkins.

"Abby, you're so beautiful. You take my breath away. You're the most beautiful woman I've ever known. Have I told you how stunning you look?" More lies. He'd actually made her believe she was beautiful. She was Cinderella, and he was her handsome Prince Charming. Having seen Tansey, she felt like one of the ugly stepsisters. Knowing the truth, she realized how denigrating his words had been, and she felt so gullible. She'd never been treated with such cruelty in her entire life.

The only thing that mattered was having him there, thinking he cared, wanting his arms around her. Wanting his love. She'd been so needy that she didn't see the truth in front of her. She hated that she still wanted his love.

Trent's words haunted her. "Of course, Abby. You're the only person in the world who didn't know. Now, we can all stop pretending."

It stung that the people she loved all her life abandoned her to help the monster with his charade. Who could she turn to? She was alone again. No one knew her anguish when Drew died, and no one knew now. And her baby girl. He'd convinced her he cared about the baby, too, that he planned on staying a part of her life until she was grown. He knew all along it would only be a matter of months before she wised up, and it would be over.

She wondered where she could find a time machine. If she could just go back one year, everything would come out differently. She could get Drew the medical help he needed to save his life. She would have been at home, delivering a healthy little girl. It would be the life they'd planned. That day last October changed everything in her world, and nothing had been right since.

She twirled her wedding ring around her finger, glad it was back where it belonged. Drew put it there, and she never should have removed it. He'd loved her, and she loved him, and what she felt for Chris, what she *thought* she'd felt for him, was not love.

So why did it hurt so badly? What had she done so wrong in her life to deserve all of this pain? "Oh, Chris, I need you. I need you so much. Why couldn't you be real? Please hold me again, and be my safe place. I don't know how to do this without you. I want to go back to not knowing what I know now. If I just go back up the mountain, will you be there waiting for me? I so much wanted it to be true. I want the things we talked about and planned. You made me believe in life, and in love, and in you. I gave you everything I had, and it was all a joke to you. Why? Why couldn't you love me back? Why did you lie to me? I trusted you so completely."

She cried until her brain was too tired to go on, and the pain in her chest was heavy, then succumbed to sleep with the tears still wet on her cheeks.

●

It was early evening when Chris returned to the house, hanging his hat on a hook inside the back door and stripping off his wet shirt. "Hi, Mama. Where's Abby?"

"I haven't seen her. I assumed she was with you. I've only been home about twenty minutes myself."

"I've been out in the south range. Two of the mares ended up out there, and by the time we got there they were already foalin'. Couldn't move 'em until they delivered. Been out there in the storm all day. I'm gonna find Abs and put on some dry clothes." He headed toward the stairs calling out her name. Passing by the den, he glanced in the door and stopped dead in his tracks. All of his awards sat out on the table. His mothers' scrapbooks lay scattered around the room and videos cluttered the floor. Panic rose in his throat, choking him.

"Abigail! Abby!" His shouts echoed through the house.

He ran upstairs to his bedroom. As soon as he saw the necklace, he knew she was gone. He sat on the bed and picked up the note, his hand shaking as he began to read it.

CHRISTOPHER

Dear Kip:

You won! You get to shout Checkmate! You got the naïve little nobody from nowhere to play along, and you beat me. I realize in your world of fame and celebrity, you have to come up with new ways to entertain yourself. Women come too easily, and you like a challenge. I now realize that's exactly what I gave you. A young widow, grieving over the loss of a husband and child with no desire to start over, and yet you managed to seduce me into your bed. I hope it's given you the satisfaction you were after.

I applaud your skill in moving me like a pawn on your chessboard, every move, every word, all a calculated part of your game. You should get an Academy Award. Oh! Silly me! You already have one of those. Next time you should enter the 'actor in a leading role' category. I'm sure it will make a nice addition to your collection of statuary.

As for me, you've taken my life from me. You had my own family betray me. I have nowhere left to go, no one left to care about me, and nothing left for me to care about. Is this supposed to be part of the game? To reduce the fool to a cipher? Couldn't you have just stopped at hurting me? Why did you feel the need to destroy me so completely?

Keep your jewels. I don't want them, and I have no use for them in my little nobody world. Besides, I can't be bought.

You've played me as smoothly as your guitar, made me trust you, even fall in love with you. In return you gave me nothing but lies. I'm tired of your game. I'm tired of being the jester in this preposterous stunt of yours. I don't even know why I'm bothering to tell you this. It's not as though you actually care, and I think for me that will be the hardest part because I've cared so much, and I don't believe I deserve to be the only one who's left hurting.

Shame on you for your deceit. But shame on me for believing in you. Shame on me for letting you into my heart and most of all, shame on me for last night. For giving myself to you so completely. The one thing I'd only ever shared with my husband, who was worthy of it. I'll never regret anything in my life so much as I do last night. You're not the man I was in love with. He was someone special. I need to accept that someone that loving and

246

kind can't exist outside of a fantasy.

I'll cry over you today, but that is all I will allow you, because you're not deserving of my tears. I promise you that when tomorrow comes, I'll have forgotten your face. I won't remember a thing about you, not even your name—whatever it is.

Abigail Lockner

You can pick up the Blazer in town. I'll park it near Main and 4th so you can easily find it, and leave the keys under the front seat.

CHAPTER 27

He blinked back the tears that blurred his vision. "Oh, Abby, you do love me. You've finally said it. That's all I wanted. Just to know you love me as much as I love you. Please don't leave me, Abs. Please don't. I need you. Don't be sorry about last night. I love you, Abby girl." He needed to find her.

"Mama! Mama!" He thundered down the stairs, shouting all the way. "Abby's gone, Mama. She's left me. She found all the awards and videos. I have to find her and explain. I love her. I want to marry her and have babies with her. Please help me find her. She's out there thinkin' I used her; that I don't really love her." His panic and despair combined to make a broken man.

"Any ideas where she is?"

"She took my truck into Lander. Where can she go from there?"

"She can't get anywhere by plane. We don't have a train. Her only other options are to find a place to stay in town or to rent a car, in which case she could be anywhere by now."

"I'm gonna have one of the hands take me into town to pick up the SUV. I'm gonna look around and see if I can find her." He frantically paced, needing to do something.

"All right. You get goin'. I'll call the motels and the bed and breakfasts in town to see if I can find her. Take your cell phone, and keep in touch."

He ran out the door, and Maddie grabbed the phone book and methodically called all the places offering lodging, only to be told no one had seen her. She called both of the car rental agencies, but they hadn't seen her either. It seemed when Abby Lockner wanted to disappear, that is exactly what she did.

Reaching the end, she called Julie. "Hi, it's Aunt Maddie. Listen, you haven't heard from Abby today have you?…No, I'm afraid there's trouble—she found everythin', the awards, the videos, all of it. She was here alone…No, she's left him…He's pretty distraught over the whole thing…Do you think Trent may have heard from her?"

Fifteen minutes later the phone rang, and Maddie snatched it on the first ring. Julie reported Abby's conversation with Trent. He heard from her sister in Canada and told Julie about that conversation as well. They knew she wouldn't head to Nashville to be with Trent, and she felt she couldn't go back home to Claire, either. No one had any idea where she would run to.

"I'm worried about her, Aunt Maddie. She's been so good for him."

"I know. I've grown to love her while she's been here. I can't remember when I've seen him more euphoric than he is with her. I just hope she can forgive him, and they can work it out. He needs her, and I have a feelin' she needs him just as much."

In town, Chris found his SUV right where she said it would be. Since it wasn't yet dark out, he cruised up and down the main streets searching for her. He stopped in at the restaurants and showed her picture, but no one had seen her today. It was early Sunday evening, and not many lingered about. Julie called him and relayed her conversation with Trent. His heart sank further. Abby was feeling betrayed by Trent and Claire, as well as by him. She would need her safe place.

He'd promised to be that for her, to protect her heart from pain, and now because of him, pain was all she had. Emptiness and pain. He could no longer justify his deceit. He knew early on that her feelings were genuine. She had told him a thousand times she wasn't interested in money. Her values were based on honesty, and kindness, and humanity. Deception didn't sit well with her. He knew, and still he didn't tell her. No wonder she hated him. He didn't deserve her after the way he behaved.

"Please, Abby girl, where are you? I have to find you, honey, cuz I need you so bad. Just let me find you." He combed the streets until one in the morning before finally heading home.

He climbed into bed, his hand resting on the pillow which had cradled her head. He wanted to see her brown curls there, to run his fingers through them and feel their softness. He smelled the lingering scent of her perfume, and it made him long for her even more. How they'd loved last night! She'd taken him into her world, and he gave himself to her so completely, leaving himself totally vulnerable. It was the best night of his entire life, and she was somewhere regretting it. He'd told her the things of his heart, and now she believed it was all lies. When the sun began to shine through his window, he roused himself from his dampened pillow.

Throwing on his clothes, he climbed into the truck, jammed it into gear and headed to Riverton Airport. If she intended to catch the morning commuter to Denver he had to stop her. Somehow he had to find a way to convince her that he loved her.

In the face of the morning sunshine, Abby determined to follow through with the things she wrote in the letter. It was Monday, the beginning of a new week and a new life. As of today, there was no Chris Adams in her life. She went to the Lander Post Office and filled in a change of address card so the rest of her identification could be picked up from General Delivery when it arrived. Without her birth certificate and driver's license she couldn't return to Canada. She remained in limbo until they arrived.

She didn't realize she was already the talk of the town. First people talked of how Chris must be serious if he brought her home to meet his mother. People who had met Abby said what a lovely girl she was, not a bit like the last one. But the people who saw her this morning had a new page to the story. Something had obviously gone very wrong in paradise.

With her credit card in her pocket, she ventured to the Chamber of Commerce, which was housed in the old train depot, and picked up a map of the town and a listing of businesses. Walking around the block, she found a hair salon called Dashboard Hula's. The name intrigued her, and an idea formulated in her head. She backed up a few steps and stood peering in the window. A new look would be appropriate for starting a new life. She walked in with her head of chestnut curls and came out a few hours later with short blonde hair.

Wandering back to Main Street, the smells from The Gannett Grill made her hungry, and she went inside the packed restaurant, ordering a burger and fries with a sprite. Grabbing the last empty table, Abby sat down to eat. Two women came in behind her, got their orders, and scanned the room for a vacancy. The taller one, a blonde, approached and asked if they could sit with her. Knowing there were no other seats available, she consented.

The women sat and introduced themselves. "Hi. I'm Tiffany, and this is Stacey. We're in town on vacation."

"Hi. I'm Abby. I'm vacationing, too."

Stacey's head jolted at the name, and her eyes narrowed as she stared, inconspicuously nudging Tiffany. Could it be the Abby they were after? The short blonde cut made the woman appear radically different.

"Where are you from, Abby?"

"Canada. North of New York state."

"We drove up from California. Needed to get away from the big city. You know, all that smog gets to you after awhile. Tiffany suggested we come to the mountains and get some fresh air. We just arrived yesterday."

"Well, you'll like Lander. It's a lovely town. The people aren't too busy to be kind. I love the place. For awhile I even thought about living here."

They chatted a bit, none of them bringing up the subject of Kip Adams. They didn't want to be obvious, and in Abby's mood she would have asked, *Who*? Her stomach was so tied in knots she couldn't eat and just sat poking at her lunch.

"It was nice to have met you, ladies. I'm afraid I have some things to do now. Have a nice stay." Abby cleared her things off the table and left the restaurant.

Maisie and Daisy gawked at one another.

"Could you believe that? We found her right off the bat without even trying. That means he must be here in Wyoming too. If everything else falls into our laps this easily, we'll be rid of her and have him to ourselves in no time at all. What's with the hair though! That's a shocker," Daisy observed.

Back on Main Street, Abby remembered the Shady Eagle was just a few blocks away. She walked there and introduced herself to Wally at the bar. She explained about losing her ID and being stuck in town for the next month or two until the replacements arrived.

"I realize you can't legitimately hire me, but if you'll take me on I'd be willing to work strictly for tips. I waitressed while I was in university, so I know I can handle it."

"I could be interested in that."

"I'm available any time."

"How about Thursday through Saturday from seven to closin'. Course now, that would mean you'd have to miss the Friday night bingo over at the legion hall, but you could still go Sunday afternoon."

"Gee, missing the Friday bingo," she said with a straight face. "It'll be tough, but as long as I can go on Sunday's, I guess it'll be okay. I think we have a deal."

Smiling, Wally completely missed her sarcasm. "All righty then, Thursday night."

She thanked him and left feeling better about herself. At least she would have money coming to give her Visa card a bit of relief.

●

Chris sat at the airport in Riverton from the time the first passengers arrived until the plane was in the air. No Abby. He drove back to the ranch feeling desolate.

Maddie was in the kitchen when he got home. "Chris, didn't Abby lose everythin' in that explosion?"

"Yeah. She just had the clothes on her back."

"Well, son, she can't travel without money or ID, and I haven't noticed any replacement documents arrive in the mail. She got somethin' in the Saturday mail. I think it might have been a credit card, but she can't go anywhere until the rest of her papers arrive, can she? They're all being sent here to Lander."

"Which means she has to be in town somewhere."

"That's what I'm thinkin'."

"Mama, you're brilliant. I'll take Julie with me. After all, what can Abs do in Lander besides walk up and down Main Street and sit in a park? I'll find her and bring her back home."

"Just remember to be remorseful. She has every right to be angry. She's in hormonal hell after losing the baby, she's still grievin', somebody's been tryin' to kill her, and she's had all she can take. She's standin' up and sayin', 'I'm not going to take any more!'"

Christopher winced, knowing Abby was stretched to the limits emotionally. "Mama, I'm gonna be on my knees beggin' her forgiveness. I'll do whatever it takes to get her back."

He called Julie, and they drove into town together. They each took a side of Main Street and walked it, stopping in stores along the way. The display in the window at Chisholm's Jewelers caught his eye, and he went inside.

"Hello, Chris. Is there somethin' I can help you with?"

"As a matter of fact, I'm looking for Abby."

"Oh, you're back together? That's great."

"Wait a minute, Sherie. What made you think we weren't together?"

Sherie Landry could not have been more surprised. Was he the only one in town unaware his love life was in a shambles? "Whole town knows, Chris. This is Lander." She watched as his shoulders drooped in defeat. "Anythin' I can do to help?" she offered.

He looked up suddenly, a glint of hope in his eye. "Matter of fact, there just might be."

●

Abby lay on the bed, wondering how she got here from where she started. She wanted to go home and end the whole nightmare.

A knock on the door roused her, and she swiped at the tears with the back of her hand. She opened the door, and there stood Mrs. Beadermeier.

"Lands sakes, child. What have you done to that beautiful head of hair?"

"Does it look awful?" Her hand shot to touch it.

"No, it doesn't look awful. It just doesn't look like you. Can I come in for a minute?"

"Sure." Abby stepped aside and closed the door behind her. "I'm not sure how you found me, or why you're here, but if Chris sent you—"

"I haven't spoken with Christopher, dear. I've come to take you home with me."

"I don't understand."

"I want you to stay at my house. You know, I have that whole house with just myself to ramble around in it. Company would be nice."

"Oh. But why?"

"I like you. You're a delightful young lady stuck thousands of miles from home with nowhere to go, and no one to turn to. Well, that's just not so. I'm here, and I want you to come home with me. I won't stick my nose in your business, but if you want to talk, I'll be here."

Touched by the benevolence, Abby started crying again. Mrs. Beadermeier sat on the edge of the bed next to her and hugged her.

"There, there now. You're not alone any more. Let's just get you home."

Abby nodded her consent as she blew her nose and tossed her few belongings into her plastic bags. In a matter of two minutes she was ready to go.

"I need to stop at the front desk and let Howard know I'm checking out."

"No need. Howard's the one who called me. He's worried about you."

"Oh. I never expected such kindness from people I hardly know."

"This is Lander, dear. Come on now, let's go."

They drove to Mrs. Beadermeier's house on Amoretti Street, and Abby was given a bedroom where she unpacked her belongings.

"Now, I want you to call me Frances. We're going to be good friends, you and I. I felt that the first time we met and you finagled those atlases for the school. You're a smart girl. I like that."

"Thank you, Frances," she smiled weakly.

"Now, why don't you come to the kitchen with me. We need to bake cookies for the Little League's fundraiser."

"Okay."

They didn't speak about the Adams or the Claytons all evening. Abby was glad she came. Frances asked her about her parents and learned her mother suffered from a serious heart disease and lived in Arizona, where it was easier to breathe. She noticed Abby's wedding ring and asked about it. Abby told her about Drew and losing their baby just two months before. Not once did she mention Chris or how he fit into any of it. Frances didn't ask. She decided the child had experienced more sorrow in a year than most people handle in a lifetime.

When they went to bed that night, the darkness of her room enfolded her, and her heart ached for Chris. "I'm so lonely for you," she whispered. She placed her hand on the pillow beside hers, and it felt so empty. She cried herself to sleep.

CHRISTOPHER

•

The Lander Millennium Park Committee gathered in the park, and as they ate hamburgers and an assortment of salads, Frances introduced her young friend and let it be known Abby was an accountant. When appetites were satisfied and the leftovers packed away, people pulled their lawn chairs into a circle to discuss business. The group's function was to raise enough money to build an outdoor theater in the park so they could invite bands and performers of a high caliber to perform. They saw it as a way to bring commerce to town and to make the arts more accessible to the locals.

Once Abby had been filled in on previous fundraising projects, she suggested, "It makes sense to me to use the arts to raise money for the arts."

"What do you mean?"

"A play, using local talent. We could do something with the teens, and maybe get some help from the high school. If you choose the right play, it could run for a number of nights and bring in a sizable revenue. I'm sure we can get a lot of volunteer help with costuming and set building. We can probably get a volume discount for printing tickets, adverts and programs."

Eyebrows raised and heads nodded. Excited chatter arose.

Frances declared, "I think it's a brilliant idea. Theater in the Park. Let's see a show of hands. Who thinks we should produce a play?"

All hands raised, and before Abby knew what was happening, people were thanking her for heading up the project. She gave a bewildered smile.

"Well, I wasn't actually going to be in town long enough for this, but if I'm here for six weeks I might as well be here for eight. All right. I guess I'm heading up a theater production." A round of applause confirmed it. She was in it now, hook, line, and sinker.

That evening she went online and ordered thirty-five copies of the musical score to *Joseph and The Amazing Technicolor Dreamcoat*. If they were going to do a play it might as well be a musical, and this one was fun.

The following morning she walked uptown to the Lander Journal office and asked them to run an article on the project. In her mind she calculated the money they were saving on advertising. She told them about her musical background and that she would be performing a role in the play as the narrator. It was a large role requiring a flexible soprano voice. She wasn't confident an untrained voice could do it justice, although she kept that to herself.

CHAPTER 28

Chris stood leaning against the corral fence when Julie drove up. She'd seen homeless people who looked better. His hair was unwashed and uncombed, his beard a week old, and his eyes bloodshot. After days spent roaming the streets of Lander, he'd given up.

"I have news." She joined him at the fence rail, but he didn't acknowledge her.

She put her hand on his arm. "Chris, I know where she is." The words sank in slowly, and he turned to look at her. "I know where she is," she repeated.

"Abby?"

"Yes, Abby. She's stayin' at Mrs. Beadermeier's." He stared as though she spoke another language. "I was there this afternoon, Chris. Let's sit down." She led him to a bale of hay and sat next to him.

"Tell me."

"She wasn't there when I went. I had a long talk with Mrs. Beadermeier, though. She said Abby's heartbroken, and definitely still in love with you."

"Abs still loves me?"

Julie draped an arm around his shoulders as they started to shake. "Yes, she loves you. She's just so hurt. She puts on a good front durin' the day, tryin' to keep busy, but every night when she's alone, she cries."

"She's cried enough tears. She deserves to be happy."

"Well now that we know where she is, you can work at that. The impor-

255

tant thing is she's not in the bottom of a canyon somewhere. She's alive and only a few miles down the road. You have to go about this slowly, though. She's hurt, and you've taken her pride as well. In her eyes you've made a fool of her in front of the entire town."

For the first time since he found her note on his pillow, he found a small ray of hope glimmering on the horizon. Now that he knew where she was, he could put his plan in motion and win her back.

Tuesday evening a knock at the door of the Beadermeier home interrupted *Jeopardy!*

"I'll get it, Frances." Abby crossed the room and went to the door. Her heart jumped into her throat, strangling her when she saw him through the screen. She froze, staring at him.

"Is Abby here, please?"

She didn't speak, and he looked at her again.

"Abby? What have you done? Oh, Abby, not your hair." His voice filled with tears, and she felt sorrow for what she'd done. "Did I do this to you?"

Stiffening her spine, she answered, "No. As a matter of fact, I don't even remember you being there. Alicia up at Dashboard Hula's did it as I recall."

"You know what I mean."

"No. I'm afraid I don't. I don't know anything about you."

"Can we at least talk? I have a lot to apologize for."

"I really don't think there's any more to say once the truth has been told."

"Please, just come out on the porch. I have somethin' to show ya."

She heard the catch in his voice, and she hated the fact that it ripped at her. Taking a deep breath, she decided to get it over with. She knew the moment would come sooner or later, but had hoped for later. Much later. Pushing open the screen door, she went out on the porch and sat down. He pulled up a chair across from her and sat.

"I'm sorry, Abby."

"For what? You owe me nothing."

"I owe you an explanation. You're right. I wasn't completely honest."

"I thought it was a rather big thing to forget."

"I was gonna to tell ya that day. If Dean hadn't come to get me for the horses I would have been there, and I would have told ya."

"You mean you couldn't find a single moment in the previous four months to mention it?" She eyed him with disdain. "Funny, cause I can think of a hundred thousand opportunities."

He leaned forward, resting his elbows on his knees as she'd seen him do so many times before. "You have every right to be angry."

"I don't need your permission."

"I'm not tryin' to imply ya do. I'm just sayin' that I understand."

"Well so do I. I understand a lot of things." She held up her fingers and counted them off. "You lied to me. You used me. You made me the laughing stock of this town. You turned my family against me. You hurt me."

"Abby, I love you."

"Don't even. You don't know what it means. Everything you've done to me speaks volumes about what you don't know."

He reached for her hand, and his eyes begged her to forgive him as he knelt in front of her. "I love you more than I've ever loved in my entire life. I want you to marry me, Abby. Please. I need you, sweetheart." He pulled the ring box from his pocket and handed it to her.

She opened it. "Is this supposed to impress me? I would have expected something much bigger from the famous Skippy Adams. This is rather small, isn't it? Or is size relative to feelings?"

"The famous Kip Adams didn't buy the ring!"

"Oh, you've resorted to thievery as a new method of entertainment? Or did you send one of your minions to buy it for you?"

"Chris Adams went to the store right here in Lander and picked it out for the woman he loves. Abigail Lockner. She would hate a gobby ring with a stone bigger than her hand. She would hate the expense of it. She's doesn't need to compare her ring with every one else's and always come out with the biggest. She wants somethin' simple that symbolizes my promise. The important thing to Abigail is that she loves the man who loves her so desperately, not the size of the stone. The important thing to Abigail is the commitment. I love you, Abby girl. Please don't turn me away. Say you'll marry me, and stay with me forever."

"You lied to me. I can't trust you. I don't even know who you are."

"But you do know me. The rest is all a facade. It's not real. It's not who I am. You know me better than anyone, Abs."

"No. You didn't trust me with the truth. It's been a lie. All of it."

"Do you remember the night you were reading that Hampton CD? Do you remember what you said?"

"Of course. I said he was hot with a really great butt, and you got mad about Oklahoma being a nice place to visit."

"That's not the part I mean. Do you remember when you said, 'How does a guy like that find a girl who will love him for himself, not for the fame or the money? Someone who he could say, 'I don't want to sing any more. I just wanna be a mailman,' and she'd say 'okay, if that's what will make you happy'. Do you remember that conversation?"

"Yes, I do."

"You were tellin' my life story, honey. Tansey married me for the money and the glamour. She didn't care about me. You know how bad I was hurtin'. At first, I thought you were jokin' about not knowin' who I was. Then, well it didn't matter because we'd only be there a few weeks, and I'd never see you again. Then I fell in love with you, and the only thing that mattered was whether or not you loved me back. I was waitin' for the words, Abby. I'd resolved to tell you when you finally said you loved me back. You never said the words until after you'd gone."

"Don't be ridiculous. I spent an entire night saying the words."

"No, I said the words. You didn't. You gave me your love, but still you never said the words. I'd decided to go ahead and tell you that day anyway, because I knew your heart and thought maybe the words were too difficult for you."

She closed the ring box and handed it back to him. "I'm sorry. I can't marry you. It wouldn't be right, and honestly, I don't think you mean it. I think you're just not used to being told no. I'm sure you can find a million women who'd be happy to take it."

"I don't want anyone but you. Please, Abby." A tear spilled down his cheek and his voice shook. "I'm dyin' without you, honey."

She felt her throat tightening and choking her. She stood and headed for the door. "I'm sorry. I can't." She ran to her bedroom and closed the door behind her.

Frances came outside and put a hand on his shoulder.

"Time, Christopher. She needs time. Don't give up on her. She's too special to let her get away."

"I love her so much."

"I have some advice for you. If you're the smart young man I know you are, you'll do exactly as I say."

"Yes, ma'am."

Abby lay in her bed, the words repeating in her mind. "You never said the words. I said the words, Abby, you didn't." Was he right? She'd spent the entire night thinking how much she loved him. Could she have thought it and not actually vocalized it? She thought she said it.

She also remembered his smart remarks about marriage. He didn't want to marry her or anyone else. If she said yes, he would find a reason to break it off before they got to the altar. She was certain of that. Well, almost certain.

The only thing certain was that it hurt. It hurt to see him. It hurt to talk to him. It hurt not to fall into his arms telling him how much she still loved him, and most of all, it hurt to turn her back on him.

Frances stood outside the bedroom door, her own heart breaking at the sound of the heart wrenching sobs coming from the other side.

Friday afternoon found a large crowd assembled at the park. The committee followed Frances' suggestion and formed an ad hoc group to make the casting decisions rather than leaving it singularly to Abby.

Abby was stunned when she saw Chris arrive to audition for the lead role, dragging his partner in crime along to play Pharaoh. Knowing she couldn't possibly work with him a few times a week in such close proximity without falling apart emotionally, she determinedly voted against him. Unfortunately, everyone else voted him in. His celebrity would provide a huge drawing card for ticket sales, and after all, that was the point of the production. She would have to suck it up for the greater good of the community.

When her back was turned, Chris gave Frances a smile and a conspiring wink.

•

Three weeks after the ill-fated night of the proposal, Abby sat in the living room trying to concentrate on a romantic suspense novel Frances had picked up at the library. The plot was too slow-moving, and her focus wandered. A knock at the door provided a welcome diversion, and she set the book aside to answer it.

Seeing her approach, Chris opened the screen door and stepped inside.

"I really don't want to see you. I get enough of it shoved in my face at rehearsals," Abby told him.

Frances stood, ready to make her exit, but Abby stopped her. "Frances, you don't have to leave. Mr. Adams just dropped by to say hello, and now he's leaving."

"Abby, I brought somethin' for you." He held a box out to her.

"I thought I made it clear. I don't want anything from you."

"This just arrived from Nashville. It's yours. I'm just returnin' it."

Taking the package, she opened the lid, and the contents broke her. It was the baby's layette and photographs. "Andrea. It's Andy's things." Tears welled up before she could stop them, and she looked up at him. "Oh, Chris. My baby, oh my baby! I miss her so much."

He opened his arms, and she sank into them, welcoming his comforting embrace.

"I miss her. I want her back. I want my baby."

"I know, sweetheart. So do I. So do I." Her held her as tightly as he could and kissed the top of her head while she keened for her dead child. She stayed in the circle of her safe place for a few minutes and wept inconsolably before pulling away.

"Thank you." Turning, she clutched the box tightly and fled to her room.

Frances stood with one arm folded across her chest, the other hand on her cheek. She stared at the floor, and the silence lengthened. Finally, she thanked him for bringing the parcel.

"That's not all. There's this as well." He opened the door and brought in a large, thin box from the front porch. "This is Abby's, too." He leaned the package against the wall and quietly left.

CHRISTOPHER

Frances stood outside Abby's door a moment before going inside. Sitting on the bed, she gathered Abby into her arms and held her while she grieved. When she was finally exhausted, Frances tucked her in and left her to sleep.

The following morning at breakfast, Frances told her about the other box Chris left. Not hungry, she went to see what it was. She opened the box and in it found a painting. Not a print, but the original, beautifully framed. Gasping in surprise as her fingers fluttered to her mouth, she remembered the day they stood in the gallery looking at it. How he knew she was hurting without her even saying a word, and how he wrapped his arms around her and let her lean into him. He'd always been there for that, simply sensing when she needed his comfort.

"What is it, Abby?" Frances came to stand quietly behind her.

"It's called *Bright Eyes*. We saw it in the artist's gallery in Niagara-on-the-Lake. We talked of how it reminded us of Andrea. He must have bought it that day. I didn't know." Her hand reached out to touch the baby in the painting as a tear trickled down her cheek. She smiled fondly at the poignant memory and decided to keep the gift.

●

Saturday night found Abby doing her usual waitressing stint at the Shady Eagle. She made a point of wearing her denim mini skirt, because she got bigger tips when she did, and she needed the money.

Chris arrived with Jeff and Julie, and they took a seat near the stage. Wally had arranged with Abby to sing that evening but seeing the Nashville trio, she didn't want to go through with it. Scheduled to go on in just a few short minutes, she worked her way to the bar to tell Wally she couldn't do it. Her attention was diverted by his voice booming through the sound system from the stage. Too late to stop him, she tried to get his attention, shaking her head emphatically.

"Ladies and Gentlemen, welcome to the Shady Eagle. Tonight we have a real treat for you. It was five weeks ago tonight that you first heard her on this very stage, and the demand to bring her back has been overwhelmin'. Our very own, Abby Lockner."

Amid clapping and cheers, she walked to the stage with dread in her stomach. As she crossed the platform he made a further announcement that stopped her dead in her tracks. "And to sweeten the pot, I've been told Abby and Chris Adams are gonna record an album of duets together. He's agreed to sing a few with her tonight."

Chris climbed onto the stage with Jeff on his heels. Passing by, he crooked a finger under her chin, lifting it back into place. "Close your mouth, Abby. It's fly season in Wyomin'," he told her quietly.

He set two stools side by side, and Jeff placed his own further back. The bar pianist sat ready, and Chris picked up his guitar. Reluctantly, she sat on the stool next to him, apprehensive about the whole situation. He handed her a headset mike and put another on himself. Jeff leaned forward from behind to slip the pack on the back of her skirt waistband.

Chris played a few chords on his guitar and turned to speak over his shoulder. "We've got a high impedance air gap here, Jeff."

"What does that mean," she asked.

"That's shop talk for 'it's not plugged in.'"

"Oh."

Jeff made the necessary connection, and the music started before she even had time to think about it. She knew her cues and her lines. The first song they did was one she'd chosen called *Stay Awhile* by the Bells. She loved the whispery, intimate quality of the piece. Maddie loved listening to them rehearse this number. It held sentimental memories for her as the song she and her husband listened to on their honeymoon.

Abby tried not to think about the lyrics, not to be affected by them, but it was impossible. The next number was *Endless Love* followed by *Let's Make Love*. And if that wasn't enough, they did *I Melt* by Rascall Flatts and finally *Let It Be Me*. By the time they finished she was fighting back the tears. He suggested she sing one on her own, and he would follow.

"I'm not playing games with you. I don't like your rules. You cheat," she said, bending the mike out of the way so only he could hear.

"Sing, Abby."

She started with *If I'm Not Over You By The Time I Get To Georgia*. He did a tender rendition of Lionel Richie's *Truly*. She sang *I'm Gone,* and he responded, *How Do I Live Without You?* With a definite trend establishing, the audience eagerly anticipated what each would sing next. Abby did *Forgive-A Mighty Big Word For Such A Small Man*. They had the full attention of the audience, who they forgot about as they sang directly to each other. He rebounded with *The Love of My Life*.

"And that's who you are, Abby, the love of my life." His voice rang out over the speakers, and the bar became silent as all eyes turned her way waiting for a reply.

"Well, that's a joke if I ever heard one. I'm sure everybody here saw you on the Flameworthy awards back in June." She turned to the audience. "Did you all get the chance to see good ole' Skippy here that night on television? Wasn't it great that he won all those awards?" The crowd applauded. She turned back, addressing her remarks directly to him again. "So you see, Skippy, they know that when asked about me, you told the entire country that marrying me would be an expensive way to get your laundry done free. Remember that?"

He had the decency to be embarrassed. The crowd cringed at the reminder, which had seemed funny at the time.

"I believe you also said you were miserable being single, but if you married me you'd wish you were dead. Shall I go on?"

"Abby, they were jokes."

"I guess we have different ideas about what's funny then, because I didn't find being humiliated in front of an entire nation even remotely amusing." Her anger built to face him down over the issue, and it no longer mattered that they had an avid audience. "To me they were just plain hurtful. I was lying in a hospital losing my baby while you were on television telling the whole world how hideous the very thought of marrying me is to you."

"Honey, I'm sorry I said those things. I wish I hadn't. Will you let me explain how it happened?"

"Don't you honey me, mister. I don't think that's at all necessary. You came out loud and clear the first time around."

"Let it be known to one and all that I made an ass of myself on network television. I admit it. I'm sorry. I wish I could take it all back. But let it also be known that I do love you. I'm crazy about you. I would give up every minute of fame, every penny I've ever earned if it would convince you to marry me and spend the rest of your life by my side."

She pushed her stool away and did a spectacular performance of N'Sync's *Bye, Bye, Bye*, along with all the band's dance moves. Now this was a performance he enjoyed, watching her dance around in that mini skirt. Realizing all the other men in the place were enjoying it, too, he sighed, shook his head, and did *I'd Miss You Babe* by Aerosmith.

Abby suggested he was unfaithful to her by singing *Who's Bed Have Your Boots Been Under,* and he reciprocated with *Truly, Madly, Deeply*. She sang another classic break up song, *Kiss This!* He very tenderly sang of how precious their love was in Hampton's, *Our Love* but she came right back with Faith Hill's, *Cry*, which showcased her voice beautifully. Then he swamped her by singing one of her favorites, the song that had made her cry when Julie sang it back at the cottage, *I Miss My Friend*. She fought hard against the tears, but she managed one more comeback by Travis Tritt called, *Here's a Quarter, Call Someone Who Cares!*

He knew time was running short and pulled his last trick out of his hat. He stood in front of her and took her hand in his, pulling her to her feet.

"Remember the day we met?" He took her in his arms and began to sway while he sang *You Had Me From Hello.*

Abby gazed up into his topaz blue eyes, getting totally lost in them and feeling the passion in his music. And it was all for her. He savored every minute of having her in his arms again. When the song finished, he bent and kissed her. She kissed him back, wanting him, wanting forever. Then she remembered and pulled away, and even though she whispered, the microphone filled the room with her agony. "I can't do this, Chris. It just hurts too much." She ran off the stage, heading straight for the ladies room.

Julie followed and heard Abby in the cubicle vomiting. "Abby, it's Julie. Are you okay?" The only response was more heaving. A few minutes later Abby came out and splashed cold water on her face.

"Abby, are you all right?"

"I'm fine."

"I'm sorry. For everythin'. He wasn't tryin' to hurt you, but I shouldn't have gone along with him. Jeff and I were both against it, but he made such a good case for himself, and he promised he was gonna tell you soon."

"What am I supposed to say to that? It's okay that you all deceived me?"

"I don't know. I only know we were becomin' good friends, and I miss you. I've been so worried about you. I can only imagine how much you must be hurtin', but I knew you didn't want to hear from me. Please, do you think you can forgive me? I'd like us to be friends again."

She saw the sincerity in Julie's eyes. "Are you going to try to convince me to go back to him?"

"No. This is about you and me. He has nothin' to do with it."

"All right. I know better than anyone how persuasive he can be." They embraced briefly in forgiveness. "Could you do me a favor?"

"Sure, if I can."

"Can you drive me home? I can't stay here. This evening turned out to be a lot more than I bargained for."

"Of course, come on." Julie took her by the hand and led her through the crowd and outside to the parking lot.

Only then did Abby start to breathe.

"I don't know what's come over me. I feel so awful." She put her hand on her forehead, checking for a fever but there was none.

"Get some sleep, and you'll feel better in the mornin'. You really look tired."

"It would be great if I could get some decent sleep. It's hard to come by these days."

"I'm sorry."

"Me too. More than you'll ever know." The car arrived in front of the Beadermeier house. "I'd ask you in, but I think I need to go to bed."

"Of course. Anythin' I can do for you?"

"No, I'll be fine. Frances will be home from her Jazz Festival meeting soon. Thanks."

"I'll call you. Maybe we can do somethin' while I'm home."

"Sure, that would be great. Night, Julie."

CHAPTER 29

Julie pulled up in front of the Beadermeier home to find Abby waiting on the porch. Skipping down the steps, she climbed in. Julie headed the car south, and within minutes they arrived at the entrance to Sinks Canyon State Park. The girls shouldered their backpacks and started out on foot along one of the many trails.

Following the Popo Agie River downstream, Abby watched in fascination as the river suddenly disappeared into fissures in the rock, reappearing a quarter mile away in a large pool. She shot two rolls of film as they hiked the four mile loop. Nearing the top of the Northern Slope, they decided to stop for a rest.

"This is the neatest place, Jul. Chris never brought me here."

"He would have gotten around to it. Mind you he's pretty fond of his own mountains."

"I don't think I've ever known anyone who owned a mountain before, except the Waltons, and that doesn't really count, does it?"

"I guess we don't think much about it because we grew up with it." They sat silent for a moment, before Julie spoke again. "Hey, Abby, I hope you don't mind. I saw the pictures of her."

From the soft tone of her voice, Abby understood. "Andrea?" She gazed across the mountains and remembered holding her baby. "I miss her, Julie. If I had her, I wouldn't be alone. She was the best thing Drew left me, and I lost her."

"I'm very sorry. She was an incredibly beautiful little girl."

"Yes, she was. Thanks." A memory brought the hint of a smile to her lips. "Do you remember the day Chris and I went shopping for baby things? We ended up in a huge fight."

"Of course I remember. You both called me for advice. I told you I couldn't get him a flight sooner than the weekend. Man, did I get in trouble for that one. For a heart stoppin' moment, I thought he was gonna fire me."

"It's hardly your fault if the airlines are booked. He can't blame you for that."

"He sure can. It's his plane."

Abby's eyes opened as understanding dawned. "You mean the one that –"

"Yeah, it's not the McGarrett's plane. It's his." Julie laid back and looked at the clouds. "I told him it was my job to look after him, and that's what I did. I've been doin' it since I was five years old, and I know what's better for him than he does."

Abby laughed as she lay down, too. "What did he say to that?"

"Not much he could say, really. How did you get him to talk to you, any-way?"

"I took his guitar away," she giggled.

"That's just like him, thinking he's all that and then acting like a little kid. Some days I think he never got past bein' ten years old. I sure do love him, though. Can't imagine growin' up without him. He always had the greatest ideas, and they always ended up with Uncle Greer paddlin' his backside, and sometimes ours too."

Abby grinned at the images in her mind, then asked, "Did you ever have a crush on him?"

"Nah, that'd be like fallin' in love with Jeff, and that would just be wrong. I've always thought of him as my brother. Heck, I never even noticed he was drop dead gorgeous until it was pointed out to me at about the age of sixteen. I simply never saw him that way."

"Boy, were you blind."

"Does it matter to you? His looks I mean. So many women are infatuated with him just because he's handsome. Like that's all that matters."

"No. Although I do enjoy looking at him, I'd have fallen in love with him anyway. It's his humor and caring ways that won me. From the moment we met, we could talk about anything and everything, or so I thought. Nothing seemed too private to discuss. There was freedom in that."

Taking a bottle of water from her pack, she took a long drink before con-tinuing. "We enjoyed being together all the time, never bored with each other. If we didn't have anything to say, we just sat quietly. But it was always easy, relaxed. I wish we never left that island. Everything was right with us there. At least I thought so at the time. Now I wonder about everything." Tears began to mist her eyes, and she pulled a plastic container from her backpack as a distraction. She took out a tart and offered one to Julie.

"It's hard watchin' you both hurt so much. I just wish…never mind." Julie bit into the tart and giggled, unprepared for the runny contents that dripped down her chin. "What the heck is this?"

"Butter tart."

"Never heard of it. It's delicious." Julie tried to lick the syrup off her face.

"It's a Canadian thing. They should be a staple in everyone's life."

Julie reached for a second one. "So, tell me about life. You're amazin', you know. Not many people would throw themselves into a community where they don't know anyone."

"I've made a lot of friends, now. I love this town. It's full of nobody's from nowhere, just like me. Of course, I'll only be here a few more weeks. Maybe I'll go to Alberta. I've gotten used to having the Rockies outside my front door, and I'd miss them."

"No chance you'll stay here?"

"No. This is his home, not mine."

"But you're makin' your own space here. Everybody loves you. You fit."

"Julie, I love it here, but I can't stay. It's too hard. Every time I see him my heart dies a little more. It's hard when the person you need the most is the one who hurt you. He's the lucky one."

"How do you figure that?"

Abby reached for another tart and stared at it. "Because when I leave he can forget about me and move on. How am I supposed to do that? I'll turn on the radio and there he'll be, or on the television, or in the papers. You see, I won't be able to forget because he'll always be there, and I'll just keep hurting every time."

"Wow. I thought you knew him."

"No, I don't know anything because if he lied about who he is, then everything else is a lie. Don't you see that?"

"Remember when we got to the hotel in Niagara Falls, and you and I had our little talk? I didn't lie to you. I told you he was a powerful person in Nashville. I told you he was far wealthier than you imagined. I told you no one gets to know the real man. You did, Abby. The guy you were with on that island is the guy I grew up with. Not the guy the magazines think he is, or the fans, or the reporters. He's just a simple, lonely guy. "

"Julie, I've seen the concert footage. I've seen the women going ga-ga over him. And who wouldn't? The man is beyond gorgeous. He's talented and smart and funny. He's every woman's dream come true." Abby stuffed half of the tart into her mouth as she leaned back on the grass.

"He's not interested in any of them, and they're not interested in him. They're in love with the image, not the man. You had the real thing. He loves one woman, and that's you."

"And I loved him. Still love him. But this is a whole new ball game. I accepted the man he gave me. But that's not his real life, is it? He's a public figure. He's out on the road for so many months a year, and away in recording studios for weeks at a time. He asked me to jump into a lake without telling me how deep it is, or about the currents, or if there are man-eating fish swimming in it. How can I make a lifetime decision when I don't have all the information I need to make that choice?"

"That makes sense, but at the same time, does any of it matter more than your love for each other? You should know, he's givin' up the business. He refuses to return to Nashville. He doesn't want to perform any more. In fact, about two hundred people are about to become unemployed."

"That's ridiculous!" She pointed a finger at Julie's face. "You've got more syrup on your chin. Music is in his soul. Julie, you have to talk some sense into him. This has got to be the dumbest thing he's ever said or done." Angry, she sat tapping her water bottle against her knee.

"We shouldn't be discussin' this. I said I wasn't gonna try talkin' you into goin' back, and I won't. You two are on your own."

"This is the first time I've talked about it. I've been keeping it bottled up."

Julie laughed. "It wasn't too bottled back at the bar, dear. But I'd say it was an improvement. You didn't bite him this time!" Standing, she pulled Abby to her feet, and they resumed their journey.

Halfway down the hillside, Abby had a dizzy spell and needed to sit. Minutes later she was sick all over a patch of phlox. Julie handed her a water bottle to rinse her mouth.

"Sorry, Julie."

Worried this was a repeat performance of the other night at the Shady Eagle, Julie asked, "Abby, are you sick?"

"No, it's just stress. I'll be fine once I leave Lander."

"I hope so." Julie kept an eye on her for the rest of the day, worried there was something more seriously wrong with her friend.

•

Abby ran into the vacationing girls from California regularly, and they became friends, going to Sunday afternoon bingo and horseback riding on a ranch south of town together.

Tuesday afternoon she was baking pies for the upcoming Jazz Festival when the phone rang. Wiping the flour from her hands, she answered it.

"Hi, Abby. This is Stacey. Listen, Tiffany and I are going to rent a boat

Thursday morning and cruise around the Boysen Reservoir. We'd like you to come along. We'll get some water skies and make a day of it."

"Thanks for thinking of me, Stacey. It sounds like a lot of fun."

Stacey hung up smiling, and bent over the small circular table in their motel room. Various materials lay scattered across the surface.

Tiffany turned her attention from the motel television and asked, "What are you doing, Stacey? Something really smells bad."

"Just a little homemade bomb. I've had enough of little Miss Abby. It's time to get rid of her for good."

"You can't be serious."

"I'm very serious. She never goes away. He bought her a diamond. The whole town's talking about it. I'm going to see to it he doesn't have the chance to give it to her. I'll plant the bomb on the boat, and we'll jump overboard before it goes off. Bye-bye, Abby."

Tiffany knew Stacey had a problem with anger management, but she hadn't realized the woman was mentally ill. Following Kip around was one thing. It was fun and gave them something to do, but this was a whole new ball game.

"If you go ahead with this, I'm not coming. I won't be part of it, Stacey. You're going too far."

"Fine. I'll tell her you've come down with a cold. One less person to have to get off the boat that way. I'll take care of the dirty work. Just don't expect that you'll get him when I'm done. It doesn't work that way."

"You know what? If this is what it takes to get him, I don't want him."

"You're such a wuss, Tiff."

Tiffany held the knowledge of Stacey's intentions inside, tormenting herself as she grappled with it. If she interfered, would she be the next victim? If she didn't tell, did that make her an accessory? Would she spend the rest of her life in jail? She only knew one thing for certain. Stacey frightened her.

•

Wednesday morning Abby climbed out of bed and headed for the bathroom. Frances stood at the door waiting for her, a white paper bag in her hand. "Here, Abby. I thought you could use this."

"Just a minute, Frances." Abby quickly closed the door and vomited. After washing her face and rinsing her mouth, she went back and opened the door. "I'm sorry, what was it?"

"I picked this up for you. Thought you might need it." She handed the bag to Abby, who opened it and gave Frances a startled expression.

"I don't need a pregnancy test kit."

"Abigail, it's not my business, but if you've been intimate with that young man, you'd better take that test. If it comes out negative, I'm takin' you to the clinic."

"But why–"

"You're bein' sick to your stomach all the time. You either eat everythin' in sight, or you can't hold anythin' down. I'm worried about you. You're pale and tired all the time."

"It's just stress. Once all my papers are here I can leave town, and then I'll be fine. Really, Frances, you don't need to worry. It's just nerves."

Frances said nothing. She turned Abby around and gave her a little push back into the bathroom, pulling the door closed behind her. Going to the kitchen, she dropped bread in the toaster, knowing it would help Abby's stomach settle.

Abby sat staring at the stick, and felt sick all over again. Two blue lines. Pregnant! Chris had given her another baby. His love was growing inside of her. If they were still together this would be the most exciting news for both of them, but they weren't. She could still hear his voice telling her he wanted to have babies with her. He wanted her to be the mother of his children. Well, at least one of them was getting their wish.

Abby went to the kitchen, and Frances saw the look on her face. Abby walked into her arms and burst into tears. Frances let her cry, then sat her at the table with the toast.

"This is not supposed to happen. I ask you, Frances, have you ever met anyone with worse luck than me?"

"Well, I'd probably have to say no to that question. You have a lot of thinkin' to do and decisions to make, dear."

"I don't know what I'm going to do. My mind is spinning in every direction at once. You had two children, didn't you?"

"Yes, my boys are grown long ago. Robert is a banker in Los Angeles, and Daniel is a professor at Columbia. Both far from here."

"Did you love being a mother?"

"I still do, Abby. It's the best thing in my life. You'll do fine. It won't be your little Andrea, but you'll have a baby in your arms. You'll be a wonderful mother, and if you need help you know where to find me. I wouldn't mind you stayin' here with me permanently if you aren't getting' back together with Christopher. Although, maybe this changes things on that front?"

"I don't know. Please, Frances, don't let anyone know about this. I have a lot of thinking to do before I tell him, and he should know first."

"Things will work out for the best, Abby. In spite of every bad thing that's happened to you, I believe the good Lord has his eye on you, keepin' watch. Maybe he decided it's time you need a blessin'."

●

CHRISTOPHER

Thursday morning Abby arrived at the Reservoir with a picnic lunch in tow. She ventured out onto the landing and watched for the boat. As it came into view from around a bend in the river, a hand grabbed her arm and yanked her back. She turned and saw it was Chris.

"Get away from me, and don't touch me."

"Abby come with me."

"No. I have plans, and they don't include you, Oh Great Conceited One."

As the boat drew closer, Stacey saw Abby and waved. She throttled back and steered for shore.

Chris lifted Abby and tossed her over his shoulder, carting her away.

"Chris, put me down now."

"No way, Abs. I love you, and I'm not gonna lose you like this." He began to run, taking her farther from the water.

As she pummeled his back, loudly demanding to be put down, a blast split the air throwing them to the ground. Stupefied, she froze before trying to pull herself away from Chris.

Chris looked back over his shoulder and saw the sky behind him filled with flying fragments, leaving pieces of burning debris littered everywhere.

"Let me go. I have to save my friend," she screeched, swinging punches to obtain her release.

"It's too late now," he shouted, trying to be heard over the sound of her panicked cries.

"I have to try. I can't just leave her out there to die. I have to save her."

"You can't save her now, honey. She's gone." He grabbed her face and held it, forcing her to look at him. "Listen to me, Abby. She wasn't your friend."

"What are you talking about? Do you think you know everything about my life? Do you think you control everything and everyone, you arrogant—" Shoving as hard as she could, she tried to topple him off of her as she struggled to get free.

Chris obliged, helping her to her feet. She tried to run back to the water, but he refused to release his grip on her. Pulling her back, he tried to shelter her from the ever-growing physical aftermath of the explosion as it continued to rain down around them.

"Abigail! Stop!" He dragged her farther away, and as the futility of the situation finally sank in, she allowed herself to be led.

"The police are on their way. They'll handle it," he told her.

Her eyes stung from the burning tears that spilled down her cheeks. "What am I supposed to do? That was my friend out there, and now she's gone. I don't know what to do."

"You never met her before you came to Lander, did you?"

She looked at him warily, wondering where the conversation was leading. "No, but I don't see what difference that makes."

"Abby, her name is Stacey Fillion. Her friend, Tiffany, told Mrs. Beadermeier that Stacey planned to kill you on that boat today. That's supposed to be you out there in a thousand pieces."

She shook her head vehemently, tears streaking down her cheeks. "You're just saying this. It isn't true. Why would she want to kill me? That doesn't make any sense at all. "

"Honey, she's the one who killed the baby and tried to kill you, four times now. She's not your friend."

"Why? Why, Chris? I want you to answer me."

Jeff arrived with the law. Deputies waded into the depths, searching for the body. When they finally dragged it in, Jeff saw what remained and turned away, flinching. While missing an arm and both legs, the rest remained intact, though burned, including his face.

Jeff turned away, cringing, and walked to Chris and Abby.

"Chris did you see who it was?"

"Yeah, we were right. She was after Abby all along."

"Can either of you men identify the body?" an officer asked.

"I'm afraid so. She was a groupie who followed our band on the road." Chris kept his eyes averted from the body, nauseous and disturbed by the ramifications of his stardom.

The deputy asked him, "This the one Ashton put on the bulletin board back at the office?"

"Yep, that's her."

Abby's legs felt suddenly weak at the shock of seeing someone die in front of her. She started to tremble uncontrollably and cry. Chris took her to a picnic table where he held her on his lap.

"I'm sorry for all she's put you through, sweetheart." He tucked her head onto his shoulder and told her the tale of Maisie and Daisy. "Somethin' obviously went wrong today, and her bomb exploded too soon. She saw you as a barrier between me and her."

"So, after all this, someone really did want me dead. I could have been the one they're dragging out of the water. She killed my Andrea, then came here and befriended me, all the while planning to murder me."

"I'm afraid that's about the size of it, darlin'." She tried to rise but he held her snugly to his chest. "Stay here, Abby. You've been through enough today. Just stay here awhile, and feel safe. It's over now. She can't hurt you any more."

She snuggled into the security of his arms, needing it. Her mind tried to make sense of everything he told her, but found it hard to grasp, in spite of what she'd seen today.

CHRISTOPHER

Police divers arrived to salvage the remaining pieces of the boat so they could reconstruct it to determine the cause of the explosion.

"Christopher, thank you for saving me again. You're always there for me no matter what, aren't you?"

"I always will be. I love you, Abby girl. If you leave me because of somethin' I've done, well, that's my own fault. But I'm not gonna let anybody take you from me like this. I'm glad it's finally over so I can breathe a little easier. It's been hell not knowin' when or if she'd strike again."

"I wish things could be different between us."

"Can't they?" he sounded hopeful.

"No. The life you offered me isn't the life you live. You didn't trust me to love you. I could say yes to the cowboy on the ranch, but that's not how your life is. Geez, Chris, I was almost killed today because of your fame. Do I want that for my life? If you had talked to me, explaining what it would really be like and how you envisioned us handling it, then maybe we could have worked it out together. But not now."

"I'm givin' it all up, Abby. I don't want it any more. I'd rather have you."

"It's not a choice between one or the other. I would hate to have you give it up. You're gifted, and what you do makes so many people happy. More than that, it's in your soul. If you stop the music, you won't be you any more. I couldn't bear that."

"I still keep your ring with me. I keep it with me all the time, just in case you change your mind." He sat for a moment, playing with her hand. "I hoped we could take it back together and exchange it for whatever you liked."

"It's perfect. If they had a thousand to choose from that one would have been my choice. You know that."

"Please, Abby, please. Say you can forgive me."

"I want to. More than you know. I can't right now. Maybe somewhere down the road, I don't know. You've hurt me so deeply."

"I'm sorry, darlin'. I'm really sorry." He pulled her head back to his shoulder and held her there. "I love you, my Abby. You're the light in my life."

"I love you, too. Too much, I fear. If I didn't, it wouldn't hurt so much." The tears on both their cheeks mingled together as they kissed, and he felt in his heart this was their goodbye. He clung to her mouth as long as he could, but finally she pulled away and stood up. "Thank you for coming."

Turning, she walked away.

•

The next two weeks the town of Lander focused on the upcoming play. Thursday afternoon was the final dress rehearsal. The first performance would be that evening. The school allowed the children in the chorus the day off in preparation.

Abby borrowed Frances' car for the afternoon to transport things to the park. As she started the engine, she flicked on the radio and adjusted the air conditioning. After a jingle for the local hardware store, the announcer introduced the next song.

"Here's a brand new one that's gonna be a huge hit."

The music started, and she slammed on the brakes in the middle of the street. By the time the chorus came she didn't know whether to break down and cry or hit somebody. She decided hitting would be an affirmative action. Putting her foot back on the gas pedal, she sped to the park.

Chris saw her marching across the grass in his direction and knew something was seriously wrong. He knew her expressions, and this one meant trouble.

She stood toe to toe with him. "How dare you!"

"What is it you think I've done?"

"What is it I *know* you've done! I heard it on the radio. You can't lie your way out of this one, and there is no explanation I will ever accept." Her arms hung stiff at her sides, her hands balled into fists, her eyes fighting the tears of indignation.

"Honey, I still don't know what you're talkin' about."

"Don't you honey me, mister!" she shouted. "I heard it with my own ears. You said it was mine, that no one else would ever have it, and now it's on the radio for the whole world." Her tirade wound down to a whispered question. "Couldn't you keep just one thing between us sacred?"

"Darlin', I hold every minute we shared sacred, but you're not makin' any sense. What are you tellin' me? You heard your song on the radio?"

"I heard it all right, and you'll be glad to know they expect it to be a huge hit."

Feeling completely blindsided, he took a step back. "I don't believe this, not that I don't believe you. How would anyone even know about it?" He stood shaking his head, trying to make sense of it. "I promise you, I had nothin' to do with this. I never sang the song for anyone but you. Believe me, sweetheart, if this is true, I'm as upset about it as you are." He pulled her into his arms and held her while they both absorbed the shock and the pain of the violation. Minutes passed before she pulled away, but he held her by the shoulders so she'd have to stay to listen to him.

"Abs, I never even put it down on paper. There were only our two tapes. I've still got my copy in my safe in Nashville. Where's yours?"

"I never got it. The day you made it was the day your little friend tried to kill me."

He racked his brain trying to recall the sequencing of events that day. "I

273

took it with me back to the cabin. That's the last time I saw it. I pulled you out of there, and I guess I left it behind. It must have been stolen."

"I'm holding you responsible. It's your world, your business. I'm simply the bystander who has once again been betrayed."

Stalking off, she tried to regain some semblance of composure as she called the cast to take their positions to get the rehearsal started. Tickets had sold out for all three performances, and the majority of the money needed to construct the amphitheater sat in the bank. Both Abby and her play were considered a success before they ever made it to opening night.

Friday morning's mail arrived with Abby's birth certificate replacement. It was the final item she'd been waiting for. Monday morning she would fly to Denver and head on to Arizona to visit with her parents. Hopefully, while she was there she could look at things from a distance and gain some perspective, because where she sat right now, she never wanted to see Lander again, or Skippy Chris Adams.

The opening night's performance went well, and she expected the same for the second night. Tug and Cree were coming to town, as well as reporters from four national magazines. In spite of her bitter feelings, she couldn't help admiring how good Christopher looked in a loin cloth, and Jeff made a very sexy Elvis-impersonating Pharaoh. Just two more evenings, and he would be out of her life for good. Except that he was the father of her baby. Her hand settled on her stomach at the thought.

Sunday night when it was all over and she'd finished packing, Frances sat her down in the living room. "Abigail, I think it's time you and I have a talk."

"Sure. What about?"

"About you and Christopher. I know the whole story. The whole town knows it. Yes, he deceived you, and you're hurt. I don't blame you a bit for that. But, Abby, when is enough, enough?"

"What do you mean?"

"Why don't you tell me all the bad things he's ever done to you."

"He lied about who he is, so how can I believe anything else?"

"And that's the only thing he's ever done wrong?"

She stared down at the hands in her lap. "Yes, isn't that enough?"

"Maybe it is, but you still love him, so there must be a reason. Tell me all the good things he's done for you."

She lifted her eyes to meet Frances' as her mind began to recount the deeds of kindness. "The good things. Well, he gave me back my life after Drew died. He loved my baby and cried with me when she died." Her chin started to quiver and tears began to fall. "He gave me his time, his affection, his humor. Looked after me when I was too sick to take care of myself. Saved me from suffocating. Wrote me a song when I lost Andy. Gave me a safe place to go when I grieved. Brought me to his home to share his private life.

He watched over me and worried about me, and he saved me again last week from being killed. He's loved me unconditionally."

"Somehow that list doesn't sound very balanced, does it?"

"Not when you put it like that. It makes me sound rather selfish. Is that what you think? I'm being selfish?"

"Your complaint is that he didn't tell you who he is. Instead, he showed you every day for four months. The stardom, all the media hype; it's utter nonsense, and he knows it. Why do you think he uses a different name professionally? It's because that's not who he really is. He gave you himself. The real Christopher. The man that will still be here years down the road, when the radio and the fans have all forgotten him and moved on to someone new. The day will come when people say 'Kip who? I don't remember him'. And Christopher will be sittin' out at that ranch, still bein' the man he's always been. The real person.

"Abby, he already had one wife who never knew the man. Never even tried to. She married his name and his money, and left him empty. Can you blame him for wantin' someone to love the real man? Maybe he never told you the rest because it's not important to him. Do you believe he loved you more than you loved him?"

She thought about it and gave an honest assessment. "No. I love him just as much."

"You just told me he loves you unconditionally. If you love him as much, why isn't your love unconditional? Make Christopher, and yourself, happy. Forgive him, Abigail."

She listened, not wanting to hear it. She was right, and he was wrong, and that's all there was to it. She didn't want to let in shades of gray, but they were there, and there were a lot of them.

Frances drove her to the Riverton airport early Monday morning.

"Here's the number of my parents place in Arizona. I don't have to tell you not to give it out. Thank you for everything, Frances. I'm thinking about the things you said last night. I don't know how I would have survived these last two months without you."

"This door is open any time you want to come back. I'll miss you. You're the daughter I never had."

"And I'll bet after all this turmoil, you're glad you didn't have any girls."

"Oh, land sakes, just give me a hug."

"Thanks, Frances. I'll stay in touch," Abby promised.

"Of course you will. I've still got your paintin'. Go on then."

Abby boarded the commuter plane to Denver. A chapter in her life was ending, and she was embarking on the next one. She hadn't even said good bye to him. She knew she could trust Frances not to tell where she'd gone. She was on her own again.

CHAPTER 30

Chris sat alone on the top of a mountain, as he had every day for the past few months. He cherished the spot where they shared their first picnic, where she'd given herself to him, and he came to be alone with her memory. She was gone from Lander, and he had no idea where. Hours dragged into days.

He couldn't retreat to his music any more. The spot it filled was vacant, along with everything else in his life. And so he sat alone, remembering the joy she brought him, her smile, her tears, the way she carried things off so artlessly. The way she looked so elegant and sophisticated in that pink taffeta dress, then turning to ask if she had lipstick on her teeth. The way he never won when she was angry with him. The way she always said, "Don't you honey me, mister!" The way she always wove her fingers into his hair when they kissed. The way she came to his bed to kiss him better after biting him. The way she bowled him over the first time he heard her sing *The Music of the Night*. Everything was Abby. His Abby.

●

Abby couldn't believe how quickly her stomach bulged with the baby. Barely four months along, and her clothes hadn't fit for weeks. She told her parents she was pregnant, but that she and the father were no longer together. She didn't tell them why or who, and they didn't ask.

Life in Scottsdale was nice, but it wasn't Lander. She loved Lander. She missed Frances. Most of all, she missed Chris.

Thinking about it provided a constant pursuit, and she admitted Frances was right. Nothing but her pride kept them apart. She understood his reason for the betrayal. She didn't approve, but she understood. He loved her, and she loved him, and between them they could work through anything that came their way. Surely there couldn't be anything worse than they already weathered together. That was the key—together. They could work it out together, not two states apart. She needed to go back. By tomorrow, she could be in his arms. Maybe she should ask him to come to Arizona to meet her parents, then they could travel to Wyoming together.

Her decision was made. She would call and set things right between them.

•

Chris heard a horse approaching up the east side of the mountain. He didn't bother to look. It really didn't matter who it was.

"So, this is where you've been hangin' out, huh?"

"Yup. What are you doin' here, Jefferson?"

"Haven't seen ya around for awhile. Ain't havin' no fun without ya."

"I'm not feelin' like fun."

"What are you gonna do? Sit up here for the rest of your life?"

He kept his eyes focused far beyond the vista. "Maybe. I got nothin' better to do."

"You've got two businesses to run. I know it's rough, but you have people out there dependin' on you to make a livin'."

"I can't sing any more. I've told you that already."

"Chris, she'll be back. She loves you. Trust in that. You have to give her somethin' to come back to." Jeff sat next to him. "Do you think she'd want ya the way ya are now? She'd take one look and run."

"I miss her so bad. I can't think of nothin' else."

"You're a sentimental man, which makes for a great songwriter, but it's not an easy way to live, buddy."

"I am what I am. And that's not enough for her."

"Now you're talkin' stupid. She knows you as well as Julie and I do, and she's had a lot shorter time to do it in. Heck, I think she probably knows ya better, bein' as Jul and I never slept with ya."

"You're not gonna either," Chris retorted.

Jeff laughed, and Chris began to smirk.

"That's the kinda joke Abby would'a made," Jeff remarked.

"Yeah. I never knew what she'd come out with next. As unpredictable as a mountain storm, that girl. Can you imagine namin' horses after Jane Austen

277

characters? Where's the cowboy in that thinkin'? But she has the most genuine heart I've ever known."

"Come down off this mountain, and be the kind of man she can come back to. She loves you too much to walk away. How's she gonna set me up with that sister of hers if she doesn't come back?" He dropped a hand on his best friend's shoulder and gave it a squeeze. "Man, did you see her dancin' in that mini skirt? Now that was a show worth watchin'! That girl sure knows how to move."

Chris glared.

"Come on. Let's go to the Silver Spur, have a beer, and bowl a game."

"Abby can't bowl. Her ball hit the scorekeeper."

"Somehow that doesn't surprise me, but I'm not askin' her. This is a guy thing. We haven't done a guy thing in too long. Come on." Jeff stood and offered a hand to his friend, who suddenly toppled over, his hat tilting down over his face.

"Come on, Chris, get up."

Christopher lay so still that instinct kicked in, and Jeff knelt to look at him. Lifting the black hat, he saw a bullet hole in Chris' forehead. Looking wildly around in an attempt to discern where the shot came from, he snatched his cell phone from his jacket pocket, and dialed 911.

"This is Jeff Clayton. I'm out at Chris Adams' ranch. He's been shot. Hurry, damn it. He's gonna die out here!"

●

Abby's father answered the phone, and held it out to her. Only one person who knew where she was. It had to be Frances.

"Abigail, dear. I want you to sit down. I'm afraid I have some bad news."

Abby heard Frances' voice trembling, and it immediately scared her. Tears started before she even heard the news.

"Frances?"

"Dear, I'm sorry to have to tell you. Christopher's been shot. It doesn't look good. They don't expect him to live." Frances heard hyperventilating on the other end and gave her a moment to let it sink in. "Abby, listen to me. He needs you now. More than he ever has before. He's been so despondent since you left that they think he won't fight. You have to go to him, dear. I know what's happened between you, but the life of your baby's father is more important than your pride."

"Of course I'll come. Where is he? In Lander?"

"No, dear, they've airlifted him to Salt Lake City. He needs some delicate neurosurgery, if he makes it there."

Abby's fingers flew to her lips and her voice rose with anxiety. "His head? Someone shot him in the head?" Her legs shook beneath her as she felt the world tip over.

"I'm afraid so."

"So we're looking at brain surgery?" She sniffed loudly through her tears.

"Julie wants to send the plane for you, but I need your permission to tell her where you are."

"Yes, yes tell her. Of course tell her. When you talk to Julie, have her tell him I love him, and I'm on my way. He has to hang on for me."

She hung up and collapsed into her father's arms. "Abigail, what's going on? Who was shot?"

"Dad, you know Kip Adams, the country singer?"

"Of course I do. Everyone does."

"Yes, everyone but me. They're airlifting him to Salt Lake City for surgery right now. It doesn't look good. They think," she broke down and sobbed, "Dad, they think he's going to die."

"Well, honey, I'm sorry to hear that, but I don't understand what that has to do with you, or why you're so upset about it."

"I love him, Dad."

"So do lots of people."

"No, I *love* him, Dad. This is his baby. I have to get to the airport. I have to tell him I was wrong, that I am going to marry him. He doesn't even know about the baby."

Don Rose listened to his daughter's words, and as incredible as it sounded, her tears told him it was all true.

"Oh, Daddy, what will I do if I lose him, too? I can't go through all this again, I just can't. I do love him. He's a wonderful man, and he loves me so much. He's been there for me through everything. He's been my strength. I need him. I can't lose him."

●

In Salt Lake City the waiting room at University Hospital was silent. Five worried people sat, paced, and sat some more.

"How long before she gets here?" Maddie asked.

Julie checked her watch. "About another half hour until her plane lands, then about twenty minutes to get here from the airport, dependin' on traffic."

"Tell me again what she said to Frances." Maddie hung all her hopes on Abby.

"She was badly shaken. She wanted me to tell him she loves him, and she's on her way. That's about it. Mrs. Beadermeier says she has more to be upset about than we realize, and that we're to look after her. She wouldn't elaborate."

CHRISTOPHER

"I hardly think Abby is the one that needs looking after when Christopher is in there…" Her voice dropped off, and she struggled to compose herself. "I'm sorry, I'm guess I'm just too worried about him to think of anyone else's needs right now."

"It's all right, Maddie. This hospital has some of the best neurosurgeons in the country in there with him right now. He'll be fine." Wendy Clayton put her arm around her neighbor and dearest friend. "He'll be fine."

Jeff continued pacing, stopping now and again to look out the window and thanking God Chris lived long enough to get here.

Julie looked at her watch again. "I think I'll go for a walk." Feeling the tension closing in on her until she was ready to suffocate from it, she wandered to the elevator bank. On the main floor she pushed her way through the front doors and sucked in the fresh mountain air. She would wait for Abby outside.

Minutes seemed like hours before the cab pulled up, and Abby climbed out. Julie ran to greet her, and they embraced. "I told him, Abby. He wasn't conscious, but I told him you love him and that you were comin'."

"What do the doctors say?"

"They won't know anythin' until they get in there and see what damage has been done. Wait a minute. Look at you." Julie looked down at Abby's stomach.

"Yes, Chris and I are having a baby. Can you believe it? He has to be okay. He's going to be a daddy."

"This is why you were bein' so sick back in Lander? I was worried somethin' serious was wrong."

"Something was. I wasn't with him where I belonged. Now, tell me what happened. All I know is he got shot somehow."

Julie related what little there was to tell as they stepped into the elevator.

"I don't understand. A bullet just came out of nowhere?"

"Jeff said he couldn't tell where it came from. He didn't see anyone. Didn't even hear the gunshot."

Abby wrung her hands together in worry, stopping to stare at her fingers. "My ring. He said he kept it with him all the time."

"I've got it here in my purse." Julie opened her handbag and took the red velvet ring box out. She handed it to Abby who slid the ring on her finger before the elevator opened on the surgical floor.

"Wait until Maddie sees you. She's gonna be so relieved you're here and very excited about the baby. How far along are you? I thought you guys didn't…"

"The last night we were together. I think that's why the deceit was so hard to take. I'm only four months, but I look more like six."

They entered the waiting room, and Jeff's eyes widened. Maddie was too happy to see her to notice the pregnancy. Abby sat beside her, and they hugged.

"Thank you for comin', Abby. I'm sure he'll fight once he knows you're here."

"I love him, Maddie. I'll never leave him again. I'm here to help him fight. Chris and I always do best when we work together." She placed Maddie's hand on her stomach. The older woman looked at her with surprise.

Abby nodded and smiled, "You're going to be a grandma. Late April." Maddie hugged her again.

"God bless you, darlin'. A baby! Wendy, did you hear that? Chris and Abby are havin' a baby!"

Wendy embraced her friend and congratulated her. Jeff took Abby in his arms. She hugged him back, and he kissed her forehead. "I know you'll save him, darlin'. He loves you more than his own life. And now a baby to hold on for, too."

"I love him the same way, Jeff. I was about to ask him to come to Scottsdale to meet my parents, when Frances called. He has to make it." She turned back to Maddie. "Chris promised you'd be a great help with a baby. I want it to grow up at the ranch, just like his daddy did."

"You're comin' home?"

"Home. It has a wonderful sound to it. Yes, I'm coming home to stay. I've missed you, Maddie, and I've been losing my mind without him. I'm sorry it took me so long to come to my senses. I should have listened more to my heart and less to my pride."

"You're here now. That's what matters. You're the reason he'll fight to live. But, Abby, we don't know the extent of the damage. We don't know if, well, there are a lot of things that could be affected by this. He might not come out of it without difficulties."

"All I need is for him to be able to nod yes to a minister. Anything beyond that we'll deal with. I love him no matter what happens. I'll look after him if that's what it comes to. I have to."

Maddie saw the engagement ring in place and knew she would stay for the duration, no matter what happened.

Seven hours later the surgeon came to the waiting room. "Hi, I'm Dr. Shumway. He's alive."

They all breathed for the first time since leaving Wyoming.

"The bullet passed along inside the top of the cranium, in a direct path between the two cerebral lobes. It scraped along the interior of the skull, and we had to clean out a lot of bone shavings. Amazingly, nothing serious was damaged. He's in recovery right now, and we'll be keeping him in intensive care for awhile."

"So, he's going to be all right?" Maddie asked.

CHRISTOPHER

The doctor folded his arms across his blue scrubs. "Don't expect a lot. He's still suffered a major head trauma. He'll be in a drug induced coma for a number of weeks while it heals. There's a lot of swelling to go down before we can allow him to wake up. If he comes out of that all right, I see no reason why he shouldn't fully recover. I'm not saying he's out of danger. We have to be careful about any infection or any intra cranial hemorrhaging. We don't anticipate it, but we aren't taking chances. We're guardedly optimistic."

Abby sat back down and cried happy tears. They had a chance after all. "How long before I can see him?"

"He'll be in recovery for about another hour, then he'll be moved to ICU. Visits will be limited to one person for five minutes each hour. You'll have to decide who goes in. Immediate family only. You've all been here a long time. Why don't you grab something to eat? By the time you get back he should be in ICU."

Abby hugged the doctor. "Thank you so much."

Julie took him aside and spoke quietly with him. He nodded and agreed to meet her in the morning.

●

He kept an eye out as he dialed the phone, making sure he was alone. If anyone overheard, it would be the end of everything for him.

"Hello."

"Job's done. Put a bullet through his head this morning. You'll be hearing it on the news. We need to complete our transaction."

"When I hear confirmation on the news, I'll be in touch with you."

"No, I'll get in touch. I'm out of here. Back in Nashville by morning."

"We'll meet soon."

"Don't forget, fifteen grand." He hung up and went to watch the television, waiting for a news bulletin.

●

Maddie wanted Abby to see him first, hoping her voice would strengthen him.

"Just five minutes," the nurse reminded her.

She approached the bed nervously, eyeing the IV pole with its numerous bags hanging on it, and noted the lines blipping across monitors. Taking his hand in hers, she kissed his cheek and put her mouth close to his ear so he would hear her.

"I'm here, Chris. It's Abby, darling. I'm wearing the ring you bought me. I'm going to marry you. I have so much to tell you. Most importantly, I love you, Christopher. I love you so deeply, and I've never stopped. I want to spend every day with you for the rest of our lives. Do you hear me? I'm here for you, and I'm ready to be your safe place. Come, and let me hold you."

She pressed her cheek tightly against his and felt his warmth. "I'm with your mama. She's very close by. We both love you so much. I need you to fight for me, sweetheart. Fight to come back to me. I need you. Don't you leave me. Don't you dare." She placed his fingers across the back of her hand. "Do you feel that? I'm wearing your ring. I'm sorry I hurt you, but I'm back now, and I'll never leave you again. I promise you with my heart. I love you."

The nurse told her that her time was up. She kissed him one more time and reluctantly left his side.

Maddie waited outside the door for her. "How is he?"

"It really scared me, Maddie. So many tubes and wires, and his head all bandaged up, but I told him I need him to fight, and that I'm going to marry him. I love him so much. I'm so sorry for the time I wasted."

"I know, honey. I've known since the day we met. He loves you, too. He needs you, Abby."

"I need him just as much."

The next morning Julie was already showered and dressed when Abby woke.

"Abby, I'm holding a press conference this morning at the hospital. It's better if the news is broken by us," Julie told her.

"Okay. Did you want me to be there?"

"Not if you can't handle it. We have to be honest but appear optimistic. The surgeon will talk about the medical aspect of things."

She thought for only a moment. "I want to be part of it. If I'm going to marry a celebrity, I have to be able to cope with this kind of thing."

Arriving at the hospital, they went to ICU to check on Chris first. Maddie embraced Abby when she saw her. "How are you today, dear?"

"I'll be fine. I'm going to be strong for him. No more tears. He can't pull on my strength if I'm wimping out, can he?" She smiled, showing her brave attitude.

The nurse told Abby she could go in. She walked to the bedside and took hold of his hand. "I'm here, Chris. I'm right here beside you. I'll bet you have a whopper of a headache coming. Remember when I had that horrid headache on the island, and you looked after me? Now it's my turn to look after you.

"You know, I think this little stunt of yours might put a damper on our recording schedule for a while. It's going to be great though, isn't it? *Kip and Abby Adams, Married and In Love.* That's what I want to call it. Maybe you can even write a song about us called that. Everyone will buy it because they'll hear in our voices how much we love each other. You rest and get better for me. I need you.

"I stayed at the Sheraton Hotel last night. Pretty fancy place, of course you know me, I'd be happy to sleep in the parking lot. I'm going to my first press conference this morning. I'll be strong and make you proud of me. I'm going to tell the world how much in love we are. It's you and me all the way, sweetheart."

The nurse signaled her time was up.

"I have to go for a few minutes, but I won't be long. If you want me, just let them know, and I'll be right here at your side. I love you, baby. Get some rest." She gently kissed his lips and left the room.

Jeff and Julie joined her to go to the conference. They met with Dr. Shumway outside the conference room and went in together to sit at the table on the dais as a unified team. Jeff sat with his arm around Abby for support. He felt her trembling and leaned to whisper in her ear. "You okay, darlin'?"

"Yeah, just a bit overwhelmed. I didn't expect anywhere near this many reporters."

"If you need me, just squeeze my hand, okay?" She nodded yes, and he removed his arm from her shoulders and clasped her hand. "And, Abby, I'm glad you dyed your hair back to brown. Much better look!"

She giggled, and Julie started the session. After introductions, she informed them Kip had been shot, then turned it over to the doctor. He told the details of the surgery and the prognosis. The floor was open for questions.

"Where was Kip when he was shot, and was he alone?"

"He was at a remote area on his ranch in Wyoming. I was with him," Jeff answered.

"Has he woken up at all?"

"We don't expect him to be conscious for several weeks. He's suffered serious brain trauma and surgery. It takes time for things of this magnitude to heal." The doctor fielded all medical questions. "He'll be kept in a drug induced coma for a number of weeks to allow it to heal."

"Abby, will this affect your plans for marriage?"

"Not at all. Kip and I will be married as soon as he's well enough. The only thing in question is the date."

"Were you at the ranch at the time of the shooting?"

"No, I was in Arizona visiting my parents." She answered calmly, and Jeff felt her relaxing.

"Where are you planning to live when you're married?"

"There won't be any changes in that aspect. We'll spend part of the year on the ranch in Wyoming and part in Nashville."

"Is it true you and he have plans to record together?"

She was taken off guard by that question. "Yes, we're going to cut an album together, although I'm wondering how you found out about it. That isn't public knowledge as far as I know."

"I'd like to ask about the allegations regarding some of Kip's music being stolen and sold to other artists."

"It's true. The song *Put Your Heart Into My Hands* was written for me when I lost my baby last spring. It was a private thing between us, and I was very distraught when I heard it on the radio."

Jeff gave her hand a squeeze and cut in, "Kip started an investigation to learn how this happened, and I'll be followin' up on it. We've also learned of other pieces he wrote earlier this year that have appeared for artist option. They have been withdrawn since he was able to prove ownership, but we will be pursuin' this to the end."

Abby hadn't known any of that. She smiled at Jeff, and he squeezed her hand again.

"Abby, we can't help noticing you're expecting a baby. Can you tell us about that?"

"Kip and I are expecting our first child in April. I'm hoping to be at home in Lander when it's born."

"Can we see your engagement ring?"

She held up her hand to show her ring, and one reporter had the gall to ask, "Weren't you surprised a man who appears on the Fortune 500 list didn't come up with a much bigger diamond?"

Her temper flared, but she kept her poise as she answered, "Kip would have bought me the whole damn mine if I'd wanted it. I have small, delicate hands, and I don't care for gaudy jewelry. I don't need a huge diamond to know how much he loves me. Money has no place in our relationship. We have a love based on friendship, and tenderness, and two souls who can't bear to be apart.

"Quite frankly, I'm appalled anyone would have the temerity to care about the size of a silly stone when my fiancé is upstairs at this very moment fighting for his life. If you have anything further to ask that is pertinent to this situation, fine. Otherwise, I'd like to get back to him."

Julie whispered in her ear. "You go, girl. Well done!" and a number of reporters applauded.

"Doctor Shumway, how long do you anticipate him being kept here in Salt Lake City?"

"We'll keep an eye on him here for two weeks, and barring any unforeseen difficulties, he can be transported to Wyoming for continuing care."

"Jeff, is this in any way related to the bombing of his home in Nashville?"

"We initially thought they were unrelated incidents, but the state police back home are in touch with the Nashville police."

Julie stepped in and took over. "Thank you for comin'. We'd like to ask on behalf of the family, that none of his friends try to visit him until he's back in Wyomin'. Only his mother and Abby are allowed in to see him for brief

285

periods of time right now."

In the elevator ride up, Abby said, "That was so weird, calling him Kip."

"You'll get used to it. We never refer to him as Chris in public," Julie told her.

Jeff tucked his arm around her and gave her a tight squeeze. "You were fabulous, darlin'. Man, I wish he could have seen that. It's one of the things he admires about you. You won't put up with crap, even from him."

"Well, what a stupid question! That guy just made me mad." They still heard the defiance in her voice.

"Yes, but you kept in control. Very nicely done." Julie gave her a bright smile.

The elevator doors opened. "Thanks. Now, if you'll excuse me, I need to go throw up!"

CHAPTER 31

The plane touched down in Lander, and an ambulance stood waiting near the end of the runway. Chris was transported the short distance to Lander Valley Medical Center along with his mother. Frances was there waiting to meet Abby with open arms.

"Oh, Frances, I'm so glad to see you."

"How are you, Abigail? Keepin' that stiff upper lip?"

"Trying. It's been hard at times, but when I've been in with him I haven't broken down."

The women climbed into Frances' car to drive to the medical center.

"You're lookin' well. How's that baby doin'?"

"I can't believe how big I am. It's so different from last time."

"Successive pregnancies do tend to show earlier."

"But this big?"

"Maybe you're retainin' a lot of fluid. You should get your blood pressure checked. How was the trip?"

"Everything went fine. It's hard to see Chris like this, but I have to be strong for both of us. Now it's all a waiting game. They're starting to reduce the drugs keeping him in the coma."

At the medical center a nurse at the front desk told them where to find Chris' room. Maddie stepped into the hallway as they arrived. "Frannie, thank you for all you've done for us, and for Abby. It means a lot."

287

CHRISTOPHER

"It's my pleasure, Maddie. Listen, I want you and Abby to stay in town at my place while young Christopher is here. Save you a lot of driving time."

Abby put her hand on Maddie's arm and asked, "I was wondering if it would be all right for Frances to go out to the ranch to pick up my necklace for me?"

"Certainly, dear. I know exactly where it is," Maddie assured her.

Abby wandered into his room and watched a nurse checking his IV drip. "How is he?"

"He's settled in real nice. The good news is we already did the MRI. It looks better than we'd expected. You should go ahead and talk to him. He can probably hear every word you say. He just won't be able to respond yet." She smiled encouragingly.

Abby settled into the chair at the side of the bed. She took his hand in her own and kissed it. "I'm here, honey. You're looking better today. I think you're getting more color in your face. I love you, and I can't wait for you to wake up so we can be married. Want to feel the ring again?" She ran his fingers over her engagement ring.

I feel it, Abby. I'm so glad you're here. I've missed you, honey. I want to hold you in my arms again. I'm so happy we're gettin' married. It's what I've wanted forever. Just keep talkin' to me. The sound of your voice is like bein' in heaven.

"I've been thinking. I was going to wait and ask you first, but I don't think you'll mind. I want to set up a scholarship fund in neurosurgery at the University of Utah."

Why would you do that? What's Utah got to do with anythin'?

"They saved your life, and I want to thank them. They took such good care of you, my love. Thank heavens Jeff was with you to call for help. If he hadn't been there, you would have died up on that mountain top. Was it our mountain you were on? The one where we made love for the first time. That was such a wonderful night wasn't it?"

Saved my life from what? What are you talkin' about? Our mountain top. It was the most perfect night of my life, Abby girl. I've relived that night so many times. If only you knew.

"Jeff called yesterday with news about our song. The police finished their investigation. You were right, it was stolen on the island, along with a number of other pieces you wrote there. Stacey Fillion sold the music to the publisher. Guess it's too late to send her to jail, but she provided justice all by herself, didn't she? Anyway, Jeff proved it was yours because he has the copies you faxed him with the dates and times of the faxing on them. They all precede the music publishers dates. So your music is all yours again.

"As for our song, I guess you know it's a massive hit. You'll receive a sizable portion of the profits from it. The guy who recorded it felt so bad when he learned it was stolen from you and wants to make financial restitution. Of course, you know I have thoughts on that. I don't want us to profit from losing Andy. I want to give it to the Children's Miracle Network. Maybe it can help save someone else's child. Funny, that charity is the brainchild of Marie Osmond. Sort of seems right after we had so much fun playing Donny and Marie. I guess I'll give her a call."

I'm glad the music is safe. But your song–Abby, I never intended that to be a hit. It was for you, a sharin' of our sorrow. I'm gonna take you back to that island someday so we can wash away the bad memories and fill it with more wonderful ones. Remember that first day when you came around the corner of the house and wanted me to get off the island? It was the first time you ever said, 'don't you honey me, mister'. I'm so glad I stayed.

"Frances is bringing my necklace back from the ranch.

Remember the night you gave it to me? I was so surprised. I don't think I've ever owned anything so beautiful. Everything you've ever chosen for me has been perfect. We've grown so close, I'm sure you can even read my thoughts sometimes."

Of course I remember that night. You put on that dress, and you looked so spectacular. I was already aware of you as a woman, not just a friend. The way your eyes sparkled when you opened the box filled me with joy. I've never been so happy to give a gift as I was that night. I was already in love with you.

"I hope you aren't going to keep me waiting too long. I want us to be married soon. You once told me you'd do anything for me. That's what I want. To be your wife. We have so much loving ahead of us, and I don't want to put it off one day longer than we have to."

Oh, baby, I want that too, more than you'll ever know. I want to hold you right now. I hear you, but I can't find my way. Is this what it was like for you after you lost Andrea? I'm tryin', honey. I'm tryin'.

She sat on the edge of his bed and kissed his lips lightly. "I miss your kisses so much. When you kiss me I can't think of anything except the kiss. I want them back. I want your mouth pressed against mine, loving me. I miss your touch. I miss your laughter. I miss you getting jealous, even though you say you aren't. I miss the way you let me win when we argue and then kiss me anyway. Thank you for giving me a chance to keep you. Drew didn't give me that chance. He died without even saying goodbye. But not you. You promised you'd stay with me, and that's just what you're doing."

Of course I'm not leavin' you. But kiss me again, Abs. It felt so good. I want more of that. And Abby, let's get this straight. I don't get jealous.

She took his hand and rubbed it over her stomach. "Remember the first time you put your hand on my stomach and felt Andy? This time the baby in there is yours. You're going to be a daddy, Chris. It makes me so happy, having your love growing inside of me. Can you feel it?"

A baby? We're havin' a baby? Abby, I love ya so much. It's the best news in the world. I'm comin', honey. I'll be a great dad, and you, well I know a baby couldn't have a better mother. Oh, honey, I want to make love to you right now.

The beeping increased in frequency. She looked at the monitor and saw the blips on the screen moving faster. "Chris, are you all right? Don't leave me now. I need you too much."

I'm not goin' anywhere, Abby. I'm just so happy at the news.

The monitor returned to a normal rate, and she relaxed. "Quit scaring me, Mozart." She placed his hand on her stomach again, letting him feel the beginnings of their child. Then she bent down and whispered in his ear, "You're mine now."

I've been yours forever. I always will be.

●

Abby hit the speed dial button on her cell phone.

"Hi, Jeff... He's doing better today... No, not because the doctor said so, because I can feel it... I'm going to lose my mind, though, I need something to do. Is there anyway I can be of use?...Yes, I agreed to do that back when we first met. I can do it here at the hospital. ... What sort of things do you suspect?"

"I'd rather let you look, and see if anything jumps out at you."

At Jeff's response her brows lifted, and then she frowned. "Okay. I'll keep my eyes peeled."

●

Julie arrived on the Gulfstream at Hunt Airfield with everything Abby needed. She'd taken all the financial records, filing cabinets and all, from Cree's office. He was away on vacation for the next month and wouldn't know the difference anyway. Her father brought the truck to transport it all to the hospital for Abby to conduct a corporate audit.

"Hey, Abby. I made it. How's our hero doin'?"

Abby lay on the bed with Chris. "Julie, I'm so glad to see you. Maybe you can talk some sense into this man. He's arguing with me again. He should know by now it's no use."

Julie looked at Chris' comatose body. "What's he arguin' about today?"

"Just about everything. If he doesn't stop, I'm gonna have to take his guitar away again. Do you hear me, Christopher? I'm going to take your guitar away if you're not nice to me."

"Well, that should pretty much take care of that problem I'd say." Julie laughed at her. "I've got everythin' here for you. Dad's gonna bring it up on a dolly." She took hold of Chris' hand. "How's it goin', Kipper? When are you gonna wake up and marry this girl? She's not gonna wait forever you know, so you'd better get a move on." She turned to Abby, and they went to stand near the door. "How have things been really?" she asked quietly.

"He hasn't gotten any worse, so that's good news. He opens his eyes, and that's supposed to be a good sign, even though he doesn't focus on anything." Her gaze drifted to watch him.

"He's had a lot of visitors though. I think I've met just about everyone who ever made a record. Alan Jackson was here to see him yesterday, a couple of the fellows from Diamond Rio stopped by the other day. Tom and Hope were here our first week in Lander. We've just had a rolling list of who's who in and out of here. So many people care about him.

"Oh, and I finally met his friend, Coby. He says that, yes, Oklahoma is a nice place to visit. He told me all about how he had to keep Chris from killing Kenny at a barbecue. He even brought his guitar with him and played for us awhile. I think Chris liked it. His heart rate increased when he heard it." They pulled chairs to the table in the corner and sat. "How are things in Nashville?"

"The office is goin' crazy. We've had to hire extra people for the switchboard to handle the calls. The new single is climbin' the charts in spite of him not bein' there to promote it. Kip has a solid fan base. They're standin' in full force to support him. Jeff made a few appearances on CMT and a few radio stations. Tug is usin' the break from Kip to push Trent. He'll be cuttin' a record by this time next year. All in all, business is good in spite of the circus."

Bill Clayton arrived with the cabinet. "Where do you want it, Abby?"

"Umm, set it here by the table. This is where I'll be working, so it's the best place for it." She grabbed the side of the table and pulled it out. Bill moved the cabinet into place.

"There ya go. That oughta keep ya busy for awhile."

"Thanks for bringing it."

Bill hugged her before sitting for a short visit with Chris.

The women resumed their conversation. "Jeff says do the last two years. He won't say what he suspects. He wants to see if you find anythin' out of the ordinary."

"Okay. Did he get that scholarship arranged with the University?"

"It's all set. It'll be awarded for the first time next spring. They're thrilled to have it."

"They deserve it. They saved my man."

"I don't know if you're interested, but there's an awards ceremony next week in Las Vegas for Billboard magazine. We have two floor tickets. He's nominated in three categories. Jeff and I can go in case he wins."

"No, Julie. I'll go. You two decide between you who comes with me. I want to represent him until he's able to do it for himself. Then he'll know I'm supporting his career, and people will see we're strong together."

"I thought you might say that. I have a feelin' Jeff wants to escort you."

"My Lord Protector."

"Yeah, somethin' like that." she smiled, and Abby giggled.

As the day of the awards ceremony approached, Abby knew she couldn't embarrass Chris by showing up in a second hand bridesmaid's dress from one of the thrift stores in town, so she and Jeff arrived in Vegas early in the day to shop. She found a beautiful baby blue strapless gown in chiffon with a fitted bodice covered in chiffon pleats and an empire waist, allowing plenty of room for the baby. The gown fell gracefully and didn't pronounce her stomach. With it, she wore the necklace and bracelet Chris had given her.

Under the bright lights she saw several musicians from the rock/pop charts that she was familiar with. Jeff escorted her to their seats in the third row on the center aisle. She felt glamorous being among these people.

"Are you comfortable enough?"

"I'm fine, Jeff. Just lots of butterflies. Maybe someday I'll get used to a social setting like this, but I can't imagine it. He really knows these people?"

"A lot of them, yeah. Just be Abby. So tell me about your sister. Is she really a lot like you, or is he just pullin' my chain?"

She laughed as the house lights dimmed. The ceremony started, and her attention was caught up for the evening. When they mentioned Kip Adams as a nominee, her hands flew to her mouth in anticipation, nervous on his behalf.

"And the winner of the Country Entertainer of the Year Award is, *Kip Adams*!"

Her eyes teared with pride.

"Accepting the award for Mr. Adams is his fiancée, Abigail Lockner."

Jeff escorted her up the stairs, and she made her way to the podium.

"I'm accepting this award on Kip's behalf tonight. As most of you know, he's still in a coma. I'm not just sure what he'd say if he were here, but what I can tell you is that he loves music. It's a part of his soul, of who he is, and he'd be happy to play and sing in a little nightclub in the middle of nowhere. What he gives you isn't a job to him. He's sharing a huge part of himself. Thanks to Billboard, to Tug Crilley, Julie Clayton, and to Jeff and the band, who all make what he does a gift of love. Thank you."

With Jeff's hand on the small of her back, they walked off stage and were swept into the press room to answer questions before returning to their seats in the audience.

Chris won the award for Country Album of the Year, and she graciously accepted it as well. When the evening was over, Jeff asked if she wanted to attend the parties. She declined, tired after the long day.

At the hotel, they went to their own rooms to get out of their formal clothes, then relaxed together in the sitting room. They shared a Chocolate Hot Fudge Mountain Sundae as they wound down.

"You were terrific tonight, and the prettiest woman there. Chris hit the jackpot when he found you. I'm glad you're gonna be my sister. Speakin' of sisters…"

She laughed and took Claire's picture from her wallet.

"Man, she really does look like you. You sure you're not twins?"

"No, but as close as twins. At least we were. I suppose it's time I forgive her."

"That might be a good idea. Nobody thought of it as hurtin' you, ya know. I guess we never stopped to realize you would be hurt. Just saw it more as protectin' him. He really is the best man I've ever known. You can't do better."

"I know that. I'm sorry for all the time I wasted."

"You had hurts to heal. I can understand why you couldn't just say, "Oh, well," and pretend like it never happened."

"Thanks, Jeff. I'm going to like having a brother."

CHAPTER 32

Weeks passed as Christopher lay in the Lander Valley Medical Center. Abby and Maddie stayed with him almost constantly, talking to him, reading to him, and helping with his physiotherapy so his muscles didn't atrophy. Abby spent her days auditing the business accounts to keep her mind occupied. Each day she lay beside him, resting his hand on her growing stomach while she napped. He gradually began to move his hand and leg on the right side of his body independently. Sometimes his hand flexed when she held it in her own. She felt certain he knew and understood.

•

The clock displayed two a.m. in bright red digits when Abby awoke startled. The cause was unclear at first, but a sense of foreboding engulfed her. Suddenly, a sharp pain made her gasp in agony.

"Maddie, Frances, help me! Something's wrong!" she screamed.

Both women bounded from their cozy beds and scrambled through the darkness to her room.

"What is it, Abby?" Maddie was at her side.

"It's the baby. Something's wrong with the baby. I have to get to the hospital. Please, help me. I can't let this happen again. Not this time. Not now." She panicked as another pain grabbed hold, stealing her breath.

Distraught at the prospect of losing the baby, she was rushed to the

Women's Services unit at the hospital. Within minutes of arriving, through cries of physical and emotional pain, she delivered the dead fetus.

Maddie and Frances, distressed by the latest turn of events, felt helpless. Both swept at tears of their own as they sought to soothe Abby, knowing all the while there was no comfort to be found at a moment like this.

"That's two babies I've lost. What's wrong with me? I'll never have children," she lamented as she curled up, sobbing inconsolably.

"There's nothin' wrong with you, honey. The last time was an accident and this time, well there's been so much stress." Frances gripped her hand.

Dr. Joel Hopkins came in to examine her, and Maddie and Frances left the room to give them privacy.

"Abby, how far along were you?" He seemed puzzled by what he read on the chart.

Abby looked at the young, spectacled doctor and answered, "Twenty-two weeks."

"The fetus was extremely small for that gestational period."

"But I've been so big."

He laid his hand on her stomach and felt around her uterus. His eyebrows rose in surprise. "Hmm. We're going to do an ultrasound. I want to take a look. Have you had one before for this pregnancy?"

"No."

As a nurse connected the portable ultrasound machine, Dr. Hopkins squirted the doppler with the cold jelly and rubbed it over her stomach, still tender from labor. She turned away, tears streaking down her face. She couldn't bear to see the emptiness that had, until moments ago, been her baby's home. How could she tell Chris she'd lost his baby, too?

"Abby, look at this."

"I don't want to see," she wept.

"I think you do. Look." Gently setting his fingers under her chin, he encouraged her to turn her head. Blinking her eyes to clear the tears away, she glanced at the monitor, and what she saw held her riveted.

"You lost a baby all right, but you've still got two more in there. You're gonna have twins."

Laughter bubbled inside of her and rang out through the room. "Maddie, Frances, come quickly," she shouted.

Alarmed, the woman rushed into the room to find Abby giggling through her tears. She pointed to the monitor, and they looked.

"Twins! Chris and I are having twins! That's why I was so big. There were three!"

The women hugged each other and Abby.

"I don't understand how this is possible," Maddie asked.

"It's fairly common when carrying multiples to lose one, for any number of reasons. When the fetus has its own separate placenta, it doesn't endanger the other, stronger babies when it aborts."

Dr. Hopkins allowed them to stay for the remainder of the procedure. He clicked the button numerous times, taking pictures. He pointed out the heartbeats, the little hands and feet, and the facial features as the women watched, fascinated.

"My goodness, Maddie. Things certainly have changed since we had children. Isn't it marvelous?" Frances commented, captivated.

"Abby, do you want to know what you're having?" the doctor asked.

She nodded.

"Only one is positioned to show, but it's definitely a boy. See? Each of these babies has their own placenta, which means they won't be identical."

Three happy women beamed at the screen. There would be two new babies to hold and rock.

The next morning Abby was released, and Maddie brought clothes to her from home. She found her way down the hall to Christopher's room and lay down beside him, wrapping his arm around her shoulders while placing his other hand on her stomach.

"Guess what, Christopher? I had a terrible time last night. I went into labor and lost the baby. It was a little boy. I can't begin to tell you how devastated I was."

You're not soundin' very devastated, honey.

"Now, I know, you're thinking I'm not sounding very devastated, but that's because I found something out. Can you guess what that might be?"

No, I can't guess. You'll have to tell me. What could possibly make you happy after losin' our son?

"The doctor did an ultrasound, and you'll never believe it. I've been carrying triplets. So we still have a set of twins on the way, and he said one is a boy."

Triplets? Twins? This is unbelievable. You'd better be takin' care of yourself. I'm gonna have a son! Abby, you're the most incredible woman I have ever known. Every time I think I have things squared away you throw me a curve. I love you.

"That's right, you're going to have a son. I want him to be everything you are. Our life is happening, Chris. Please wake up, and share it with me. Share in my joy. We're starting our family. Your mama was with me, and she saw pictures of the babies. She's here now. I'm going to let her tell you they're the most beautiful babies she's ever seen. I love you, Chris. I love you so much. Thank you for the gift." She kissed his mouth, and his heart rate elevated. It was a good sign.

The telephone rang, and Abby answered it, her voice so jubilant she almost bounded through the phone. "Hello?"

"Abby?"

"Yes."

"This is Hope McGarrett. You're sounding particularly happy this morning. Is he awake?"

"Hi, Hope. No, he's not awake yet, but I'm confident it will happen soon. We just got some incredible news!"

"Great! Is it something you can share?"

"Thought you'd never ask. Chris and I are having twins. We know one is a boy, but he couldn't tell about the other one."

"That's wonderful. No wonder you're so happy. Can I tell Tom?"

"Sure. I'm so excited I want the whole world to know."

Hope laughed. The excitement was contagious. "Any news on Chris?"

"Whenever I kiss him or give him happy news, his heart rate increases, so I'm sure he's hearing me. He keeps his eyes open for long periods now. He's gaining more use of his right side, and he's starting to make sounds. It shouldn't be much longer before he's back with us."

"Soon then. Let's hope very soon. Kenny was talking about heading out there next week."

"He's coming here? I hope I don't hyperventilate when I see him, pass out, and miss the whole thing. That's just my luck."

"Abby, dear, you don't need Kenny. You've got Kip Adams, and most of the women in America would give anything to be in your spot."

"I know. I am lucky, aren't I?

"You know it, girl."

"Thanks for calling, Hope."

"I'm glad for the good news. Our prayers are with you both. Tell him we love him. I'll call again next week."

Abby spent her days working on the books, and most things fell into place. The only problem she found was a charitable donation made at least once a month, sometimes more, to the TA Fund, and there was never a cashed check as a receipt. She got on the phone and called Jeff.

"Jeff, what is the TA Fund?"

"Never heard of it. Why?"

"There are frequent donations to it listed, but no receipts. I might not worry, but these are big amounts. The smallest I've seen so far is twenty thousand dollars."

"How long has this been goin' on?"

"Looks like it started October of last year."

"I'll make some phone calls and get back to you."

"Thanks, Jeff."

●

297

CHRISTOPHER

LaDona Spencer scrutinized the phone bill that just arrived in the post, finding a long distance call she didn't recognize. Anyone who stayed at the Blue Spruce Bed and Breakfast was supposed to use a credit card to make long distance calls. She picked up the phone and dialed. When it was picked up at the other end, a feminine voice answered with a distinct Southern flair.

"Hello, this is LaDona Spencer. May I ask who I'm speakin' to please?"

"This is Tansey Adams. What can I do for you?"

"I'm sorry. I must have a wrong number." LaDona hung up the phone and thought for a moment, then picked it up again and called the sheriff's office.

"Fremont County Sheriff's Office. How can I direct your call?"

"Hi, Jen. This is LaDona. I'd like to speak to the deputies working the Chris Adams shootin'."

"Hi, LaDona. I'll put you right through."

She waited while Jennifer forwarded the call.

"Deputy Ashton. How can I help you?"

●

Jeff pulled out his key and let himself into the mansion. Chris had never asked for it back, and he hadn't offered. He figured you never knew when something like this could prove useful. Like today for instance.

He knew the house well, and knew exactly where to find the sexy blonde. Excitement propelled him up the staircase three steps at a time. He strode down the hall to the double doors, and without bothering to knock, he flung them wide open and entered.

"Hello, Tansey."

"Jeff."

"Surprised to see me? Don't feel the need to get dressed on my account."

Tansey and her lover came out of their momentary shock and floundered for the sheets to cover themselves.

"What's this about, Jeff? I don't recall inviting you."

Jeff looked at them with disgust, glad Chris wasn't here to face the betrayal. "Just thought I'd pay a little courtesy call. Let you know the game is over."

"What are you talking about?"

"You might want to put your pants on, Cree, before the police get here. Tansey, you can stay naked. Everyone knows you're a slut anyway. No surprise there."

Cree sat staring at him, not wanting to accept the truth. "Police? Since when did it become an offence to sleep with a woman?"

"Oh, it's not, unless you're helping her to embezzle thousands of dollars

298

from your employer."

"I don't know what you're talking about. Get out, Jeff." Tansey let the sheet drop, exposing her breasts.

Jeff snorted with disgust. "Those things don't work on me, Tans. You and your boyfriend here are going to jail."

"Jail! I'm sure I don't know what you're talking about. I've done nothing wrong."

Cree sighed with resignation. "It's over, Tansey."

She looked at Cree with astonishment. "Have you been stealing Kip's money?" She turned to Jeff, seeking absolution. "I don't know anything about this. I'm not involved."

"Like hell you're not," Cree bellowed.

"Tell it to the judge, Tans. And as for you," he directed his attention to Cree, "you're supposed to be one of his best friends. He's trusted you and was always more than generous with you. She's a selfish little leech. What's your excuse?" Hearing the police arriving in the downstairs foyer, he called for them to come upstairs. "I just wanted the satisfaction of seeing this go down."

●

Hours later, the phone rang and she grabbed it on the second ring. "Hello?"

"Abby? You're a genius, girl."

"Why? What did you find out?"

"I contacted the bank and asked them to search through our cashed checks for the month. They found one for the TA Fund. You aren't going to believe this. Chris has unknowingly been making donations to the *Tansey Adams Fund*."

"Oh, My Glory! Didn't he already give her a huge divorce settlement?"

"Seventeen million."

She gulped. "Dollars?"

"We're not talkin' horse feed here, Abby."

"Who signed the checks?"

"This is what's gonna be bad for Chris. It was Cree."

"Isn't he supposed to be a good friend? I've met him. He came to Salt Lake City with Tug, and to the play here in Lander. Remember?"

"Yeah. we met him when we first came to Tennessee. Chris hired him as his financial manager from the start. Shoot, now that I think about it, he's been managing my money, too. Dang it all! Looks like I'm going to need you to audit my accounts too. I never got as close to him as Chris did, though. They hang out together a lot, even vacation together sometimes. It's gonna be a long time before Cree sees another vacation."

"So, what's going to happen to Tansey? Is she culpable in any way?"

"Sure is. They've already been arrested and are going to jail for embezzlement."

"Good!" She mentally filed the information. "I'm glad to help. I need to protect the interests of my children's father."

●

Abby lay on the bed with Chris' hand on her stomach, as usual. It comforted her to have it there, giving her a sense of sharing it with him. She heard a noise and looked at the door.

There stood Kenny Hampton.

Her face broke into a huge smile. "I'd recognize that black hat anywhere." She climbed off the bed and went to greet him.

"Hey there, Abby. How you holdin' up?" He wrapped his arms around her, and gave her a warm hug.

"Really good. Did you hear the news? About us having twins?"

"Yeah, Hope told me. I think that's great. How's my buddy doin'?"

"Honestly, I'd hoped he would have woken up by now, but he hasn't. I have faith it'll happen soon, maybe by the New Year.It sure would make a terrific Christmas present. We're pretty sure he hears us." She took Kenny's hand and led him to the bed.

"Chris? Kenny's here. He came all the way from East Tennessee just to look at you layin' in a bed. Maybe I'll let him take pictures, so he can show everybody. Maybe even send copies to the *Enquirer*."

Kenny was surprised by her good natured teasing and understood why Kip loved her. He laughed and reached down to take his friend's hand. "Hey, buddy! How you doin'? Your song is knockin' the rest of us off the charts, and you're not even out there pushin' it. I'm gettin' a bit ticked off about it."

Abby smiled. "Chris, I'm getting tired of waiting for you. I mean, I know I'm havin' your babies and all, but I can't do it alone. Kenny's come to take me back to Nashville. I'm going to marry him and be Abby Hampton!" She looked at Kenny and winked.

"The hell you are!"

They were so startled by the harsh, raspy whisper that they couldn't react. Both sets of eyes turned to see the patient awake and glaring at them. In their joy, they embraced.

"Get your hands off my woman, Hampton."

Kenny started to laugh, and Abby started to cry. She threw herself on Chris and hugged him, and kissed him, and cried some more.

He drew a deep breath and struggled to push the words out. "Abby, I'm definitely not jealous."

"Of course you're not, Mozart. Not a bit." She smiled and kissed him again, tenderly this time. "Welcome home, sweetheart."

•

"Jeff, he's awake! He's awake! Come home." He replayed the joyous message, allowing the impact to penetrate his stunned disbelief. Did he hear right?

Euphoric, he leaped into the office corridor, shouting for everyone to hear, "He's awake. He's awake." Cheering erupted, and celebratory pandemonium reigned. Julie ran out of her office, and her brother picked her up and twirled her around, both of them laughing through their tears. "He's awake, Jul. Let's go home."

•

Two weeks were spent with Chris learning to use a walker before graduating to a cane. His voice gradually grew stronger until he sounded like himself again. All the physio Abby and Wendy Clayton had consistently provided, helped him regain the use of his motor skills at a quicker pace. When he reached a point where they felt his therapy could be continued from home, he was released. On a wintry January morning he finally returned to his ranch with Abby by his side.

Early that afternoon, Jeff, Julie, and Trent burst through the kitchen door of the ranch house together. Only Trent stopped to take his shoes off.

"Where are you, Chris?"

"We're in the den," Abby called.

They came in, all talking at once. Abby was surprised to see her cousin.

"Am I forgiven, Abby?"

"Seeing as how I'm going to marry him, I'd say you're forgiven. But don't ever do it again." She opened her arms, and he lifted her in the embrace.

"Wow, you're huge. Are you sure there's only two in there?"

"Trent, I'm having two so I can give one to you."

"Not on your life, cousin dear. You're welcome to keep them both."

She turned in time to hear Jeff telling Chris the news from Tennessee. "The police in Nashville got a call from the state police here. It seems La Dona Spencer had a lodger who made a long distance call from her house the day of the shooting. Guess who he called?"

Chris shook his head, not having a clue. "Who?"

"Tansey. Now she's charged with conspiracy to commit murder as well and the embezzlement. She was pretty quick to give up the name of the paid assassin. Said she never got her money's worth."

301

CHRISTOPHER

"What I don't understand is, if she was already embezzling his money, why would she want to kill the meal ticket?" Abby puzzled.

"Because of you, Abby. She thought she was the main beneficiary of Chris' will. She wanted to cash in before he cut her out to put you in. She didn't know he already changed it to include you and Andy when he was in Nashville last June. She's also been paying premiums on a two million dollar life insurance policy on Chris." Jeff shook his head, unable to comprehend such vicious greed.

"Chris, I brought ya somethin'. Watch this." Julie popped a video into the VCR and turned on the television. He saw it was a press conference.

"Abby, can we see your engagement ring?"

"Weren't you surprised a man on the Fortune 500 list didn't come up with a much bigger diamond?"

"Kip would have bought me the whole damn mine if I'd wanted it. He knows me very well and knows that I wouldn't have accepted anything larger than this. I have small, delicate hands, and I don't care for gaudy jewelry. I don't need a huge diamond to know how much he loves me. Money has no place in our relationship. We have a love based on friendship and tenderness and two souls who can't bear to be apart. Quite frankly, I'm appalled anyone would have the temerity to care about the size of a silly stone when my fiancée is upstairs at this very moment fighting for his life. If you have anything further to ask that is pertinent to this situation, we'd be glad to answer, otherwise, I'd like to get back to him."

He reached out and grabbed her hand. "Come here, Abby girl." She knelt next to him as he lay stretched out on the sofa. "I knew I could count on you to be my safe place."

"All ways, always."

CHAPTER 33

"No, Abby. I won't allow it, and that's the end of it."

"But the Neat Repeats Boutique is my favorite store," she lamented.

"It may be, dear. But we're talking about your weddin' dress. You and Julie are gonna take the Gulfstream, go to Salt Lake, and buy a brand new gown. Besides, I doubt the boutique has many gowns in their inventory for a women in your condition."

She heaved a sigh. "I suppose you have a point. All right."

The flight to Salt Lake City a week after Chris' arrival home had to be wedged into the whirlwind of activities for the upcoming wedding. The women found a shop with a varied selection of maternity bridal gowns, and Abby found one she fell in love with. Julie bought two dresses identical in style to Abby's in soft baby pink, one for herself and one for Claire.

With the wedding a mere week away, Claire arrived. She cried when Abby forgave her and asked her to be the maid of honor. Chris was busy matchmaking, continually finding reasons for her to be with Jeff. When it came down to it, she wasn't complaining. Jeff was handsome, talented, and funny. All in all, a pretty hot property as far as she was concerned. She privately predicted many visits to the Adams' ranch in her future.

•

CHRISTOPHER

Pink and white roses decorated the church for the early afternoon wedding where four hundred guests sat in attendance. Chris had reserved every motel and B&B room in Lander to accommodate his Nashville guests, grateful it was the middle of winter and not tourist season.

Abby arrived at the church wearing a floor length white strapless gown covered in European lace, scalloped along the top edge of the snugly fitted bodice, the skirt falling from an empire waistline. A matching lace bolero jacket completed the ensemble. Around her neck she wore her sapphire and diamond necklace. Julie put her hair up the same way she wore it on her birthday, with the rosebuds tucked in.

Chris couldn't believe she was even more beautiful than she'd been that night in Niagara Falls, but as he watched her father bring her down the aisle to him, his heart pounded madly, and her beauty left him breathless. The minister was saying something, but Chris couldn't take his eyes, or his mind, off of Abby.

"I, Abigail Elizabeth Lockner, take thee, Christopher Kendall Adams to be my lawfully wedded husband. To have and to hold, to love and to cherish, for richer or for poorer, in sickness and in health as long as we both shall live."

Chris took her small hand in his. "With this ring I thee wed, and with all my worldly goods I thee endow. My precious Abby, please accept this ring as my token and pledge of my eternal love for you. My world was empty without you, and I thank God each day for bringin' you into my life. I promise to cherish you forever." He slid the delicate gold band on her finger.

She looked at the ring on her hand, then smiled into his eyes. Claire handed his ring to Abby. "With this ring I thee wed, and with all my worldly goods I thee endow. My darling Christopher, please accept this ring as my token and pledge of my eternal love for you. A year ago I died. With you I was reborn. I treasure your love and promise to never betray it. I give myself to you completely." She slid the ring onto his finger.

"By the powers vested in me, I now pronounce you husband and wife."

Chris gazed into her moist eyes with tears in his own. "I love you, Abigail Adams." He cupped her face in his hands and settled his mouth on hers. His wife. He was kissing his wife.

"I love you so much, Mozart, or Skippy, or whatever your name is," she grinned.

He chuckled as he took her mouth again and sealed it so she couldn't say another word. Her perfume filled his senses. Her tongue touched his in such a way that it ignited his passion, and he wanted to kick everyone out and start the honeymoon right there. She would be his tonight and every night, so long as they both should live, and he wouldn't have it any other way.

Thousands of bright lights twinkled over the heads of the guests as they found their seats for the reception dinner. The large, new barn had been transformed into a fairyland of tiny glittering lights and flowers, giving the evening a romantic ambience.

Jeff stood at the microphone making his toast to the bride. "Last summer when Abby first came to the ranch, she helped with the birthin' of two colts. Chris let her name them, and she did. She called them Mr. Knightley and Mr. Darcy. Now that Abby is the one havin' the babies, Chris is terrified she's gonna name one of them Mr. Bingley."

Everyone laughed, and she turned to Chris and stuck out her tongue.

"Abigail Adams, who now bears the same name as one of our proudest, strongest first ladies of the United States, is also a first lady. She is the first lady of Chris' heart, and I don't think anythin' can ever change that. She's spontaneous, she's compassionate, she's funny, she's honest, she has the most generous of hearts, she sings like a bird, but most importantly, she loves my best friend in a way I've never seen love happen before.

"Ladies and Gentlemen, raise your glasses to our own first lady, Abigail Adams." The crowd stood and toasted her with their champagne, then sat back down. Jeff continued, "I'd like to take this opportunity to announce that the winner of the Weddin' Pool from last summer's barbecue is Trent Roblin. Here you go." He handed Trent an envelope, thick with hundred dollar bills. "Enjoy it."

Chris' head swiveled in shock, receiving a round of laughter from the guests. He grabbed the microphone and stood, pushing Jeff down into his seat. "I can't believe you guys had a pool goin' on me, and I didn't know about it!" The Nashville people chuckled again. "Seriously, I want to thank you all for bein' here with us today.

"Last summer I wanted a vacation where I could be totally isolated. My manager, Tug, found me such a place. I went to a little island in Ontario, and it wasn't long before this little brunette showed up on the scene and told me I needed to vamoose off of her island. That was my first encounter with the sweetness of my wife's personality."

She grinned at him.

"From that moment on she changed my life. She had a tragic year filled with loss, but she allowed me to be part of her world. She brought me her tears and allowed me to help put her heart together again. The stories are true. She didn't know I was Kip Adams, at first. I was just Chris from Wyomin', and I knew when she fell in love with me that she loved the man, not the celebrity. In fact, she has no trouble whatsoever puttin' me in my place. But she makes me laugh each and every day, and now she's givin' me children. She's the light of my life, and I love her more than I ever dreamed it was possible to love. I'd like to formally introduce her." He took her hand, and she stood. "I'm proud to say, this is my wife, Abby Adams."

She confiscated the microphone from him. "I just want to thank Kenny Hampton for what's happened today. Chris didn't have the least bit of interest in me as a woman until I said Kenny was a hot babe. From that moment on, he was determined to win my heart. It was also Kenny who helped bring Chris out of his coma."

Kenny stood and took a bow, and people chuckled. "Thank you, Kenny. You'll always hold a special place in my heart."

She blew him a kiss before turning to her husband. "Being your wife is a sacred thing to me. I hope to always be worthy of your love, because my happiness depends on it. I'm glad you stayed on the island and saved me. You became my safe place, and I love you so much." Her voice broke. Taking her hand, he pulled her onto his lap. He passed the microphone to Jeff while he kissed his new wife tenderly. They sat with their foreheads tipped together. "I love you, Chris," she whispered. She kissed him hard and hugged him tightly, then laid her head on his shoulder. Everyone cheered and clapped and women wiped away tears as they watched love happening in front of them.

He reached over and took the mike back from Jeff. "You people are gonna have to carry on without us for awhile. We have some, uh, business to take care of." He tossed the mike back, lifted her in his arms and carried her out of the barn and into the house to the sound of clapping, laughter and plenty of male encouragement.

Upstairs in their bedroom, he kicked the door shut behind him and lay her on the bed, instantly on top of her. "I love you, Abs. I need you, honey."

Although swept along by his kisses, she foolishly asked, "Can't we take our clothes off first?"

"No time. Can't wait." He shimmied up her dress and consummated their marriage. "Oh, Abby. Abby, I love you so much. I love you, sweetheart." His breath raced along with his heart. "My sweet wife. I love you, wife."

She kissed his neck, the scent of his cologne drawing her uncontrollably to him. "I love that word." Her fingers ran through his hair. Minutes later they lay still, panting, sweating. She looked at him, lying next to her and smiled. "Well, husband, if memory serves me right, you were a much more considerate lover before we got married."

He groaned and pulled her closer. "Sorry, honey. I didn't mean to be so selfish, but it has been over six months now."

"I'm not complaining. It was sexy having you want me that badly. I've never been ravished before." She giggled as she stroked his cheek with her finger.

"Sweetheart, if I took you every time it crossed my mind, we'd never leave the room."

"Sounds enticing, but we do have a few hundred people out there. We have to go back."

"Not yet. If we went back now, they'd all say, 'Poor girl, her husband obviously isn't gonna make her happy in the marriage bed.'"

"They'd all be wrong then, wouldn't they? I love you, Chris. I love every touch from you. I cherish every kiss. I love being married to you. And they'll all say, 'Wow, that guy must be quite the stud. How many kids do they have now, twelve or is it thirteen?'"

Laughter burst from his chest, and he bent to kiss her rounded stomach. "Do you know how badly I wanted to do that the last time you were pregnant? I found you so sexy then, just like I do now. You're very beautiful. Abby, I love you, and our children." Then he made love to her again, taking their clothes off, taking all the time in the world, taking the opportunity to leave no doubt about his prowess. An hour later, after showering together, they dressed and joined their guests, him without his tie, shirt collar open, and her with her hair down.

People danced, laughed and had an all round good time. Abby danced a Texas two step with Kenny, and Chris kept a close eye on them, one eyebrow raised. At the end of the dance Kenny pulled a card out of his inner jacket pocket and gave it to her. She opened it and saw he'd written inside what he'd bought them for a wedding present. It would be delivered to their Nashville home when they bought one. She squealed with delight and hugged him.

Jeff dropped a hand on Chris' shoulder. "She's married to you, buddy. Cool down."

Kenny danced Abby across the floor to where Chris waited.

"Chris, wait until you hear. Guess what Kenny got us as a wedding gift?"

"I can't imagine."

"A pool table!" she bubbled.

His face fell, and Jeff howled with laughter. Kenny wasn't sure what it all meant.

Jeff dropped an arm around his shoulders and strolled off with him. "Kenny, my friend, you're a genius. Have you ever heard of a game called Beaver Billiards?"

●

March winds blew, and April tried to push her way through. Abby struggled to make her way across the wet, muddy stable yard and pushed open the stable door. "Chris! Christopher!" she called out in a strained voice.

"What is it, honey?" He stepped out of a stall and saw her doubled over in pain. Immediately dropping what he was doing, he ran to her side. "The babies?"

She nodded, and he picked her up, carrying her toward the truck. She shook her head no. "There isn't time. I'm going to have them here!"

"But mama's not home, Abby. You can't do this."

She punched his shoulder and shouted, "Just get me in the house, and get these babies out. Now!"

"What are you mad at me for?"

"Because you got me this way. We are never having sex again! I mean it, Christopher. It's over." Her voice rose in volume and temper.

He got her to their bedroom and set her on the bed. She screeched with pain, and he tried not to panic, having never delivered a human baby before. He went to the linen closet and grabbed a few thick towels to spread under her, then ran across the hall to grab his mothers' sewing box. Between contractions he managed to get her undressed. Another contraction came and refused to let up. The baby was already crowning when he got into position.

"Push with the next one, honey."

"Don't you honey me, mister." She felt a burning sensation as the opening dilated. With all the energy she could muster, she pushed, and the head was delivered. "What is it?"

"I can't tell from the head, Abby, but its got lots of hair. You ready to push again, honey?"

He rotated the head, and when she pushed again the shoulders came out, and the baby slid into his hands. "It's our little boy, honey. We have our son." He tied and cut the cord. It opened its mouth and hollered as Chris gave him to his mother to hold for a few minutes.

Abby giggled with relief as she looked at him. "Oh, listen. He sings just like his daddy."

Chris frowned at her. "Thank you, darlin'. It's nice to know you appreciate the way I support this family."

Another contraction hit, and he quickly took the baby, laying him in the bassinet beside the bed. The placenta delivered quickly, and the next baby was hot on its trail.

"I can see the head. We're almost there. Okay, sweetie. You can do it."

She pushed hard, and the baby was delivered in a single push. Tired and relieved, she lay back, trying to catch her breath.

"She's a darlin', Abby. Our daughter is beautiful like her mama."

"It's a girl? We have a little girl?" Tears of joy brightened her eyes, and she looked at the painting on the wall of *Bright Eyes*. Chris finished the delivery and wrapped both babies in soft flannel receiving blankets before removing the soiled linens. After making sure Abby was taken care of and comfortable, he put their daughter in her arms, and he held their son.

Moving around to the other side of the bed, Chris quickly called Abby's obstetrician to bring him up to date. Dr. Timmons assured them he would come out to the ranch to check on both Abby and the babies in a few hours with instructions to call if anything seemed amiss. Wyoming doctors were accustomed to home births and took it all in stride.

Chris looked at the tiny face with the dark blue eyes peeking at him from under a mop of dark hair. "Hello, Mr. Bingley. I'm your Daddy."

"Silly man," she said affectionately. "I was thinking of naming him Kendall."

"After me?"

"Of course. After the love of my life and his dearest friend. Kendall Jefferson Adams."

He kissed her with adoration, then he looked back at his little man. "Hey, cowboy. You're mama's given you quite a name to live up to. Kendall was my Grandpa Christopher's name. And your Uncle Jeff is gonna love you." As he cuddled his son in his arms a thought occurred to him. "Wait a minute! Abby, you're not plannin' on callin' him Kenny are ya? Because–"

Her laughter cut him off. "No, I'm going to call him Kendall. Believe me, I know who his daddy is."

"Just wanted to make that clear! But I'm not jealous, so don't even suggest it."

Her daughter looked up with the same dark blue eyes as her older brother, her hair a lighter shade of brown. Her little red face scrunched up and let out the littlest mewling cry they'd ever heard.

"Hmm. I've heard her mother make that little noise before. Speakin' of which, you were just kiddin' about the no sex thing back there, weren't ya?"

"This is not the time to ask a woman a question like that, darling. However, seeing as I have a problem keeping my hands off you, I'd say it's a safe bet it will happen again. You did say you wanted a whole passel of kids if I remember correctly. Just give me a week or two to recover first."

"Hey, Abs, is it possible to get pregnant when you're nursin'?"

"Yeah, it's possible, but it's easier if you put the baby to bed first." She grinned at him, and he laughed.

"I love your mind."

"I know. It's my most attractive feature. Now what are we going to name our daughter?"

"Well, there is a name I like, and I think it goes well with Kendall." He looked at her hopefully.

"Okay, what is it?" She put her daughter to her breast, bending to kiss the precious tiny head.

"How 'bout Keeley?"

"Hmm. Not at all what I expected from you, Mozart. But I love it. It's perfect.

"You choose the middle name."

"Frances," she offered.

"After Mrs. Beadermeier?"

"Yeah, she did a lot to help us get back together. When are you going to start calling her Frances instead of Mrs. Beadermeier?"

"Never! That woman wields a mean pointer. I've been clipped enough times to know. But I agree, Keeley Frances Adams. Kendall and Keeley. We're a family, Abby. I love you so much. This is the greatest thing anyone's ever given me." He kissed her, long and sweet. "Thank you, darlin', for our son and our daughter." He kissed the babe in her arms and the one in his own. "My heart feels like it's gonna explode, I'm so happy. How are you, my love? Are you all right? You must be so tired."

"No, I'm actually feeling quite wonderful. I love you, Chris. I'm in love with our children. I'm in love with our life. I'm so glad you went to that island to get away from women."

"And found the only one that mattered. Which reminds me, I have somethin' for you." He pulled a packet of papers from the drawer of his night table and handed them to her.

She opened them and stared in disbelief. "I don't understand. How?"

"When Jim and Gilda went to Australia last summer, he made some important business connections. Too good to pass up. They're movin' to Australia in May. Jim talked to me when they came for the weddin', and I was more than happy to buy the island for you. For us. So we'll always be able to go back to our beginnin' and remember how wonderful it was when we fell in love."

"I love you, Christopher."

He kissed her lips and whispered, "I love you, Abby girl."

Printed in the United States
37885LVS00002B/16-33

9 781595 070739